Prais

'S... ...eat plot twists, and lashings of Homburg-hatted,
...suited, shiny-shoed Cary Grant ambience'
Daily Mail

'[A] compulsively readable melodrama about life in the Manhattan
publishing world of the 1950s … [Rindell] does it with such high
style and draped in such alluring, gin-soaked detail'
Booklist

'Think of it as the publishing industry's take on Mad Men: a
gripping fictional dispatch from the world of talented writers and
editors with big dreams, secrets, and booze bills'
Entertainment Weekly

'*Three-Martini Lunch* captures the excesses as well as the inhibitions
of New York City in 1958, from the eponymous meals of the big
Manhattan publishing houses, to wild drinking-and-drug bouts in
Greenwich Village, to the lingering paranoia of McCarthyism, to
the casual racism, sexism, homophobia and anti-Semitism among
the professional class'
NY Journal of Books

'*Three-Martini Lunch* is a gripping study of the ways in which
people betray others and themselves in an effort to carve out places
for themselves in a competitive and unforgiving world'
S...

SUZANNE RINDELL is a doctoral student in American modernist literature. Her first novel, *The Other Typist*, has been translated into fifteen languages. Before she turned to writing, she worked at a New York literary agency and lived in a cheap apartment above a funeral home. She still lives in New York, although no longer above the funeral home, and is currently working on a third novel.

suzannerindell.com
@SuzanneRindell

By Suzanne Rindell

Three-Martini Lunch

a&b

Three-Martini Lunch

SUZANNE RINDELL

Allison & Busby Limited
12 Fitzroy Mews
London W1T 6DW
allisonandbusby.com

First published in Great Britain by Allison & Busby in 2016.
This paperback edition published by Allison & Busby in 2017.

Published by arrangement with G. P. Putnam's Sons, an imprint of Penguin
Publishing, a division of Penguin Random House LLC.

A CIP catalogue record for this book is available from
the British Library.

10 9 8 7 6 5 4 3 2 1

ISBN 978-0-7490-2079-8

Typeset in 10.5/15.5 pt Adobe Garamond Pro by
Allison & Busby Ltd.

The paper used for this Allison & Busby publication
has been produced from trees that have been legally sourced
from well-managed and credibly certified forests.

Printed and bound by
CPI Group (UK) Ltd, Croydon, CR0 4YY

To Amy Einhorn and Jake Morrissey,
formerly 'work-wife' and 'work-husband'.
It is only fitting a book about publishing be dedicated to editors

'Nobody ever became a writer by just wanting to be one.'

– F. SCOTT FITZGERALD,
in a letter to his daughter and aspiring writer, Scottie

1

CLIFF

Greenwich Village in '58 was a madman's paradise. In those days a bunch of us went around together drinking too much coffee and smoking too much cannabis and talking all the time about poetry and Nietzsche and bebop. I had been running around with the same guys I knew from Columbia – give or take a coloured jazz musician here or a benny addict there – and together we would get good and stoned and ride the subway down to Washington Square. I guess you could say I liked my Columbia buddies all right. They were swell enough guys but, when you really got down to it, they were a pack of poser wannabe-poets in tweed and I knew it was only a matter of time before I outgrew them. Their fathers were bankers and lawyers and once their fascination with poetic manifestos wore off they would settle down and become bankers and lawyers, too, and marry a nice debutante. If I'm being honest, I'll admit I was mostly pissing away my time in school and not trying very hard, on account of the fact I'd lost the interest. With every passing day I was becoming increasingly convinced academia was for the birds, and the more time I spent below Fourteenth Street, the more it was becoming obvious to me that the Village was my true education.

When I finally threw in the towel and dropped my last class at Columbia, My Old Man came poking around my apartment in

Morningside Heights. He *ahemed* quietly to himself and fingered the waxy leaves of the plants in the window and finally sat with his rump covering a water stain on a hand-me-down Louis XVI sofa my great-aunt had deemed too ugly to keep in her own apartment. Together we drank a couple of fingers of bourbon neat, and then he shook my hand in a dignified way and informed me the best lesson he could teach me at this point in my life was *self-reliance*. His plan mainly involved cutting me off from the family fortune and making long speeches on the superior quality of *earned pleasures*.

Once My Old Man broke the news about how I was going to have to pave my own road, it was all over pretty quickly after that. I threw a couple of loud parties and didn't pay my rent and then the landlord had me out lickety-split and I had to go looking for a new place.

Which is how, as I entered into my study of the relative value of earned pleasures, I found myself renting a one-room studio in the Village with no hot water and a toilet down the hall. The lid was missing on the tank of that toilet and I remember the worst thing I ever did to my fellow hallmates was to get sick after coming home drunk one night and mistake the open tank for the open bowl. But even without my whiskey-induced embellishments the building was a dump. It was a pretty crummy apartment and when it rained the paint on the walls bubbled something awful, but I liked being near the basement cafes where people were passionate about trying out new things with the spoken word, which was still pretty exciting to me at the time. In those days you could walk the streets all around Washington Square and plunge down a narrow stairway here and there to find a room painted all black with red lightbulbs screwed into the fixtures and there'd be someone standing in front of a crowd, telling America to go to hell or maybe acting out the birth of a sacred cow in India. It was all kind of bananas and you were never sure what you were going to see, but after a while you started to come across the same people mostly.

I had seen Miles, Swish, Bobby, and Pal around the Village, of course, and they had seen me, too. We were friendly enough with one another, all of us being arty types. I knew their faces and I knew their names but the night I really entered the picture I was in such a sorry state, it was a real act of mercy on their part. I was slated to read my poems for the first time ever at a place called the Sweet Spot. Earlier that afternoon I had been looking over my pages when it suddenly struck me they were no good. The discovery had me seized up with fear until my whole body was paralysed and I sensed I was rank with the stench of my impending failure. The poems were bad and that was the truth of it. My solution was whiskey, and by six o'clock I had managed to put down half a bottle before the poems finally started to look better than they had at 3 p.m. In my foolish state I decided finishing the other half of the bottle would be the key to gaining at least a few more increments of poetic improvement. By the time I took the stage I could barely hold myself upright. Somehow I managed to get off two poems . . . more or less . . . before I heard the wooden stool next to me clatter to the ground as it fell over and I felt the cold sticky black-painted floor rise up like a swelling wave to my hip and shoulder and, seconds later, my face.

When I came to I was lying on a couch in Swish's apartment with the whole gang sitting around the kitchen table, talking in loud voices about Charlie Parker while a seminal record of his spun on a turntable near my head. After a few minutes Pal came over and handed me a cool washcloth for my bruised face. Then Bobby whistled and commented that I had '*some* kind of madman style' in an admiring tone of voice that made me think perhaps the two poems I could remember getting off hadn't been so bad after all and maybe it was even true that in getting wasted I had actually made the truest choice an artist could make, like Van Gogh and his absinthe. I could see they were all deciding whether I was a hack or a genius, and the fact they might be open to the second possibility being true fortified me and filled me with a kind of dopey pride. Then Swish boiled some coffee on the stove and brought it over to me. He told me his religion was coffee and he couldn't abide his guests adding milk or sugar and so I shouldn't ever expect him to offer any of that stuff. The coffee was so thick you could have set a spoon in the centre of the mug and it would've stood up straight and never touched the sides. Later when I learnt more about Swish he told me that was how you made it when you were on the road and once you'd had your coffee like that everything else tasted like water. I guess some of Swish's romantic passion about cowboy coffee wore off on me, because after that night I sneered at anything someone brought me that happened to have a creamy shade or sweetened taste.

Swish's given name was Stewart and he was nicknamed Swish because he was always in a hurry. He was one of those wiry, nervous guys with energy to spare. After I'd taken a few sips of Swish's coffee and managed to work my forehead over some more with the washcloth, I was feeling well enough to join them at the kitchen table and dive into the talk about Dizzy Gillespie and Charlie Parker, and all of a sudden it was like I had always had a seat at that table and had just never known it. The frenzied tempo of their chatter was contagious. They conversed like musicians improvising jazz and I hoped some of this would find its way into my writing. Between the five of us we finished off a pot of coffee and two packs of cigarettes and fourteen bottles of beer and shared the dim awareness that a small but sturdy union had been formed.

Swish regaled us with his adventures riding the rails across America like a hobo and about the year he'd spent in the Merchant Marine. Even though he'd never finished high school he had still managed to feed his mind all sorts of good solid stuff. In talking to Swish I realised all those guys at Columbia who thought they had the edge over you because they went to Exeter or Andover were all pretty much full of horseshit because here was Swish and he was better read than anybody and his education had been entirely loaned out to him from the public library for no money at all. I worried that maybe I'd offended Swish because I said something to set him off and he went on to give a big argumentative lecture all about John Locke and Mikhail Bakunin and about Thoreau. But my worries about having offended him were unfounded because I later realised Swish was one of those guys with a naturally combative disposition.

After he'd finished harping on old Mikhail's theories about anarchy, I asked Swish what he did for a living now that his hobo days were over.

'Bicycle messenger,' he replied. 'Miles here is, too.'

I regarded Miles, who seemed like an odd fit for this group. He was a slender, athletic-looking Negro with sharp cheekbones that would've made him appear haughty if they had not been offset by his brooding eyes. He wore the kind of horn-rimmed glasses that were popular all over the Village just then. He nodded but didn't comment further and I gathered that being a bicycle messenger wasn't his primary passion and figured him for a jazz musician. He had the name and the look for it, after all.

Anyway, the topic of conversation turned to me and what

my ambitions were, and sitting there at the table I already felt so comfortable and everything seemed so familiar, I found myself confessing to the fact I'd recently come to the conclusion that I'd decided to become a writer. Only problem was, ever since I'd arrived at this decision, I'd been having a spell of writer's block.

'I'll tell you what you do,' Swish said, his wiry body tensing up with conviction. 'You hop on the next boxcar and ride until you're full up with so many ideas you feel your fingers twitching in your sleep.'

'Well, I for one think a good old-fashioned roll in the hay would do the trick,' Bobby chimed in. 'It's important to keep the juices flowing.'

'Says the fella who's so busy balling two girls at once he can't make it to any of his auditions,' said Swish. I asked them what they meant. It turned out Bobby wanted to be an actor but his great obstacle in achieving this ambition was his overwhelming beauty. Under ordinary circumstances this wouldn't be a problem for an actor but in Bobby's case it kept him far too busy to get onstage much. Wherever he went, loud-shrieking girls and soft-spoken men alike tried their best to bed him and because Bobby liked to make everyone happy he went along with all of it and was loath to turn anyone down. He was presently keeping two girls in particular happy. One girl lived with a roommate over on Morton Street and the other lived in the Albert Hotel on East Eleventh and this left Bobby constantly hustling from one side of the Village to the other.

Bobby's recommendation that I ought to ball a girl (or two or three) to get over my writer's block appeared to disturb Pal's sense of chivalry and make him shy: he shifted in his chair and set about studying the label on his beer. He was by far the quietest and most difficult guy to read of the pack. Later I found out Pal's real name was Eugene and he was named after the town in Oregon where he was born and, as far as first impressions go, he often struck people as something of a gentle giant. He was a couple of inches over six feet and had the sleepy blue eyes of a child just woken up from a nap and when he read poetry or, even when he just spoke, his voice was always full of a kind of reverence that made you think he was paying closer attention to the world than you were.

'How 'bout it, Miles?' Swish said, continuing the conversation. 'What do you think helps with writer's block?'

I didn't know why Swish had directed the question to Miles. It unnerved me that after I mentioned dropping out of Columbia, Bobby had let it slip that Miles was due to graduate from that very institution come June. The lenses of Miles's glasses flashed white at us as he looked up in surprise.

'Well,' he said, considering carefully, 'I suppose reading always helps. They say in order to write anything good, you ought to read much more than you write.'

'Oh, I don't know about all that,' I said. I was suddenly in an ornery, contrary mood. The way he had spoken with authority on the subject antagonised me somehow. 'The most important thing a writer's gotta do is stay true to his own ideas and write. I don't read other people's books when I try to write, I just read my own stuff over and over and I think that's the way the real heavyweight authors do it.'

Miles didn't reply to this except to tighten his mouth and nod. It was a polite nod and I sensed there was a difference of opinion behind it and I was suddenly annoyed.

'Anyway, fellas, I think I've given you the wrong idea about me because I'm not really all that stuck,' I said, deciding it was time for a change of topic. 'I've written piles and piles of stuff and I'm always getting new ideas.'

This was mostly true, and the more I thought about it now the more I began to think perhaps it wasn't writer's block at all but more a case of my energies needing to build up in order to reach a kind of critical mass. Back then everyone in the neighbourhood was talking about a certain famous hipster who had written an entire novel in three weeks on nothing but coffee and bennies and about how he had let it build up until it had just come pouring out of him and about how the result had been published by an actual publisher and I thought maybe that was how it might work for me, too. If I just soaked up the nervous energy of my generation and let it accumulate inside me until it spilt over the top, I was sure eventually a great flood would come. Swish and Bobby and Pal all seemed like part of this process and I was very glad they had inducted me into the group. Even Miles was all right in the way that a rival can push you to do better work. Perhaps it was the mixture of the whiskey and coffee and beer and bennies but I suddenly had that high feeling you get when you sense you are in the middle of some kind of important nerve centre. I closed my eyes and felt the pulse of the Village thundering through my veins and all at once I was very confident about all I was destined to accomplish.

2

Looking back on it now, I see that New York in the '50s made for a unique scene. If you lived in Manhattan during that time, you experienced the uniqueness in the colours and flavours of the city that were more defined and more distinct from one another than they were in other cities or other times. If you ask me, I think it was the war that had made things this way. All the energy of the war effort was now poured into the manufacture of neon signs, shiny chrome bumpers, bright plastic things, and that meant all of a sudden there was a violent shade of Formica to match every desire. All of it was for sale and people had lots of dough to spend and to top it off the atom bomb was constantly hovering in the back of all our minds: its bright white flash and the shadow of its mushroom cloud casting a kind of imaginary yet urgent light over everything that surrounded us.

Shortly after the fellas revived me at Swish's apartment, I fell in regularly with the gang and soon enough I found out Miles was a writer, too. I should've known all along because everyone who was young and hip and living in New York at that time all wanted to do the same thing and that was to try and become a writer. Years later they would want to become folk musicians or else potters who threw odd-shaped clay vases but in '58 everyone still wanted to be a writer and in particular they wanted to write something truer and purer than everything that had come before.

There were a lot of different opinions as to what it took to make yourself a good writer. The people in the city were always looking to get out and go west and the people out west were always looking to get into the city. Everybody felt like they were on the outside looking in all the time; really it was just that the hipster scene tended to turn everything inside out and the whole idea was that we were all outsiders together.

I had always scribbled here and there but I didn't try to write in earnest until I left Columbia and got cut off and moved to the Village and this was maybe a little ironic because My Old Man was an editor at a big publishing house. He had wanted to be a writer himself but had gone a different way with that and had become an editor instead, although he never said it that way to people who came for dinner. When people came over for dinner he mostly just told jokes about writers. It turns out there are lots of jokes you can tell about writers.

I had a lot of funny feelings about My Old Man. On the one hand, there was some pretty lousy business he'd gotten into in Brooklyn that he didn't think I knew about. But on the other hand, he was one of those larger-than-life types you can't help but look up to in spite of yourself. He had a magnetic personality. Back in those days My Old Man was king of what they called the three-martini lunch. This meant that in dimly lit steakhouses all over Manhattan my father made bold, impetuous deals over gin and oysters. That was how it was done. Publishing was a place for men with ferocity and an appetite for life. Sure, the shy, tweedy types survived in the business all right but it was the garrulous bon vivants who really thrived and left their mark on the world. Lunches were long, expense accounts were generous, and the martinis often fuelled tremendous quantities of flattery and praise. Of course all that booze fuelled injuries, too, and the workday wasn't really over until someone had been insulted by Norman Mailer or pulled out the old boxing gloves in one way or another.

I was passionate about being a writer and My Old Man was passionate about being an editor and you would *think* between the two of us this would make for a bang-up combination, but my big problem was that My Old Man and I had our issues and I hadn't exactly told him about my latest ambitions. He'd always expressed disappointment over my lacklustre performance in school and now that I'd dropped out and was spending all my time in the Village, he thought I was a jazz-crazed drunkard. His idea of good jazz was Glenn Miller and it was his personal belief that if you listened to any other kind you were a dope fiend of some sort.

But whether or not My Old Man ever helped me out, I was determined to make it as a writer. In fact, sometimes it was more satisfying to think about becoming a writer without My Old Man even knowing. I'd written a couple of short stories that, in my eyes, were very good and it was only logical that in time I would write a novel and that would be good, too. I thought a lot about what it would be like once I made it, the swell reviews I would get in *The Times* and the *Herald Tribune* about my novel, the awards I'd probably win, and how all the newspaper men would want to interview me over martinis at the '21' Club. But the problem with this is sometimes I got so caught up in my head writing imaginary drafts of the good reviews I was bound to receive, it made it difficult to write the actual novel.

On days when I was having trouble punching the typewriter, I began to find little errands to run in the evenings that usually involved going down to the cafes in order to tell Swish and Bobby and Pal something important I had discovered that day about writing and being and existence. After I had delivered this message of course it was necessary to stay and enjoy a beer together and toast the fact we had been born to be philosophers and therefore understood what it was to really *be*. Sometimes Miles was there and sometimes he was not and I didn't always notice the difference because he was so reserved and only hung around our group in a peripheral way.

But Miles *was* there one afternoon when I went to a cafe to write. I had decided my crummy studio apartment was partly to blame for my writer's block and that I ought to try writing in a cafe. After all, Hemingway had written in cafes when he was just starting out in Paris and if that method had worked for Hemingway then I supposed it was good enough for me. The cafe I happened to choose was very crowded that day and the tables were all taken when I got there but I spied Miles at a cosy little table in the far corner of the room and just as I spotted him he looked up and saw me, too.

'Miserable day outside,' I said, referring to the rain.

'Yes.'

Miles and I had never spent time together on our own and naturally now that we were alone there was an awkwardness between us and it dawned on both of us how little we truly knew each other. I squinted at the items on the table in an attempt to surmise what he had been up to before I had come in.

'Are you writing something, too?' I asked, seeing the notebook and the telltale ink stain on his thumb and forefinger.

'I'm only fooling around,' Miles answered, but I could tell this was a lie because peeking out of his notebook were a few typewritten pages, which meant whatever Miles was working on he cared about enough to take the trouble to type it up.

'I see you own a typewriter,' I said, pointing to the pages.

'The library does,' he said, looking embarrassed. I couldn't tell whether the embarrassment was due to the fact that he was too poor to own a typewriter or because it was obvious he took his writing more seriously than he'd wanted to let on.

'They charge you for that?' I asked, trying to make conversation.

He nodded. 'Ten cents a half hour. It's not too bad. I've taught myself to type at a fairly good speed now.'

'That's swell,' I said. 'Say, do you mind if I settle in here and do a little scribbling of my own?' I asked, finally getting to my point.

'Of course not,' Miles said, pushing a coffee mug and some papers out of the way on the table. He had a very polite, formal way about him and it was difficult to tell whether he truly minded. But whether he minded or not didn't matter because after all he'd said yes and I needed to write and there really weren't any other tables and I wasn't going to go look for another cafe because by then it was really coming down cats and dogs outside. I pulled out my composition book and fountain pen and set to work staring at the thin blue lines that ran across the white paper. About ten or so minutes passed and I had made a very good study of the blank page. Then my nose started to itch and my knee began to bounce under the table. I looked up at Miles and watched him scrawling frantically in his notebook. I was curious what it was that had gotten him worked up in a torrent like that. He was so absorbed in his writing he didn't notice me staring at him. Finally, I asked him what he was working on. The first time I asked he did not hear me so I cleared my throat and asked again, more loudly. He jumped as if I'd woken him out of a trance and blinked at me.

'It's a short story, I suppose . . .' he said. This was news to me because, like I said, nobody had bothered to tell me Miles wrote anything at all, let alone fiction. Between his attending Columbia and writing, I was beginning to feel a little unsettled by all the things we had in common. Something about Miles was making me itchy around the collar.

'I don't know if it's any good,' he said.

'Say, why don't you let me have a look at it?' I replied, catching him off guard and reaching for the notebook before he could put up a fight. 'I know good fiction. My Old Man is an editor at Bonwright.' His eyes widened at this and I knew it had temporarily shut him up. I flipped the notebook open and moved my eyes over the tidy cursive on the page.

It wasn't terrible. Miles was a decent enough writer, all right – save for the fact that he wrote in a careful, old-fashioned voice, and that was probably on account of him being an educated Negro. All the educated Negroes I'd ever known were always a little stiff and took their educations a little too seriously in my opinion. But all and all, I could see he had a way with words and it wasn't half-bad. I had to admit I liked the story okay. It was about two boys on the war front who discover they're half-brothers but they've always been competitors and don't like each other. When they get into a real bad scrape one has the option to let the other die and be off the hook for the death, but he hesitates.

'How are you going to end it?' I said, coming to the place where the cursive trailed off.

Miles shrugged.

'Maybe just like that,' he said. 'It was the hesitation that interested me.'

I shook my head. 'He should hesitate all right,' I said. 'And decide against his better sense to save his brother. But then when he does, the other fellow shoots him with the dead German's gun, like the sucker he is.' Miles looked at me with raised eyebrows. I could see my suggestion was unexpected.

'I suppose that would . . . make quite a statement.'

'Exactly,' I said, feeling magnanimous for loaning out my superior creativity. 'It's not worth writing if it doesn't make a statement.' Miles looked at me and I could already see he wasn't going to write it the way I suggested, which was a mistake. It was a good twist and I had made a nice gift out of it for him and it was awfully annoying that he wasn't going to take the wonderful gift I had just bestowed upon him.

'Well, anyway,' I said, 'suit yourself with the ending.'

I handed the journal back to him and attempted to get back to work. Miles sat there a moment looking at me with a wary expression on his face. Then he turned back to his own work. We were silent together and all at once the words started coming and I found I could write and for several minutes the only sound you could hear at our table came from the scratching of our duelling fountain pens.

But it was no good. I had helped Miles along with his plot and now I couldn't get it out of my head. I was off and running and writing something but soon enough I realised I was just writing his story all over again, but better. The thing that really got to me as I wrote was that it really *ought* to have been *my* story in the first place. You should always write what you know and I was something of an authority on unwanted relatives, but of course Miles couldn't know that. Now that he had started writing that story, I couldn't go and write anything similar, even if he *was* going to botch the ending.

'How'd you come up with the idea for that story, anyway?' I asked, feeling irritated that I hadn't thought of it first. Miles looked up.

'I was trying to remember some of my father's stories about the Battle of the Marne; that's why I picked the setting. And the idea of brothers and all the rest of it' – he shrugged – 'just came out of my imagination. Like I said, I'm not sure it's any good. I usually can't tell about my own work until several drafts and a few months later.'

'Well, it has potential. I wouldn't take it too hard,' I said. 'You strike me as a guy who works pretty hard at it, and that's what counts, right?'

Miles looked at me, not saying anything.

'Say, I'm thirsty,' I said. 'Why don't we order up something stronger than coffee?'

After a brief bout of resistance he could see I wasn't going to take no for an answer. We spent the afternoon drinking and talking about the Pulitzer and the Nobel and the differences between French writers and Russian writers and to tell the truth I had a decent enough time talking to Miles. I decided it would be fine if we ran into each other on our own again, so long as I didn't have to sit across from him as he scribbled away in his notebook, writing the kind of stories *I* should've been writing but with all the wrong endings.

3

After that day in the cafe with Miles, I decided to try to jump-start my writing by going on a bender and hitting each and every party I could. The idea was, I was a young guy and I ought to be gathering experiences and then once I had a bunch of wild stories inside me the writing would just flow. This had an unfortunate side effect other than the obvious, because besides hangovers this was also how I made the acquaintance of a one Mr Rusty Morrisdale.

Rusty Morrisdale was the assistant to a very important and well-known literary agent who, before the war, had been credited with making a handful of writers very famous. Rusty's boss was quite old; no one knew exactly how old the famous agent was and just like the man's career his age had become the stuff of legend. I won't mention his name here but if you know anything about publishing at all then you will know exactly whom I mean. According to most people in the industry, you were not an important writer unless this literary agent had discovered you and anointed you and introduced you to all the best editors. Anyway, that's what they all said and here Rusty was, the personal secretary to this man.

I think it must've been because of Bobby that Rusty came around at first. Rusty was a scrawny, rat-faced dandy of a kid who acquired

his nickname by virtue of his rust-coloured hair. I mentioned Bobby
was beautiful in a way that even guys who went around with girls
noticed and Rusty was not the sort to go around with girls at all and
so was even more likely to pay his respects to Bobby's beauty. There
was something kind of dopey and all-American about Bobby, and
yet he and his lopsided grin were difficult to resist. He was a tanned,
gangly kid who looked like he had spent half of his youth going to
Sunday school and operating farm equipment and the other half
stealing eggs out of chicken coops and lamming from the police
for petty crimes. He'd taken the bus to New York from Utah and
was desperate to do anything or know anybody who might scrub
some of that squeaky Salt Lake rime off his skin. Bobby had great
intellectual aspirations and always wanted to talk about important
books but, unlike Swish, if you actually entered into a conversation
with him you discovered he had not read that many important
books so much as seen and admired their jackets. I'm guessing Rusty
saw Bobby from afar and got the bright and thoroughly unoriginal
idea it might be nice to bed him and after getting a little closer to
Bobby and speaking with him, this desire had only increased in
both magnitude and intensity.

When a guy named Rex Taylor who I'd been pretty chummy
with at Columbia invited me to a house party he was throwing,
I invited Bobby. He'd recently broken things off with both of his
girls and was primed for some fun. It was always a smart thing if
you were going to a party to invite Bobby, because all the prettiest
chicks flocked to Bobby and if you were standing next to him it was
like they were flocking to you, too. He was supposed to go drinking
with Rusty that night and he told Rusty he couldn't go because now
he was going to go to the party with me, but then I guess Bobby felt
pretty bad about leaving Rusty out in the cold like that because he

ended up telling Rusty he could tag along if he liked and of course Rusty liked. It was a BYOB party and when Rusty met us at my apartment he showed up carrying six bottles of eighteen-year-old Scotch and so we thought maybe in the end it was all right to have him along. I didn't know who Rusty was or who he worked for then, but I figured the math was right because anyone who showed up places with six bottles of eighteen-year-old Scotch was OK in my book and so we loaned him a shirt and helped him peg his pant legs to match ours and then set out as a group to find the party.

Rex lived rent-free in a swanky brownstone on West Seventy-Fourth Street. His parents owned the building and evidently his old man felt differently than mine did about the value of earned pleasures. The Taylors were old money and their fortune slid from one generation to the next with ease. My family was old money, too, but only on my mother's side. This meant My Old Man had come up in the world. He had that way about him that people who are raised poor and come into money later in life do in that sometimes he was a spendthrift and other times he was a tightwad. He blew hot and cold when it came to giving me money and I guessed this was partly because of that business out in Bensonhurst. In any case it was irritating because it meant he was an unreliable source of income. Sometimes when he was in a generous mood after having drunk a lot of martinis with his lunch or else wine with his dinner he would remember how he had been the recipient of a lot of people's benevolence and then he would soften up and slip me fifty bucks here or there but I always had to ask.

Together Bobby, Rusty, and I rode the train up from the Village, carrying two bottles of Scotch apiece. Bobby got the idea to open one of his bottles and we passed it around some on the train, our breath coming alive with the hot caramelised odour of malt and oak as middle-class businessmen with their newspapers and umbrellas frowned at us and scandalised mothers scooted away from us and hugged their children tighter. At Forty-Second Street, a real-life Indian got on the train wearing a beaded belt and a feathered headband and long black braids and all of that business and Bobby, already feeling warm and friendly from the Scotch, held out the opened bottle to the Indian and said, 'Little sip of fire-water for ya, Chief?' Bobby could be as obnoxious as he liked because somehow it still came out charming. No one ever said no to Bobby and neither did this Indian. The Indian regarded Bobby with a black-eyed stare, then nodded in a serious way and took a decent-sized swig of the bottle and handed it back to Bobby. Then he wiped his mouth with the back of his hand and stared straight ahead again as stoic and sombre as anything and it struck me we had just had ourselves an uneasy sort of peace-pipe ceremony the way heroes did in all the westerns. We got off the train at Seventy-Second Street and it looked like the Indian was continuing on and I felt a little embarrassed when Bobby stood on the platform and raised his hand and said 'HOW' in a deep voice because I doubt the Indian liked that but then maybe he got it from people all the time and was used to it. Then the train doors closed and the Indian slid sideways out of our view and we went above ground where it smelt like wet leaves because we were so near Central Park and we walked westward for a few blocks until I finally recognised Rex's brownstone.

I'd only been to Rex's pad once before and that was for another house party and much of that night had been lost to my crummy alcoholic memory. But even if I'd forgotten what the brownstone looked like, we still would've been able to tell which one it was by the coloured Christmas lights blinking like a hundred tiny Roman candles going off in every window and by the sound of Latin jazz drifting into the open street. The music was some sort of bossa nova business: the sound of a xylophone being busily worked over a few sassy chords on the piano, some easy bongo drumming, and the steady shake of maracas throughout, all punctuated by the occasional angst-ridden blast of a trumpet or sax. It was frenetic and easy all at the same time.

Once inside we looked for Rex so we could present him with the six bottles of Scotch, which at that point had transformed into five and a quarter bottles of Scotch.

'Rex!' I shouted.

The record player was turned up full blast and Rex was in the living room tinkering with it to see if he could make it go even louder. We shouted our hellos and Rusty was quick to jump in and take credit for having brought the booze. Later I came to find out that Rusty hadn't even paid for the Scotch at all but had swiped it instead from a delivery intended for his employer's wet bar. He was very proud when he told the story about swiping the Scotch to me and Bobby because he bragged that the famous literary agent trusted him so much he didn't even bat an eye when Rusty blamed it on the delivery boy, he just picked up the telephone and had the delivery boy fired right then and there. Rusty avoided mentioning this was the same six bottles he had 'generously' brought to Rex's party but the math was the same and once you got to know Rusty better it was hard to picture him paying for anything at all, let alone six bottles of very expensive Scotch, and so it didn't take a genius to figure it all out.

'Make yourselves at home, fellas!'

Rex always had a generous indifference about him and never went in much for who paid for what. The volume on the record player suddenly got louder and Rex smiled at us. We asked Rex a few more questions but he just went on smiling and shook his head as though he couldn't hear what we were saying over all the music and commotion, and finally just waved an arm in the direction of a table overflowing with bottles of every sort of liquor. We understood from the wave that we could deposit our bottles there if we liked or we could keep them to ourselves; it didn't matter much to him what we did as long as we were having a swell time and enjoying all of Rex's unearned pleasures.

It wasn't very long until we were surrounded by girls, most of whom made it pretty clear as they clambered over one another that all the fuss was for Bobby. A lean and wiry brunette with heavy black eye make-up gave out a hoot of recognition and threw her arms around Bobby to hug him hello, then simply remained hanging on his neck as though her body were some sort of soggy scarf that had been knotted there and forgotten. A second girl – a chubby bottle-blonde who was pretty in a way but had a piggish sort of nose – stood off to the side touching Bobby's shoulder and trying in earnest to have a conversation as he nodded and smiled and tried to listen with one ear. But it was a shy toffee-skinned girl standing in a corner who ultimately caught Bobby's eye and who I could tell Bobby would probably ball before the night was over. I glanced over at Rusty and could see his jaw clenching and I could tell already he'd fallen in love with Bobby's beauty in a way that reduced him to feeling stingy and mean about things. He was watching the coloured girl with a look of pure hate in his eyes and I could only guess about the kinds of ugly names he was probably calling her inside his head just then.

The roof of Rex's brownstone had a pretty decent view and later that night Rex and Rusty and I and also Bobby and his coloured girl all ended up on it. The three of us stood there drinking and talking and flicking cigarette butts off the top while Bobby nuzzled and necked with his girl until he had her in a corner pressed up against the roof's ledge. Bobby was always a man for steady progress and eventually he worked that coloured girl's skirt up enough to expose the majority of her toffee-coloured buttocks and it wasn't long afterwards that he began to press himself against her and the slow peal of a zipper sounded. We adjourned to the other side of the roof in order to give Bobby some privacy to do what he needed to do with the girl. I had tried to get the little plump blonde girl up on the roof for myself but once I'd gotten her alone she kept talking on and on about the boy she was going steady with and so eventually I got bored and gave up and had decided smoking cigarettes on the roof with Rex and Rusty wasn't such a bad idea after all. It was a nice night out, one of those unreal reprieves from winter when you find you hardly need your coat, and we smoked in silence and looked up into that vacuous space above New York where the stars are supposed to be. We tried to relax and there was a lot of sighing but it was difficult. It was clear from the sneer on Rusty's face he was sore about Bobby and the coloured girl, and his bitterness smouldered in a way that filled the air all around the three of us. Then finally someone spoke and it was Rusty and he was asking me what I did for a living.

'Cliff here is going to be a writer. An important one,' Rex answered for me, and in his voice I heard the pride he had for his friend and immediately felt myself cringe with embarrassment.

'That true?' Rusty asked.

'That's the idea, I guess,' I said, not catching on to how the bitterness in Rusty's sneer had twisted into something else now and he had suddenly perked up with alertness, his eyes as clear and sharp as a hawk's. He looked me over, studying me from head to toe with what I took to be a freshly interested appraising air. I had no clue why I suddenly interested him so much. He narrowed his eyes and smiled and when I looked at him again it struck me that the expression was the Machiavellian smile of a tiny tyrant. The moans of Bobby's coloured girl grew louder and floated over to us from the other side of the roof and we all did our best to ignore it. Then Rusty cleared his throat and looked me in the eye and told me in that deliberately slow, over-articulated way he had what it was he did for a living and who he worked for. He paused and waited for the information to blow me over sideways as he knew it would. I must've had a look of great hunger on my face after he told me this because the tiny tyrant's smile stretched wider and his eyes narrowed in increased smugness and I became vaguely aware of the fact he knew he had me on the hook then.

Rex rejoined the conversation and changed the topic and we all went on talking amiably as ever about baseball and about communism and about whether or not the two things could ever exist simultaneously together in a single culture and it was a good talk and all real groundbreaking stuff, but when I think really hard on the origin of things I realise that night on the roof was when all the trouble with Rusty truly started. He knew he had me on the hook, and *I* knew he had me on the hook, and the only person who didn't know it was Rex because Rex didn't care about who wrote what or published it and how. The only thing Rex cared about was would the Cubans ever really have a league as good as the Americans.

4

Once I found out about Rusty's boss, I kept my eyes peeled for Rusty in the Village. Besides Rusty, there were a handful of young publishing types who ran around the hipster scene. You could tell them apart from the other Village kids because they wore turtlenecks and jackets and glasses and skewed more to the bookish side of things. They arrived in New York on Greyhounds from all over America with an air of great optimism about them; young, single people willing to live in terrible apartments and work for peanuts so long as Manhattan dazzled them with her bright lights and taxi-horn siren song. Mostly the publishing folks were young men but there were tons of young women who worked in publishing, too, mostly as typists and secretaries. They came to the city after graduating from Vassar or Mount Holyoke or some women's college in the Midwest whose name you were bound to forget two minutes after it was mentioned. Generally, they tried to behave like the good girls they had been brought up to be and confined themselves to women's hotels uptown so you weren't as likely to see them down in the Village as you were the fellas. Mostly these girls were waiting to meet their husbands. Once that happened they were destined to quit working and return to the suburbs from whence they came and throw bridge parties and tell one another stories about the madcap year they lived as single gals in the city.

But there was one girl who Swish started bringing around on a regular basis and that was Eden. He had met Eden as he was cutting through Central Park and riding his bike very fast through a section where bikes aren't really allowed and where Eden was sitting on a park bench reading a book and as he dodged between a schnauzer and an old lady Eden yelled after him to slow down. Like I said, Swish was always in a hurry, but he was never in too much of a hurry to enter into a great debate with a willing adversary over his 'goddamn God-given rights', as he liked to call them. Differences of opinion excited him and arguing was like making love for Swish: he did it with passion and vigour and really it was his way of loving you and loving all the differences. When Eden yelled at him, Swish circled back and the way Eden tells it Swish was already wearing an eager grin as he turned and pedaled furiously back to her. The way *Swish* tells it, his grin got bigger when he saw the book in her hands was *The Secret Agent* by Conrad because there were few things Swish loved more than a book with a plot that revolved around a bunch of anarchists. When he saw the book he knew right away to invite her to the Village to come hear Pal's first poetry reading.

I guess I didn't think much of Eden when I first met her because even though Swish had twigged to her the way he did I took one look at her dark hair combed into a tidy ponytail and her sweater sets and figured she was only slumming it and as soon as some nice bond salesman proposed, that would be the last we saw of her.

'Hey, Cliff!' Swish shouted to me that evening as I strolled into the San Remo. 'Over here!' He was standing at the bar with Eden. The San Remo was one of Swish's favourite watering holes, as it was always buzzing with lively debate and on any given day you could find someone willing to engage you about politics or art or philosophy. Swish made the introductions and I shook hands, finding Eden's how-do-you-dos every bit as buttoned-up and boring as her sweater sets.

Eden was very petite with elfin features. She had pale skin and large black eyes. Later, people would say she looked a little like Audrey Hepburn but that was only after she went and got her hair cut very short. When I bumped into her again later that year, I saw right away Eden had reinvented herself with that haircut. She was all right to look at before, but afterwards she was *really* something because the thing about Eden that got everybody in the end was her style. She became one of those sharp-looking chicks with very dark hair and her bangs cropped in a very precise line high up on her forehead, running around the Village in boat-neck shirts and black capri pants, shimmying to jazz with a mysteriously aloof, blasé look in her eye.

But that's not how she was on the day I first met her. On the day I met Eden she hadn't transformed yet and her ponytail swung high atop her head and her Sears, Roebuck & Co. sweater hung lumpy and dull on her small frame and she looked like any other girl you might see walking the street in Des Moines or Wichita or what have you.

'We were just talking about Sputnik,' Swish said, by way of inviting me into the conversation. Back in those days Sputnik was one of Swish's favourite topics of conversation because Swish loved a good conspiracy theory and they had just announced in January that the satellite had burnt up as it fell from orbit and re-entered Earth's atmosphere. The physicists said this was to be expected but Swish insisted this was proof it had never existed in the first place and the whole business was a hoax. I'd had an earful of these theories because Swish could always manage to bait someone into a debate on the topic: young and old, liberal and conservative. Space travel was getting to be the great leveller of our generation.

'I mean, c'mon,' Swish said, making his argument to Eden now. 'That

Khrushchev is one mad cat! Mad enough that no one'll call his bluff, but you can see it in his eyes. The whole thing was a big theatre production.'

'Do you really think so?' Eden asked. I could see from her expression she was less concerned with the question of Khrushchev's sanity than she was with Swish's. Swish often had that effect on people, especially girls, and it was really too bad because it was only a question of too much intensity and sincerity because beneath his wiry, paranoid-seeming exterior he was really a sharp and decent guy.

'You bet I do!' Swish replied. 'These governments, they have to control people somehow, brainwash them with patriotism and get them to comply, get them to pay their taxes and never ask where their money went when all they ever do is build more and more missiles. Right, Cliff? You agree, don't you?'

I'd been over this with him before and grown tired of the subject and I decided to say so. 'I don't know, Swish,' I said. 'I don't know about any missiles and maybe I should've lived during a different time because I can't seem to get very excited about the Soviets one way or another. But Russian poets, on the other hand . . . now, that's a conversation I'd be willing to weigh in on . . .'

At this, Eden whirled about and her eyes lit up. 'You like Russian poetry?'

'Well, I like Pushkin, of course,' I said, naming the one poet everyone knew so as to not make her feel too dumb. 'You?'

'Oh yes,' she said. 'And Tsvetaeva and Akhmatova and Pasternak, too.'

This caught me off guard. She was far smarter than I'd expected and I wondered if she hadn't just said some kind of sentence in Rooskie.

'Keep it down,' I said jokingly, 'too much of *that* jazz and they'll arrest us for communism.' I decided it was time for another subject change, so I asked, 'What do you do in the city here again?'

'Oh. I'm a secretary at Torchon & Lyle.'

'Really? You don't say.'

Torchon & Lyle was one of the bigger publishing houses in midtown. The only one bigger was Bonwright, where My Old Man worked. I wasn't all that surprised but I could see she wanted me to be impressed, so I played along.

'Do you like it there?'

'I love it,' she said, nodding so vigorously I thought her head might come unhinged from her neck. 'It's why I came to New York – my goal is to become an editor someday.'

Eden was quick enough to catch the look of surprise that crossed my face.

'You don't think I would make a good editor?'

'No, I do; you seem to me like a regular go-getter. That's swell. I thought most girls were just waiting for a ring.'

'Well, I *am* waiting for a ring,' Eden said. 'On the telephone. From my boss. Telling me I've been promoted.'

I took a closer look at her face.

'What was your name again?' I asked.

'Eden,' she said, putting out her hand. 'Eden Katz.'

'Well, then, I'll be sure to keep an eye out for Eden Katz, future star of publishing,' I said. We smiled at each other. She really *was* quite attractive once you'd had a chance to get a second look at her. In any event, before I could get too far considering the possibilities, Swish cut back in, putting a hand on Eden's shoulder to remind everybody who'd brought her around in the first place, irritated that we'd managed to steer the conversation away from Sputnik for so long.

5

EDEN

When I first began my employment at Torchon & Lyle, I attended as many of the company's parties as I could. If I am being honest I will tell you I was hoping to get a glimpse of all the famous literary people it publishes. Of course I was only hired on as a secretary but that didn't matter much, because even the lowest-ranking secretary in the typing pool had a standing invitation to the parties. I remember thinking at the time that this was very generous of them but now I see it was less a matter of generosity and more a matter of practicality: secretaries are good if you want to fill up a room with fresh-faced, warm bodies and in a pinch a secretary can be asked to lend a hand if the caterer turns out to need an extra smiling waitress here or there to walk around with a tray of drinks. This happened to me on a few occasions and each time it did, it made me realise it was no small feat to cater a publishing party and an even bigger feat to keep the publishing types' glasses full.

Back in those days, publishing parties were great lavish affairs, with pigs-in-a-blanket and stuffed olives and lots of other fashionable little canapés, and of course an open bar with 'enough gin and Scotch to wash an elephant', as Truman Capote might say. If you were a single girl who had to pinch pennies just to pay the rent on her room at the Barbizon, it was a rather clever trick to skip dinner and fill up at the parties. Most of the parties happened on weeknights and if you played your cards right you could arrange it so you only had to buy a couple of cans of soup or beans for Saturdays and Sundays. It was a funny thing indeed to go from one night eating water biscuits heaped with miniature mountains of jewel-toned caviar and devilled eggs dusted with iron-red paprika to the next night eating nothing but canned beans on stale toast, but publishing is a funny business that way. If you worked in publishing you did it for the exciting books and authors and all the parties that went along with them; you didn't do it for the groceries your paycheck bought and if you didn't understand that much going into it, then you were a silly little fool. I should know. I was a silly little fool. I would go to the parties and if I wasn't asked to help the caterer I'd get to floating dreamily around the room with a cocktail in my hand feeling like Dorothy Parker and eventually I'd get so carried away that by the end of the night I'd even pay the extravagant sixty-five cents it cost to take a taxi back to the Barbizon. Then the weekend would roll around and I'd wonder why I had so little money that I had to cancel my visit to the hairdresser and be very careful at the grocer's. My poverty was a subject of great mystery to me and I rarely thought of it in connection with Torchon & Lyle.

Part of the reason for this is because on party nights I rarely felt poor; I felt young and lucky and full of potential, like the ingénue in a magazine serial who'd come to take on the city as a single girl, only instead of imagining myself engaged to a swell young businessman by the story's end I imagined myself one day being promoted to editor, which was my true dream. There was certainly something very electric about those evenings. Even now I get a little impressed when I picture myself attending those parties, those restaurants and private clubs and wealthy people's apartments that were all such a far cry from my life in Indiana. The men were all artfully unshaven and the women were all very tanned or else very pale; there were practically none who were a normal colour in between. The banquet rooms were wallpapered in oriental landscape patterns and had fashionably speckled wall-to-wall carpeting that made your ankles wobble just the tiniest bit if you were wearing ladies' pumps. I found it all very exotic. As far as the famous literary people went, sometimes when the party was very good or the host was very important you would spot one or two here and there, but you usually didn't get to talk to them. The big name authors were often flanked by their editors, and their agents, too, if they had them. You'd see them standing off in a corner holding a drink while either their editor or their agent murmured something in a low tone. No one dared cut in on them and it was difficult to eavesdrop. Of course all this only heightened the mystique. The editor would talk and at regular intervals the big name author would nod with a glazed, far-off look and a clenched jaw and he would appear very intellectual about whatever it was that was being said.

No matter how many of these soirees I attended, each time I decided to go to another I was always very nervous and I routinely spent a great deal of time picking out my outfit the day before. This was silly because usually as soon as you mingled about and talked to people you realised they were nervous, too, and if we were smart we could have all just made a mutual pact to be easier with one another and not to get so worked up about things. People seemed more relaxed after their second or third drink but if you were to observe closely you would see it wasn't really a question of them being more at ease so much as it was a question of the volume being turned up more loudly on their nervous laughter, which made them sound like they were having the time of their lives but also made them sound slightly maniacal, like mental patients wandering around a carnival.

Once I became a veteran of these parties, I noticed there were really only two main types of personalities: nerves brought out eager comedy in some and cattiness in others. Just like me, most of the people at the parties were employed as somebody's secretary or else somebody's assistant and had come hoping to rub elbows with the giants of the literary world. If you do the math in this equation you are destined to realise that, more often than not, the eventual result of any given party turns out to be a bunch of people's secretaries meeting a bunch of other people's secretaries, and all too often that really *was* what it boiled down to. That fact alone should take some of the glamour out of my memories but somehow it doesn't. I suppose this is because a handful of those assistants went on to become important editors with a lot of power and you can see how people take it when you drop into the conversation that you met the important editor way back when.

What I'm getting at is that publishing is quite a heady business. If you aren't careful, then you can let the sparkle of a certain famous name or the memory of holding a glass of champagne on a starlit terrace with a lovely view of the park wipe out all the long hours spent writing reader's reports in your room with its one small window pointed into an air shaft while your nylons dried on the radiator and you ate beans on toast and wished you could afford a few eggs or even a can of sardines to go with it.

In any case, at that time I was over the moon to have any job at all, but especially one in publishing. It was what I had set my sights on and the entire reason I'd moved to New York. Most jobs are gotten by referral and when it comes to publishing houses this is especially true. I was lucky enough to arrive at the offices of Torchon & Lyle with a letter of introduction in hand from one of their former senior editors, and I was very aware this was an extremely unusual situation – and therefore an extremely *fortunate* situation – for a girl from Indiana to have fallen into her lap.

A man named Mr Hightower referred me to Torchon & Lyle. Mr Hightower was a Fort Wayne native, a lifelong bachelor who had left his publishing career in New York in order to care for his ailing mother. I can't remember precisely what his mother had; cancer of the pancreas, I think it was. Once he'd gotten settled back into life in Indiana, Mr Hightower was invited to teach a few seminars on popular literature at the local women's college, and this was how I made his acquaintance: I was his student.

I took his seminar in the fall of my senior year, and then I took it again in the spring for no credit at all. I was not his only repeat student, though I am certain I'm the only one who retook the course based on my fascination with the subject. Despite the fact he'd never married – or perhaps because of it – Mr Hightower was what was referred to as *a ladies' man*, and as it was a ladies' college, I don't think I'm jumping to conclusions when I say this motivated a surge in class enrollment. In those days it wasn't uncommon for girls to have crushes on men twice their age. We all pictured riding off into the sunset with a middle-aged Clark Gable, I suppose. In any case, the young ladies of my college were taken with his debonair, middle-aged ways, with his steely blue eyes and the white streaks of hair just over his temples. I suppose he *was* good-looking in a certain fashion . . . but I wasn't so much enraptured with his looks as I was the stories he told about working in the publishing business.

Mr Hightower told marvellous stories. Most of them involved a great deal of martinis with this-or-that famous author, and ended with him outsmarting somebody in a business deal. But the stories I liked best – the stories for which I repeated the seminar – were always about finding a gem of a manuscript in the unsolicited submission pile. According to Mr Hightower, he had been responsible for publishing several unknown writers who later went on to become great authors.

It occurred to me that something downright magical had happened when Mr Hightower discovered these authors. And then, not too long after that, a little voice inside me said, 'I could do that!' I suppose that's awfully cocky of me to think, but my gut feeling was that I *could* do it, if given the chance. The sheer notion of reading a book *before it was a book* made me dizzy with excitement, and I realised I ought to follow where this feeling might lead. I began to linger after class, asking Mr Hightower more and more questions about his publishing days.

The funny thing about people is that when you take a special interest in something they know all about, they take a special interest in you. Mr Hightower answered my questions with enthusiasm; his supply of anecdotes seemed never-ending, and he was happy to share them. Occasionally when our conversations threatened to carry on long after class had ended, we adjourned to the student coffeehouse, where Mr Hightower took off his cuff links and rolled up his shirtsleeves, as though to signify that now we were really going to get down to business. He often loosened his tie and leant his elbows on the table and spoke in deep, confiding tones. There were whispers from the tables all around us and looking back on it now I see it was very likely the entire campus believed we were having an affair.

I don't know what Mr Hightower thought of me as far as the prospect of an affair was concerned, but as for myself I was completely naïve to the idea. In those days I was still very ignorant about most things having to do with sex. The truth was the only thing I was conscious of wanting from Mr Hightower was his expertise on all the major publishing houses in New York, and on discovering good writers and about becoming a successful editor. As the semester wound down and graduation drew near, I informed Mr Hightower of my plans to go east in order to try my own hand at publishing. I remember it was after class on a Friday, following his last lecture of the year. I worked up my nerve to tell him and when I did, he looked at me with surprise, then shrugged.

'I think that's a fine idea, Eden,' he said, packing up his things. 'A very fine idea, indeed. Of course you know Rome wasn't built in a day. You'll have to start at the bottom and prove yourself. But having said that, I think you'd make a fine editor – someday. Women of your generation are doing all kinds of surprising things.' He stopped packing up his briefcase and patted me on the shoulder and looked at me with glassy eyes and for the first time the realisation dawned on me that he would be sorry to see me go. While plenty of girls had crushes on him, I don't suppose there were that many other students who'd taken as strong an interest as I had in his professional life, and when I left Fort Wayne there would be one less inquisitive thread tying his past to his present.

He was still holding my shoulder when his gaze turned thoughtful. His eyes roved slowly over the entirety of my person, from my carefully combed ponytail to my blouse to my black wool pencil skirt, registering each in turn. His upper lip twitched faintly and his hand involuntarily squeezed my shoulder. He moved as though to say something. But just as abruptly as the impulse took hold, he abandoned it; he stopped himself short and relinquished his grip. 'Ah, to be young again,' he finally said in a resigned, trite voice, sighing and returning his attention to the buckle on his briefcase. He looked at me one more time as he made his way out the classroom door and gave a little strange half-smile of defeat.

'Tell you what,' he said, mashing a slate-grey fedora down on his head. 'You've been a sterling student. I'll write you a letter of introduction. That ought to help you get your foot in the door to start.'

The next time I saw Mr Hightower it was in the stadium, over an expanse of green lawn steaming with the heat of high noon, just after the last graduation speech had been given and the caps had been thrown in the air. The initial hullabaloo had started to break up and all the parents had begun to mill about, each family hollering out the name of their newly anointed alumna. I turned my head and saw Mr Hightower striding towards me with a businesslike expression etched into his distinguished features. I was expecting an envelope containing the letter of introduction he had promised, and was surprised when he handed me not one but two.

'I took the liberty of writing one in the name of Eden Katz, and one in the name of Eden Collins.'

I squinted into the sun. My surprised hands accepted the envelopes and turned them over, puzzled. A daunting insecurity dimly formed itself in my brain. Was I so unmemorable a student that my professor had never been sure of my name? I looked up at Mr Hightower with a confused smile.

'It was the best approximation I could think of,' he said, as though that explained it.

'Oh!' I murmured, still not understanding but wanting to. I continued to look at him with wide eyes. I must've looked pretty stupid about it all because he seemed to read the bafflement on my face. My parents, who had been standing by my side just moments before Mr Hightower's arrival, were now at least ten paces away from us and were busily chatting with Dolly Worthington's folks.

He gave them a nervous glance, then leant in and lowered his voice.

'Publishing is a pretty friendly business to . . . all types,' Mr Hightower confided. 'But even so, some circles are friendlier than others and with the ones that aren't, you'll want to play your cards right.'

'Oh,' I said softly, my stomach still a bit uneasy from the surprise of it. Knee-jerk decorum compelled me to say *thank you* but I was having trouble getting the words to come out. 'Oh, I see,' was all I could seem to muster. I stared down at the envelopes in my hands.

'Now, if you take one of those letters – maybe the one written in the name of "Collins" would be better in this instance – over to Torchon & Lyle, where I used to be a senior editor, well, then my name should open some doors for you,' Mr Hightower instructed. 'Got that? Torchon & Lyle – they're in the book, of course. And be sure to ask if you can see Miss Everett, on the fifth floor. She's in charge of hiring all the secretaries and the readers, and she's liable to look out for anyone I'd recommend.'

As it turned out, graduation day was the last time I saw Mr Hightower. Once my parents had joined our conversation, he shook their hands and complimented them for having raised such a studious, hard-working daughter with such lofty ambitions. 'Let me assure you, you've done a wonderful job, Mr and Mrs Katz.' He didn't say another word about the two letters of introduction and I was nearly convinced I'd hallucinated the whole conversation until I got home later that evening and pulled both envelopes out of my purse.

I won't bore you with the details of the summer I spent working as a clerk at the five-and-dime to save up for the Greyhound ticket that eventually took me the distance from Fort Wayne to

New York. A few months after graduation, I found myself sitting in Miss Everett's office at Torchon & Lyle. I watched as she lit a cigarette, unfolded a sheaf of typewritten paper and held it away from her face, almost at arm's length, and proceeded to move her eyes over it with a careful, clinical sort of interest. I'd handed her my resume, and one of the letters. Despite Mr Hightower's enigmatic admonishments, I'd decided I would only use one of them.

'*Eden Katz.* How exotic. *Katz* . . . that's not German, is it?'

'Oh. Well . . . my grandparents came over from Vienna.' There was a long pause. 'Before both wars,' I added. 'I suppose it was sometime around 1910.'

'I see. And you say Horatio is a . . . friend? . . . mentor? . . . of yours?' she asked. There was a cool lilt in everything Miss Everett said, a lilt that in my mind seemed somehow linked to the ash-blonde tint of her poodle-cut hair. I later found out the tint came from a bottle and the lilt had been achieved by indirectly memorising lines from Ingrid Bergman pictures.

'Horatio?' I repeated, peering around the office. I was having trouble concentrating. My head was still spinning with the euphoric realisation that I had finally made it through the doors of a publishing house, and my knees were still quivering from the elevator ride up to the fifth floor.

Her lips moved to form a thin, stabbing sort of smile. 'Horatio Hightower? The man who was kind enough to write this letter for you?'

I began to put two and two together as I recalled the name stenciled on Mr Hightower's briefcase in gold lettering. Mr H. I. Hightower. *Aha! So that's what the first H stood for.* 'Oh!' I said aloud. 'Oh yes, of course – Mr Hightower! He taught a seminar on popular literature at my college, you see, and he has been very encouraging ever since I told him about my interest in publishing. He's a wonderful professor.' Miss Everett gave me a look. There was something vaguely dubious in it, something that puzzled me.

'Can you type?'

'Why, yes . . . I think I was up to eighty words per minute the last time someone timed me.'

'Take shorthand?'

'Yes; my mother made me take a summer course.'

'That was very prudent of her,' Miss Everett said. She smiled that same thin-lipped stabbing smile and the word *implacable* sprang into my head and floated up invisibly between us. There was an oscillating fan sitting upon the bookshelf behind her. Every time the fan pivoted in Miss Everett's direction, the papers on her desk fluttered under their paperweights but not a single curl of ash-blonde hair wavered from the confines of her carefully pinned-up hairdo. I suspected a rather large quantity of Aqua Net had been involved in their arrangement. She discreetly exhaled a breath of smoke from her cigarette and, with a gesture that struck me as very familiar and well practised, delicately fished a stray filament of tobacco from the tip of her tongue. Then she leant back in her swivelling chair and regarded me with an air of cold calculation. Her silence seemed to carry on forever, but I'm sure in reality it was only seconds before a loud rap sounded at the door and a young girl rushed in with a slip of paper in her hand and a pencil tucked over her ear.

'I'm sorry to interrupt, but Mr Pierce said I was to deliver this phone message to you immediately.' The girl held out the slip of paper. Miss Everett rose from her chair and snatched the paper away from the girl with a frown.

She eyed the message. 'Of course he found a way out of that lunch.' She read from the note in a high, mimicking voice. '"*Would you mind terribly going in his stead?*" Hmph. Little surprise. I should've planned for it from the start.' She touched a hand to her shellacked curls and then looked at me as though she had forgotten I was in the room. 'Tell me, dear, have you gone to lunch with many writers?' she asked. There wasn't much question in it; she already knew the answer.

I shook my head.

'Well, don't if you can help it. Most of them are either fools or madmen.'

I took this as an attempt at humour, and forced a little laugh. I watched as she pulled her gloves on and gathered up her purse. As Miss Everett neared the open door, she stopped. She turned and gave me one last icy evaluation.

'Mabel,' Miss Everett said, still staring at me, and I realised she was addressing the girl with a pencil tucked over her ear.

'Yes, Miss Everett,' the girl said.

'Show Miss Katz to Personnel. We'll have her start as Mr Frederick's new secretary.' Then a second idea appeared to occur to her and she snapped to attention. 'No! Wait. Isn't *Mr Turner* also looking for a new girl right now?' Mabel nodded hesitantly. A curious expression appeared on Miss Everett's face. Finally, she said, 'Yes, that'll be better for you, dear. Let's have you start there.' She carefully fixed a hat over her hairdo and departed without another word.

6

Rising in front of the entrance to the Torchon & Lyle building on Fifty-Eighth Street was a large phoenix cast in copper. For being stationary, it nonetheless implied a great deal of motion; its wings stretched wide as if to take flight, its neck arched to strike downward at a serpent or some such creature with its beak, and one talon lifted free into the air while the other still touched the ash heap from which it perpetually rose. I've been told that since my time at Torchon & Lyle the company swallowed up many of its smaller competitors until the whole outfit was so big it was forced to relocate slightly uptown to a more modern and muted-looking glass skyscraper where there is no mythical phoenix poised to take flight out in front. This is one of the more tragic outcomes of progress. The old building was all limestone and brass with that giant terrifying phoenix you had to step around to enter the revolving door. Somehow I wouldn't want it any other way.

Most of the phoenix had turned the milky green colour of pale jade, save for one spot on the first knuckle of the phoenix's lifted talon. In contrast to the rest of the statue this one spot gleamed with a well-polished brilliance, and eventually I discovered an old office superstition was responsible for it. The superstition went that if you touched the statue's talon before entering the revolving brass door in the morning, then you were protected from being fired for the rest of the day.

No one could tell me how this superstition got started, but the logic made sense somehow. After all, the phoenix was Torchon & Lyle's colophon. A silhouette of it rode the lower spine of every book the publisher printed. It appeared again in the middle bottom of every book's title page. I must say, even in miniature silhouette the Torchon & Lyle phoenix was a beautiful, powerful-looking creature, with flames burning brightly from the tips of its wings like stray feathers licking up in the wind, so you can imagine the statue version was that much more impressive, standing as it did fifteen feet tall. Though I didn't know about the superstition on my first day, when I saw the people walking ahead of me pause to give the statue a strange abbreviated rub, I found myself standing at the base of the phoenix reaching up to touch its talon.

'Oh!' a girl next to me said. 'You already know about the phoenix!'

'I'm not sure I do. What about it?' I asked.

'That it's good luck,' the girl said. She explained about the superstition while I nodded.

I looked more closely at the girl. Her face was scrubbed clean and, except for a swipe of very red lipstick, she could've just as easily been taken for a high schooler as a secretary. She wore her hair in a ponytail that fell in a straight line and was the colour of wheat. The heavy weight of it caused it to swing subtly as she talked and moved her head, shimmering slightly with every perky tremor.

'Whose secretary are you going to be?' she asked.

'Mr Turner's,' I said.

'Oh, in that case you'd better rub it twice.' She reached for my hand and put it back on the shiny spot on the phoenix's talon. 'He's famous for being awfully strict with his girls.'

'I'm Judy,' she said when I had finished rubbing the talon to her satisfaction. We shook hands. 'I'm on three,' she continued as we proceeded into the building and stepped into an elevator. 'Come and find me at lunchtime; I'll give you the tour!'

'Won't they have already given me the tour?' I asked.

'Not if you're Mr Turner's girl. He's always in early and he's dreadfully serious. He'll want you to get to work right away and the other girls on that floor will steer clear for a few weeks – just until it's safe. Don't take it personally.' The elevator ticked off the third floor with a cheerful ding and the doors slid open. 'See you at twelve-thirty!' With that, Judy stepped out and merged into a stream of girls scurrying about, tugging off gloves and unpinning hats and removing the stiff vinyl dustcovers from a row of typewriters.

When the elevator chimed its announcement of the fifth floor, I stepped off and reported to the same personnel office where I had ended up at my previous visit. In short order, I was told Mr Turner was located on the sixth floor and I was to occupy a desk right outside his office. I oughtn't bother to knock and introduce myself, the other girls in the typing pool told me; he didn't like to be disturbed and would call for me when he had need of me. I went up to six, did as instructed, and spent the morning arranging and rearranging the contents of my new desk.

With several hours surrendered to the art of aimless sorting, my stomach had begun to launch into a minor soliloquy of grumblings. The clock on the wall showed twelve-twenty before I got my first glimpse of Mr Turner himself. He was a tall, stiff-jawed man with wire-rimmed glasses and pepper-grey hair. He came out of his office with a stack of manuscripts in one arm and a pile of correspondence in the other. He carried an air of cold, calculated precision about him that put me in mind of a Swiss watch.

'Miss Katz,' he said, and my spine straightened, surprised to hear him speak my name so forcefully when we had not yet been introduced. 'All of these need to go back to from whence they came. Very short and concise notes of declination will do just fine.' He transferred the stack of manuscripts onto my desktop with an efficient grace. 'And these,' he continued, holding out the pile of correspondence, 'want for a reply. I'll dictate my responses later this afternoon.' He paused and glanced at me over the rim of his glasses. 'You do take dictation, don't you?'

'Oh yes,' I said. Mr Turner had a curious effect on people. It was clear he was rigid and uncompromising, but seconds after meeting him I found I desperately wanted to win his approval.

'Fine. Let me make one thing clear: I don't know you, and I didn't pick you to be my secretary. Miss Everett did,' he said, crisply pronouncing her name *Miss Ev-er-ett*, with equal emphasis on each syllable. 'You have her to thank for that. But she knows better than to send me dunces, so that must mean you must've impressed her somehow. As for my expectations, I don't enjoy excuses, and I expect you to prioritise my assignments before anything else you might receive from the typing pool. You'll find I run a very tight ship here. I'm sorry to say you won't be able to take any long lunches or indulge in any afternoon shopping trips on account of my being asleep at the wheel. The bar is certainly *not* open in *my* office. However, I will tell you this: if you understand this business is all about working very hard and spending long hours doing it, we'll get along just fine. Got that?'

I nodded.

'All right.' He glanced at his watch. 'You have one hour for lunch, so you'd better get to it. I expect to start that dictation precisely at one-thirty.' He turned and strode back into his office, shutting the door behind him with the same air of forceful efficiency with which he'd emerged.

I stood up from my desk and, feeling a bit wobbly-kneed, gathered my things.

When the elevator doors slid open on three, I found Judy standing there waiting for me.

'There you are! Twelve-thirty on the nose,' she said, holding up her wrist as if to prove it. 'Well, if there's one thing I can say about Mr Turner, it's that you sure can set your watch by him!' She motioned for me to step off the elevator. 'C'mon. I'm sure he reminded you: we don't have all day. We'll start the tour here and I'll give you the skinny on who does what.' Clutched in her left hand was a white paper bag marked with two small grease spots. She unrolled the top and reached into it. 'Speaking of skinny, you *are*, awfully . . . Here's something to fatten you up.' She handed me a pastrami on rye and kept what looked like turkey for herself. Just peering at the paper wrapper rendered translucent by all that oily meat and mayonnaise gave me indigestion. I would've much rather had the turkey, but I accepted the sandwich gratefully.

Between bites, Judy gave an otherwise steady monologue as she took me around. Torchon & Lyle's offices took up the better part of seven floors of the twenty-four-storey high-rise. 'We're the second-biggest publishing house in New York,' Judy announced proudly. I learnt where to make coffee and how to make it in a specific fashion so that nobody would complain. She told me which of the other secretaries you could trust to help you out of a jam if you botched a task, and which of them offered to send out for the lunch order but then pocketed your extra change. Judy also repeated details about each of the editors – not so much what authors they'd edited and what they'd published – but rather personal details that would help me handle myself. *Alcoholic* . . . she said, pointing to one editor's office . . . *works better in the afternoons, best not to approach him in the mornings if you see his hand shaking* . . . *Shrewish wife* . . . she said of another, *we've all got to pretend like we don't know he sleeps in his office most nights.* She rolled her eyes as we passed another. *Editor-in-chief's nephew* . . . she said, thumbing towards another office, *rarely in and practically useless but be careful what you say in front of him; it all gets back to the Big Cheese.* When she got to Miss Everett's office, she stopped.

'And I take it you've already met Miss Everett,' she said, and paused. There was a cautious note in her voice, and I found myself thinking of the phoenix and how Judy had instructed me to rub its talon twice. I waited for Judy to go on but she didn't.

'Yes; Miss Everett was the one who hired me,' I finally said. It was an unnecessary statement, but I couldn't think of anything better and the silence of Judy's pause was beginning to unnerve me. She glanced at me and smiled stiffly.

'Well, something about you must've caught her attention if she chose you to be Mr Turner's girl,' she said. Like a dummy, I mistook her warning for a compliment. I shrugged and smiled and felt my cheeks colour.

'Perhaps she likes her girls to be ambitious. I told her I wanted to become an editor,' I confessed.

'Oh! You *told* her that? That's awfully bold!' It seemed there was more Judy wanted to say on this subject, but she took a quick glance at her watch and flinched.

'Golly! Time flies. Better be getting back to your desk or Mr Turner will have your head. He's a stickler, but I'm sure you know that already. I'll walk you back to the elevator.' As we walked, I thanked her for her hospitality. 'Don't mention it!' she said, waving my gratitude off. A ding sounded and the elevator doors opened. Judy gave my arm a friendly squeeze. 'You'll see – it's really swell here. Once you figure out who to steer clear of, it'll all be cake.' The red lipstick she was wearing earlier in the day had now been mostly rubbed off by the bread of the sandwich she'd been eating. I stared at the freckled apples of her cheeks and sincere blue saucers of her eyes. We smiled at each other as the doors slid shut.

I was still smiling when the elevator stopped on four, and a rather rotund, red-faced man in a plaid sports jacket stepped on.

'Well, don't you look jolly!' he said, noting my expression. As he spoke, a strangely sweet yet rank, overripe scent filled the elevator. I realised with a shock he must've been drinking during the lunch hour, and not in moderation. He leant towards me in a mock confidential manner, the alcohol causing his features to slide into an ugly leer. 'Oh, don't pull a serious face on my account! I like a girl who knows how to have a good time.' He winked and then suddenly declared, 'You're new. Whose girl are you?'

'I work for Mr Turner.'

'Ah. Well, he's no fun. Not compared to Yours Truly. I see I'll have to come visit you on six more often just to save you from that sourpuss.'

We were alone, and an uncomfortable silence filled the elevator as he continued to regard me. I forced a smile. When another ding announced we had reached the sixth floor, I felt myself exhale.

'Oh, but where are my manners! And I call myself a gentleman,' he called after me as I stepped through the elevator doors. He gave a little bow in my direction, swaying a little as though the elevator car were really a small boat pitching upon a rolling wave. 'Harvey Frederick. Pleasure to meet you!'

Before I had a chance to acknowledge his introduction, the elevator doors slid shut. I recalled on the day of my hiring Miss Everett had mentioned a 'Mr Frederick'. And to think everyone seemed to pity me for having been assigned to Mr Turner! Surely working for Mr Frederick could be far worse. Perhaps Miss Everett had done me a great favour, and a surge of gratitude passed over me as I made my way back to my desk.

7

The next morning I made sure to stop and rub the phoenix's talon, happy for my new career and hopeful to keep it. Mr Turner stuck his head out of his office exactly three times that day: once to give me some reports to type up, and two additional times to enquire with great irritation why I wasn't finished yet. Rising to his challenge, I picked up the pace, completed the task in no time flat, and knocked on his door. I figured since he seemed to be in a great hurry, he would want to know the instant I was done.

'Somebody *ought* to have informed you, Miss Katz, I loathe unnecessary interruption. You are never – *ever* – to knock on my door if it is not open,' he scolded me. 'If it's an absolute emergency you may buzz me on the intercom.'

'I'm sorry. I didn't know,' I said.

'Well, now you do,' he sniffed.

My cheeks coloured and I left his office immediately, closing the door behind me.

During the months that followed, though I got used to my duties, I found Mr Turner impossible to please. There were a great many annoyances in his life that I was personally responsible for, according to him.

'For God's sake!' he complained on one occasion, nearly giving me a heart attack as he burst through his office door and shook an angry finger at the radiator near my desk. 'Why do you insist on letting that infernal thing clang away until we are all deaf instead of calling for the janitor?' Sure enough, I listened, and the radiator was rattling ever so slightly. But it was hardly the kind of apocalyptic racket Mr Turner was ranting about. I'd hardly noticed it myself, and I couldn't understand how he'd managed to hear it from all the way inside his office, behind a closed door. Fearing both Mr Turner's sensitivity and his wrath, I called for the radiator to be fixed immediately, and stood over the janitor while he worked.

I would have believed he hated me, save for the fact I knew it was much more likely he didn't care about me at all.

'He's just like that,' Judy remarked, during one of our quick lunches together. She looked thoughtful for a moment and frowned at the half-moon lipstick stain rimming her paper coffee cup. She wiped at it with her thumb. 'He's like that, but . . . perhaps a little more so with you.'

'Why more so with me?' I asked.

Judy shrugged. 'Oh, I don't know,' she said, and changed the subject to an evening radio soap she'd recently begun to follow. Judy lived in a women's hotel similar to the Barbizon, but with a few more niceties. She had a radio in her room, and there was even a big black-and-white television in the lounge the girls could gather around to watch things like *American Bandstand*. I had none of these distractions, but that suited me; Mr Turner let me take the slush pile home with me, and I spent my evenings reading manuscripts.

'If any of them show promise, you are to write up a reader's report and submit it to me,' he had instructed. 'Then I'll be the judge of whether they are worth our time.' I'd written up a small handful of reports, but so far nothing I liked tickled Mr Turner's fancy. That's the thing about taste: it's rarely shared, and Mr Turner made it clear he did *not* share mine. But if Mr Turner did not want to play mentor to me, that was all right, because Miss Everett seemed to want the job.

By the time I'd been at Torchon & Lyle for a few months, Miss Everett had cultivated a habit of calling me into her office once or twice a week for the purposes of having, as she called it, 'a little professional chat'. She did this so regularly, I soon had the walk to her office memorised: the sailboat paintings that hung on the wall in the corridor that led to Miss Everett's door with their flaccid cheerfulness; the plant that sat on her window ledge with its waxy-leaved tendrils curling down into the slats of the radiator below it; the pungent, lingering tang of the Russian dressing I knew Miss Everett used on her daily salad. Miss Everett would sit just as she had on the day of my interview, leaning back in her oversized swivel chair, levelling a cool stare at me. 'I take it, Miss Katz . . .' she always began when we sat down for one of our little professional chats. Miss Everett had a peculiar habit of phrasing her questions as observations. I don't know whether this was a calculated manoeuvre, but the result was it made it difficult to introduce information not contained in her observational statement lest it sound like you were disagreeing with her. Even now, my brain is still filled with examples of these conversations.

'I take it, Miss Katz, you are enjoying your time here at Torchon & Lyle?'

'Oh yes, ma'am.'

'I take it you've been enjoying all the book signings and publishing parties?'

'Oh absolutely, ma'am.'

'I imagine our little soirées must be rather different from what you're used to in Iowa.' (Miss Everett often used the state names Indiana and Iowa as though they were entirely interchangeable, and I knew enough by then not to correct her.)

'Oh, you bet they are, ma'am,' I said with what I hoped sounded like sincere enthusiasm. Gushing was not a disposition that came naturally to me, but I pressed on. 'I have to pinch myself half the night to keep from thinking I've dreamt the whole thing up!'

'Hmm, yes. Isn't that something. I heard from a colleague that you've managed to turn up at every single party he's been to in the last week and a half. What a busy little bee you've been.'

'I thought it would be a good way to get to know who's who – you know, in case it comes in handy down the road when I've been promoted to editor.'

'That's very ambitious of you. Of course, there's more to this job than socialising, you know.'

'Yes, ma'am.'

'After all, you *do* want to be an editor and not a debutante, is that correct?'

'More than anything, ma'am.'

'More than anything?'

'Oh yes.'

'Mmm. "More than anything" sounds rather extreme. I'd be mindful, if I were you, of anything that implies you'd be willing to go to *immoral* lengths . . .'

I nodded with all the vigorous sincerity I could muster. I was glad to have her on my side, despite her odd preoccupations with certain subjects. For instance, Miss Everett seemed particularly concerned with giving me advice about how to be 'a proper lady' and about how to avoid wanton behaviour. She told me about other girls she'd hired in the past, girls who'd disappointed her by finding themselves *in the family way*, and unwed to boot. Miss Everett said no matter how nice, one simply couldn't keep a girl on staff once she'd gone and gotten herself in that sort of situation. I think she felt she was giving me a thoughtful warning – the kind of warning where, if I ever did find myself in the family way, Miss Everett could tell herself, *Can't say I wasn't generous . . . After all, I warned that girl.*

The funny thing was, whenever Miss Everett launched into a lecture on the value of not giving in to a man's demands, I always found myself staring at her carefully lipsticked mouth and imagining her at home, dressed in a chiffon peignoir, eating bon-bons and reading a Harlequin pocketbook. Picturing her like this, it was a challenge to take her seriously. There was an air of profound loneliness about Miss Everett, an impression that some sort of yearning had ripened on the branch and then was left to go rancid. I immediately chastised myself for these thoughts; after all, she was being generous with her time, and a willing mentor was certainly nothing to sneeze at. The very fact she – a woman executive – existed at Torchon & Lyle gave me hope that I might someday make editor after all.

8

One morning, when I reached up to rub the shiny talon of the phoenix, I was startled to see a dark hand appear next to mine. I turned to see a young Negro man in horn-rimmed glasses. He was strikingly handsome, with high cheekbones and a tall, athletic build.

'Oh!' I said. 'You must work at Torchon & Lyle.'

He smiled politely at my surprise. 'In a roundabout manner. I'm a messenger boy,' he answered, then nodded in the direction of the phoenix hovering over us. 'But I suppose I like it enough to want to keep my job.' We turned back to gaze again at the phoenix.

'It's silly, isn't it? I'm not at all superstitious,' I lied, suddenly feeling the need to explain myself.

'Neither am I,' the young man said. 'But I like a good ritual.' He put a finger to the bridge of his nose and pushed his glasses up. He regarded me through the lenses. There was a glimmer of shy, bookish intelligence in his eyes. It was a kindred glimmer, one I recognised in myself.

I thought to ask him about what it was like to be a bicycle messenger for Torchon & Lyle; whether he ever got sent out on any odd deliveries or else brought things to famous authors' houses. But I was too timid to ask. So the young man and I stood there staring at each other, a pair of awkward smiles on our faces, neither one saying another word, until finally we both nodded and turned to go through the revolving door and into the building. He went downstairs to the mail room, and I waited for the elevator to go up.

Later that afternoon I was typing up some dictation I'd taken earlier that morning, when Mr Turner emerged from his office and tossed something onto my desk. I recognised the reader's report I'd written a few nights prior, recommending a novel I'd found in the slush pile. I braced myself for him to announce what terrible judgement I had, but the criticism never came.

'This one isn't half-bad,' he said, frowning. 'I pulled the manuscript and I agree it has promise. The quality of your report itself is middling, but I expect you may improve over time if you're to be a reader from now on.'

'Reader?' I repeated in disbelief. My heart leapt and I couldn't help but smile. 'Am I being promoted to reader?'

As he caught sight of my smile, Mr Turner's frown deepened. 'It's more work, but not more money – understand?'

'Oh yes, sir! I'm still very honoured! I . . .' I hesitated, searching for the correct word '. . . I accept!'

Mr Turner gave me a disdainful look, and I understood my naked enthusiasm, coupled with the presumption I was somehow entitled to accept or decline the position, had annoyed him.

'Fine,' he grunted. 'You can start with these.' He placed a small stack of manuscripts on my desk. 'And get in touch with the author of that unsolicited manuscript.' He pointed back to my reader's report.

'Oh, I will, sir! Right away,' I said. He vanished into his office, the door swinging shut behind him.

I didn't care if he'd been annoyed by my eager attitude. I was a reader! I was one tiny step closer to becoming an editor. Perhaps rubbing that statue was lucky after all. As I looked the submission log over in search of the unsolicited author's address and telephone number, I picked up the telephone to dial someone else entirely.

'Judy?' I spoke into the receiver. I could hear the clackity-clack of her uninterrupted typing.

'Mmm?'

'Say, let's go for a drink tonight. I've got something to celebrate!'

Later, when I told Judy the details, she was happy for me and eager to celebrate, but I had to twist her arm to get her to go down to the Village.

'Why not let's go to a bar here in midtown, or else on the Upper East Side?' she complained, slicking on a fresh coat of red lipstick once the clocks had struck five and we were riding the elevator down. 'That's where all the eligible bachelors are.'

'It's fun in the Village; you'll see,' I promised. 'There's a real energy. I've met the most interesting people down there. You never know who you might meet: a painter or a musician or a poet!'

Judy snapped her compact shut and slipped it back into her pocketbook. '*That's* what I'm afraid of.'

'Oh, c'mon, Judy! Who knows? The next Hemingway or Salinger could be down there, and Torchon & Lyle might someday publish his book!'

'You forget,' she said. '*You're* in it for the books. *I'm* in it for a husband.'

She sniffed and pretended to pout, but followed me in good humour out to the street to catch a taxi. We rode down Fifth Avenue to Washington Square, giggling with excitement as the wedding-cake arch loomed into view. I had decided on the Minetta

Tavern, over on MacDougal. It was cosy inside, dim, with lots of dark wood and a black-and-white checkerboard floor.

'How do you know about this place?' Judy asked, raising an eyebrow as we walked through the door. We pulled out two stools at the bar and wobbled onto them in our pencil skirts. I explained about the day I'd met Swish, and how he'd introduced me to a whole slew of bohemian cafes below Fourteenth Street.

'I wish I could come down to the Village every day after work,' I said. 'There's always something interesting going on – some poetry reading or improvisational band or . . . well, some of it I don't even quite know how to describe!'

'Yes, well, going out can get expensive,' Judy said. 'Especially if you're not out with the kind of gentleman who knows he's supposed to foot the bill.' I could tell she had not liked the sound of Swish one bit.

'Well, I'm not interested in him like that.'

'So?' Judy said. 'He still ought to treat. It's what a fella does.'

'Anyway, you'll find it's not at all expensive down here. Most of the readings and art shows and music are free. It's the time, not the money, that I can't spare. Too many manuscripts to read!'

Judy rolled her eyes. 'You and your career gal ambitions,' she said in a mock-scolding voice. 'What *am* I going to do with you?'

Just then I felt someone brush by my elbow.

'Say – Eden, right?'

I looked in the direction of the voice and saw a man with a slight build, sandy hair, and pale blue eyes.

'Oh! Yes,' I replied. 'How good to see you again. Judy, this is Cliff.'

'How d'you do?'

Judy shook his hand and gave him an appraising look, but

almost immediately her gaze slid to another boy standing just over Cliff's shoulder, and she blushed.

'This is my buddy Bobby,' he explained. 'Bobby, meet the gals.'

Bobby grinned in an extremely charming, lopsided way. He was tall and very good-looking, with the kind of relaxed, slouchy posture that suggested he was very reassured about how good-looking he was, too.

'Listen,' Cliff continued. 'We were just headed over to Chumley's. There's a playwright who wants a few actors to do a cold reading of his new play, and Bobby is going to volunteer.'

'What d'you say, Judy?' I asked. I wanted to go but I wanted her to feel comfortable, too.

'All right,' she agreed, still smiling at Bobby in a wistful fog.

The play was fairly awful. It was obvious the playwright fancied himself some variety of absurdist, like Ionesco or Beckett, but possessed only a fraction of the talent. However, Bobby read his lines with fierce commitment, and the whole room sighed dreamily every time it was his turn to speak. When it was all over, we clapped Bobby on the back, and the boys suggested we relocate to the Cedar Tavern. I hadn't planned on taking a tour of all the bars in the Village, but it seemed like that was what the night was shaping up to be. Once at the Cedar, a third man came over to join us. I was startled to recognise the bookish-looking Negro with horn-rimmed glasses.

'I saw you this morning in front of the phoenix!' I exclaimed. He smiled and the sense of camaraderie we'd shared earlier that day returned.

'You've met?' Cliff asked.

'Well, not formally,' I said, realising we'd never introduced ourselves. 'I'm Eden.'

'Miles,' he said, extending a polite hand. We chatted a bit.

'How long have you been a bicycle messenger?' I asked.

'For almost a year. I only do it part-time,' he said. 'I'm still in school.'

'Oh!' I said, cocking my head in confusion. He didn't appear young enough to be high school age.

'College,' he said, reading my misapprehension. 'Columbia.'

I was impressed, and was about to say so, but just then a stranger spilt a drink on Judy's lap, and she leapt up from her bar stool. I could see she'd had enough. It was nearly two o'clock in the morning. Cliff and Bobby wanted to go to yet another bar for more drinks, and looked slightly disappointed when Judy and I excused ourselves.

'Time for us career gals to turn back into pumpkins,' I said, 'or it'll take a whole lot more than coffee to wake us up in the morning.'

In the taxi on the way back uptown, Judy sat dabbing her skirt with a handkerchief.

'Was it terrible?' I asked.

'Not terrible,' she said. 'But I'll send you my dry-cleaning bill.' I asked her what she thought of them.

'Well, that Bobby is about as handsome as they come,' she said, still blotting away at her skirt. 'But he's not marriage material. You can see he's more trouble than the devil himself! And Cliff . . .' She considered for a moment. 'Well, he might be different. He seems like he's from a nice family, and a college boy, too: I noticed a class ring!' I was glad she liked Cliff. I liked him, too. 'But I don't know . . .' She qualified her endorsement: 'He runs around with so many Village kids . . .'

'More of them might've gone to college than you'd think,' I murmured, lost in thought and watching the city flying by outside

the taxi window as we zoomed up Third Avenue. 'Miles told me he's
due to graduate from Columbia this June.'

'Who's Miles?'

'That young man I was talking to just now.'

'The Negro?'

I nodded, and she sighed.

'Oh, honestly, Eden . . . hipsters and Negroes! Don't you *ever*
want to get married?'

9

MILES

A few weeks prior to my graduation from Columbia, my mother surprised me by pressing a small nickel-chrome key into my palm and telling me a secret.

This happened in our family apartment in Harlem, but I wasn't living there at the time. At Columbia, I had worked out a way to stretch the scholarship money to afford a room in one of the dormitories, thinking – with that tragically flawed logic of mine – that not living on campus was all that stood between me and making friends. As it turned out, it was a pathetic room and I hated being in it. I was profoundly lonely and I had no roommates to speak of; no one in the housing office wanted to make any assumptions as to how another student might feel about sharing a room with a coloured boy. They had resolved this predicament by giving me my own room. I was well aware they could have done much worse by me, and I felt guilty each time I looked at the cramped, windowless space and wondered if my room wasn't really a broom closet they had converted at the very last minute in the hopes I wouldn't notice – or, at the very least, that I wouldn't be brave enough to raise a ruckus upon making such an observation.

In any event, this rather sad broom closet of a room was where I was when the telephone in the hall rang and one of the young freshmen – I was the only upperclassman on my floor – began hollering for me. 'Tillman!' he shouted. 'It's your ma on the horn!' I got up from my bed, grateful for the chance to leave my room, and thinking my mother was simply calling to check in on me.

'Miles?' she said.

'You gotta stop by the house this afternoon.'

'What time?' I asked, knowing better than to ask the reason.

'I got some errands to run right quick, but why don't you c'mon over now. I be back real soon.'

Her command that I come over was nothing unusual, but her urgency was. 'Is anything wrong?'

'No, no, nothing's wrong. But ever since I woke up, I been thinking about somethin' and I needs to talk to you. Your brother's out playing with the neighbourhood boys, and be best to talk before Wendell get home.'

'All right,' I said. 'I'll see you in a bit.' I hung up and walked back to my broom closet to put some shoes on. The dormitory halls were full of that particular manic energy that occurs at the end of a school year, when half the students are whooping with hilarity over having already finished their exams and the other half are still studying like mad to pass them. It was the season when clothes and books are being boxed up and old hot plates are left abandoned near the trash chutes by virtue of some undergraduate's careless thought that some custodian might want to adopt what he, the undergraduate, no longer wants to transport elsewhere.

Walking from Columbia to Harlem was mostly a matter of descending the hill that separated the stony Gothic facades of Morningside Heights from the green streetlamps and brownstones of Harlem, and the most pleasant route to take was through Morningside Park along the eastern side of campus. It was a warm day; little beads of sweat tickled my temples as I ambled down the sloped path. A hot day meant, of course, that Harlem would be busy with people sitting outside on their stoops, fanning themselves and gossiping. There would be greengrocers pouring buckets of ice over their produce, pushcarts selling ice cream, and children dancing spastically in front of gushing fire hydrants, cheering and laughing – and, of course, eventually booing in protest when the firemen came to shut the spouts down again. I had these sights and sounds memorised; together they made up my childhood.

'Hey, Miles,' a young woman called to me from her stoop, flirting out of pure boredom.

'Hey, Sherrie,' I called back. 'Hot enough for ya?' At this, she rolled her eyes, nodded, and shrugged, all the while continuing to fan herself. Then she gave me that uneasy look I knew well, looking me up and down more critically from out the corner of her gaze. I sensed she wouldn't engage me further. None of my peers from the old neighbourhood knew what to make of me, especially the girls. I was tall, I ran track and field; the girls would flirt, but most would stop short of any real overture. I knew on instinct it wasn't because I had a girl, although I did: I had a lovely girl named Janet who I sometimes took out for egg creams and long walks through the little botanical garden at the northernmost end of Central Park, near the Harlem Meer. No, it was because to them I was a curiosity, intriguing but vaguely unsettling.

I was accustomed to their standoffish treatment. In those days, I straddled more than a handful of worlds, which is also to say I belonged wholly to none. I had been born in Harlem but sent to school on the Upper East Side. This had been arranged when a schoolteacher at P. S. 24 had noticed my 'outstanding aptitude' and petitioned a series of Manhattan church organisations on my behalf. Charitable donations were given, mostly by elderly white widows whom I have never met but to whom I have been made to write thank-you letters. I remember the way my former Harlem classmates used to see the eternal heap of Latin books in my arms and eye the burgundy blazer of my private school uniform with suspicion. That was the first time my life took on a split nature. Little did I know this is all too often what it means to grow into adulthood, and that my sense of self would fracture yet again, and again, in the years to come.

Around the time I turned fourteen, my father died. Capable as she was, my mother could not bear life without a man, and three short months after my father passed away a small tyrant named Wendell had taken up residence on my father's old La-Z-Boy. My mother never took the trouble to marry Wendell, but over the years she began referring to him as my 'step-daddy', a label I more or less accepted despite the fact I never much liked or respected the man. Wendell was a mean-spirited individual whose face was defined by the kind of pinched features that made all who glanced at him do a kind of double take, thinking he had just tasted something bitter. This perception was not wholly inaccurate, for the bitter thing Wendell had tasted was life. His perpetual mood was one of deep aggrievement. In his telling of it, the world was against him and was hell-bent on keeping him down at all costs. He was short and balding – he wore a soiled grey newsboy cap to conceal this latter fact – but he had the kind of wiry, intensely strong musculature that comes from a lifetime of exerting one's body out of pure spite. I will grant he possessed a sizable store of raw intelligence, but his ignorance coupled with his stubborn hatred of educated men meant this mean, sprightly intelligence bucked around like a wild bull in a very small pen.

Being smart only made Wendell angrier about the bitterness of life, and he used his cunning mostly to exact revenge on those he perceived had slighted him. Unfortunately for me, he perceived that I was his chief offender. And now the fact that his hatred had begun to attach itself to Cob, my seven-year-old brother, with near equal force, rendered me perpetually nervous and protective. No fistfight had ever broken out between us, but I spent the latter half of my adolescence lifting dumbbells should one finally erupt. *Be best to talk before Wendell get home,* my mother had said on the telephone. I hadn't the slightest idea what my mother wanted, but I was happy to comply with her request that we talk before Wendell was due back.

With this in mind, I wound my way through the streets near the park, north into the heart of Harlem, past the Apollo Theatre with its neon sign and its marquee bearing the names of jazz musicians preferred by the white weekend crowds in large black letters, followed by lesser-known performers that were preferred by the locals in smaller letters just beneath. I turned a few more corners and neared my mother's apartment on 127th Street. The familiar look of it gave me a friendly feeling, the old brown stoop with its park-green painted rails and tall rectangular windows like the features of a face I knew more intimately than my own. Once inside, I trooped up to the fourth floor, my footsteps pounding a satisfyingly loud beat on the rickety wooden stairs. When I got to my mother's apartment I put my key in the lock, then halted and knocked cautiously on the door, just in case Wendell was inside. When no sound stirred within, I finished turning the key and let myself in.

I sat down at the kitchen table to wait and considered eating one of the apples perched in a bowl in front of me, then thought better of it. Four years ago, when I'd managed to secure my room in the university dormitory, Wendell had reacted as though this development was a personal victory of sorts. During the intervening years, he had grown increasingly prickly about my visits, demanding that I knock instead of letting myself in and that I stay out of the ice-box, the contents of which my mother stocked and paid for but that he inexplicably considered his sole property.

In recent months, my mother had grown even more jumpy than usual about me and Wendell occupying the same room. We hadn't discussed whether I would move back in after graduation. The idea was I'd eventually marry Janet – no rings had been exchanged, but Janet and I had discussed as much – and we'd find a place of our own, but I had to save up the money first. Despite her abundant love for me, I knew my mother was dreading the prospect of my coming back home to live, even for a temporary time, fearful that the relationship between me and my stepfather would eventually arrive at a point of violent impasse.

I heard the sound of the front door. 'Ma?' I called.

'C'mon and lend a hand, Miles,' her voice commanded, breathing hard. I found her laden with grocery bags and moved to lift the heaviest ones from her arms. Together we carried everything into the kitchen. Then she pulled an apron over her head, sighed, and fished something out of the front pocket.

'Here it is,' she said, exuding the same air of terse efficiency with which she had surely executed all of the afternoon's errands, and placed a small nickel-chrome key into the palm of my right hand.

I blinked at it. 'What is this?'

'Your daddy gimme that key,' she said. 'I promised I would give it to you soon's you old enough.' Having off-loaded her charge, she dusted her hands together with two claps as though brushing away an invisible layer of flour, and turned back to attend to the groceries laid out on the kitchen table. 'Woke up with my mind set on that key this mornin' and figure it's a sign. Figure now's as good a time as any. You know, I guess mothers, sometimes we blind to our babies. But jus' lookit you now,' she said, not actually looking at me. 'Gettin' ready to graduate. You grown.'

I continued to gaze at the foreign object in my palm with incredulity. 'I don't understand,' I said.

'Hmph. Not sure as I do, either,' my mother said, her back still turned to me as she lifted canned vegetables into a cupboard. She produced a knife from a drawer, cut open a gunnysack of potatoes, and counted under her breath. '*Shoot!*' she exclaimed. 'That no-good cheater promised me it was always ten to a bag.' My mind reeling with questions about the key, I watched as she loaded nine potatoes into the dark recesses of the larder. 'I don't want you to get your expectations up, now. You know how it was for your daddy when he get sick. He was babbling clear outta his mine. By the end I don't know that sweet fool knew his rightful name.'

My hand trembled. 'What . . . what does the key open?'

My mother sighed, and finally turned to face me. 'Don't go gettin' no ideas. Ain't no gold bars stacked up in a safe nowheres.' She peered meaningfully into my eyes, as if to will me into tamping down an invisible mountain of wild, optimistic hopes. I didn't harbour any delusions that our family possessed secret riches, but it was useless to say so to my mother, so I gave a solemn nod in acknowledgement. 'You remember your daddy always goin' on about his army days? Well,' she said, her eyes turning glassy and sceptical as she glanced at the key. 'When he die, he lay there on his deathbed, his eyes wanderin' all over the ceiling like he seein' nothing and everythin' all at the same time. Then suddenly he looks clear as lightning and he grab out for me. I give him my hand and I feel something sharp and when I open it I see that key. The key's got to do with yo' daddy's journal, see.'

'Journal?' This was the first I'd ever heard of my father having kept a journal.

She shrugged. 'He say he kept hisself a record of all the things he did in the war, and all the other soldiers he knew and battles they fought in, and he left it in an old army locker on his way out to the Pacific. He always meant to go back an' get it so's you and Cob could read all 'bout his adventures, but never had the chance.'

I blinked.

'When he was dyin', he tell me, "Mae, we done somethin' good with Miles. He got his funny ways but he bright as the sun. That boy goin' to be a college boy, sho' as the day I was born. When he get done with his schoolin', you give 'im this. I wants him to know my stories, and be proud."'

'He wanted me to . . .' I paused, trying to fight my way out from under an avalanche of confusion '. . . read his diary?'

My mother *tsked*. 'I reckon that's the way of things. My guess is you better go fine it first.' She paused, then added, 'That is, *if* there's anything to fine. That's why I say I don't want you to get your 'spectations up, now. Maybe that key don't lead nowhere but to a dying man's loony business.'

She lifted the heavy lid of the stovetop and reached for a roll of green-backs bound in a rubber band that lay dangerously near the flickering blue flame of the pilot light. 'Lucky your step-daddy never take an interest in doin' any of the cookin',' she said, pulling the rubber band off the wad and counting. 'There,' she announced, handing me the majority of the roll. 'I done saved you up a hunnerd dollars for your trip.'

'My trip?' I stammered. My head was swimming. I looked again at the key and then the wad of dollar bills. Never in my life had I ever held so much money in my hands at one time.

'Yes, indeedy, son. That locker he mention gotta be at an army base som'ere out in Californ'a. He deploy there, but he don't come back through the same facility, on account o' his early discharge. I 'spect that's the place he meant. That's a start.' She pointed to the bills. 'But you best save up more. Might take you some time to do the lookin', and I hear Californ'a an expensive place.'

'You want me to go to California?' I found that my brain, meticulously educated though it had been, often had to work hard to catch up with my mother, whose shrewd, all-business mind often shot right through the most complicated details at lightning pace. 'But what about Janet?' I stammered.

'Janet already waitin' for you, son,' my mother said. 'She wait some more.' She sighed. I knew my mother was not overly fond of Janet. Janet, like me, was something of an outsider within our neighbourhood, and the same thing – education – that made my mother so proud of me was the very attribute that caused my mother to label Janet 'uppity'. But at the same time she was impatient for me to marry, and she couldn't understand why I was dragging my feet.

'See here,' my mother said now, taking my face between her hands. Her palms were dry and warm against my cold, clammy cheeks. 'You go look for yo' daddy, you have yo'self an adventure! An' maybe when you come back, you be ready to do some plannin' finally. It's time someone lit a fire under yo' ass, my boy! Get you to makin' some choices in yo' life! If that girl won't do it, I will.'

I tried to look her in the eye, but eventually I glanced away and stared at the chipped tiles and permanently soiled grout of the kitchen floor, afraid to let my fear show. There had been rumours surrounding my father's discharge – rumours that had swirled through the neighbourhood but that I'd never discussed with my mother – and the idea of my father's words sitting somewhere in a footlocker choked me with excitement, but it felt like the dangerous kind of excitement, the kind that could lead to deep disappointment. I bit my lip and didn't know what to say. My mother's posture relaxed and she heaved a sigh.

'Will you think on it?' she asked.

I nodded. 'I'll think on it,' I said, and reached to hand the wad of dollar bills back to her.

'No,' she said. 'You hold on to that. You gon' need it. I know you come around.'

10

When my mother handed me a key and told me to go look for my father, she of course did not mean look for his body. We both knew where that could be found: buried in a remote corner of the Woodlawn Cemetery in the Bronx, by that time for some seven years. My father had been accorded a military funeral, and this had left a deep impression on me. I was fourteen and overwhelmed by what I saw that day, mesmerised by the bugler who played taps and downright baffled by the riflemen who shot off a rigid, violent, ear-splitting salute to a man who I'd rarely ever glimpsed in an army uniform. Later, my mother never let me forget: he'd served with the Harlem Hellfighters during the First World War, and was one of only a handful of Negro men who had the distinction of having served during both wars. 'Don't you forget,' she would say, 'yo' daddy a war hero.' I did, however. I did forget.

It was difficult to picture. According to my mother, my father, a mature-looking teenager, had lied about his age to enlist at age sixteen. He had seen trench warfare in France, but of course this was long before I was born. In all the time I knew him, he was a sweet, doddering man who worked at a radio repair shop on 125th Street. The fact he remained active in the National Guard was a detail I mostly forgot about, only to be abstractly reminded when he disappeared one weekend a month to do his service. When the Japanese bombed Pearl Harbour and my father's regiment was reactivated, I was flummoxed to watch him pack his bags and ship out. He may have been a precocious teenager in the First World War, but the man I knew when the Second World War broke out seemed to me to be too old, too kind, too fatherly; what on earth was this peaceful, soft-smiling man going to do in the war?

I didn't have to wonder about this question for very long. Two months after he left, he came back to us from Okinawa in plainclothes, having been abruptly given an honourable discharge. My father never discussed the reason – not with me, at least – but in the years that followed his death, my mother insisted it was on account of disability. It was his lungs, a respiratory complaint he'd picked up in the gas-filled trenches of the Marne that ultimately rendered him useless in the humid South Pacific. There wasn't a government man alive, my mother used to say, who wanted to be responsible for a used-up forty-year-old coloured soldier whose lungs weren't working right. Whatever the reason for his discharge, it seemed to drain a little bit of his spirit out of him. He seemed to be overwhelmed by some sort of nebulous, unnamed sadness.

I possess only a dim memory of the day he returned; I remember thinking it was funny that he knocked on our front door as though he did not live there, and that his clothes were filled with a melange of strange odours I later came to identify as the olfactory cocktail that makes up the scent of travel: cigarettes, stale beer, mothballs and musty upholstery, fried food. He came home, but never completely. Thereafter, he spent the bulk of his hours in the same threadbare flannel trousers and dingy white undershirt, listening to radio dramas and coughing a small piecemeal rainbow of red and yellow fluids into a handkerchief. He didn't talk about the Pacific, but sometimes he told stories about his glory days in France. I am ashamed to say I was dubious of these stories. I didn't pay very close attention, listening to them with the same indifference I had for his frequent retelling of the various plot twists that had occurred earlier in the afternoon on *Ma Perkins* and *Young Doctor Malone*. I have a vague memory of him talking about what it was like to be coloured and in the army, about what it had been like to fight alongside the French and to see the English Channel.

I remember my father best with a soft expression and a grizzled beard – prematurely grizzled, I now realise (he was only in his late forties when the cough began to get the best of him). He didn't bring home anger, or any traumatic traces of the bloody battles he'd seen. There were no night terrors, no trembling hands. Quite the contrary: despite my father's respiratory ailment, I can only conclude he evidently still had enough breath in him to sweet-talk my mother, as a few years after he came back from Okinawa, Cob was born. If anything, my father was lacking only in assertiveness. An honourable discharge meant he was eligible for the G. I. Bill, but my father took advantage of none of it. He sat in his chair, friendly enough yet inert, worrying the upholstery of the armrests with his restless thumbs and smiling a dazed smile at my school reports. I moved around him in our cramped living room as though he were a piece of forgotten furniture.

As much as I found him a kind and patient man, a vague air of shame followed him wherever he went. I could not puzzle it out. I could not puzzle it out, that is, until one day when I was eleven and a man named Clarence came knocking on our door.

'Mel-vin Till-man!' Clarence sang out in a slurred voice when my father answered the door. 'Got a hug for an old war buddy?'

I remember watching Clarence, shiny with perspiration, ripe

with body odour and visible dirt on his clothes, lurch for an embrace. I was vaguely horrified, but my father tolerated and even hugged Clarence back, clapping him on the back. He invited Clarence in and offered him a beer, which Clarence happily accepted.

'This here yo' boy?' Clarence asked when they had settled into the living room, where I was curled up in an armchair, reading a book.

'Miles, say hello to Clarence,' my father said, nodding. 'Clarence was a Hellfighter like yo' old man. One of only a few fellas who lasted in the Guard as long as I did!'

I shook hands timidly, then pretended to resume my reading, hoping they would permit me to stay so I could eavesdrop a little. I couldn't understand how or why my father was friends with a man who, had I seen him outside on the street, I would've taken for a vagrant and a wino. They caught up on old times. It was plain Clarence wanted something, but was putting on some sort of mad tap dance. Finally, once the beer ran out and the conversation wound down, Clarence darted his eyes over to where I was still pretending to read, then looked back at my father and cleared his throat.

'I ain't gonna lie, times has been rough,' Clarence said. 'I wouldn't mind some of yo' good hospitality, Melvin. I wouldn't mind it one bit.'

My father hesitated. I knew he was thinking of what my mother would say.

'You remember how I was always on yo' side, don't you, Melvin . . .' Clarence said, pressing my father in a low voice. ''Bout all tha' business surrounding yo' discharge . . .'

I looked up, and my father's eyes shot to my face.

'We don't need to discuss that, Clarence,' he said quickly. I could see there was something between them that had caused my father to recoil. 'I sup'ose we can always make room on our sofa,' my father said, as though to change the subject. 'Mae won't mind.'

But of course my mother *did* mind. She let Clarence stay, but late at night I heard my parents arguing in hushed voices. My parents rarely argued, and the sound of it put me on edge. I couldn't sleep, and decided to creep quietly into the kitchen for a glass of milk.

It turned out, creeping quietly was unnecessary; our houseguest was awake. The light was on in the kitchen. I found Clarence rummaging through the ice-box. He spun around when he heard me come in.

'A'most gave me a case o' palpitations, boy!' he scolded. He straightened up and looked me over from head to toe. 'Say, you oughta be able to tell me: whatchu got in here worth eatin', son?'

I shrugged. 'You could fry up some eggs.'

He shook his head. 'I don't wanna wake up the house with all that sizzlin' grease and cookin' smells,' he said. When he talked, I could see his teeth and tongue were slightly purplish, as though stained by wine. I wondered where he'd gotten it. He'd told my father he was down on his luck and flat broke.

'Ma made some ham-and-potato casserole,' I said.

'That'll do.'

I skirted around him to retrieve a glass of milk, my stomach turning at the rancid smell of cheap, sugary wine sweating through his pores. My mother didn't allow food or drink in any room but the kitchen, so I sat down dutifully at the table, trying to finish the glass I'd poured as quickly as possible. Clarence scooped a mound of cold potato casserole onto a plate, helped himself to a fork, and sat down across from me.

I watched him eat, bits of slobbery cheese sticking to his unkempt beard. He caught me watching him – very likely a disgusted expression on my face – and looked up. A hostile, wicked smile slowly stretched over his features.

'Yo' daddy ever tell you 'bout his army days?' he asked.

'I suppose,' I said, shrugging.

'I bet he din' tell you ever'thin'.'

I finished my milk and moved to wash the glass and go to bed. 'Now, hang on a minute there, son,' said Clarence. He refreshed his plate with a second helping. 'Don' rush off. Chew the fat with me a bit.' I didn't want to, but I sat down, feeling arrested by Clarence's demand. 'Tell me about you. You gotta girl yet?' I shook my head.

'Guess you still too young to be much interested in that yet. What's yo' best subject in school?'

'Latin,' I replied. This was true; I had worked so hard to catch up to my private school peers, I had surpassed them.

'*Latin!*' Clarence hooted. 'What's a nigger boy like you doin', fooling around with Latin?'

I stiffened at the slur and didn't answer.

'When they start teaching Latin at ol' P. S. 24?' he asked, still laughing at my expense.

'They don't,' I said. 'I go to Warner Academy.'

At this, Clarence stopped laughing and narrowed his eyes at me. 'What's that?'

'Private school,' I said. He proceeded to ask me questions about my schooling, and I haughtily explained the circumstances.

'Huh,' he grunted when I'd finished my explanation. 'Sounds to me like you think yo' better than us, boy.' I widened my eyes at the accusation. 'Yeah,' he continued. 'I see the way you been lookin' at me, actin' like I'm gonna give you a case of them head-bugs or somethin' . . . You think yo' shit don't stink.'

By this point, his eyes had turned eerily black and the expression on his face had grown hard and bitter.

'But I'll tell ya something, boy . . . you may think yo' something special, but you just a chip off the ol' block. Your mama tell you your old man a war hero. Sure – he march up Fifth Avenue in that fool parade with the rest o' us, but that about it. He ain't seen no action in the Pacific. Ever'body know yo' father discharged for bein' a coward and a thief.'

'He saw action in France in the first war,' I said, 'and he was discharged for his health.'

'Hah! That disability an act of mercy; they couldn't charge him with nothin' else.' Clarence leant forward on his elbows and licked his lips. The lamp over the kitchen table threw long, ugly shadows down his face, and I realised he was winding up for some kind of final blow. 'He such a coward, he murdered a man just so's they wouldn't have no proof o' his thievery,' Clarence growled in a low, confiding voice.

I got up from the table, trembling, and stormed out of the room. I lay in bed for the rest of the night, hurt and confused. I didn't believe Clarence's story; he was a drunk and a bully. Nonetheless, he had struck some kind of chord. There *was* something funny about my father's discharge. A disability discharge made sense on the surface of things: my father was old by active duty standards, and there was no question his respiratory ailment was real. And yet, there had always been something slightly discomfiting, an unanswered question that hovered like a dark cloud. I couldn't shake the image of my father in the living room, his eyes snapping instantly to my face as he rushed to say, 'We don't need to discuss that, Clarence.'

Staring up at the ceiling of my bedroom, only a ten-year-old boy, I was suddenly afraid to learn the truth, and this fear remained with me into adulthood, long after my father passed away.

Clarence stayed with us for a full month, well past the point of his welcome, as far as my mother was concerned. Late at night, I could hear her complaining about him, levelling some kind of accusation I could never make out, not even with a water glass pressed against my bedroom wall.

As my mother's resentment mounted, eventually my father had a falling-out with Clarence, and I assumed it had to do with her objections. I could never be certain what the straw was that broke the camel's back. I caught a few fragmented lines of the final fight between my father and Clarence, but they were cryptic, my father demanding over and over again, 'Explain to me what these bars doin' in yo' things!' Clarence, for his part, adopted a stance of indignation over the violation of his privacy, until finally he gathered his belongings and I heard the front door slam.

I never knew what my father meant by *bars*. It didn't make sense. As far as I could tell, Clarence hadn't stolen anything from my parents, apart from copious amounts of food and beer.

Either way, Clarence must have left the neighbourhood not long after leaving our apartment, because although I expected to cross paths with him at some point, I never saw him again.

After the incident with Clarence, I avoided the subject of my father's discharge at all costs. I never asked my father anything about his years of service; I never asked my mother, either. I pushed Clarence's words to the back of my mind, where they remained for years, until my mother turned to me that hot afternoon in June and handed me a key.

'Aren't you afraid to go all the way across the country to California?' Janet asked me as we sat at a drugstore counter on 125th Street once I had announced my plan.

Her brooding eyes bored holes into my own. *Yes* was the true answer: I was afraid to go. I was also afraid *not* to go.

'I know this will upset our plans a bit . . . It will take us a little longer to save up for a place of our own, but it's something I have to do.'

She closed her eyelids as though they were suddenly very heavy, and briefly lifted a hand to her temple. Then she dropped the hand and opened her eyes again. 'All right,' she said in a meek voice, shrugging and shaking her head. 'If it's something you have to do.'

'I think this will help us in the long run,' I said, reaching across the table to touch her hand where it had fallen. 'I think once I've done this, I'll be ready . . . for the next steps to come.' I did not say *marriage*, but of course marriage was what I meant, and Janet knew it, too. She looked up, and smiled weakly.

'Then I guess I ought to wish you good luck.'

I squeezed her hand and leant across the table to give her a grateful peck of a kiss. This move was only moderately successful. Her lips were cold and waxy, and smelt a bit like the peculiar clay used in ladies' lipstick. She smiled, though, and I smiled back, already feeling guilty for the slight shimmer of relief I felt upon having resolved to go to California after all.

11

The money my mother had given me was a start, but if I was going to make it all the way out to California, I'd have to scrimp as best I could. Summer loomed closer, and I graduated from Columbia. My mother attended the ceremony with a mixture of pride and dread on her face as she fanned herself in the humid sun, for graduation also meant the end of my life in the dormitory, and that meant I was coming home to stay under the same roof as Wendell.

For income, I had my part-time job as a bicycle messenger. The pay was modest, but I was having little luck finding much else – college degree be damned – so I asked the messenger service to increase my hours to as many as they would allow. I was paid weekly, and every Friday I added to the roll of bills I kept hidden in an old boot in the corner of my closet, but the saving was slow going.

One morning, however, the heavyset dispatcher sent me on a delivery that changed my fortune in a rather unexpected manner. It was – I realise looking back on it now – the second time within the space of a month that someone handed me a key and altered my prospects.

'Be careful with this one,' the dispatcher advised me, chewing on a toothpick and handing me a slip with an address scribbled on it. 'Character named Augustus Minton, but likes for his help to call him "Mister Gus". He's a grumpy sonofabitch, but he's richer than God. He writes a whole heap of them dime-store books under some other name – for kicks, I suppose – but he comes from important family, so we're under orders not to rattle his cage. The old fart doesn't get around too good, so if he doesn't hear you buzzing, you're to go around to the side entrance and use this key to let yourself in.'

He handed me a house key and an envelope, eyeing me over from head to toe. 'Hmph. I know you're one of those book-smart Negroes and all, but I don't expect you've ever been anywhere that compares to his house. Try to behave yourself. With any luck, you can leave the package downstairs and you won't have to talk to him face-to-face.' He paused and rubbed his chin. 'Now that I think about it . . . maybe I'll phone over and warn him. Wouldn't want the codger to be surprised by seeing a Negro in his house and have himself a heart attack.'

The dispatcher shuffled away. The top flap of the envelope was open, and a quick peek inside revealed the package contained a slender manuscript written under a curiously quaint nom de plume, 'Francois Reynard'. I had seen this name before, on bookshop shelves and even, sometimes, at the drugstore. He was the author of short, noir-style mysteries, the type of fare popular in the 1930s and more often than not snatched up by Hollywood and turned into movies.

I memorised the address; it was on the Upper East Side. I tucked the key into my vest pocket and pedalled off on my bicycle. Messenger boys were indispensable to publishing houses in those days. It seemed an endless stream of copies wanted dispatching all over the island of Manhattan and occasionally across the Brooklyn Bridge. Memos, typed carbons, and signed contracts whizzed between skyscrapers, brownstones, and mansions alike. A great many authors lived in New York at that time and quite often correspondences between writers and editors were ferried directly back and forth by messenger.

I rode uptown and found the town house more or less as I had imagined it: a rather large, stately brownstone on East Seventy-Eighth Street near the park. It was a corner building, the kind with a servants' entrance around the side. After two attempts at the bell, I went to the side entry and tried the key. Once inside, I found myself in a narrow hallway. I followed it blindly into a foyer where my shoes echoed loudly on the pure white marble floor. A package wrapped in brown parchment was laid out on a small console table. I assumed it was intended for me, or rather for the publishing house that employed me, and I moved to collect it.

'Who's that? Who's there?' came a voice. I froze.

'My name is Miles Tillman, sir,' I called back. 'I'm a messenger. Torchon & Lyle sent me.'

'You're not the regular boy,' the voice said. The timbre of it sounded tight, full of tension, as though he were holding back a wheezing cough. I was sure he was lying down and had been napping. I could hear him catching his breath from some remote back bedroom and I understood I had clearly woken him by ringing the bell and upset his regular routine. 'Well?' the voice demanded. 'Come on up here.'

'Sir?'

'You're here in my house: I need to get a look at you!' he snapped. 'Don't dawdle. I'm not getting any younger.'

I set the package down, put a hand on the cold marble banister, and looked upwards in the direction of the voice. There was nothing to do but go. I reached the top of the stairs and was met with a hallway that extended in both directions. I hesitated, considering which way to turn.

'Faster, boy!' he snapped. 'You lack confidence. I can hear your mincing little step on the rug.'

I moved in the direction of the voice, and found my way to the most cavernous, sumptuous, bizarre-looking bedroom I have ever seen. It was a veritable sultan's palace. Every inch of the place was covered in velvets and silks. Cushions were piled in heaps amid animal skins stretched out all around the floor. I looked up and noticed there was no visible ceiling, just billowing swags of ruby-coloured silk ascending, tent-like, to an apex from which dangled a strange-looking glass chandelier. Aesthetically speaking, the room charged headlong towards a state of gaudiness and then veered away at the last second. Until that day, I had never realised there existed people wealthy enough to bring the entire museum home with them.

Sure enough, as I looked around, I saw several objects that very likely had, on some occasion, once been exhibited in an actual museum. Marble sculptures perched on ionic pedestals. Baroque figurines were arranged in clusters here and there on a fireplace mantel. Dark, jewel-toned Renaissance paintings hung on the walls, the ripples of muscular human and animal flesh so real and vivid, they threatened to topple right out of their gilded frames.

'They're copies,' Mister Gus said, catching me gazing at the paintings. 'But quite accurate, I assure you. That's a Titian.' I nodded absent-mindedly. 'Don't nod as if you know who that is,' he snapped in a petulant voice. 'You don't know who that is.' My eyes sought out the source of the voice. The room was big, dim, and ornate, and it took me some seconds before my gaze landed on a small face frowning at me over a mound of bedcovers.

His brittle visage hovered over the bed, and I was struck by how it was possible he could appear paler than the white bedsheets. He was very much how I expected him to look, only smaller. He had sunken-in, skull-like features, the kind wherein the cheekbones and jawbones encircle each side of one's face like two angular, upside-down trapezoids. His chin was very pointy, his eyes were a faded blue, his skin bore a mottled map of age spots. His lips had thinned to the point of becoming a taut line. You could see, though, from the dark pepper still present in his wiry eyebrows and in the dark fringe of his lower lashes, that once upon a time he had perhaps reminded people of Errol Flynn and had been something approaching handsome. Now he glared at me, waiting for me to speak.

'That's a Caravaggio,' I said, pointing to another painting in a far corner. This was a lucky observation. Once, when I was fifteen, I found a large book that had been abandoned under a bench in Central Park. Inside the book was a series of translucent envelopes filled with glossy black-and-white photographs of the great paintings of Western civilisation. I took the book home, extracted the photographs, and pasted them up all over my bedroom walls with Scotch tape. They gave me great pleasure to look at, and they hung there until two years later, when my stepfather ripped them down in a routine fit of drunken irritation with me. The Caravaggio had been one of my favourites; I had taped it to the ceiling over my bed and memorised its shapes and lines, but I had never seen it in colour and hadn't understood all that I was missing. I stared at it with fascination now. It was like seeing a friend you thought you knew and realising there were still a great many secrets you had yet to discover about each other.

'Hmph,' he said. 'When they telephoned to warn me you were

coming, they said you were an educated Negro. I didn't know how to picture that until just now.' He pointed to another painting over his shoulder, on the wall to the right of his bed. 'Do you know that one?' he asked.

'No, sir,' I admitted. He smiled instantly, a smug, gratified smile.

'Then I guess there's still some difference between us after all,' he said.

'Yes, sir.'

'Don't *agree* with that, boy!' he snapped. 'I just insulted you. Never agree with a man who insults you.'

'Yes, sir.'

He huffed and rolled his eyes. 'Oh, I can see you are going to be trouble already,' he scolded. 'Don't you know enough not to abide a man who insults you?'

'With all due respect, sir,' I said, 'insults are relative. They depend on what a man aspires – or *doesn't* aspire – to be.' Mister Gus looked at me a long time, his left eye squinting a tiny bit more than his right.

'I believe,' he said finally, 'that *you* just insulted me.' Only as he said this did I realise how brazen I had been. I thought about my job and swallowed, waiting for him to speak again, my pulse thundering in my ears. It would not take much for him to telephone the publishing company and have me fired. 'Hmph,' he said. 'Well. At least I can see you're not going to be boring. Come here; let me get a look at you.'

I drew closer to the bed. He must've been one of those old people who is perpetually cold; the blankets were tucked up to his chin. All of his body remained concealed beneath and only his long, spindly fingers curled over the folded edges of the cool white sheet. His eyes studied me, and I got the impression he was calculating a long and complicated math equation.

'Your name again?'

'Miles Tillman, sir.'

'Hmm, well. I suppose I'm stuck with you instead of the regular boy, so you'll have to do. I assume you read the paper from time to time?'

'Yes.'

'Don't say "yes" so quickly, you dunce,' he barked. 'You don't even know which paper I mean!'

'I assumed you mean do I read The *Times*,' I replied.

'Of course you did. But there are lots of papers these days. You shouldn't assume. Only fools assume,' he said emphatically. 'Are you a fool?'

'No, sir,' I replied. He fumbled for a scrap of paper on the nightstand and handed it to me.

'Well, if you read the paper occasionally that means you *ought* to be able to find your way to the news stand. Now,' he said, 'there's the list of all the papers I want.'

I blinked at the scrap of paper, slowly comprehending I was being sent on an errand for him. The chicken-scratch handwriting revealed a long list of newspapers. It occurred to me it might be easier to bring him the whole news stand, wooden booth and all, but I didn't say so.

'And here,' Mister Gus continued, huffing as he reached back to the nightstand to retrieve a glass. In it were a couple of bills and a few nickels and dimes. I realised he had been waiting to assign someone this task and must have counted out the money sometime earlier, perhaps even the night before. I wondered if the previous messenger boy had been routinely sent on this errand. He dumped the contents into my palm. 'And don't go thinking you can pocket some of this for yourself; I know the cost, and

I've counted out exact change. When you return, you'll get your proper tip, but not before then.'

I made no move to go and simply stood there, dumbstruck.

'Well? Go, boy!' Mister Gus shouted. 'Hurry up, now.'

'Don't you' – I hesitated – 'have some live-in help?'

'Hmph!' he grunted. '*Greta*,' he grumbled, grinding teeth that I could only presume were dentures. 'Useless! Gone out. Grocery shopping, she says, but she dawdles and takes her time . . . hiding from me, that's what she's doing. Do you know, she's taken to bringing my meals while I'm asleep. Puts the tray on the bed and then rings a little bell *after* she's hurried out of the room so I won't have a chance to complain about her awful cooking. Hmph. Thinks that's crafty!'

I wasn't sure what to say to this. As Mister Gus glared at me, I began to sympathise with his housemaid's strategy.

'Well?' he said with irritation. 'Go already!'

I unfroze, went downstairs and around the corner – making sure I took the key with me – and bought the newspapers. The news stand attendant appeared to be familiar with my laundry list; he took one look at it and stacked the papers in a neat pile without checking twice and confirmed my suspicion that I was not the first messenger boy Mister Gus had sent on this errand. When I returned, the old man had propped himself up on the pillows and was waiting.

'Set them here, boy,' Mister Gus said, patting the bed beside him, and I did as instructed. He pulled one of the papers into his lap, squinting with milky eyes to make out the headlines. 'Your tip is on the nightstand,' he said, not glancing up from his reading. I looked, and in my absence an envelope had appeared – extracted, I assumed, from the nightstand drawer, where it had likely been pre-counted, ready and waiting. I was surprised to see it was an envelope, for that meant paper, not coin.

'Thank you, sir,' I said.

'Felston was the regular boy they sent here,' he said. 'I trusted Felston.'

I didn't know what to say to this idle remark, so I remained silent.

'But I understand he quit recently.'

'Yes, sir,' I said, for this was true. Bill Felston was a very handsome messenger boy who had recently quit to marry a girl in New Jersey and take over her family's gas station.

'Hmph. Well, we had an arrangement, Felston and I,' Mister Gus remarked. 'Delivery or not, he used to drop by with the papers. You see, I like my papers. And Felston, well, I believe Felston liked his tips.'

'I see,' I said, not knowing where this was leading. Mister Gus paused and lowered his paper, looking me over with scrutiny. His eyes travelled up and down the length of my body twice, then he grunted.

'I suppose you're not a total barbarian after all,' he said. 'You might do.'

'Do what, sir?'

'I like to have my papers – all of them – brought to me every day. If you know anything at all about old men, then you know we don't require much sleep, so bring them as early as you like; I wake with the proverbial cows, as they say, long before dawn. If this is amenable, you may start tomorrow.'

'Oh. I . . . I . . .' I stammered.

'That is all,' Mister Gus said. 'If you want the money – and let me tell you, you'd be a fool not to, boy; being a Negro messenger boy, I hardly expect you're rich – you'll come back tomorrow.' He waved a hand as though to shoo me away. I turned and made my way down the stairs, collecting the package I'd originally come to retrieve on my way out.

Once outside, I opened the envelope Mister Gus had handed me, and found two dollars tucked neatly inside. My weekly salary working as a part-time messenger boy was fifteen dollars. An extra two dollars per day was nothing to scoff at; if I were to perform this service every day for a week, I would make nearly double my pay. I had a funny feeling about this proposed arrangement, though. I couldn't put my finger on exactly why, but I knew my uneasiness had something to do with Mister Gus. I knew he was what was in those days called 'a confirmed bachelor', and I suspected that, despite his cantankerous manner, he liked receiving visits from messenger boys every bit as much as he liked receiving his actual stack of newspapers. Even so, if I took on this extra chore, the arrangement promised to bring me one step closer to California and to my father's journal. As I pedalled away that afternoon, I found myself making plans to stop by Mister Gus's town house first thing the next morning.

12

It had been a little while since I'd gone down to the Village, and I found myself missing the scene. Try as I might, I'd never been able to get Janet to come along. We were inverted images of each other in some ways, Janet and I. I had been elevated in the world through my scholarships, while hers was a tale of reversal of fortune. Her father had run a successful general store in a little town upstate and paid for her to have a private education, until one day the general store burnt to the ground and her father, tragically, with it. At sixteen, Janet was sent to live with her aunt and uncle in Harlem, where she helped to care for their four children. Like me, she was considered something of a misfit, and mostly kept her nose in a book.

In any case, while she liked to read every bit as much as I did, she had very conservative tastes and claimed the atmosphere in the Village wasn't to her liking. I attempted to lure her below Fourteenth Street by telling her about the exciting things that went on, the poetry and the jazz and such. She argued that Harlem had plenty of jazz without the indecency and all the people yelling about their dangerous political ideas. I could've pointed out Harlem had those latter things, too, if only you knew where to look for them, but I knew it would do no good. It was just as well. I figured I would enjoy the Village while still a bachelor, and give it up once we were married.

So I strolled the Village's hodgepodge of crooked streets alone. I appreciated the artists and the bohemians, the long-haired hipsters in their undershirts and rolled-up denim jeans, the girls who walked around in painter's smocks and ballet flats. As a young coloured man, I had a certain amount of anonymity. It wasn't that people in the Village treated you as though you weren't coloured; it was more a question of the fact that, to the kids of the Village, being a writer or artist or politico came first, and all the rest of it came second.

One evening, after finishing a shift at the messenger service, I took my throbbing calves down to a little cafe on MacDougal to unwind and read a book. I was reading about the Imagist poets and sipping a glass of cheap red wine, when a band of rowdy young men burst in. It was clear they had been drinking somewhere else before their arrival. They were giddy, whooping it up in booming voices. I recognised one of them and realised it was Bobby.

'Hey! Miles!' he called out in friendly recognition when he saw me. 'Hey, fellas, come over here and meet my pal Miles.' I didn't recognise any of the others. I looked around for Swish, Pal, and Cliff but didn't see them anywhere. It was clear this was a new band of friends who had probably picked up Bobby only hours earlier. I would venture to guess they'd gotten his attention by sending over drinks. With Bobby, that was often the way he acquired new acquaintances: people sent him drinks or bought him things. He never asked for such generosity, but his handsome face did. Bobby had a perpetually rumpled, appealing air about him that put people in mind of James Dean.

Now he came over and began to make introductions. I don't recall the names of all the guys, but I remember there was a pair of young men named Andrew and John who had been all-Ivy gridiron champions at Yale, and these two seemed to be the group's leaders.

They were friendly enough but not the sort of fellows I liked: they were a privileged, pampered lot, making the rounds of New York's most notorious neighbourhoods as though Manhattan were some kind of personal playground intended to be enjoyed by them alone. To a native New Yorker, this attitude of novelty can be particularly irksome, but I pushed it aside and smiled and shook hands with each of them in turn.

'You boys look like you're ready to get up to some trouble tonight,' I said in an attempt to make polite conversation.

'We're going to go get some kicks at the Hamilton Lodge Ball,' Andrew said. '*You* oughta come with us! You can show us the way around Harlem.'

This was an assumption. I had not volunteered the information that I was from Harlem, much less that I knew my way around.

'Oh, I don't know . . .' I said, but Bobby cut me off.

'C'mon, Miles! It'll be fun.'

'C'mon, Miles,' the group chorused in varying degrees of sincerity. I very badly wanted to say no, but I couldn't see much of a way to flat-out decline at that point.

'C'mon, Miles,' Bobby repeated. 'You *do* know Harlem better than all the rest of us, and besides, have you ever been to the Hamilton Lodge Ball? It's supposed to be *some* scene. We'll get a story or two out of it. Don't you want to do something adventurous?'

'I have a fiancée,' I said.

'So do most of these fellas,' Bobby said, thumbing over his shoulder. 'Like I said, we're just going to get a load of the scene. It's harmless.'

I looked at him. Bobby had that somewhat sheepish, slightly guilty look that all young scoundrels have about them; there was a devilish twinkle in his eye that appeared to be forever paired with his humble smile, which said, *Don't blame me! I didn't do anything!* He smiled now and I sighed, realising he wasn't going to give up.

'All right,' I relented, in spite of myself. 'Why not?'

After a few more beers, the group staggered outside, splitting up as we piled into a series of taxicabs. I rode with Bobby, wondering the whole time what it was I'd let myself be talked into.

The Rockland Palace in Harlem hosted the Hamilton Lodge Ball every year. The dance was infamous for over-the-top revelry and for the large number of attendees dressed in drag. Astors and Vanderbilts had famously attended in years past. I had never been to a single one, and as we rode along in the taxicab I worried about the consequences of turning up at such a party. If I were to be sighted at the ball, it would embarrass my proudly middle-class Harlem family and make me more of an outsider in my neighbourhood than I already was. But at the same time, I reasoned, whoever reported seeing me there would have to admit *he'd* been there, too. There was, at least, a kind of mutual safety in that fact.

We stepped out of the cab onto 155th Street, under a black awning that led into a tall brownstone building flanked with three sets of double doors and a giant arched stained-glass window. Frantic band music shrieked and roiled from deep within, and we each paid our entry fee to a six-foot-tall Miss America lookalike who stood holding a cashbox at the door. I could instantly see why she had been picked for the job: her facsimile was meticulous, and she was an impressive sight no matter what the truth was beneath her evening gown.

I followed Bobby inside. It was difficult to ignore the multitude of appreciative smiles he received as we moved deeper into the crowd. He smiled back in a careless, come-what-may manner. The space itself was a mixture of a dance hall and a theatre, with a small balcony of loge boxes along two walls. I was immediately gripped with the sensation of being in a fishbowl.

'You know, Bobby, I might beg off early; I'm feeling tired,' I said as we stepped further into the darkness. I was hardly dressed for this, and not in the mood for loud people. There was just enough light for me to see the whites of his eyes as he rolled them at me.

'Stop being a square. Take it easy!' he said. 'Let me buy you a drink and then if you want to go, go.' I was taken off guard. I'd never in my life witnessed Bobby buy anyone a drink. He'd never needed to. The fact he had money in his wallet that he might actually spend fascinated me. As far as I knew, he'd never had a steady job.

Bobby made good on his word and I soon had a beer in my hand. It was humid in there; the heat and perspiration of bodies pushed up together in a confined space had already begun to dominate the atmosphere. Despite the thick heat, hordes of people were dressed to the nines. It was oddly touching. Well-coifed queens – who, if they couldn't be called beautiful, could at least be called *statuesque* – floated about, festooned in mink stoles and mermaid-tail dresses. Women with short hair shuffled about in tuxedos; I glimpsed a pair of women in matching suits kissing at the bar. Scores of people were arrayed in masquerade costumes. Others skulked about the darker corners of the room in plain clothes, some of them genuinely interested in the scene, others just taking in the freak show, as I'm sure the Vanderbilts and Astors must have done. Tourists to the carnival. I found myself inexplicably embarrassed to realise we were among their number.

'Let's go up to the boxes,' Andrew suggested to the group, and John moved towards the staircases, clearing the way with his tank-like posture. We climbed up and found our way to a loge box, where Andrew seemed to already know people. As I was introduced around for the second time that night, I realised I was meeting a dozen or so men who would soon have jobs selling stocks or bonds or something of that ilk on Wall Street. Some of these boys were simply having a laugh, trying to create the madcap memories they would recall when their lives had gotten boring and grey. Intuition informed me, however, that a small minority among them – a few of the quieter, sober-eyed fellows – were laying the foundation for the split nature of their future adult lives.

'What do you think?' said Bobby as we looked down over the riotously colourful throngs on the dance floor below. 'Awfully wild scene, but impressive all the same. Look at all these *characters*! These cats go all out.' I surveyed the panorama down below. Half-naked bodies intermingled with the formally clad. Headdresses bobbed high over the crowd as people milled about. It *was* pretty wild. And beautiful. And obscene.

I finished my beer in record time and we hadn't been there longer than thirty minutes before Andrew got his hands on a purple feather boa and had draped it around his shoulders. He sat perched atop the seat back of a settee in our loge, teetering ever so slightly as he presided drunkenly over the small kingdom of our box. He was making fun of it all, I understood. But the vehemence of his glee made me wonder if there wasn't a bit too much protest in it. If someone were to press him on this subject, however, he would very likely retaliate with surprising viciousness. I felt a slight tremor of revulsion.

'Where are you going?' Bobby asked, seeing me turn away.

'I might roam around a bit,' I replied.

'Down in the trenches?' he asked with one eyebrow raised.

I nodded and made my way towards the stairs. I wondered if he intended to follow me, but he stayed put. I was simply relieved to be away from John and Andrew and the band of merry men they led. I was sorry I'd come. I would kill some time by making a few rounds of the scene downstairs, I told myself, then I would go back up to the loge box and bid Bobby goodnight.

Once downstairs, I wandered the floor aimlessly, awash in a

disorienting sea of cologne, body odour, and sickly-sweet perfume. A tall man dancing with an even taller drag queen backed into me and spun around just in time to spill beer down the front of my collared shirt.

'Sorry, fella!' he bellowed.

The drag queen – a brunette with snow-white skin and a drawn-on mole over her lip – tittered nervously, anticipating my aggravation. She was mistaken. I generally avoided fights as a personal rule, and now, at the Hamilton Lodge Ball, the last thing I wanted was to draw attention to myself by starting a brawl.

I waved my hands and shrugged to signal my lack of desire for a confrontation, then moved away to find something to mop the beer off my shirt before the stain set permanently. A hand appeared holding a clean white handkerchief.

'Here, take this,' a voice said. I looked up, following the hand that held the handkerchief. A young man with strawberry-blonde hair and hazel eyes stared back at me. He was about the same age as me, conservatively dressed – his manner of dress made me think he might be a clerk at a law firm or an insurance company – and he appeared every bit as out of sorts with our surroundings as I was. I regarded the handkerchief and smiled politely.

'I couldn't,' I said.

'Please.'

'All right.' I took the handkerchief and began to dab at the dark-hued stout stain as best I could.

'That's not going to do it. Try some of this,' he said, offering his drink to me. 'It's club soda.' He took the handkerchief back, handed me the glass, dipped the handkerchief in it, then patted at the stain. His methods, though not a complete solution, were substantially better than mine. The shirt might be salvaged after all.

'Thank you,' I said in a quiet voice as he performed his ministrations diligently. He smiled.

'You look about as comfortable here as I do.'

'I was just about to say something along that line.'

'I don't know what I'm doing here,' he said, laughing.

'Some friends talked me into it,' I said. 'They're . . .' I glanced up at the loge box where I'd left Bobby and his troupe of ne'er-do-wells. Andrew's behaviour had escalated: now he was shouting rude things to passers-by down below and pouring beer on anyone who dared to ignore him. 'They're here on a lark, I guess. To tell you the truth, they're not really my friends. A pack of hyenas, more like.'

'That's too bad,' he said, following my gaze to the loge box and frowning as Andrew dribbled beer onto a queen's very elaborate – and likely very *expensive* – *wig*. I shrugged. 'I'll admit, it's not really my scene, either,' he continued. 'Too ostentatious for my taste, too much rouge and lipstick. None of it is really my . . .' He searched for a fitting word.

'Shade?' I provided. We both chuckled.

'Yes. But there's something about the boldness and the bravery of it . . . something I wouldn't make fun of,' he said.

'I wouldn't, either. True bravery is rare.' We locked eyes and stood there, not talking.

'Would you like to get a drink?' he asked. He held up his glass of club soda and rattled the ice. 'Not this jazz, but a real one?' I nodded, and he turned and moved in the direction of the bar, and I followed him.

Just before we drew up to the counter, however, I glanced again at the loge box and saw Bobby looking down at me. He had spotted me in the crowd and was watching me with a curious, amused smile. There was no malice in it, but it bothered me all the same, and I felt a cold jolt of something. I froze mid-step. I tapped the young man on the shoulder.

'You know, on second thoughts, I don't know about that drink . . . I'd really better be going,' I said. I watched the young man's brow furrow in confusion. I looked at his intelligent hazel eyes and tasteful suit and immediately felt sorry, but there was nothing to be done for it. I managed to make things even worse by adding insult to injury. 'I apologise if I've been' – I paused – 'less than clear.' He remained where he stood, the surprise and dismay written on his face, looking at me and saying nothing.

'Thank you again for your help,' I concluded, holding out a hand. It looked formal and awkward, hovering there in the air. He held me in his gaze for a moment longer, then shook my hand coldly – there was something tremendously empty and angry in it – and turned, abruptly disappearing back into the crowd.

I stood there feeling lousy, although I couldn't say exactly why. I looked up to where Bobby had been watching us but it appeared he was now engaged in a conversation with Andrew and John, who clapped him on the back and doubled over in laughter at something he said. I wondered if the joke wasn't about me. Annoyed, my impulse was to leave without saying goodnight, but no sooner had that thought flitted through my brain than I ruled it out. At this point, if Bobby didn't see me depart alone, he might make other assumptions about when and how I'd left.

I moved to climb the stairs back to the loge box to make my farewells.

13

CLIFF

A guy could write all he wanted, but when it came to getting published it was always better to know somebody. I didn't really want to get chummy with fellas like Rusty Morrisdale but, considering who his boss was, it wouldn't hurt to be friendly. Literary agents were more rare in those days and only the really important writers were represented. If Rusty's boss represented me, I was sure to become a big deal. Once this idea occurred to me, I spent hours picturing the famous literary agent magnanimously placing a hand on my shoulder and choosing me as the next great torchbearer of the written word. And sooner or later the famous agent was bound to go to lunch with My Old Man; My Old Man had lunch with everybody who was anybody, and Rusty's boss was definitely a somebody.

I spent a lot of time imagining the details of how that lunch would go. In my fantasies I pictured the famous literary agent eating a steak and smoking a cigarette and talking about the *absolute genius* of a young client of his in urgent, earnest tones across a white-linen tablecloth as my father smiled and nodded and then eventually froze when the important literary agent said the young prodigy's name was Clifford Nelson and that he assumed it was no relation, of course. In some variations of this fantasy My Old Man would simply freeze upon hearing his son's name and in others he would choke a bit on his martini mid-swallow and dribble gin on his expensive silk tie but either way it was very good to fantasise about and it was a satisfying way to pass the afternoon, especially after spending all morning staring into a blank notebook and drinking coffee until the clock struck noon and the time finally came to tip some whiskey into the coffee mug and *Irish it up*, as Swish often phrased it in that wry winking way of his.

Of course, the problem with getting discovered by Rusty's boss was that it meant first getting discovered by Rusty. I'd have to find him, and I'd have to be friendly about it. I decided my best bet was to go around the Village looking for Bobby because after all Rusty had taken a strong interest in Bobby. If I hung around Bobby long enough, Rusty just might turn up again.

That afternoon I didn't find Bobby or Rusty but I *did* find Swish at the White Horse. He was drinking a beer with a pale-faced kid I had never seen before. The kid's face caught the cold late-afternoon light coming in from the window and gave off a milky bluish glow. It was always dim and slightly moist inside the White Horse and the wooden floor creaked when you walked on it but nevertheless there was something homey about all this and it was a favourite spot for hipsters to convene and argue about politics and philosophy and poetry. I guessed that was what Swish and this pale kid were doing now and I got a beer for myself and joined them. They were sitting at a booth and as soon as I approached, Swish looked up and smiled and scooted in to make room for me.

'Hey, Cliff, old buddy old pal. Sit on down and meet Gene,' Swish said, nodding to the pale-faced kid. 'Gene here went and bought an ancient printing press for a song from some crazy old ex-Bolshevik and is gonna start up his own literary magazine.

Rented out a basement on Bleecker for the operation and everything.'

Gene smiled sheepishly and shrugged. 'Swish and I have been coming up with names. I've decided to call it *The Tuning Fork*.'

I asked him a few questions about the whole business and he began to explain more about his plans for the print run. I was impressed by his ambition but also by his modesty and shyness. He had an unassuming way about him. It wasn't just that he was pale, either; there was a curious lack of colour, like an albino but not quite, from his mousey hair to his washed-out hazel eyes that peered at you through a pair of delicate-looking wire-rimmed glasses.

'We need top-quality submissions for our first issue,' Gene said.

'I told him you're a writer,' Swish added. Now it was my turn to smile sheepishly and shrug.

'Would you care to submit something?' Gene asked. 'A story or maybe an essay? No pressure, of course. It's just that Swish here tells me you're a swell writer with real ambitions, and we'd be happy to have something from you.'

'Well,' I said, turning the proposition over in my mind. 'All right.' It would be fun to be part of a new literary magazine starting up and Gene seemed like just the kind of person who might actually succeed with a magazine. You had to have energy to start something like that, but you had to have a steady quality about you, too. Most kids in the Village who tried to start magazines had the energy but not the steadiness, and this was why you saw so many new magazines come and go after only a handful of issues. They were flashy, rebellious-looking magazines and their covers were bursting with vibrancy and jazz and had a kind of manic quality about them you knew could not be sustained.

Looking at Gene, I figured that his literary magazine would

be quieter and more understated but would still have plenty of youth and energy in it. I only had two stories on hand at the moment. One was something I had written a few years back about a boy leaving a girl and acting like it didn't matter when really it was tearing him up inside. It was a little like that Hemingway story 'The End of Something', but instead of going on a fishing trip together the couple is at a baseball game and after the boy breaks things off with her the girl leaves for good during the seventh-inning stretch, while the boy lets her go and stays and sits there like a stoic watching the end of the game even though he's all torn up inside. I had originally written the story back in prep school but I had worked on it over the years and made it better and better, but so far it had failed to gain traction with any of the literary rags I'd submitted it to. Perhaps Gene would see it for what it was and notice the great potential those editors had failed to spot.

The other story was about two young guys who ride the rails as hobos and the big con they pull on this little town in the Midwest. They get everyone to buy tickets for a fake lottery. The two guys are real sneaky about it, too, because they never overtly discuss their plan in public but instead they leave hobo writing in discreet places around the town buildings and it ends with them back on the train, drinking whiskey and laughing about how they managed to pull the wool over everybody's eyes. During their time in the town one of the guys balls a farmer's young, pretty daughter but later as he sits drinking whiskey with his friend and laughing he realises he can never go back to the town again because of the con they've put over on everyone. He likes the girl and the realisation he can never see her again makes him profoundly sad but he carries on and never admits this sadness to his friend. The truth was I'd gotten the bare bones of the story from Swish.

It was one of the stories he liked to tell from his old hobo days because it had a kind of punch line to it and everyone who heard it always laughed. Of course I'd changed the names and altered some of the details, but Swish never really asked me about my work anyway and so I thought it was no big deal if I didn't tell him his story had been the original inspiration, just in case it made things funny between us.

It was true that the seedling of my idea had come from his anecdote, but a seedling is just a seedling and what mattered more was what a writer did with it after it was planted and I wasn't sure Swish would understand this. In any case, I decided to give Gene the first one.

'Sure,' I said. 'I think I have something.' Gene and I made arrangements to meet up the next day and he gave me the address of the basement workshop on Bleecker and I promised to bring over a freshly typed copy for him to read.

Suddenly the memory of sitting in the cafe that day with Miles flashed into my head and I wondered if Swish hadn't recommended that Gene ought to ask Miles to contribute a story, too. It didn't appear Swish had thought of it and I considered whether I ought to bring it up. But then Miles seemed awfully private with his stuff and it wasn't my job to go around advocating for him anyway. If a fella wanted to get people to read and acknowledge his work, then that was on *his* shoulders. I decided to keep quiet about Miles and anyway I was glad to have happened upon Swish and Gene and was feeling optimistic that Gene would like my story.

'Cheers to both of you,' said Swish, raising his glass. It was plain he was happy to have fostered this connection and we were all excited to think Gene's new literary magazine might actually amount to something.

* * *

The prospect of having my writing appear in print had put me in a fine mood. It was still early in the day, and I was feeling a little happy-go-lucky and maybe also a little foolish. I say foolish because in my stoned state I decided to go up to midtown and visit my father's office at old Bonwright. I was burning to tell him that my story was going to be published in a literary magazine and I figured I could casually drop it into conversation.

Professionally speaking, it was best to get to My Old Man in the afternoon if you wanted his good favour. Even though I had only observed things from a distance, I did know *something* about how editors worked and generally the rule was that there were editors who it was better to approach in the morning and editors who it was better to approach in the afternoon. And even if I didn't know about editors, I knew about My Old Man and I knew he was definitely the type to approach in the afternoon, after he'd had a nice steak and a few martinis in him and was feeling jolly and affable.

It was a quick jaunt up to midtown and to the high-rise where My Old Man worked. I got off the elevator on the seventh floor and looked for my father's secretary in her usual spot amid the hustle and bustle of the typing pool but there was nobody there. This was odd, because in all the time My Old Man had worked at Bonwright he'd always had the same girl, Francine, and Francine guarded his office in that funny watchdog way that only older broads who've worked for the same boss all their lives have about them. She was tough and kept a careful eye on his door and I knew My Old Man liked it that way.

His door was open a crack and I pushed it the rest of the way open. There was an air of real chaos inside. My Old Man was pacing in front of the window while arguing with someone on the telephone and intermittently smoking a cigarette and gulping down a glass of Scotch. His desk was buried under a rippled mountain of heaped-up papers and the mountain was crumbling one binder-clipped manuscript at a time.

'No,' he was saying into the telephone. 'No, no, no. I've already had two temps in here; I'm telling you now, I need another. I was told the girl from the temp agency – what's the name of the one they were going to send? Barbara? – I was told *Barbara* would be here already . . . What? . . . When? That is unacceptable! I don't care if she's on another job; send someone else in that case. What? . . . I don't know what was requested . . . Well, whoever you send, I'll tell you this much: she'll be here come Monday or I'll inform our personnel department that Bonwright is no longer doing business with your agency.'

I stooped to pick up some of the papers that had fallen and put them back on the desk and when I did My Old Man turned around and noticed me. I was only trying to help but nonetheless he frowned with irritation and waved a hand as if to shoo me away. My stomach sank. It was plain that I had miscalculated and instead of picking a very good time to share my news with him I had wound up picking a very bad time and it was not likely that it would go very well for me. Finally he hung up the phone and sighed and drained the last of his Scotch.

'Yes? How much do you need, Clifford?' he said once he'd swallowed the Scotch and slammed down the glass. He stubbed out his cigarette with an angry jab. 'Make it quick. I haven't got time to fuss over your financial problems today.' My father was famously friendly and charming to everyone except me.

'I haven't come for money.'

'Well, now, there's something new.'

'Where's Francine?' I asked, not ready to launch into the real reason for my visit.

'*Mrs Edmund Roper* quit last week,' he said, lighting another cigarette. He pretended to look at his watch with a mocking expression. 'I expect she's on her honeymoon right about now. She got married, if you can believe it.'

'At her age?' I said. I was blown over by this news, because Francine was a steely old battleaxe of a woman and I couldn't for the life of me picture her married, much less on her honeymoon.

'It turns out she found herself a nice old widower,' he said with a bitter expression, 'and left me here to rot.' He made a gesture towards the disarray on his desk and crossed over to the bar-cart in the far corner. 'I suppose it's my fault,' he said, pouring himself another Scotch. He poured a few fingers into a second glass and I assumed this one would be for me so I went ahead and sat down in a chair. 'Back when I could've had any girl at all, I chose *that* tough old bird to be my secretary, thinking, "Well, here's one I won't have to pretend to romance", only to have her romanced out from under my nose! Hasn't anyone any loyalty any more?'

'Well, she *was* with you for around fifteen years, wasn't she?'

'That isn't the point, Clifford.' He put the second glass down in front of me and sighed.

We sat and drank the Scotch and then drank two more and I listened to My Old Man let off steam about his responsibilities at the office and about coping without Francine. As his face turned pink and I felt my cheeks begin to glow with the warmth of the Scotch, I changed the subject to baseball and which Yankees were rumoured to be doing well at spring training. After a while he loosened his tie and sat further back into his chair and together we chatted away. When he seemed relaxed I thought again of bringing up my lucky news, as it was sure to impress him.

'Say, I've been thinking,' I said, 'about all that jazz we discussed after I told you Columbia was all washed up and that I'd had enough.'

'Good,' he said. He stiffened a bit in his chair. 'Have you come to your senses about finishing your schooling?'

'Not exactly,' I replied. 'I've been thinking about doing a little writing.'

His brow furrowed. 'Hmm,' was all he said.

'Why the face?' I pressed. I knew things were beginning to take a sour turn and my visit wasn't going to go as I'd planned but I didn't care. I was irritated because here was a man who had spent his whole life helping writers who were strangers and now that I wanted to become one of them you would think he would encourage his own son. 'Writing is hard work,' I said, trying to keep the terrible defensive whiney tone out of my voice.

'It *is* hard work,' he agreed, 'and even so, it takes a great deal of talent. Not to mention a good deal of patience and experience. Take it from me, as I know something about the subject: the world doesn't need another failed writer, Clifford.'

I stared at him, feeling punched in the gut. I couldn't believe my ears. The poisonous words *Like you?* sprung to my lips but I held them in.

'Your mother and I are hoping that – if you refuse to finish your schooling – you will find practical employment.' He looked at me, and I could tell he was trying to muster some variety of fatherly encouragement. It didn't flow naturally between us. 'I have every confidence you can,' he finally finished. He gave a tight-lipped smile. 'Now, I ought to be getting back to work, Clifford. Without Francine here, this place is an absolute zoo.' He paused and pulled a few greenbacks out of his wallet. 'Your mother says you haven't phoned her in well over a week.'

'You know I don't have a telephone in my, *ahem*, new situation,' I said, glaring at him.

'Ah, yes,' he said, looking both irritated and embarrassed. 'Well, here you are. That's all I've got at the moment, I'm afraid.' He held out two fives and a ten.

He might as well have said *Run along now, sonny* for how crummy he made me feel. I knew as well as he did it was Friday afternoon and nothing ever happens in publishing on a Friday afternoon and the only work he was going to get done was to finish the bottle of Scotch and maybe pick up the phone and yell at a few more people. I wanted to say something else but it wouldn't come, so I snatched the dollar bills from his hand and charged out of his office without saying goodbye.

Later that evening I went looking for Swish but found Bobby and Pal instead. I had checked into all of our regular haunts and found them both leant up against a pillar in the tiny underground triangle of space that made up a club called the Village Vanguard listening to musicians blow some jazz and waggling their heads in spastic syncopation. There was a funny asymmetry about the picture the two of them made: tall, towering Pal bobbing his head shyly, his long eyelashes shading his deep-blue eyes from the glare of the stage lights, and Bobby with his sleek silhouette and his sexed-up panther posture, winking at anyone and everyone who made eye contact with him. They were a study in contrasts; the introvert and the extrovert, like one of those science models that had been turned inside out in order to show you both sides of a human at once.

'Boy oh boy, could I ever use a drink,' I said when I approached. I was still sore about My Old Man.

'Here, have this,' Pal said, handing me a full beer. 'I'll go get another.' He moved across the room towards the bar and I thought, *Leave it to a guy like Pal to give you the very beer in his hand and not think anything of it.* Guys like Pal were worth their weight in gold and didn't even know it and it was a shame the whole world couldn't be populated with men like that.

I stood leaning against the pillar, drinking Pal's beer and talking to Bobby as he surveyed the room the way he always did, deciding which girl he was going to ball that night. Just as I was beginning to relax and forget about My Old Man, I caught a glimpse of someone I had not seen on the other side of the pillar. I flinched because it was a surprise there was anyone there at all and it turned out the someone was Rusty.

'Say, I remember you,' Rusty said in greeting. 'You're the fella who's going to be a big important writer,' repeating the thing Rex had said while we sat smoking on Rex's roof. I recoiled at this. If he was going to mock me, he could have the courtesy not to do it to my goddamn face. But then he straightened and looked at me with a sincere expression and said something that changed everything.

'Maybe you ought to give me some of your work to read sometime,' Rusty said. I stood there blinking stupidly because I had expected Rusty to taunt me like he had at the party but not to make an actual offer to do me any favours. He saw the surprise written all over my face and smiled, but it was a twisted smile because Rusty had a very unappealing manner of pursing his lips awkwardly when he was enjoying something. 'Write down your address,' he said, handing me a little notebook and pencil from his pocket. 'I'll drop by sometime.'

I looked at Rusty with his big ears that stuck out too far from his head and his puckered smile and realised I did not especially want him coming by my apartment building and dropping in unannounced, but I also thought, *What the hell?* – because here was this guy who was the assistant to New York's most famous literary agent and anyway I'd be a fool not to take him up on his offer. That had been my plan when I'd started the day, and now here I had come full circle back around. I took the notepad and scribbled down my address and handed it back.

'When do you think you'll come?' I asked.

'Oh,' Rusty said in a vague tone, 'sometime.'

14

EDEN

During my next chat with Miss Everett, I announced the good news. I knew she would be glad for me, and perhaps even take a little pride in my accomplishment. But as soon as the words – 'I've been promoted to reader!' – left my lips, I realised I'd misjudged things. She simply froze, her expression utterly blank. Then, very slowly, tiny increments of adjustment took place. Her spine stiffened where she sat, and the arch of her left eyebrow floated upwards.

'My, but what an ambitious little thing you are,' she finally remarked. There was a perplexing quality to her voice, a slightly patronising tone I hadn't heard before, and a wide, closed-mouth smile spread across her lips. It was one of those expressions where you can't tell at first if it is in fact a smile or a grimace; the whole of her face pulled at it, and I was suddenly reminded of a violinist tightening the strings of his instrument. '*Reader*, and in only a few months, Miss Katz. We had all better watch out; I suppose you'll just make editor yet.'

I waited for her to comment further, but she abruptly returned her attention to the badly stacked pile of manuscripts lying on her desk. 'Mabel!' she called in a loud voice. The door swung open and Mabel materialised, as if she had been lying in wait like a jack-in-the-box poised and ready for someone to turn the crank. 'I don't understand *why* I'm still looking at these manuscripts when I asked you to remove them and type up my editorial letters over half an hour ago,' Miss Everett said to a rapidly wilting Mabel.

'I thought you wouldn't want me to interrupt your chat with Miss Katz,' Mabel said in a small voice.

'If I didn't want that, I would've told you so,' Miss Everett said. 'Besides,' she continued, 'let's not lose our heads and act like little fools. Miss Katz is not so important that we should neglect our work, even if she *has* been promoted to reader.'

'Reader! Oh, Eden – that's just what you wanted! Congratulations,' Mabel said, turning in my direction with wide eyes.

'That'll do, Mabel!' Miss Everett said, abruptly lifting the pile of manuscripts and heaving them into Mabel's arms. Miss Everett had scooped up the pile with careless effort and now as Mabel took them a thick section of the bottommost pages escaped her grasp and slid to the ground. 'Oh, for the love of Pete,' Miss Everett sighed as Mabel stooped to pick them up. She shook her head and glanced again in my direction. 'Now, if you'll excuse us, Miss Katz, we're quite busy down here. I'm sure you have quite a lot of your own work waiting for you upstairs, and Mr Turner will be wondering where you've gotten off to.'

'Yes, ma'am,' I said. I nodded and smiled, then beat a hasty retreat, hopscotching over the papers strewn about the floor on my way out.

First one week, then two . . . then eventually four whole months went by and Miss Everett did not ring for me to come down to her office for one of our chats. I began to worry I'd lost the only champion I'd truly had. I figured her silence meant she had written me off as an ingrate.

But then one day the telephone on my desk buzzed and I answered it to discover not Mabel but Miss Everett herself on the other end of the line.

'Hello, Miss Katz,' came the cool lilt, sharpened and slightly tinny through the telephone. 'I was wondering if you might have some time to dash downstairs. I have something for you.'

'Oh! Of course,' I said, nearly knocking over a paper cup of cold coffee with my elbow. 'Right away.'

Miss Everett rang off. I quickly surveyed my desk. In front of me, the electric typewriter hummed a quiet whir. I had been in the middle of typing a letter for Mr Turner, but I didn't want to keep Miss Everett waiting. I switched the typewriter off, tucked some files away in a drawer, and headed for the elevator.

Once I reached the fifth floor, I made my way down the hall, past the row of gilt-framed sailboats and their maritime cheer, towards the familiar and increasingly strong odour of Russian dressing. Upon reaching Miss Everett's office, no sooner had I touched the doorknob than the door flew open and Mabel emerged, charging forth with her usual harried speed.

'Oh!' Mabel exclaimed with affable surprise. 'Gosh! I nearly ran right into you, Eden! Go on in; she's expecting you.'

I stepped cautiously into the room and found Miss Everett waiting for me with her hands clasped neatly on the desk before her. This was unusual. Almost always when I entered Miss Everett's office she was lost in a whirlwind of busyness. She had a habit of keeping me standing about awkwardly for several minutes before asking me to have a seat.

She smiled – not the violin-string smile but rather a much softer cousin to that smile – and waved a friendly hand to a chair. 'Well, Eden,' Miss Everett began. 'I must say you've made good use of your time here. I've thought some more about your promotion, and I'm really quite impressed.' Her face contorted and she managed to produce the soft smile again.

'Thank you, Miss Everett.'

'In the spirit of *mentorship*, I've decided to provide you an opportunity to keep that marvellous upward momentum of yours going here at Torchon & Lyle. During our last chat, Eden, you said you were not overburdened with your new responsibilities but were rather enjoying them. I take it that is still the case?'

I nodded. 'Oh, sure. I've found I can get the extra work done easily if I just use some of my weekend time.'

'And you don't mind that?'

'No. I shouldn't . . . I mean, I suppose I figured that's just what editors *do,* and if I want to be an editor I'd better get used to the hours.'

'Very mature, and you are quite right to take the long view. Now I'm even *more* certain I was right to pick you for what I'm about to suggest.'

'And what's that?'

'Well, I've decided to let you take charge of some of these,' she said, pushing a stack of manuscripts towards me across the desk. Surprised by this sudden development, I eyed them with disbelief. 'I think it's safe to assume that Mr Turner is a very busy man,' she continued. 'Probably too busy to properly give you all the details about his opinion of your reports. How will you ever learn to write a tip-top report if you don't have guidance? You see, this is how we can be of mutual help to each other, Eden. I'll allow you to read and write up reports for a few of my manuscripts each week. And I'll personally review your reports and tell you exactly what I think of them. You stand to learn a lot this way.'

I didn't quite know what to say. The pile of manuscripts loomed large, and her words swam in my ears: *I'll allow you to read . . . I'll tell you exactly what I think of them . . .* I understood she was giving me more work, and I also understood that Miss Everett had managed to very neatly tie something important together in how she'd framed our discussion: she had bound my desire to become an editor to the additional pile of manuscripts that now sat before me. I'd said I wanted to be an editor – *more than anything,* I'd claimed. Here was my chance to prove to her I'd meant it.

'Thank you,' I finally said.

'Of course.' Miss Everett waved a hand. Her freshly lacquered nails flashed in the light like five tiny pools of crimson blood. 'Don't mention it. You've made your ambition plain, and I want to do whatever I can to nurture it and see you down your proper path.' She returned her attention to her desk and began shuffling various papers around. It was clear our meeting was over. I rose from my chair and reached to gather the manuscripts into my arms.

'Oh – one last thing, Eden. I only have two rules about the manuscripts I'll be giving you. The first is that you let me know straightaway if there's going to be a delay in finishing a report; that way I can take matters into my own hands and finish your reports for you, if need be. And second is that you never, under any circumstances, remove these manuscripts from the office. I had one girl who took them home and left them on a city bus – can you imagine? I simply can't have them vanishing on me, and I need for you to work on them here.'

The stack Miss Everett handed me was sizable, and taking them home would allow me to continue working on them at night. I was about to mention that Mr Turner allowed me to take manuscripts home overnight and even over the weekends, but I didn't want to come off sounding rude or disrespectful. The manuscripts were very heavy in my arms and my stamina was already flagging when I thought of the long evenings of work that stretched before me, so I simply nodded.

15

I quickly became acquainted with the office rhythms in a new, more intimate way. Miss Everett's decree that the manuscripts – *her* manuscripts, at least – should never leave the premises meant staying long after all the other secretaries, readers, and editors had packed up for the day. Coming back from the ladies' room, I often encountered the sight of my desk lit up and looking like a lonely castaway amid a dark sea. I got a lot done during these evening sessions, but I can't say I was ever one hundred per cent at ease. There was something discomfiting in the atmosphere once the lights had been turned out. I would feel the echoing cavern of the sixth floor spreading out around me, the crinkling rustle of each manuscript page I turned growing louder by the minute. The best way to describe how I felt was *haunted*. I was acutely aware of being isolated and yet not alone. At nine o'clock each evening, an elderly Swede named Olaf came to empty the waste bins and wash the coffee pots. When I glimpsed the pupils of his eyes, milky blue with advanced cataracts, I understood how it was the glass coffee pots never seemed to get completely clean. There were often stirrings, too. Editors who came back to retrieve a bottle of Scotch or to hang about their offices with the lights turned out while having a nightcap with a lady friend. These were the editors I thought of as the company's 'wolves'; they were lonely men who prowled about, using the office like it was some sort of private back room at Sardi's or the Algonquin. But then I identified a species of even lonelier editors, too – the ones who worked too hard or had fights with their wives. These editors ultimately resigned themselves to sleeping on the scratchy upholstery of their office sofas for the night. Torchon & Lyle during the afterhours was a place heavy with silence and yet thick with restless activity.

One night I was reading at my desk, when I looked up to see a blonde apparition moving towards me. Recognising the jaunty step, I realised it was Judy. As she drew nearer, I was astonished to note she looked every bit as fresh and perky at nine o'clock at night as she did at eight o'clock in the morning.

'I thought I'd find you here!' she exclaimed. As she stepped into the pool of light around my desk I noticed that the bright swipe of lipstick she habitually wore had been recently reapplied. 'Mabel said Miss Everett had piled more work onto your shoulders.'

There was a pitying tone in her voice that irked me. 'Oh, I don't mind,' I said. 'I take it as a compliment she trusts my taste. Would you know what, she doesn't even bother to read the ones I say are bad? She trusts me that much.'

Judy nodded sweetly, still looking at me with the kind of expression one wears when trying to help a lost child. I didn't understand Judy; she never seemed to acknowledge that this was how I was going to make editor. But at that moment she appeared to detect my irritation with her sympathy, because suddenly her face relaxed and she laughed.

'Say, don't look so glum; I've come to rescue you! Want to take a little break? I'm awfully thirsty myself.'

I looked at the pile of manuscripts, which somehow appeared every bit as mountainous as they had hours earlier when I'd set them on top of my desk with a plop. I realised in the course of the last couple hours my vision had gone a little blurry. 'That might be nice,' I murmured, then brightened and looked at my watch. If we went very quickly for a cup of coffee, I could be refreshed and back at my desk in a little over half an hour. 'What time is it? Is Schrafft's open much longer?'

'Oh. I thought we might go somewhere else. I had something a little stiffer than coffee in mind.'

'Stiffer?'

Exactly two vodka martinis and one hour later, I reluctantly said goodbye to Judy and forced myself to return to the office. Going from the noisy, fusty warmth of the little Irish bar where we'd been drinking back into the echoing isolation of the office was like going from a steam room into an ice-bath. The fuzzy feeling that had come over me in such a comfortable and inviting wave at the bar now seemed more like a disjointed jangling in my head.

When the elevator doors opened on six, I stepped off but was immediately brought up short. From across the floor I could make out a dark figure hovering over my desk. As I squinted at the bulky shape, I realised I was looking at Mr Frederick. His head turned, and as the alcoholic glisten of his watery eyes flashed, I understood he was looking in my direction.

'Ah, Miss Katz – there you are! I've been looking for you,' he said in a slow, thick voice.

'For me?'

'Yes! I promised I was going to visit you, and here I am . . .'

'That's very . . . uh, *thoughtful*.'

'Exactly! I'm a very thoughtful man. Ask anybody! Ask 'em all!' I had no clue who it was that constituted the phantom population he thought I ought to ask, but I didn't enquire further. As I approached my desk, Mr Frederick stepped nearer to the desk lamp and I was able to make out his expression. He lurched close enough for me to smell his breath, and stared into my face for several seconds with an anaesthetised smile plastered stupidly upon his face. Then his features fell downcast and he frowned. He jabbed a finger at the pile of manuscripts on my desk, and from the state of disarray I could see he had been searching around my desk only moments earlier.

'Yes, I came to see *you* . . . but you weren't here,' he said. 'Where were you?'

'Oh, I stepped out for some fresh air.' As soon as I said it, I was sorry. My heart was not in the lie, and I could tell from Mr Frederick's expression he knew this was so, and that he could guess exactly where I'd been.

'Aha! "Fresh air", eh?' He winked. 'I *knew* you were a girl who liked to have a good time,' he said. His finger made a poking, prodding beeline to my ribs. On automatic impulse, I recoiled and raised my hand to swat his finger but stopped in the nick of time.

'I'm not trying to get fresh,' he said, holding both hands in the air innocently. He wavered there for a moment, tipping drunkenly on his feet, then dropped his hands to rub his sizable belly. 'I am nothing if not a gentleman. Ask 'em. Ask 'em all! A gentleman, through and through.'

'Of course,' I said. 'I'm sorry.'

'Yes . . .' he said, placated by the opportunity to remain chivalrous. 'I do believe you young people nowadays are oversexed. You're always getting the wrong ideas . . .'

'You're so right, I apologise,' I repeated, suddenly sensing my opportunity. 'It's past my bedtime, and I'm positively bleary-eyed.

I'd really better be getting home.' I departed with sufficient haste to thwart the next sentence forming on his lips.

I hurried out, taking the stairs, and snuck back into the office again at five in the morning in a desperate attempt to finish my work from the night before.

Soon enough, this became a routine; once initiated, the game of cat-and-mouse between Mr Frederick and myself proved difficult to call off. Mr Frederick was now sharply attuned to my existence, much in the manner a mosquito – having been shooed away before completing its first full sip of blood for the night – is extremely sensitive to the presence of a warm human body in a confined room. He began seeking me out persistently, especially during the afterhours. My regular manoeuvre – cutting out quickly and then making up for it by returning to the office at four or five o'clock in the morning – was beginning to take a toll. When Judy commented on the dark circles under my eyes, I nearly began to cry as I explained about my situation.

'Oh, he's shameless,' Judy rolled her eyes and proclaimed when I described yet another night of being chased around my desk. 'And there's no telling what he'll do. He's done some perfectly wicked things to girls at the annual Christmas party – you know, put them in funny positions and then the next day claimed it couldn't be helped because he was too drunk to be held accountable for anything and that it was only meant in good fun anyhow. I think he knows he can't be fired. If I were you, I'd steer clear of him at all costs.'

'I'm trying, but it's awfully difficult to manage when Miss Everett has me working on all those manuscripts and he knows I'm practically chained to my desk.'

'I don't get it,' Judy said, her ponytail shimmering as she gave a disapproving shake of her head. 'Why don't you just take them home? She'll never know the difference.'

I turned Judy's suggestion over in my mind and realised I was sorely tempted.

That evening Miss Everett came by my desk a few minutes just prior to five o'clock, as she usually did, freshly spritzed with a generous dose of Chanel No. 5. I knew she was preparing to leave the office for the day because a silk handkerchief was tied over her hair and she was holding a pair of cat-eye sunglasses in her hand. She chatted with me in a friendly manner, during which my conscience kicked in and I changed my mind three or four times about whether or not I had it in me to go through with my plan. Finally, she wrangled an armful of manuscripts out of her ostrich-skin handbag and deposited them in a breezy manner on the corner of my desk.

'Just a few more for you to have a look at,' she said. 'I expect you're getting to be quite the expert. It may look like a lot, but it shouldn't take you very long to decipher whether they're good or not. You're clever; you'll be done with them in a jiffy!'

I looked at the pile she had left behind. God knows what was in there. The stacks of pages Mr Turner handed off to me were often quite slender, and even when the manuscripts these stacks contained weren't very good, they were never very bad. I believe he employed some sort of system whereby he winnowed them down himself first and had me read only those manuscripts he wanted to consider in earnest. In contrast, the piles Miss Everett gave me were utter chaos, containing a range of things from romances to detective novels to how-to manuals. I had sympathy for the fact that Miss Everett was treated by her colleagues as a sort of editorial catch-all; for instance, she was made to edit cookbooks and children's books –

subjects her male peers assumed she liked, because, after all, she was a *woman* – when in fact she had zero interest in either. They piled all their undesirable projects on her, and now in turn she was piling her undesirable projects on me.

I attempted to take Miss Everett's manuscripts home with me for the first time that night, my heart in my throat the whole time. After she departed, I waited a solid hour just to make sure she wasn't coming back. I think I was waiting until that vapor trail of Chanel No. 5 finally dissipated.

16

Taking the manuscripts home wasn't *so* terrible, I reasoned. After all, I was able to get them done more efficiently when I didn't have to worry about Mr Frederick turning up, and I was never late meeting any of the deadlines Miss Everett set for me. What she didn't know couldn't hurt her.

Then one day I got caught. My bad luck in bungling the whole thing started straightaway. If I'd been paying better attention, I would've noticed Miss Everett was not wearing the silk handkerchief she usually tied over her hair when she came upstairs to say goodnight. But I didn't. Instead, I packed up even earlier than was my fashion, and by 6 p.m. I was already riding the elevator down to the lobby, clutching the stack of manuscripts she'd handed me only an hour earlier. Unexpectedly, the elevator stopped on the fifth floor. The doors opened, and who should be standing there but Miss Everett.

'Oh!' I exclaimed. She looked at me with a flat curiosity. She stepped in and the doors closed. Clutched in Miss Everett's hand floated the silk handkerchief. Clearly she'd come back to retrieve it. Instead of tying the handkerchief bonnet-style over her hair, she set about rolling it into a tube and tying it around her neck, cocking it to one side like a fashionable airline stewardess. I inhaled and noticed her Chanel No. 5 had been freshly reapplied. She was going somewhere, I realised, somewhere for a night out on the town. We glanced at each other. I cleared my throat.

'Already done for the day, Eden?' Miss Everett asked in a surprised tone.

'Not exactly, I suppose.' I forced a meagre smile. 'I'd thought I might dash across the street to have a cup of coffee at Schrafft's.' As soon as it left my mouth, we both knew it was a lie.

'I hope those aren't *my* manuscripts.'

I glanced weakly in her direction and tried to comment, but nothing came out.

'I thought I made it clear, Eden: I really can't have them going anywhere. Not even across the street to Schrafft's.'

'I'm sorry,' I said. 'I'll go upstairs and put them back right away, Miss Everett.'

'Good,' Miss Everett said. 'I don't give you that much to do, and I trust you don't mind working a little late tonight; I need a couple of those done by tomorrow morning.' She produced a compact from her handbag and proceeded to powder her nose. When she was done, she snapped it shut and sighed. 'And don't worry. I won't make a big fuss over your taking them to – where was it, my dear? – *Schrafft's*, did you say?' The manner in which she said *Schrafft's* turned my stomach. She was letting me know she was onto my lie. I nodded. She tucked the compact neatly back into her purse. With her lips freshly ablaze with Revlon Red and her skin powdered white as snow, she levelled a cold blue stare in my direction. 'It just can't happen any more. I'd hate to think you already knew that and were just disobeying me. Which is why I'm *sure* it was just an honest misunderstanding. Wouldn't you say that's just what it was, Eden – an honest misunderstanding?'

'Yes. Of course.' The elevator dinged, and the doors opened to reveal the empty, echoing marble lobby. I stood there, motionless, feeling like a prize idiot.

'Well, then, goodnight, Eden,' Miss Everett said, stepping off the elevator. She turned and watched me with a dubious expression as the doors slid shut, as though to ensure I wouldn't attempt to hop off at the last minute. I felt like a naughty child who'd been sent to the principal's office. I pushed the button for the sixth floor.

I felt the elevator car ascending and that familiar, even push of the floor against my legs that always made my knees all wobbly. Physically, I was rising. But internally my spirit was sinking.

I was alone for less than an hour when I heard the elevator doors slide open again. Somewhere in the pit of my stomach, I knew it was Mr Frederick. On automatic impulse, my hand reached out to switch off my desk lamp, and I held my breath as darkness rushed in around me. A stupid, wild idea occurred to me. As swiftly as I could manage, I dove under my desk and pulled the chair in tightly behind me.

I could hear his heavy breathing from across the room. I knew from the sound of it he was quite drunk. He staggered in the direction of my desk. To my surprise, he did not switch on a single light as he made his way across the office floor. This both frightened and relieved me. I wasn't sure yet if darkness would prove to be my enemy or my ally.

When he got to my desk he grunted as he pushed manuscript piles around. I could just picture his hands as he rifled through my things: his reddish skin and bloated fingers, each knuckle twinkling with a spray of strawberry-blonde hair, his fat ring finger squeezed too tightly by a gold wedding band. He was making a mess of my desk, but I kept mum as he continued his sloppy rifling. At one point, however, he must've been leaning too far, because he appeared to lose his balance and staggered closer to the side of the desk, kicking me with the toe of one of the shiny black oxfords he always wore. The kick was sharp and unexpected. My eyes watered. I was able to muffle a cry, but by then it was already too late.

'Hey!' Mr Frederick exclaimed. Suddenly I felt a hand clamp down around my ankle. A peal of wicked laughter rang out as he tugged at my leg. 'I see you!' he sang out. When I didn't immediately emerge, he started pulling harder.

'Ouch,' I cried. I felt the hand reluctantly release my ankle.

'All right, little missy, I've caught you now! C'mon out of there!' he roared. The manic, sing-song tone of his voice turned my stomach.

I pushed the chair away, rolled onto my knees, and crawled out from under the desk. My stomach was churning and I was sweating. I stood up and attempted to smooth down my rumpled clothes, hoping to gather some dignity and regain control of the situation, but Mr Frederick didn't wait for me to speak. Instead, he launched his body at me like some kind of crazed animal.

'C'mon, now,' he panted into my ear. 'I *know* you're the kind of girl who likes to have a bit of fun. Heh, we can crawl back under your desk together if you like!' His breath was hot with bourbon, and before I knew what was happening, his hands went racing all over my body, moving roughly over my blouse and skirt. I felt Mr Frederick's tongue in my ear. I tried to push him away, but as I struggled, Mr Frederick got the upper hand and kissed me full on the mouth.

Suddenly the overhead lights switched on. I broke away from

Mr Frederick to see a slim man in a tidy grey suit. He was frowning with what looked like disgust.

'What's going on here?' asked Mr Turner. His voice was flat and stern, and something told me what he had said was not really a question.

17

I woke up feeling very rough. I'd gotten home late, and tossed and turned all night long, thinking about how much I ought to explain to Mr Turner – and plotting to petition Miss Everett in the hopes she might help me – and I'd worked myself up into such an exhausted lather, I'd gone and slept through the shrill ringing of my alarm's tin bell. When I finally roused myself, I got dressed as quickly as I could and hurried to Torchon & Lyle. My walk was a near run, and at one point I accidentally kicked off my ballet flat and had to go hopping after it on one foot as it skittered into a gutter filled with dirty water.

I made it to Torchon & Lyle in the nick of time. I pushed through the revolving door and in my haste I neglected to rub the phoenix's talon. Later it dawned on me what I'd forgotten to do. I hustled through the lobby and rode the elevator up to the sixth floor. When the elevator dinged and the doors slid open, I took a deep, hopeful breath and plunged forth.

To my surprise, there was a strange girl sitting in my chair when I arrived.

'Oh!' I exclaimed. For a moment I considered perhaps I'd gotten off the elevator on the wrong floor. I blinked and looked around at the other secretaries, at the placards bearing the editors' various names next to their respective doors – but no, all this was right and familiar and just as it should be. It was only the girl sitting at my desk that was unfamiliar. 'Oh!' I exclaimed again. 'I'm sorry – am I late? Were you sent to fill in?'

'Not to *fill in*,' she said in a snide voice, with an impatient roll of her eyes. She sniffed and returned her attention to the magazine she was reading. 'Go on in,' she instructed. 'Mr Turner said to send you in as soon as you arrived.' She did not bother to introduce herself, although it was clear she knew exactly who *I* was. I stood there in a sudden fog, baffled. My head began to throb terribly. I took a closer look at the girl. She was short and stocky, and wore glasses that straddled a wide-bridged nose. Her honey-blonde hair was held back by a white headband. Despite her squat dimensions, she had the well-polished look only produced by money. Her nose was peppered with freckles that had likely been acquired on the golf course at her parents' country club; the skin of her arms glowed with a Bermuda tan; the pale pink cashmere sweater that was buttoned cape-style over her shoulders could only have come from Bergdorf's. She was definitely the daughter of some business acquaintance who had long ago asked Mr Turner to supply her with a job appropriate for a freshly graduated college girl. My stomach sank.

'Well?' the girl said, looking up at me through the thick lenses of her glasses. Her flat, blue, magnified eyes inspected me. 'Aren't you going to go in?'

'Oh,' I said. I had been standing there, staring. 'Yes . . . Are you sure you don't want to buzz him?'

She shook her head. 'I said he's expecting you.'

My hand trembled as I knocked on Mr Turner's door. I had been told to never – under *any* circumstances – do this. 'Come in,' his voice commanded. I turned the knob. Mr Turner's office was sleek and modern, done up in a sort of minimal style that was quickly becoming all the rage. I walked in and padded quietly across the black wall-to-wall carpet. A giant painting hung on the far wall depicting a jumble of triangles, zig-zags, and squares, all in primary colours. I regarded the painting with a sense of unease; the shapes looked about as jumbled up as my stomach felt. Mr Turner was seated in front of a smoked-glass desk in a white leather chair, busy filling out a set of forms from the personnel department. He scribbled what I took to be his signature on the last form, lifted the pages, and tapped the edge of the stack on his desk, then tucked the group of them into a manila file folder. 'No need to sit, Miss Katz,' he said. 'I'm afraid this won't take long.'

I swallowed the lump in my throat with difficulty and remained standing.

'What I have to inform you is quite simple and should come as no surprise. Your employment at Torchon & Lyle is terminated, effective immediately.'

I gasped. 'But . . . that can't be!'

'I assure you, it is. We'll need you to gather up your personal effects and see Miss Everett with this paperwork on your way out of the building.' He handed me the manila folder. I looked at it. Along the top of the filing tab someone had typed the name EDEN KATZ, and I realised I was holding my own personnel file.

'But . . .' I stammered. 'Have you talked to Miss Everett? I know how it looked when you saw me with Mr Frederick, but you've got it all wrong! He's chased other girls around their desks, too – I'm *sure* you know that. And I would never . . . please, Mr Turner, talk to Miss Everett! If you talk to Miss Everett, I'm sure she'll vouch for me!'

Mr Turner didn't answer at first. He levelled a long, hard stare in my direction. In that moment I rather think he hated me; I had never seen anyone's eyes so full of disdain and detachment at the same time. 'I *have* talked to Miss Everett,' he said. 'But even if I hadn't, I certainly don't need her approval to dismiss an employee. It's quite simple. She has informed me there is no earthly reason why you needed to be at the office so late at night unless you were up to no good, and I can't abide immoral girls, Eden. I suggest you take your wild-woman behaviour elsewhere. We simply can't condone it here at Torchon & Lyle.'

I was stunned. Nothing Mr Turner was saying made sense. My mouth moved but no words came out. Miss Everett had said *there was no earthly reason I needed to be at the office so late at night.* I was being blamed for Mr Frederick's advances, as though I'd invited them.

'But . . .'

'That's enough, Miss Katz! You're excused.'

I don't remember leaving the building, but the next thing I was aware of was finding myself on a bench in Central Park. I was in such a daze I barely registered the familiar shape of Judy as she came huffing along the path after me, awkwardly cradling a cardboard box in her arms. I realised she must've been trying to catch up to me for a few blocks, but being lost in a state of shock I had marched on, blind and deaf to her pursuit.

'I thought you might be headed here,' she said once she'd caught her breath. 'They wondered where you'd gotten off to so quickly, and I volunteered to come after you.'

For a second my heart leapt, seized by the sudden idea that perhaps Miss Everett had successfully made the case to Mr Turner that I ought to be kept on; but then Judy set the cardboard box beside me on the bench, and I caught sight of the contents: my pocketbook, the ceramic mug I'd brought in for drinking coffee, the African violet that had sat in a little yellow pot on my desk.

'Boy, was that something! Mary Sue said you tore out of Mr Turner's office so fast you practically left behind a trail of rocket fuel. You sure do know how to make an exit, Eden.' Judy sat down with the box between us and sighed. 'I'm awfully sorry it happened, though.'

My eyes filled with tears. I realised I felt sorry for myself, and was annoyed. I clenched my teeth.

'Oh, Eden . . . It's not your fault, you know,' Judy said, fishing in her purse and producing a handkerchief. As she handed it to me I noticed what appeared to be a ketchup stain on the bottom corner. 'I'm sure she planned on it . . . you know, that whole business with Mr Frederick.'

Avoiding the ketchup stain, I wiped my eyes and looked at her in confusion. 'What do you mean?'

'Miss Everett,' she said matter-of-factly. 'I'm sure she wanted Mr Frederick to come around and bother you.'

'Why would she want that?'

Judy looked at me in disbelief. The red line of her mouth puckered in a scornful way. 'Because, dummy, Miss Everett likes her job and doesn't appreciate you sniffing around as though to take it.'

'But . . . but . . . I wasn't trying to take her job,' I said. Judy rolled her eyes and shrugged at this. 'And besides,' I argued, 'I was *sure* she liked me! I got this job on recommendation from a trusted source.' Judy looked at me with curious eyes.

'What do you mean?'

'Mr Hightower wrote me a letter of introduction. He said they were good colleagues. I thought she wanted to help me.'

'*Horatio* Hightower?'

I nodded.

'Oh, well,' Judy said. 'That settles it. She didn't just want your resignation; she wanted your head!'

'I don't understand,' I said. I suddenly felt very tired.

'Miss Everett and Mr Hightower worked side-by-side for years. She was always after him to marry her, but he never would!' Judy said, suddenly breathless. 'I think he knew if he did he'd be in for a lifelong headache.' She elbowed me and gave a wink, then turned thoughtful and gazed off into the trees. 'She probably figured you got the recommendation by going to bed with him.'

'Judy!'

'I'm not saying *I* think you did, just that Miss Everett probably thinks that!' she said, waving her arms defensively. 'She has an awfully low opinion of women.' Judy paused to consider. 'I'd wondered why she'd assigned you, of all people, to Mr Turner. I guess now we know she was out to get you.'

'How's that?'

Judy peered down at her feet and shrugged. 'Well, just that everybody knows Mr Turner is funny about Jews.'

I blinked. 'What do you mean?'

'Oh, you know; he's just funny about them. Some people are.' I looked at her, horrified, but she didn't notice. Instead, Judy suddenly sat up straight and snapped her fingers. 'Say!' she exclaimed. 'Boy oh boy, that Miss Everett, now that I think about it – she's a sly one! I'll bet she framed you up good and proper right from the very start.'

My stomach turned over, and Judy continued.

'Think about it: she paired you with Mr Turner, thinking he'd hate you instantly and find some reason to fire you. But then, when you surprised her by getting promoted to reader, she figured she'd better up the ante, so she gave you all those manuscripts to work on and didn't let you take them home, *knowing* Mr Frederick was bound to come around. She *wanted* Mr Turner to catch you in the act! She made *sure* it would look like something immoral was happening!' Judy was suddenly breathless with the momentum of her own conclusion.

'You sound impressed,' I said. By this time I was nauseated.

Judy shrugged again. 'Well, she may be a bitch, but she *is* clever, that's certain.' She looked over at me, paused, and reached out a hand to pick out a tree blossom that had fallen in my hair. 'Anyway, you shouldn't feel so bad about it. It's not your fault, and in any case there are other perfectly nice companies where you'll likely fit in better. You were kind of barking up the wrong tree to begin with.'

'What does *that* mean?'

'Nothing. It's just that, well . . . you know how it is, Eden. Who knows – maybe Miss Everett won't even be able to poison those, ahem, other places against you.'

'Those *other* places?'

Judy looked uncomfortable. She cleared her throat. 'Of course, I've always been a friend to you, haven't I?' she asked. I nodded. 'And that won't change. We'll still go for martinis and chew the fat. That is, if you want to.' Again all I could do was nod. Judy smiled. 'Listen, it's going to be all right. I pinky swear, it will be. But I better be getting back,' she said. 'Here' – she picked up the cardboard box from where it rested on the bench and set it gently in my lap – 'let me know if you think you left anything else behind. I'll try my darnedest to retrieve it for you.'

With her final promise still hanging in the thick space between us, Judy patted me on the shoulder and strode off. A crisp spring wind kicked up and a shower of blossoms were shaken loose from the tree branches above, resulting in a brief flurry of white petals that fell softly around me. I sat there trying to take in everything she had said.

18

I was determined to find another job in publishing. I typed up letters on creamy stationery I couldn't afford and sent out résumés to other publishing houses. And then I waited.

All at once spring slid into summer, and the pace of the city changed. With nothing to occupy me during the daytime, I took aimless walks and spent long hours hanging about the main branch of the public library in Bryant Park, growing increasingly nervous about my rapidly dwindling savings. After a month of receiving no response to the résumés I'd sent out, I telephoned Judy one Friday, feeling discouraged and a little depressed.

'I've heard nothing,' I complained. 'Not a single peep.'

'I'm not surprised,' she said, then hesitated.

'What do you mean?'

'Well, to be honest, Betty said she overheard Miss Everett talking to someone on the phone about you. I think maybe she's calling around town,' Judy said in an apologetic voice. 'I *told* you when she had it out for somebody she could be vicious.'

I didn't even know what to say to this.

'Listen, I'd better go,' she said. 'I've got a ton of typing to get through. It was swell hearing from you, Eden. I hope you find something!'

I hung up and sat staring stupidly at the wall of the telephone lounge for several minutes. Miss Everett was *calling around* to poison people against me. After I'd worked so hard. Everything Judy had told me in the park had been true: Miss Everett really *was* out to get me. I had been blind. Purposefully, stupidly blind.

I needed a drink.

It was a foolish impulse, but I put on a fresh blouse and skirt anyway and took the subway down to the Village. It was still early in the afternoon, and if I had been being straight with myself, I couldn't really afford the drink. By virtue of extreme resourcefulness and discipline, I'd managed to save a bit of money, but without my regular paycheck – meagre though it had been – I was going to go broke in no time. Still, I took the train downtown and found my way to the Minetta Tavern, where a bartender named Sal wiped the perspiration from his upper lip and shoved a paperback into his back pocket long enough to make me a deliciously cloudy, olive-juice-laden martini, the toothpick spear of jade-green olives winking their red pimento eyes at me. There is a sense of inherent embarrassment that comes with drinking in the middle of the day, and I was relieved when the bartender didn't want to talk. He retreated back into his corner and promptly returned his attention to the paperback. He only came out again when I waved him over to request another round. Two was my limit – financially speaking, that is. Since moving to New York, I'd certainly developed a taste and tolerance for one or two more, but my wallet hadn't. After whiling away the better part of an hour and a half, I paid and rose to go. But as I moved to make my exit, the tavern door opened. The afternoon sunshine was so bright, I couldn't make out much more than a silhouette.

'Why, hello there,' a voice said. The figure moved inside.

'Oh – you again!' I said, surprised to have run into Cliff a third time. I laughed, momentarily forgetting my depressed state.

'Were you just leaving?'

I nodded.

'Stay and have a beer with me.'

'I really oughtn't,' I said, biting my lip and mentally counting the money I had left in my pocket.

'Say,' Cliff said, as though an idea had just dawned on him, 'it's a weekday, isn't it? Shouldn't you be at Torchon & Lyle, slaving away in the typing pool? What are you doing here in the middle of the day?'

I felt my smile crumple. 'Oh. Well, the truth is' – I paused, alarmed to feel my throat was constricting; I fought it off and collected myself – 'I was fired.'

Cliff regarded me for a moment, his blue eyes hovering on my own. 'Well, in that case, you *have* to stay. I can't think of a better reason to have a beer.' I hesitated. 'C'mon,' he cajoled.

'All right,' I said. We sat down and Sal came back over. I wasn't much in the mood for a beer, so I ordered a third martini.

'I suppose I ought to ask you the same question,' I said to Cliff, once we had settled in and were sipping our drinks. 'What are you doing here in the middle of the day?'

'I spent the whole morning writing,' he said, 'so I figured I owed myself a reward.'

We chatted for a bit about our passions: writing for him, editing for me.

'I suppose I've been a little fool. I came to New York really believing I was meant to be an editor,' I said, suddenly feeling very sorry for myself.

'You're not giving up already, are you?'

I explained to him about Miss Everett and Mr Turner, and about what had happened with Mr Frederick, leaving out the part about the two letters Mr Hightower had given me and what Judy had said about 'Mr Turner being funny about Jews'.

'Listen,' Cliff said, 'it's too early to throw in the towel. Something'll open up; it's a question of timing. Gals are always getting engaged and leaving publishing houses. Why, just the other day I went to Bonwright to see My Old Man and his secretary – an old battleaxe! – quit to go marry some old widower. Can you imagine, at her age?'

'Your father works at Bonwright?'

He nodded. 'Roger Nelson.'

'Oh,' I said, impressed. 'He's well-known.' Cliff looked both pleased and irritated to hear I'd recognised the name. I began to worry that it wasn't what I'd said but *how* I'd said it – with a tiny hint of a slur. There is an exponential difference between a second martini and a third martini, and I'd been foolish to order it; the third martini had begun to take its toll. I felt very self-conscious around Cliff, and I didn't want to embarrass myself. I decided to go home.

'Good luck, Eden,' he said as I left. 'Don't give up.'

'I won't,' I replied.

19

On the way back uptown I wondered if it was true. The optimism I possessed when I'd arrived in New York had fallen into some dark, irretrievable place, like a key dropped down a sidewalk grate; I'd begun to doubt I'd ever get it back again. Then a funny thing happened on my way back to the Barbizon.

A bit more sober but still very warm and slightly pink-cheeked, I passed a beauty salon and peered into the window. I'd passed by before and knew it was a cheap place that smelt of permanent solution and bleach. A young hairdresser was stooped over the back of a barber chair, leaning idly on her elbow while she flipped through the pages of a magazine propped open in the empty seat. She yawned with boredom. I could see someone had instructed her not to sit while on the job and she was waiting out the end of the day, which was likely near now. All of a sudden, an impulse seized me. The bell over the door tinkled as I pushed my way inside.

'Cut it short,' I said, once she'd scrambled to scoop up the magazine from the empty chair and I'd climbed in. 'I need a change.'

'How short do you want?' she asked, looking at my long black ponytail with the sceptical expression of someone who is uncertain whether or not she is talking to a crazy person.

'*Very* short,' I said. She raised her eyebrows, a bit frightened.

'Say, I'm not trying to chase away business, but I'm new here. Are you sure?' she asked, biting her lip. Across the room a woman was gossiping to a manicurist. They paused and turned to look me over, intrigued.

'I'm sure.' I glanced at myself in the mirror. A reckless fire smouldered in my eyes.

'Would you mind picking out a photograph at least? Something for me to model the cut on,' she said, handing me the magazine she'd been reading. I took it and turned a few pages, then stopped.

'*That*,' I said, pointing to a starlet in a Max Factor ad.

'Boy, you weren't kidding!' she exclaimed. 'That *is* awfully short.' She tried to smile, but when she picked up the scissors and comb, her hands were trembling slightly. She took a breath and set about her work. I didn't watch. Eventually she needed to reach around to the other side of my head and pivoted the chair away from the mirror. She frowned. Her brow furrowed. She bit her lip. When she was done, she took a step back and looked me up and down very carefully, squinting. Then she giggled with proud delight.

'Gosh!' she said, covering her mouth.

The haircut was striking: suddenly I looked very modern with my dark hair clipped close to the back of my neck and my bangs trimmed across my forehead in a tidy black line. I had wanted to emulate a New Yorker, and now that I had failed in all the important ways I had finally – and ironically – gotten the trick of it, if only on the surface. The manicurist in the salon whistled and winked, exclaiming, 'It's *Roman Holiday* all over again! Look out, Gregory Peck!' I thanked the hairdresser and paid for the cut and left in something of a daze.

I bought a bottle of vodka on my way home – another purchase I couldn't really afford, but I was so far down the rabbit hole, I figured I may as well reach the bottom – and snuck it upstairs into my room at the Barbizon. I sat on the floor and stared at myself in the mirror, taking swigs directly from the mouth of the bottle and breaking down in sobs until I could barely breathe. Finally, I passed out lying face down on the rug, my skin hot and sticky with the brine of evaporated tears.

It was not until I woke up and looked in the mirror the next morning that I realised: my hair *was* different. But moreover: *I* was different. I looked like a new person. And just at that moment I remembered something else, a seemingly tiny insignificant detail I'd forgotten about. I flashed back to that day on the university lawn. Mr Hightower had written me *two* letters of introduction. I had given one to Miss Everett. The other was still tucked away in my underwear drawer along with my passport.

An idea occurred to me.

20

MILES

The day after the Hamilton Lodge Ball, I was preoccupied with the worry that someone from our neighbourhood had seen me there. Janet was not one to jump to conclusions, but I pictured the gossip reaching my mother, and the look that was likely to appear on her face. I knew I would never be able to convince her it was all a big mistake. Unable to put this worry completely out of my thoughts, I decided the best thing to do would be to go straight home after finishing my messenger shift. If she had indeed heard about it, she wouldn't have to say anything; I would know. My mother was capable of many feats, but hiding her disapproval was not one of them. Besides, I reasoned, it was time I paid some attention to my younger brother, Cob. 'Cob' was a nickname; his given name was Malcolm. He was called Cob because by the time he was three years old he'd adopted a habit of smiling so wide, folks liked to say you could fit a whole corncob in there. He was an impressionable boy on the verge of turning eight that year. To look at Cob made one's heart fill with joy; there was still a happy, unspoiled innocence about him. It was an innocence that made me glad, but also nervous. Wendell despised teenagers, and every year Cob inched closer to adolescence he likewise unwittingly inched his way closer to becoming a scapegoat for Wendell's wrath.

As it turned out, it was a good evening to spend some time at home, because Wendell was not around. According to my mother, Wendell had left the apartment that morning with his rod and tackle in tow. This meant he was likely to spend the entire day fishing at the East River and wouldn't come home until after sundown. I never understood the men who did that – men who sat sipping a bottle of beer wrapped in a brown paper bag, staring sullenly at their giant fishing poles jerry-rigged to the fence along the East River. But if there was any man who was suited to this curious variety of sport, it was Wendell.

'Miles!' Cob shouted when he saw me come in the front door. He charged at my body like a small bull and wrapped his arms about my waist. Poor vision must've run in our family: I also wore glasses, but Cob required Coke bottles so thick, it was a wonder he could see anything at all. The doctors said that if he wore them throughout his youth, he might be able to get on without them as an adult. In the meantime, the glasses were an obstacle to his popularity in school. He had always had a strong affinity for insects, and I sometimes wondered – perhaps insensitively – if it wasn't in part because of his awkward resemblance to a praying mantis.

'Hey, Cob,' I said, hugging him back. 'Tell me something: what day is it tomorrow?'

'Friday.'

'It's not the weekend yet, then, is it? You done your schoolwork?'

He sighed and shook his head. He was a good kid. Whether he did his homework or not, Cob still maintained the stunningly beautiful quality of never lying about such things.

'How about we do it together?' I said.

He gave his assent in a vigorous nod. 'And then after I can show you the new bugs I caught?' he prompted. If there was one thing

Cob cared about, it was adding to his insect collection and showing it off to people. He knew the world's geography in shockingly precise detail, but only in terms of what beetle lived where and which butterflies migrated with the seasons. For birthdays, my mother traditionally gave him socks and footballs, but I had taken to giving him heavy hardbound books on entomology, and while he showed little interest in the socks or the footballs, he never expressed disappointment with the books.

'Go fetch your books and bring them into the living room.' I nudged him into motion and he ran off to find his schoolbag. I moved in the direction of the kitchen to find my mother.

'Ma?' I called, feeling slightly apprehensive.

'In here.'

I found her at the kitchen table peeling carrots.

'I hear you say you gonna help Cob with his schoolwork?' she asked with no further greeting.

'Yes,' I said, relieved by her tone; I knew no malicious gossip had reached her ears.

'Good,' she replied. 'I was helpin' him last night, but Wendell was in one of his moods, so we had to quit.' This, I knew, was getting to be a common occurrence. Whenever my mother paid attention to Cob, Wendell grew blindingly jealous and got into one of his 'moods', as my mother called them. The fact that a grown man should be jealous of a mother paying attention to her seven-year-old son baffled me, and the fact that my mother – a strong-willed woman and breadwinner to boot – should cater to these childish tantrums baffled me even further.

'I remember when I used to do my schoolwork in the living room when I was Cob's age,' I murmured, half to myself. 'Father never got in a mood. He had so much *curiosity* about what I was studying,' I said, recalling the way I'd sit cross-legged on the floor next to my father's easy chair. It was a pleasant memory, the way he would lean over my shoulder and watch me solve algebra problems and balance chemical equations as if I were performing one magic trick after another.

My mother chose to ignore my digression.

'Who that old man you runnin' errands for in the mornings?' she asked. My sense of alarm perked up again. She meant Mister Gus. I'd told her a little bit about the extra money I was earning. 'That a lot of money to pay for jus' bringin' him the daily paper,' she said now, frowning. 'You know, they gots paperboys for that. Why don't he jus' subscribe?'

'He says subscriptions make newspapermen lazy,' I said, repeating a line from one of Mister Gus's tirades. 'He doesn't want any paper thinking they've got him on the hook.'

She grunted. 'Sounds like you got yo' hands full with that one.' She twisted from where she sat at the table in order to heap the carrot peels into a small rubbish pail. 'Well, just don't let him take advantage of yo' time or yo' kindness. Rich white folks always trying to take *advantage*!' For a moment I worried she was implying something sinister. I knew some part of my recent employment was a function of Mister Gus's loneliness, but I had not yet admitted as much to myself outright.

I glanced at my mother, nervous. But then I reminded myself of the time she had worked as a personal nurse to an elderly lady on the Upper East Side. The woman had requested my mother take on more and more work, yet was often forgetful when it came time to pay my mother. Finally when the old lady passed away, a tally of her outstanding debts was revealed. My mother's name was not listed among them. Even now, years later, I could see it still galled her to be reminded of how she had worked like a dog and been shorted nearly two months' pay – two months she could not afford.

'I'll be mindful,' I said.

'Be mindful all you wants,' my mother said. 'Just get yo' money up front.'

I spent the rest of the afternoon in the living room with Cob, the two of us crouched over the coffee table, going over parts of speech and then afterwards the finer points of 'borrowing' when subtracting two-digit sums.

'Are you going to California to look for Daddy's journal?' Cob asked while in the middle of working out a math problem.

'Ma told you about that?' I was surprised and faintly annoyed. I was nervous enough about how things would turn out; I didn't need to be nervous for two. Cob nodded, and my stomach lurched with a sense of responsibility for him.

According to my parents, I'd had another brother, too: an elder brother named Marcus who as a boy of only six had drowned in the East River as a result of accepting a neighbourhood dare. He died shortly after I was born, and I'd developed a kind of reverse magical thinking about this fact, as though my coming into the world had accidentally pushed him out. A photograph of him hung on the wall in my bedroom. From this image I was able to extrapolate all sorts of memories, with no true gauge, of course, to measure their accuracy. Every once in a while, I talked aloud to his photograph in a familiar manner, the way children sometimes do when they are confiding secrets to a favourite rag doll or asking favours from an invisible god. I had the details of that photograph memorised. Marcus was a handsome little boy, with a confident smile and his shoulders thrust proudly backwards, and I wondered sometimes whether, if he had lived, he might've become the man I know my father was hoping one of us would become.

There were times, too, when I imagined the day of the tragedy. On late summer afternoons when there was nothing to do and the heat of the day was trapped in the apartment, I would lie around my bedroom, watching dust motes falling idly through the air, and allow my eyes to slide shut despite the fact I was hardly sleepy and not in need of a nap. My waking dream was always the same. I envisioned Marcus picking over the steep boulders of the urban shore as other boys jeered at him and egged him on, his small, tough little body easing into the filthy waters and then pushing off into the current. The way I pictured it, he must've been a brave kid, the kind of kid who would not have been able to turn back defeated. The challenge was to swim clear to the opposite shore and back again. Of course no child in our neighbourhood had any business being in the water, let alone a six-year-old. The sum total of a Harlem kid's swimming experience was generally limited to a handful of summer days spent splashing chlorinated water into one another's faces in a rec pool packed with hundreds of other children, the pool shallow enough to stand on the bottom and so packed with bodies you couldn't reach out an arm without touching someone else. But heroic leader that I imagined Marcus to be, I theorised he'd been completely lacking in fear. In my most morbid musings, I wondered if he'd been surprised, in those final moments, to feel his head dipping under the water for longer and longer periods, until he had been swept all the way downstream, past the tip of Randall's Island, and he finally failed to come up altogether. I used to lie in bed and stare at that photograph, searching Marcus's face for some kind of sign, as though somewhere in the gleam that shone within his eyes was a hint of premonition, a signal that he understood his fate was already sealed. I considered whether, if he were in my place, Marcus would make the trip out to California now.

'Are you going to go?' Cob repeated his question. I considered how to reply. I thought some more about how different things were when I used to do my schoolwork with my father leaning over my shoulder and smiling in proud amazement every time I wrote a sentence or solved an equation. There was a particular sensation that went along with it – a sensation I wouldn't trade for the world – and I wished Cob could somehow know it, too. But he never would.

'Maybe,' I said finally. This was honest. 'If I can manage it.'

'Ma says you're going to bring back Pa's journal,' Cob said. Then he gave a shy smile and peered back into the open pages of his schoolbook, shrugging. I could see he wanted something; he always got shy when he wanted something. 'And maybe . . . if you go . . . you could bring back some bugs, too,' he suggested. 'I've never been able to catch a monarch. Lots of monarchs migrate through California.'

'Do they?' I asked. He nodded enthusiastically. 'Well, I, for one, would like to know more about that,' I said, and sat back, listening to my kid brother explain to me all about the beauty of love and death within the insect world.

21

I was more than a little shocked one morning when I arrived at Mister Gus's town house to drop off the usual stack of newspapers, only to find him downstairs in the kitchen fumbling with a coffee grinder over a pot of boiling water. I froze where I stood, the key to the servants' entrance still in my hand and the bundle of newspapers under my arm. An involuntary gasp escaped my lips. I had never so much as seen him out of his bed, much less standing and roaming about. He cut an eerie figure. Upon hearing my gasp, Mister Gus whirled about, his eyes flashing.

'Well?' he demanded.

Well, what? I thought to myself. I was where *I* had promised to be; *he* was the one breaking with expectation. He attempted to work the grinder but his hands trembled and he fumbled it. 'Do you need any help, sir?' I asked. He looked even frailer out of bed than in, if that was possible. His pin-striped pajamas drowned him; he was thinner than I'd thought, and I could see he was suffering from a slight hunchback.

'I'm trying to make some coffee,' he said in an impatient huff. 'Some *decent* coffee, for a change! Greta's gone.'

Greta was the woman who brought Mister Gus his breakfast and cleared it away, changed his sheets, did his laundry. The manner in which he had pronounced those words, *Greta's gone,* made me think she was not coming back and that I ought not ask questions. If she was on an errand, he usually said: *Greta's out.* I had no idea what had happened, but I knew enough to intuit it had to do with Mister Gus's irritable tirades and her diminishing success in avoiding all contact with the man.

'Here,' I said, moving to help him. I took the coffee grinder out of his hands, and after a moment of hesitation he relented and sat down to watch me. I ground up several tablespoons of coffee, then dumped them into the boiling water and immediately switched the burner off. 'Do you have . . . ?' I asked, but before I could finish my sentence I'd found a lid. I rummaged around some more as the coffee brewed and found a ladle. 'And . . . here you are,' I said, ladling fresh coffee into a baroque-looking china teacup.

'Hmph,' Mister Gus said, glaring at me and reaching for the teacup. He continued to glare at me as he let the coffee cool down. After what seemed an eternity, he brought the cup to his lips and took a sip. 'Hmph,' he repeated, but this time there was a slightly different tone in it. He sipped, then sipped again. 'Hmph. Not bad. Not outstanding. But not bad.'

I knew I had won a small but sure victory.

I was still smiling when my eyes fell upon an automatic coffee maker. It looked brand-new and state-of-the-art. It also was unplugged and coated in a fine layer of dust.

'But why . . .' I began. 'Sir . . . why wouldn't you simply use this?' I moved to stand near the machine, pointing in disbelief as though I had just found a unicorn roaming the kitchen.

'*Tsk!*' Mister Gus hissed scornfully. 'You sound like Greta! My niece in California sent that contraption to me. Don't know why I didn't put it straight into the bin, infernal thing! Why on earth would I use *that*? I said I wanted a *decent* cup of coffee!'

'Have you ever tried it?' I ventured.

'I don't need to,' he snapped.

'But if you use the machine, all you have to do is add the coffee and push a button.'

Mister Gus shot me a look that silenced me.

I sighed. 'Would you like me to carry this upstairs on a tray for you?' I asked, meaning the coffee and the newspapers. He replied with a grumpy nod, and off I went, with Mister Gus trailing very slowly behind me, his feet shuffling softly over the rugs.

By the time I set the tray on his bed and arranged the papers the way he liked them, he still had not caught up, and I realised he was likely having trouble on the stairs. Nervous, I went to go check on his progress. I walked to the top of the sweeping half-circle staircase and looked down.

There he was, doggedly climbing one stair at a time and pausing, trying to conceal his heavy breathing. I knew if I offered to help him he would refuse. I padded down the stairs with a quiet, businesslike demeanour and slipped an arm under his armpit. To my surprise, he did not resist or chide me or even – as I'd worried he might – protest my touching him. Together, we worked our way up the stairs at a fairly efficient, steady pace.

'Thank you,' he said in a hoarse voice once we'd reached the top. It was the last thing I'd expected him to say; I thought, for a brief moment, that I was hearing things. I nodded and allowed him to shuffle the rest of the way into his room on his own, following him for fear he might yet fall.

'You know,' he said, once he had settled himself back into his immense pile of pillows and blankets like some kind of bird roosting in a nest, 'you could come round more often and do things like that – the coffee, I mean. I've got a girl coming to drop off my meals, but I haven't found a full replacement for Greta yet.' I looked at him, taken off guard by him for the second time that morning. 'I'd pay you,' he said.

I cocked my head, considering. I would have to cut back on the hours I worked as a messenger, but this only made practical sense, for my messenger work paid less than half as much. Mister Gus, for all his bluster and prickly edges, was beginning to grow on me.

'Fine. Never mind!' Mister Gus snapped, assuming my hesitation was leading to a declination.

'No,' I said. 'I'll do it. I'd like that.'

He looked at me, his eyes opened wide and watering with tears. He gave a small, tight, grateful nod. Then he looked away.

22

As I soon learnt, the list of neglected items that needed fixing in Mister Gus's house was endless. Over the years, he had become something of a recluse, and his interest in seeing to it that things were properly maintained had waned in equal proportion to his interest in welcoming strangers into his home.

'Sir . . . when you go downstairs, why don't you use the elevator?' I asked. Two days prior, I'd opened a Gothic wooden door at the far end of one hallway that led to what I thought was a closet and discovered a beautiful brass birdcage-like piece of machinery.

'It's broken,' Mister Gus snapped.

'I can call to have it repaired,' I offered.

'I'm sure whatever is the matter with it is quite complicated. And besides, I don't want some greasy *fix-it man* traipsing in here while I'm trying to read or nap,' he said. There was a note of anger in his voice, but the more closely I listened, the more I realised the anger was only a mask; beneath it was fear. Mister Gus, perhaps reasonably, was afraid he might be taken advantage of. He was extremely leery of new acquaintances, and before Greta left, she had gossiped to me about an unfortunate incident involving a man who had visited the house on the pretext of representing the fundraising committee for the Metropolitan Opera but who turned out to have no affiliation with the Met and ten sticky fingers. It wasn't until hours after he left that Greta noticed a pair of silver candlesticks and cut-crystal ashtrays from Tiffany's had gone missing. Greta was sure there were other things missing, too, but as she went through an itemisation of objects she couldn't locate or account for, Mister Gus wouldn't directly acknowledge any of it. He was embarrassed, she reckoned. *Fundraising, indeed . . .* was all he'd muttered under his breath.

'I can make sure the repairman only comes during a time I'm here, and I can monitor him if you like,' I said. Mister Gus regarded me warily from out of the corner of one eye.

'Fine,' he said, jutting out his chin and rolling his lips into a fine line. 'If you're going to be stubborn about it.'

I telephoned several elevator repair companies – an act that represented a significant victory in and of itself, if only because Greta and her predecessors had all been barred from getting half as far – and hired the one that struck me as most reputable. In the meantime, I tinkered with other broken items in the house, replacing lightbulbs, ratcheting up a bit of leaky plumbing, and oiling hinges. Mister Gus treated all this work as though it were invisible. My main duties – according to Mister Gus – involved making coffee, bringing and clearing trays of food, fluffing the seemingly infinite number of pillows on his bed, and drawing his bath.

I was in the kitchen one morning when a slightly mischievous mood came over me. My gaze fell on the automatic coffee maker, and on impulse I plugged it in. Would Mister Gus honestly be able to tell the difference? I filled the coffee maker with water and grounds, and in a flash, lovely dark droplets of coffee began to dribble out. It smelt good. I tasted it, hoping it would be passable, and the flavour was absolutely fine. Perhaps even better than the coffee I typically brewed. When I brought it upstairs and gave it to Mister Gus, he drank it and seemed pleased, evidently unable to detect any difference whatsoever.

'What's that smile for, boy?' he snapped.

'Nothing, sir. Only that it's a nice day out.'

'Hmph. I wouldn't know,' was all he said. All the rest of that week, I continued to make his coffee in the automatic coffee maker.

On the following morning, I got up the nerve to ask him about the person who had given him the automatic coffee maker as a present. The longer I worked for Mister Gus, the more I wondered where his relations might be, for they seemed conspicuously absent from his life.

'You said your niece lives in California. Do you see her very often?'

He looked at me, startled by the question. For a moment I thought he was about to tell me to mind my own business. 'Hmph,' he grunted finally. 'Never,' he said. 'I've never seen her!'

'Never?'

'No. Not even when I lived out in California myself,' he said. Then he looked at me with a sort of crooked smile. 'You didn't know that, did you? – that I lived in California? Hah. Hollywood, as a matter of fact. Wrote scripts for the talkies! What a time that was! What a town.'

'But your niece moved to California and you never visited each other?'

He shot me a dry look. 'Her father didn't approve of my having contact with her. He stopped speaking to me years ago.' I did not ask him why or what the falling-out had been about; I suspected I already knew the answer.

'Where does he live?'

'Manhattan,' he grunted.

I was stunned. All this time, Mister Gus had a brother who lived in town, yet he never saw him!

'Haven't the faintest what he's gotten up to,' he continued. 'I assume he's still alive; I would've heard about it otherwise. Someday we *will* have to deal with the sticky matter of our family trust, after all. My niece sends a Christmas present every year, though,' Mister Gus said. 'Every year, without fail. Never met her, but still she does it. Must feel guilty.'

The light was draining out of his eyes, and he suddenly looked wan. 'Now leave me in peace, boy. I'm tired,' he said. I obeyed, and he rolled over as though to sleep. I padded quietly out of the room, a tray of empty dishes clutched in my hands.

A week or so later, after two visits from the repairman, the elevator was running again. It hadn't, according the repairman's best guess, been used in several years. At first Mister Gus pretended indifference to the elevator's revival, but it wasn't long before he began using it every day, sometimes twice a day. It was as though he had just gotten part of himself back, and in some ways perhaps this was an accurate assessment, for the elevator meant Mister Gus was able to visit floors of his own town house he had all but stopped living in.

It also meant it was not uncommon to come in during the mornings and find Mister Gus out of bed. Nonetheless, I was shocked again one morning when I found him standing in the kitchen. This time the surprise was not finding him out of bed; it was the fact that he appeared to be operating the automatic coffee maker.

We regarded each other in silence for a solid minute, until finally he turned back to the machine and resumed his business.

'Don't think I don't know you've been using this all along,' he said, nodding towards the coffee maker.

I'd been caught. I couldn't think of what to say. I wondered if this turn of events meant I was about to be fired. To my astonishment, he began to chuckle softly. I chuckled back, and we stood there in the kitchen, both of us amused with ourselves.

23

CLIFF

I was staring into the terrible pure white space of my notebook when the electric buzzer sounded. The first time it sounded I ignored it and thought some kid was just pranking or else some shady type was trying to get into the building because that was always happening, but when the buzzer sounded again I understood someone was really at the door ringing for me. I went downstairs to check and there was Rusty standing on the stoop. Rusty cut a peculiar shape and I recognised his silhouette immediately. The thing about Rusty was he looked an awful lot like a rat. Later I found out he really was a rat, so this resemblance turned out to be fitting but even if he had turned out to be honourable it would've been hard to see that was the case because he bore such a strong resemblance to a rodent. He had the beady eyes of a rat and his ears stuck out from his narrow head. He was short and slight and always wore sports jackets that looked two sizes too big and hung in a funny way on his slouchy shoulders.

I was surprised by the unannounced visit but of course I was glad all the same because the second I saw Rusty I couldn't help but think about the famous agent and fantasise about what he could do for me if Rusty ever introduced us. I didn't know what Rusty wanted but the last time I'd seen him at the Village Vanguard he had said he would like to read my stories sometime, which I thought was something you say to people to sound polite when really you are giving them the runaround. Now I considered that maybe Rusty wasn't as bad as I'd first thought because perhaps he had followed through and shown up on my doorstep that day on a mission to read my stories after all. I invited him upstairs and said I could put some coffee on and we could put some Irish in it if we wanted to and Rusty accepted.

Once we got upstairs I busied myself in front of the hot plate and set about boiling the coffee. Instead of sitting in the armchair I offered him, Rusty remained standing with his coat and gloves still on and poked around the apartment with a bizarrely uninhibited air, opening drawers and rifling through bookcases as though it were his job to find out what they contained. I realised he was making me feel jumpy; I felt like a Jew being visited by a Nazi officer sent to harass me on some sort of trumped-up state business.

'I've been meaning to read this,' he said, holding up a nice hardback copy of Emerson and looking at me expectantly. It was pretty quiet except for the burbling of the coffee on the hot plate and I wished I'd thought to put some bop on the record player just to have something blowing in the background. Rusty was still holding the book as I thought this, displaying the cover to me in a possessive way and waiting for my approval.

'You can borrow it if you like,' I heard myself offer. I don't really know why I said it except maybe I do know because I wouldn't have said it before finding out who Rusty worked for. He did not appear very surprised by this offer and he slipped the hardback into the funny little blue bag he always carried around with him and I knew by the way he did it that was going to be the last I'd ever see of old Ralph Waldo and his take on self-reliance.

'*Some* place you got here,' he said. It was the kind of remark that could've been a compliment as easily as a slight, but there was

no confusion about the way Rusty meant it when he said it now. I
didn't reply. Instead I put two mismatched mugs of coffee on the
table and poured a little whiskey into each. Rusty picked up the
mug that didn't have a chip at the lip and sniffed the contents and
then reached for the bottle of whiskey to pour some more. When
his mug was finally full of greater parts whiskey than coffee he sat in
the chair and inspected me over the rim of the mug. I felt his eyes
raking over the contours of my face and did my best not to make
eye contact. Finally, he spoke.

   'You're not exactly good-looking,' he said in a matter-of-fact
tone. Before I could reply he took another slurp from the mug
and continued. 'But you're not exactly wretched-looking either, are
ya?' If anything was ever a rhetorical question, I figured this was it.
Increasingly uncomfortable, I sipped my own coffee and turned a
vague, polite smile in Rusty's direction.

   'You're one of those neither-here-nor-there guys,' he finally
diagnosed. An awkward silence ensued.

   'Say,' I said, when my patience could take me no further. I
suddenly felt very shy. 'I think I've got some copies of those stories
I mentioned around here somewhere.' I got up and went over to
the stack of milk crates where my typewriter was set up in front
of a little folding chair and pretended to rifle through an old shoe
box filled with papers. The truth was I had recently typed up fresh
copies of my stories for the express purpose of bumping into Rusty
again and I knew exactly where they were. I set the copies down on
the table in front of Rusty. They were originals and not carbons,
because I thought on the off chance Rusty liked them enough to
give them to the famous literary agent it would be a poor thing if
the man had to read carbons and in the worst-case scenario might
lessen the literary agent's opinion of the content itself.

'Swell,' Rusty said, levelling a lazy stare at the pile of papers on the table. He did not pick them up right away and instead sat there staring into his mug and swirling the dregs of the Irish coffee around. He had finished the coffee and whiskey in record time and I resisted offering him another mugful. Like all writers, I wanted him to read the stories and see how strong they were and I didn't mind if he was buzzed because I wanted him to feel good while he was reading them, but not so stoned he wouldn't be able to pay attention as the stories deserved.

If you know any writers at all, then you know writers are funny about the conditions under which their work is read. But as of that moment Rusty did not appear to be interested in reading anything. The copies were on the table and I was feeling sicker with every second that passed when his hand did not make a single twitch to pick them up. I could not think what he had come for if not for the stories, although I *could* think what, and I did not want to imagine it in any detail. Rusty helped himself to another drink and make snide observations about my apartment and habits. The afternoon pressed on with a dogged atmosphere. The clock was ticking and all around us the air was going stale.

Suddenly Rusty got up from his chair at the kitchenette table – which was really just a card table with a bedsheet thrown over it – and made a big show of rolling his eyes and stretching and yawning. 'It's rather boring here, don't you feel?'

'Now, hold on just a minute—' I started to say, feeling pretty sure I'd just been insulted: first about my crummy apartment, then about my looks, and now about my supposed lack of stimulating entertainment. But the objection halted on my lips the moment Rusty picked up the typed copies from the kitchen table. He rolled them up until they were tight as a baton and put them in his blue bag. I was working up the nerve to ask if that meant he planned to read them later but Rusty paid me no mind as I began coughing and switching my weight over my feet like a nervous boxer and instead he was already digging through the pile of clothing on the floor by the mattress, looking for my jacket.

'Here,' he said, holding my jacket out to me now that he'd located it. 'Put this on. I feel like seeing a matinee.' When he mentioned the matinee there was something imperial in his manner and I realised arguing with him was futile. He had declared what we would do and he hadn't even asked me about it because he already was sure he didn't have to ask me about it. I knew who he worked for and he knew what I wanted from him and even though it had never been openly discussed, the arrangement couldn't be clearer.

Of course I paid for our two tickets to see the matinee. And a round of drinks at the bar next to the movie house. And another round of drinks at a funny little bar on the West Side that was full of sailors whose ship had just pulled into the docks in Hell's Kitchen and who were whooping it up over the fact they'd been out to sea for four months straight and they only had one week of shore leave before they had to go back out. It was getting late – almost two in the morning – but the evening roared on and I found myself obliged to buy drinks for Rusty and myself and also for the occasional merchant marine or longshoreman Rusty insisted merited a free pint of beer. I was spending all the money I had and there wasn't going to be enough left over for my rent and I knew this was not good, but by then the aura of Rusty's boss had gotten a hold over me and I was powerless to break it. Rusty was attentive about mentioning the famous agent's name just enough to keep me in the game. A few times he took the baton of rolled-up manuscript pages out of his bag and set it on a bar table here or there, as though to remind me he might read them. Or perhaps to remind me he might abandon them. Every time he did this I looked at the tight roll of Eaton's bond paper I had worked so diligently to type as it unfurled like a bird trying to work a broken wing and I disliked Rusty a little more. Twice I watched from across the room as someone set a beer down on it like it was a curling coaster. When a fight broke out between two sailors I nearly joined in just to release some of the steam inside me.

It was turning into a doozy of a night. Rusty, for his part, showed no signs of slowing up. Frequently during the course of the evening I saw him open a little tin case he kept on a chain around his neck and each time he opened it he extracted a little balled-up scrap of paper and I knew then I would probably be seeing the sun come up over Manhattan before the time finally came when I could make my way home. I found out later he had an aunt who was an asthmatic and he'd been regularly stealing the paper strips out of her inhalers ever since he was fourteen and then it made a little more sense why Rusty was the way he was because you had to wonder what taking bennies for all those years straight could do to a person.

Sure enough, the sun was yawning over the top of the Empire State Building with the cold blue light of dawn when Rusty and I finally found ourselves in the back of a taxicab headed home. We rolled down the windows and lit a couple of cigarettes and quickly finished them. Some drivers minded and some drivers didn't and when the driver didn't seem to mind we lit a couple more. Rusty started talking about the famous agent again and what it was like to work for him and as he talked his hand slid onto my knee and I let it rest there, cold as his fingers were. There was a sort of soggy lightness to Rusty's hand that made me sick to my stomach – not because I disliked homosexuals per se, because if I'm being honest I will tell you at that point in my life I'd already been to bed with a man before and I knew what it could be like when it was good – but rather because I had a flash of the kind of lecherous old-man homosexual Rusty was destined to be later in life. It was all as clear as if I had just seen it in a crystal ball and I gave a shiver and looked out the cab window and tried to focus on the tops of the buildings that were now belching steam in preparation for another busy city morning.

When we pulled up in front of my apartment building Rusty was continuing on because he lived across the bridge in Astoria and as I got out of the cab he leant over and tugged on the tail of my shirt and said, 'Be a pal and spot me a dollar for the cab, will ya?' He was drunk and you could hear it in his voice.

'I only have a five.'

'Spot me a fiver, then.'

By that point I had ceased to be thrown by his blatant requests and with a weary automatic mind I reached into the worn lining of my back pocket and extracted the very last five-dollar bill I had and handed it to him. I knew it was more than the taxi ride would cost but I also knew if I saw him again he wouldn't bring it up and neither would I and this way I would never ask Rusty for my change back.

'Thanks,' he said, and for the first time that night I thought I detected an actual note of gratitude. He patted the rolled up baton of paper that had miraculously managed to find its way back into his bag. 'Let's talk some more about your writing soon. I see great things happening.' This was the first direct mention of my writing he'd ever made to me and I stood there blinking. 'Great things!' he shouted, and with that he pulled the taxi door shut and waved. The driver pulled away in the direction of the East River and everything that lay beyond its dun-coloured shores.

24

EDEN

I began to put a plan of action together. For my idea to work, I would have to iron out certain wrinkles. My Social Security card, for one. During my first week at Torchon & Lyle, Miss Everett had sent me on my lunch hour to get mine. (It had taken several hours of waiting in line to obtain it, in fact, and when I got back to the office, Mr Turner was so irate over my absence he nearly fired me on the spot; another subtle hint that perhaps Miss Everett had meant for me to lose my job right from the start.) I would need a new one now, in a different name. A driver's licence and birth certificate wouldn't hurt, either. I asked around the Village, and finally a sculptor with whom I'd become acquainted told me of a small husband-and-wife operation somewhere on the Lower East Side that could produce the articles in question.

'Couple of old Poles,' he said. 'Nice enough. Professional. Discreet. Got real good at filing documents back in the Old Country and ran a regular printing press during the war.' He handed me a card with the name of a Judaica shop printed in raised gold lettering. I flinched when I saw the name of the shop and what they sold, instantly worried. I wondered what they would think of my proposed name change.

'So I just . . . walk into the shop and ask at the counter?'

He nodded. '*Discreetly*, of course. It'll cost you, though, and the price is not negotiable. No exceptions.'

'How much is it?' I asked. He took the card back and wrote down a sum on the other side. I looked at it; the figure was daunting, and I was living on my meagre savings account by that point.

A fresh start would not be cheap, but after mulling things over for a few days, I decided it was worth it. I made the journey down to the Lower East Side, found the shop, and enquired at the counter. A hollow-cheeked woman with her hair drawn into a tight silver bun looked me over with cold, black, untrusting eyes and gave me a series of reluctant instructions. She frowned at the two names I'd written down – the old and the new – and raised an eyebrow, but didn't say anything. I wrote down the rest of the information she asked for, handed over my money, and was told to return in two weeks' time.

'Two weeks?' I asked.

'Yes,' she replied in an unfriendly, stoic voice. I couldn't help but notice she had a heavy Polish accent. 'Is soonest we can have it ready.'

She frowned at me again and I worried that my impatience was all too obvious; two weeks seemed like an awfully long time to wait.

In the meantime, my girlfriend Diana came from Indiana to visit. I must've started to transform into quite the bohemian, because when she stepped off the bus at Port Authority she took one look at me and suddenly I saw it all there in the gaze of her surprised eyes: my sleek little haircut and my tidy black capri pants slung loosely on my hips and the dark sophistication of the pair of sunglasses I'd fished out from the lost-and-found bin at the library. I'd been self-conscious about being fired and had told no one from home and thus was dreading my friend's visit because it meant facing facts about my having come to New York only to fail. But as Diana made her way down the steps of the bus I knew I needn't have worried. Before stepping off the last stair she paused and stood there looking at me, taking it all in. All she could manage to say was 'Oh . . . but you've gotten so slim!'

I laughed and she laughed and as her eyes travelled from my head to my toes I understood she was noticing all the differences. Diana had always been very fashionable by Indiana standards and I saw she was wearing a travelling suit that had very likely been ordered from the Sears, Roebuck & Co. catalogue for the express purpose of this trip. Ordering from the Sears, Roebuck & Co. catalogue was a popular way of picking out your wardrobe back in Fort Wayne and Diana had probably been pleased with the suit when it had arrived in the mail, but now I could see she was having a change of heart as she glimpsed her matronly silhouette reflected back to her in the giant black lenses of my sunglasses. She wasn't envious of me, for she looked equally unsure of my own gamine shape. This was before women regularly wore trousers outside of the house and here I was wearing them in the middle of Manhattan. I don't think she so much admired me as I had knocked her off-balance. She was recognising a change, indirectly registering a difference between the provincial and the cosmopolitan.

We spent the weekend taking in all the sights. It made me feel funny to be with Diana, as though I were in two places at once. I remember quite clearly there was one point when we were walking along a sidewalk on the Upper East Side and we passed by a bar that, coincidentally enough, flew the cream and crimson flag of the Hoosiers on a little flagstaff over the door.

'Say,' Diana pointed. 'Would you look at that!'

I laughed. 'Didn't I tell you?' I said. 'All of the nation – all of the *world*, actually – lives in New York. You can find everything here.'

Diana lingered in front of the bar, looking at the flag, and it dawned on me that no person is as poetically homesick as someone who has come to New York for the first time and glimpsed a small vestige of her home state.

'Wouldn't you like to go in there some night,' she said to me, 'and meet a man from Indiana? Oh, wouldn't that be something? You'd be in stitches laughing together about the coincidence.'

I nodded, mostly to humour her.

'And then you could get married and move home,' Diana continued, breathless with the new, exciting plot she was hatching for my life, 'and whenever you had people over for dinner you could tell them all about how you both moved a thousand miles away only to wind up meeting each other in a bar in New York.' She turned and studied my face for the appropriate level of enthusiasm.

I thought about all the interesting people I'd met in New York, especially the ones I'd met in the Village. Considered together, they certainly constituted a pack of oddballs. But even the strangest ones, even the ones who made me uncomfortable – like the female poet, for instance, who was locally famous for having adopted a habit of squatting down and urinating in the streets on her psychiatrist's advice that doing so would free her of kowtowing to this-or-that Freudian tendency – seemed like preferable dinner dates compared to the middle-class Midwestern folks who would attend this hypothetical soirée.

'Yes, that does sound nice,' I lied. We continued walking and spent the afternoon at the Metropolitan Museum, where Diana found the civilisation of ancient Egypt only slightly less interesting than that of Bloomington, Indiana.

When I took Diana back to the bus station early Monday

morning, she hugged me and then stepped back for a moment and regarded me with a sweet and sorrowful sigh. I understood then the sigh meant she was not coming back to the city and at the same time she was resigning herself to the fact that I had changed in a way that meant I was in New York to stay. We had been good girlfriends all through our school days and had even gone to the same college together, but now we would go our separate ways and that was just the way it was.

'Goodbye, Eden! Don't forget to write,' she said. 'Promise you'll tell me the second you get engaged, and I'll do the same.'

Wanting to be pleasant, I agreed, but the truth was, I had little interest in this pact. As I waved goodbye to Diana that day at the bus station, I figured I might as well also wave goodbye to things like pot roasts and French tulle wedding gowns and Sunday bridge games and all the other things I was sure would be in her future but not in mine. I imagined all the coffee-scented pecks on the cheek I would never receive as my husband brushed toast crumbs from the corners of his mouth and made his way out the front door in the mornings, and as I imagined these kisses I shivered, for I felt their presence pass over my skin in a tiny phantom parade. I didn't exactly envy Diana this life; nonetheless I felt a little mournful to think of things this way. It was a little like being at someone's funeral, and in a way I suppose I was mourning a version of myself that would never come to be.

I walked back from the bus station to the Barbizon. New York was having a hot summer that year and the afternoon sunshine poured over the city streets thick like amber honey and the pink faces of the people I passed gleamed with a sheen of sweat. I turned a corner and passed a pair of Hasidic men who looked particularly hot and uncomfortable under the weight of their heavy wool suits and black felt hats, the curls of their long *payot* sticking to their cheeks. Fort Wayne and the Midwest suddenly felt farther away than it ever had, and I didn't know who I was or how people saw me any more; I was neither here nor there. I looked at my watch and calculated which towns Diana's bus might be passing through at the present moment.

In Central Park, I sat down on a bench. I gave myself permission to be desperately, hopelessly homesick as I counted off sixty seconds according to the second hand of my watch. Then I got up and forced myself to let it pass.

25

Two weeks had passed, which meant it was time to pick up my papers. It was the first thing I thought of, before I even opened my eyes that morning. I got up, got dressed, and decided to take the bus from the Barbizon down to the Lower East Side. It was a slow slog with a lot of stops, and took a very long time. I could've taken the subway, I suppose, but for some reason I was in the mood to stay aboveground, to look out the window as the scenery changed and really *see* it: the way one Manhattan neighbourhood slides into the next, a hundred villages, each of a different character, all piled up on one island. Eventually the stone high-rises and brownstones of the East Sixties gave way to the colourful commercial awnings and more industrial buildings of the Thirties and Twenties and the brick tenements at the outskirts of the Village, until we had trundled all the way down to Houston Street, where the bus finally turned and continued east. We passed Katz's Delicatessen, and although I was no relation, I was well aware of the irony. Seeing that familiar name in bold vertical letters on the red-and-white sign sent a pang through my body.

The peculiar feeling stayed with me as I dismounted at the bus stop and made my way down Orchard Street, passing bakeries selling knishes, their signs in the windows written in both English and Yiddish. This was simultaneously exotic and familiar. My grandmother had made knishes, and both of my grandparents could understand Yiddish. To me they had spoken English, but to each other they spoke a mixture of German and Yiddish – until the war came, that is. Once the war came they dropped the German altogether and spoke only Yiddish in hushed tones, when strangers were not around. I tried to picture them here, skirting the murky puddles that perpetually lined the narrow, uneven streets of the Lower East Side, the two of them moving through the hustle and bustle, street vendors shouting prices after them. When they'd immigrated, they'd passed through New York, and then Chicago, but only briefly. To them America meant wide-open spaces, and they'd gone to Indiana in search of those spaces, settling on Fort Wayne because it was also the location of Indiana's oldest synagogue.

It was funny to have left the Midwest for New York only to have things turned against me. I thought of my parents back in Indiana now: working and shopping, joining the local Lions Club, volunteering for the Salvation Army. Both of them the American-born children of immigrants, they were much more intent on assimilation to Midwestern life than their parents, going about their daily business with an air of cheerful, determined obliviousness that only the very self-conscious possess. There were still little incidents, here and there. My parents' application to join the country club was refused. Someone scratched a Star of David into the paint of our old Hudson while my mother was inside shopping at the Kroger. There was a birthday party from which I'd been purposely excluded. I remember once going to synagogue and seeing freshly spattered egg yolks dripping down the outside wall. The war certainly ratcheted up the tension; I was aware there were certain families in town that felt the war was 'our fault'. But despite all these memories, my parents did a proficient job of shielding me from anything more than this, keeping these incidents far out on the periphery of my childhood, and I very much felt Indiana was my home. They'd found a way to be 'the Katzes' of Fort Wayne, Indiana, and so it was with a sense of shame now that I had failed to make it as Eden Katz in New York City. Had they known what I was about to do, I believe it would've broken their hearts.

It was a different thing to be Jewish in New York than it was in Indiana. You would think it would be easier, but that was exactly the assumption that had landed me in trouble in the first place. It was only easier in a different way. It's a myth that people who live in cities are naturally more open-minded, more accepting and tolerant of difference. The truth is, whatever people are, be it saints or bigots, they simply are these things, and the city – by smashing all those different kinds of people up against one another – just makes people's tolerance (or lack of it) all that much more pronounced. Unlike me, Miss Everett had known the secret of this, and how to capitalise on it. I felt I only had two choices: go home with my tail between my legs, or stay by any means necessary and fight.

The shop was dark and cool on the inside, if a little musty. I stood there a moment listening to the quiet. On the far side of the cramped little space a man called to me from behind the counter.

'Hello,' he said. He had a heavy Polish accent and was mostly bald, with a mottled map of liver spots gathering where his hairline used to be. I looked around for the woman I had spoken to before, but she was nowhere to be found. 'Can I help you with something?'

'I . . . was here two weeks ago,' I said.

'Ah.' He held up a finger in the air. 'I thought it might be you,' he said. He turned to pull back a heavy navy curtain that led to some kind of back room.

'I spoke to a woman last time . . .' I continued, anxious to establish that he and I indeed understood each other. 'She took my information, but she didn't say much. She seemed a bit cross . . . I was afraid I had offended her,' I said, trying to move towards him through the space and nearly knocking over a basket filled with stacks of dark velvet yarmulkes.

'That was my wife, Agata,' he said, grinning and waving a dismissive hand. 'She is never smiling. Nothing personal.' He gestured for me to follow him behind the curtain to the back room. 'I know what you are here for. Come, come!'

I followed. The thick, chalky smell of dust filled the air. My eyes worked to adjust to the darkness.

'You can call me Leo,' he said once we were behind the curtain. I nodded. We were in a storage room of some variety. It was no doubt the place where Leo and Agata took breaks from minding the shop. There was a table with a plate of half-eaten food, what appeared to be chicken and orange peels, and a soap opera squawked from the speakers of a large wooden radio sitting on a shelf. On the wall was a curiously antique-looking painting in dark, heavy colours. I squinted and realised I was looking at the Virgin Mary. On an adjacent wall was another surprising object: a giant baroque silver cross, slightly dull with tarnish.

He saw me frowning at the cross in confusion and chuckled.

'We're Catholics,' he said.

'But . . .' I tried to work this out. 'You own a Judaica shop,' I said.

'Business is business.' He shrugged. He walked over to a heavy oak desk, opened a drawer, and held up a tall envelope. I understood on instinct that inside it were all the documents I'd requested. 'Before the war, we ran a little rare-books shop. Quiet place. Too quiet! There was an antique printing press in the back,' he said. 'Then the war came. That press was the real business. Everyone wanting papers! We got hundreds of people out of Nazi territory . . . for a price, of course.'

'And you came to America and opened a Judaica shop?'

He shrugged again. 'Why not? We already had the stock. You see, some people were grateful. Grateful for their lives! Others . . . left us things to hide and never came back. Beautiful things!' he said, and opened a drawer full of ornate silver kiddush cups and gilded menorahs, waving a hand. 'Was dangerous to hide them! And now . . . now, why should they go to waste? They are part of a great tradition. Gold! Silver! Beautiful things! Someone will be proud to own such beautiful things.'

'*For a price*,' I said.

He narrowed his eyes at me. 'For a price, yes. But is things used for old traditions and very useful to new people. Is good for making important memories all the same.' He opened the tall envelope and slid the documents out onto the desk. Lifting what appeared to be a Social Security card high into the air – I presumed it was the one I had requested – he said, 'Sometimes is important to remember a culture, sometimes is important to forget it, eh? Reminds me of the old days.'

'Is that what I ordered?' I asked in a cold voice. I reached out a hand as though to offer to take it. He held it away, hesitating.

'I don't understand. This is *America*, is fine for you here! Okay, not perfect, but is fine!'

'It's for a job. I want to apply for a new job.'

'What kind of job?'

'In publishing.'

'Hah!' he laughed and bent over to slap his knee. 'In *publishing*? Is lots of Jews in publishing! Tons! You are looking in wrong places. I take your money, but you don't need new name. Is madness.'

'I need a new start,' I said, angry at what he was implying. 'It's not that I hate my name. There's someone who . . . Well, anyway, the point is I want to start over.'

He narrowed his eyes and looked me over from head to toe. 'My wife say she think something funny about you. She didn't understand you – a nice girl! – what you are up to.'

'I haven't done anything illegal, if that's what you mean,' I snapped.

Leo raised his hands over his head as if to say *Don't shoot the messenger.* 'I mean,' I added more meekly, wilting with the realisation, 'except for . . . well, this.'

'What do I care about your business? Your business is your business.' He dropped his hands and brought the long envelope over to me. '*My* business is papers.'

'Thank you,' I said, taking them. I opened the envelope and inspected the various documents. It contained everything I needed to start over again, to apply for jobs in a new name and have a fresh beginning. I thanked him again and turned to leave. Before I was out the door, however, he said something that echoed in my mind during the whole ride home.

'Congratulations,' Leo said. 'You are now what we in the business call a "ghost".'

I looked at him, considering what to say. But then I thought to myself, *Ghosts have no words.* So I said nothing, turned, and left.

That night, as I went to sleep feeling a fresh wave of victory and rebellion against Miss Everett, I couldn't quite decide how to feel about Leo and Agata, whether I regarded them as merciful or mercenary. That was the thing about people: most are a combination of the two, with variously good and bad results.

26

I sent my résumé bearing my new name to Bonwright first. I suppose this was because Bonwright was a large company, and the conversation I'd had with Cliff that afternoon in the bar had left Bonwright fresh in my mind. It wasn't that I expected to work for Cliff's father per se. In the time it took me to acquire a new Social Security card, I fully expected Roger Nelson to have already found a suitable replacement, so I was extremely surprised to receive a telephone call one morning requesting I come in to have an interview with him specifically.

'Oh yes,' the woman in charge of hiring said urgently over the telephone, 'I'm afraid Mr Nelson is getting frustrated with the temporary girls he's been sent. He wants to find somebody permanent right away. These temps are awfully inexperienced, and you say you have a letter of introduction, so that's promising. How soon can you come in to meet with him?'

'Oh. I assumed I'd be interviewing with a personnel manager first,' I said, resisting the urge to bite my nails.

'Typically, yes,' the woman said. 'But seeing as how he's in a bind, Mr Nelson is looking to hand-pick someone. Let's see . . . How does tomorrow at one o'clock sound?'

I hesitated. What if Mr Nelson hired me? What would Cliff say?

Surely we would bump into each other again. Cliff didn't know I'd altered my name. Already things were getting tangled.

'That would be fine,' I said, pushing my misgivings aside. I wanted the job, and what's more, I needed it.

'Marvellous. I'll put you on the books. You'll report to Roger Nelson's office; he's on the seventh floor. There's a temp named Barbara – goodness, you'll see what I mean about the temps! – who will receive you when you get there.'

I remember that night feeling to me like the longest in the history of time. I was so relieved when morning finally rolled around, I hardly noticed the oppressive heat as I got dressed and ready. When I left the Barbizon at noon it was already shaping up to be another hot, thick day and I was sweating when I came up from the subway. Without quite remembering the walk, I was suddenly standing in front of the towering high-rise that housed Bonwright. I gazed up at the dignified gold lettering stamped into the limestone facade and at the rows upon rows of great glass windows rising into the air like a small army advancing upon the sky. I took a deep breath. There was nothing left to do but go inside.

I stepped towards the giant revolving door. The lunch hour was beginning for some and ending for others, and a parade of secretaries – most of them belonging, I presumed, to Bonwright but also to the law firms and accountants' offices that likewise occupied offices in the high-rise – were flowing in and out of the building in a steady stream. For the briefest of instants I swore I saw Judy, her clean wheat-coloured hair pulled high into a ponytail and a swipe of bright red lipstick on her mouth. I was so convinced it was her I had to restrain myself from calling out a greeting, reminding myself Judy could not possibly be here. And really, though I was desperate for a friendly face, I had to admit it was better not to know a soul here. It was my only chance for a fresh start.

I rode the elevator up to the seventh floor, where a receptionist with a pinched voice greeted me tersely, saying only 'Name, please?'

'Eden Collins,' I answered. It sounded very strange to me. But then, I suppose it ought to have sounded strange.

'Yes,' the receptionist said, following her finger across an appointment calendar. 'Miss Collins. I see you're on the books.' She pivoted in her chair and stood up, gesturing for me to follow her around behind a wall, where I encountered the familiar scene of a typing pool. The doors of the executives lined the perimeter of the large, open, square bullpen, each editor's name indicated in stylish silver metal letters. Girls sat rowed up at typing desks, each of them likely seated closest to the editor she was assigned to assist. The steady hum of typewriters and chatter filled the air.

'See that girl sitting in the far corner there? She's temping as Mr Nelson's secretary today; go check in with her and she'll notify you when Mr Nelson is ready for you.' The receptionist snorted to herself. 'Or she'll *try*.'

'Thank you,' I said. I walked in the direction she pointed. The room smelt of stale coffee and typewriter ink – a familiar smell, one I'd memorised during my time at Torchon & Lyle. Once across the room, I cleared my throat. 'Eden Collins to see Roger Nelson,' I said to the temp sitting behind the desk. She looked up, and I found myself staring into a pair of big brown eyes and an explosion of bleached-blonde hair.

'Oh!' she jumped up, and for a split second a rush of panic came over me, as the neckline of her dress was so low it appeared her breasts were going to spill out of her blouse and I might have to catch them. She put out a nail-polished hand for a handshake.

The breasts miraculously bounced in place but did not spill over, and I breathed an inward sigh of relief. 'I'm Barbara,' she said, pronouncing it 'Bawb-rah.'

'Eden Collins,' I repeated, shaking her hand.

'Oh yeah! Of course!' she said. 'You're on the calendar.' She put one finger in the air, then spun about and took a few steps to fling open one of the executive's doors. 'Mis-tah Nelson? Eden Collins here to see you.'

'Barbara, dear, I've shown you how the intercom works. Remember yesterday when we went over it again?' a man's voice called back. He sighed.

'Oh! That's right!' Barbara said in a chipper voice. With one heavy movement of her shapely arm, she slammed the door shut. I watched as she leant over the desk (I wondered again at the neckline of her dress) and pushed the button for the intercom. I heard a muffled buzzing from behind the door.

'Yes?' came the voice over the intercom, followed by another heavy sigh.

'Eden Collins is here for her interview,' Barbara reported.

'All right,' he said. 'Send her in.'

'Sure thing!' Barbara replied enthusiastically. She rose and opened the door again, gesturing for me to follow. 'Mr Nelson, Eden Collins,' she announced. 'Whoops! 'Scuse me,' she added, bending over to pick up the nail file where she had dropped it on the floor. There was a slightly clownish air about Barbara's dumb-pinup routine that made you wonder if she wasn't doing it on purpose.

I peered at Roger Nelson as he stood up from behind the desk, curious to see whether he bore any resemblance to his son. He was more substantial somehow, as though he were made of heavier bones. He wore a well-tailored suit and what appeared to be an expensive silk tie. His hair had receded to leave only a half-ring of silver that ran from his ears down and from which the rest of his head rose in a very smooth, shiny dome.

He had the kind of eyes I'd always inwardly described to myself as 'Santa Claus' eyes. They were a radiant cornflower blue and caught a slight twinkle in the light, an effect that seemed more pronounced given the reddish hue of his face. It was easy to take stock of all the details, because for the moment he was not looking at me. His gaze was steadfast on Barbara's backside as she bent over to pick up the nail file.

'Thank you, Barbara,' he said. Behind me, Barbara made her exit, pulling the door shut behind her.

He leant over the desk to shake my hand. I noticed a slight paunch around his middle.

'Well, Miss Collins, I understand you have a letter of introduction.'

I nodded and reached into my pocketbook for the letter. He read it over quickly, his eyes darting from side to side over the page.

'This recommends you very highly.' His smile stirred up a swarm of butterflies in my stomach. He cleared his throat. 'My last secretary worked for me for fifteen years. I trusted her to read all my manuscripts, and the office ran like a well-oiled machine – a quality, I'm afraid, that has been lost since her departure. I assume you have secretarial training of some variety? You know how to take dictation and type and all that?'

'Yes, sir.'

'Hmm. And you like reading? If I assign you editorial duties – I'm not promising we'll make you a reader right away – but if I ask you to read the occasional manuscript here and there, you could read the manuscripts I assign you at a fairly speedy clip?'

'Oh yes!' I exclaimed, then tried to rein in my enthusiasm so I wouldn't start babbling about my former responsibilities at Torchon & Lyle. 'That's the part of the job that interests me most.'

'What's your favourite book that's come out recently?'

We chatted for a while about books and what made for a bestseller. I explained about the course Mr Hightower had taught on popular fiction. I told him about the novels I'd loved best as a teenager, and later as a young woman in college. At one point I caught myself rhapsodising about the first time I read Katherine Mansfield and Carson McCullers but then I glimpsed a slightly disinterested frown cross Mr Nelson's face. I remembered whom it was I was talking to and threw in some mentions of Hemingway and Joyce for good measure, and he seemed to approve.

'Well, Miss Collins, I'll admit, I like you for this position. But I want to make certain you know what you are getting yourself into . . . Your office etiquette must be impeccable, and the reading, it's a great deal of work – most of which I expect done after regular work hours. You understand that?'

'Oh yes, sir.'

'And this is your first job?' he asked.

I hesitated. I only hesitated for the briefest of moments, but still I hesitated. I was about to tell a lie. I did not take it lightly.

'Yes,' I said, finally. 'That's right.'

'Hmm,' said Mr Nelson. 'Well . . .' he trailed off, then gathered himself. 'I had been hoping for someone with previous experience, but you seem like you have half a brain, at least. I guess we'll just hope you catch on quickly. I can't very well keep Barbara.' He smiled to himself. 'I'd like to, but I can't. As wonderful and as *gifted* as she is, I'm getting far too behind on work. Reader's reports in particular.' He looked me over quickly. 'You *do* look like the type to read a lot.'

I wasn't sure whether this was a compliment or an insult, but then he smiled and I smiled back. Mr Nelson had an audacious charm about him that was difficult to resist. There was something dapper yet very masculine about him. He held up a finger as though he'd had an idea.

'Have you eaten lunch yet, Miss Collins?'

'Oh . . . no,' I answered.

'Neither have I.' He smiled. 'I have just the plan.' He leant over and pushed a button on the speaker box sitting on his desk. 'Barbara? Put down whatever file or report you're currently destroying, sweetheart. We're going to lunch. Steaks on me!' I looked at him, baffled.

'We'll have a little lunch,' he said. 'The three of us, to celebrate the changing of the guard, so to speak.'

'You mean to say I'm hired?'

'You can start this afternoon.'

Just like that, in an absolute daze, I found myself following Mr Nelson and a delighted, giggly Barbara downstairs to the lobby, where we caught a taxi and rode all the way down to Delmonico's.

I had heard of Delmonico's, but I had never been there before. It was a dark-panelled sanctuary filled with bankers, lit with that incandescent brand of chandelier light that only very expensive restaurants seem to have. Mr Nelson did all the ordering for us, which meant that three martinis appeared almost immediately, followed a little later by three medium-rare steaks, creamed spinach, and potatoes au gratin.

While Mr Nelson had conveyed an air of regal authority in the office, this quality expanded even further in the restaurant so that he was positively leonine, presiding over the dining room, one of his commanding, heavy, paw-like hands laid upon the table at all times. He was friendly with the staff, all of whom seemed to know him very well. The maître d' had rushed to greet us as we walked in the door, not batting an eye to see Mr Nelson in the company of not just one but two young ladies. When our steaks arrived to the table, the chef came out, dressed in his white smock and chef's hat, to enquire whether they were done to Mr Nelson's liking. When we finished the main course, the maître d' came back over and chatted for a while with Mr Nelson, at which point Mr Nelson casually pulled out a cigar from his inside jacket pocket.

'You don't mind if I smoke this, do you?' he said. The corners of the maître d's mouth twitched. It was plain that he *did* mind.

'Certainly, Roger,' he said, then gave a little stiff bow and scurried back to the host desk.

As Mr Nelson puffed away on his cigar, he regaled us with stories about the time he'd gone on a drinking binge with Raymond Chandler and when he'd gotten into a bit of trouble during one of William Faulkner's visits to New York. I listened to these nervously, for one thing had become glaringly obvious during the course of lunch: Barbara didn't quite understand that my being hired meant her temporary assignment was at an end and that this was a farewell lunch. She called him 'Roger', as opposed to 'Mr Nelson', and patted his arm affectionately at regular intervals, as though they were a couple entertaining and I was a guest.

As lunch was winding down, she excused herself and went to the ladies' room, leaving me alone with Mr Nelson.

'Did you have a pleasant lunch?' Mr Nelson asked.

'Absolutely lovely,' I replied. 'Only . . . I don't think Barbara understands her assignment is over.'

'Yes,' he grumbled. 'She's not catching on. How unfortunate. I ought to have had the agency call her. Anyway, it's too late for that now.'

The bill arrived, a slip of paper upon a little silver tray, and he reached for it. I watched him sign it, wondering how he was going to clear up the confusion with Barbara.

'Well,' he said, glancing at his watch with an air of finality, 'I'd better be getting back to the office. You can follow along when you're through here.'

He stood up and straightened his tie while I blinked at him, uncomprehending. *When you're through here*, he had said . . . We had finished our meal; I couldn't think of what else there was to do or why I wouldn't simply follow along with him. But he spoke again and the mystery was dispelled.

'If you would, please let Barbara know she's no longer needed. When you've done that, come back to the office. You can pick up your employment card from Personnel and get settled into your new desk this afternoon.'

'Me?' I asked. 'Tell her?'

'Yes,' he said, ignoring the shock in my voice. 'You can do that, can't you? Thank you, Eden. I'll see you in a little while, and we can get to work.' With a serious nod, he hustled across the room and slipped out the door. I dimly glimpsed him waving an arm to hail a cab.

I turned back, mustering my courage. *The whole point of a temporary girl is that you're only temporarily needed*, I told myself. *Barbara can't possibly be too disappointed.* What a strange day it was turning out to be!

The maître d' came over with a plate of crêpe Suzette and set them on the table before me. 'Mr Nelson asked that we send you ladies out some dessert,' he said.

'How thoughtful,' I muttered in a flat tone. I was aware I sounded ungrateful. 'Thank you,' I added.

I looked up to see Barbara returning from the ladies' room, her hair smoothed and her lipstick freshly applied.

'Where's Roger?' she asked, innocently peering around with bright, hopeful eyes.

'Barbara,' I said, 'please have a seat.'

Feeling terrible, I slid the plate of crêpe Suzette closer to her. Perhaps she had a sweet tooth and they would make her feel better. I took a breath and delivered the news.

27

Barbara did not take the news very well. She tried to avoid making an out-and-out scene, bless her heart, but nonetheless she sniffled into the white cloth napkin until little rivulets of mascara trickled down her cheeks. I escorted her back to the ladies' room, where the two of us attempted to patch up the damage with the combined contents of our purses.

'I'm no dummy,' she insisted, accepting my powder compact and dabbing under her eyes. 'I *know* I make a lousy secretary. I wasn't in it for that anyhow. It's only that . . . Oh, he left without even saying goodbye! *That* certainly sends a message.' Her face crumpled again and she let out a soft wail. 'I suppose that's when you know you haven't the slightest chance of holding a fella's attention any more.'

With a shock, I realised she'd been gunning to become his mistress. In fact, perhaps she already had – in some capacity or another – but she wanted to make it a regular habit. I decided the less I knew about that, the better.

Later, on the curb outside Delmonico's, Barbara and I said goodbye to each other. I think, had we been closer to midtown, she might've followed me back to the office, just to see if there was still a glimmer of hope. But we were about as far downtown as we could be. I was beginning to learn that Mr Nelson did nothing by accident.

* * *

I was soon to learn Barbara was not the only one who admired Mr Nelson. In fact, Mr Nelson's overwhelming charisma was perhaps the most defining characteristic of his personality. He was well-respected among his colleagues. He could calm the finickiest, most neurotic of writers with a single pat on the back. Agents loved him; other editors wanted to be him. His lunch-dates were notoriously long, and yet most people he lunched with expressed disappointment when it was finally over. I knew this was so because when they didn't want lunch to end they often made excuses to return with him to the building and have one more drink in his office. When they emerged, they shook hands with Mr Nelson, still reluctant to go, and promised to have their girl set something else up again soon.

'Wonderful,' Mr Nelson would say. 'Have your secretary call Eden here. She's a whiz with my calendar.'

This was another clever ploy, because there was very little I could do with Mr Nelson's calendar; it was perpetually overbooked.

It was Mr Nelson's job, I realised, to be popular, and he was accomplished at it. If he had a fault, it was that he was perhaps a little *too* good at being popular; it was plain that he thrived on his popularity, and that he was very aware of how other people regarded him. I wondered if this wasn't because he'd 'married up', so to speak. Like most men who possess a larger-than-life personality, Mr Nelson had crafted a sort of mythology around his success. 'Pulled myself up by my own bootstraps', he would say, and then proceed to recount a long list of working-class jobs that had led him from newsboy to ice-truck driver to senior editor. But this was only the partial truth. His wife, Doris, I learnt, was a well-coifed silvery blonde whose handsome middle-aged face often graced the society pages. She was from one of New York's oldest families; in marrying her, Roger Nelson had made a powerful social alliance – an alliance that was fairly against the odds – and it was obvious that Mr Nelson enjoyed dropping the names of his in-laws as well as their illustrious ancestors into conversation.

It was not clear, however, how much he cared for actually being married.

Mr Nelson's office was large and included a sofa. He kept a drawer with a change of clothes and a little shaving kit. On nights when he worked late, he slept in his office instead of making the commute home to Connecticut. When Mr Nelson didn't stay late, I assumed he went home.

One morning, however, I came in early to discover my telephone was already ringing. I hurried through the large empty bullpen of the typing pool, anxious to silence its shrill ring.

'Roger Nelson, please,' came an older female voice. His door was open a crack, and I could see he was not in his office, but somehow, on instinct, I knew I could not say as much. There was something in the caller's voice, thin vibrations that revealed a kind of irritable, uptight strain, that made me think it was possible to get my boss in trouble.

'He stepped out momentarily,' I said.

'Oh,' said the woman. 'This is Mrs Nelson. He called last night to say he was working late. I assume he stayed overnight in his office, and I'm calling now regarding a personal matter.'

'Oh – of course! Mrs Nelson, how lovely to hear your voice. You just missed him; he stepped out for a fresh shirt,' I said. Unfortunately, all signs pointed to Mr Nelson not having been anywhere near his office in the last twelve hours. I silently prayed she would not call back before Roger was able to make it in.

'I see,' she said. 'Please tell him I phoned.'

'I will,' I said, intending to introduce myself and elaborate, but she had already hung up. I could tell she was not interested in knowing who I was; perhaps she thought I was yet another Barbara. I looked up to see Mr Nelson standing over my desk. I hadn't heard him come in. I jumped.

'That was my wife?' he asked.

'Yes,' I said.

'And you told her I'd stepped out for a fresh shirt?'

'I did.'

His posture relaxed. 'Yes. Very good, then.' He smiled at me awkwardly. 'Thank you, Eden.'

We never discussed this exchange further. The day I'd comforted Barbara at Delmonico's, I had decided it was best not to stick my nose into whatever it was Mr Nelson did outside working hours. For the most part, I liked working for Mr Nelson. He received the house's most literary submissions, and there were often very good manuscripts to be found in his slush pile. Though I had not yet been officially promoted to reader, he gave me quite a lot of manuscripts to take home and read, and he trusted my appraisal of their quality and promise.

During my first month or so at Bonwright, I was happy with our arrangement. I was reading plenty of high-quality stuff, and Mr Nelson had already acquired two manuscripts on my recommendation. He praised my 'sharp eye', and I felt quite proud of myself. But then a small detail came to my attention: Mr Nelson had a habit of praising my editorial taste only when we were in his office, alone. In the typing pool, or in front of colleagues, he never let on that I had done any of the reading, let alone had the 'sharp eye' that had resulted in the acquisition of the manuscript in question.

I decided one day to ask him if I couldn't officially be made a reader. I plucked up my courage and knocked on his door.

'Why, you've only worked for me for a few weeks, Eden,' he exclaimed, as though surprised. 'You want a promotion already?'

I didn't point out that it had been more than a few weeks. 'I'm not asking for a raise,' I said, trying to sound cheerful. 'I was only thinking . . . since you have me reading so many manuscripts . . . perhaps I could officially be made a reader. You know, in title.'

His lips twitched with irritation and he frowned. 'I think it's rather soon for you to be asking me this, Eden. During your interview, I meant it when I said there would be light editorial duties but that I couldn't promise to promote you to reader right away.' He shuffled around a few piles of papers on his desk as though he were suddenly very busy. 'Frankly, I don't understand you career gals these days. My last secretary, Francine, used to read almost all of my manuscripts. *She* worked for me for fifteen years and never once asked me to officially make her a reader.'

'Oh.' I bit my lip, thinking carefully of how to proceed. In the instant that had passed since I'd broached the subject, one thing had become very clear to me: my ambition was not the asset I had thought it would be. Mr Nelson wanted the kind of secretary who would remain by his side in a permanent capacity, reading manuscripts but never asking to be acknowledged as a reader. He wanted a girl who would get settled and stay put, one who he'd never have to replace.

'Look,' he said now, sighing as if to let go of a great irritation, 'I can't offer you advancement at the present moment. But if you earn it through hard work, perhaps we can work something out.' He paused, giving me a serious look. 'If you work very, very, *very* hard, we can revisit this subject at a later date. Do we have an understanding?'

'Yes, Mr Nelson,' I rushed to reply.

'If you want me to take you in earnest, you mustn't botch a single task I give you – is that also understood? I can't very well give you more responsibility if you aren't ready for it.'

'Of course!'

'Fine, then . . .' He grunted. He pulled a cigar out of his desk drawer, clipped it, and set about toasting it with an elegant gold-plated lighter. I got the sense he was getting ready to dismiss me, but he seemed lost in thought, as though he had something more to say to me that he hadn't quite worked out yet.

'You know, Eden, I'm sure you think being an editor is very glamorous, but it's a lot of hard work, and not all of it is quantifiable. For instance, you haven't any clue what it's like trying to keep some of these authors happy. You have to flatter them in a serious manner and know how to stroke their egos! Oh, it's not a woman's job, that's for certain. Men can hardly trust the word of a woman; that's just science.' He shook his head and shrugged.

'I'm sure you're right,' I said. 'But perhaps I can be taught, at least somewhat. I've learnt so much just by watching you handle people. You're very good at it.'

This was true. It was also meant to flatter him.

'Yes,' Mr Nelson said, smiling with smug satisfaction as he lit his cigar and coaxed it by puffing on it. 'Well, at least you have a good sense of things. Back to work now, shall we?'

I agreed, and left his office to finish the tasks waiting for me at my desk.

Later that evening, I telephoned Judy. I hadn't talked to her in a while and wanted to catch her up on things.

'Oh, that's wonderful news about Bonwright, Eden!' she said. 'I knew Miss Everett couldn't poison everyone against you for ever.'

'Well, perhaps not,' I said. 'But, it's not exactly as you might think . . .' I confessed the truth about Mr Hightower's two letters of recommendation, and about my name. 'I just felt I deserved a fresh start,' I explained lamely.

'You do,' Judy replied, her voice sincere. 'I'm glad you rolled up your sleeves and did something about the situation! To be honest, the last time we talked, I was a little worried you'd give up and go back to Indiana. Girls in New York are so funny that way; you can never tell which ones have come here just so they can turn around again and leave.'

I agreed with her, and we discussed New York's peculiar social gravity, gossiping about girls who'd stayed and girls who'd turned tail and run.

'Well, I think I'm here for good,' Judy said. 'I'd like to have a house in the Hudson Valley or maybe in Connecticut or Long Island, but I can't imagine going much farther than that, and of course that's only if I'm married. Speaking of which, still have your heart set on books instead of boys?'

'Yes, I'd still like to be an editor someday,' I said. 'Only the road there is a bit bumpier than I thought it would be.'

'How is – what's your boss's name? Mr Nelson?'

'Oh, all right, I suppose. He has me reading a lot, and the work is top-drawer. He's just . . . well . . .' I hesitated, then told her about his reaction when I'd asked to be officially made a reader.

'It sounds like he wants a career secretary,' she diagnosed.

'That's what I'm afraid of,' I said.

'Well, you can't blame him,' Judy pointed out. 'It's a reasonable thing for an executive of his stature to want.'

'I suppose,' I said. 'I suppose I'm only hoping for peace of mind that, if I work hard, I can move up.'

'For now, Eden, maybe it's just best to settle in and be thankful you have a job!'

'You're right,' I said. We gossiped for a few more moments and eventually made a date to go out for martinis the next week. It was nice talking to Judy again. And she was right: I *was* lucky to have a job.

28

I held up my end of the bargain: I worked hard. At the office, I typed and filed, took dictation and ran the mimeograph, dispatched correspondence, and made sure Mr Nelson's office was never lacking coffee – or any other variety of beverage, for that matter. I skipped lunch; I was alert at every moment. In the evenings, I stayed up all night reading manuscripts and scribbling down notes, which I typed up during the early hours of the mornings, before any of the other secretaries had arrived.

Unfortunately, however, my plan backfired, if only for a brief spell. I worked so hard, I wound up running down my immunities and catching a terrible flu. I went into the office one morning in a state of denial, working as best I could for a few hours; but when my temperature spiked and I began seeing spots, I waved the white flag of surrender. I got another girl to cover my desk and poked my head into Mr Nelson's office to tell him of my illness.

'Flu, Eden? Why, it's summertime. How unusual,' Mr Nelson said, not looking up from his desk.

'Yes,' I said. 'It's certainly unexpected.' Despite having the shivers, I could feel the heat of the fever rushing to my cheeks and forehead. My perception of things began to blur. I was dizzy and wobbled a bit in my heels. I knew I couldn't stay standing up for very much longer. Mr Nelson glanced up and sighed.

'Well, then, Eden, I suppose you may as well go home early today and rest up over the weekend. We've a lot to do next week.'

'Thank you, sir,' I managed to say. I staggered out of the office and back to my desk to gather up my things, everything around me appearing like a bizarre, faraway dream.

I'd made it all the way to the elevators when suddenly my constitution failed me. I realised I was going to faint. The elevator doors opened just in time to reveal a familiar-looking young man with sandy hair. As I lurched forward, he automatically moved to catch me and I fell into his arms.

'Cliff?' I murmured, confused. Perhaps I was hallucinating. I struggled to get my feet back under me. But it was no good; I had lost all my strength. He looked down at me, equally confused, still holding me in his arms.

'I thought this sort of business only happened in the movies,' he said, smiling, his blue eyes twinkling. I tried to laugh off my embarrassment but wound up coughing instead. The dizziness intensified as the effort of coughing overwhelmed me, and I began to see black spots. My eyelids fluttered as I fought the urge to let my eyeballs roll back in my head.

'Oh boy,' he said. 'You're not foolin'. We'd better get you to a doctor.' He bent over and I felt him slip an arm under my knees as he lifted me more fully off the ground.

'No doctor,' I murmured, dimly fearful of the extra expense. 'Home, please. Just put me in a taxi. I'll be fine.'

'Where's home?'

'The Bar . . . bi . . . zon,' I said. Then I gave up and let the darkness close in around me. I heard the bright ding of the elevator. The last thing I remember thinking was that it sounded so very far away, as though it were at the end of a long tunnel.

When I came to, I was in a strange room. I blinked and took in my surroundings, trying to remember what had happened. I was in what appeared to be a small studio apartment. There was a kitchenette at the far corner, and it was hot and sunny in the room. Curiously, the whole place carried a distinctive scent that reminded me of a theatre playhouse, like a combination of fresh paint and ancient dust and mildewed costumes. There was visible evidence of the paint smell, as the entire room – even the wooden floors – had been painted entirely black. The furnishings were both spartan and chaotic: a mattress lying in the centre of the room, a couple of mismatched bookcases and bureaus, and finally a pair of folding chairs and a card table upon which sat an old-model Smith Corona typewriter. A heap of books lay on the floor near the window, piled in such a careless, haphazard way as though to suggest their owner was less interested in reading them and more interested in starting a small bonfire.

For a fleeting moment I believed it was a weekday, and felt my body jolt more awake with cold panic. The sun was streaming in the windows; I would be late for work! But then it dawned on me that it was Saturday, and I relaxed. I sighed and lay there, gathering my thoughts and trying to recall the blurry events of the day before.

'Say – you're awake,' a voice called from across the room as the front door opened. 'That's swell. I was just beginning to worry you'd gone comatose on me, and it would've been a real drag to figure out what to do with you then.'

The door closed and I found myself looking at the familiar sandy-haired, blue-eyed young man.

'Oh, it *was* you!' I said. 'I thought I'd hallucinated that part.'

'I didn't take you to the Barbizon after all,' Cliff said, stating the obvious and looking sheepish. 'You kept mumbling, "No doctor", but I was pretty sure you were going to pass out cold and I thought I'd better keep an eye on you. Gentlemen aren't allowed upstairs in the Barbizon, you know. So I took you here.'

'Oh!' I said, seized by a fresh rush of embarrassment. 'I fainted on you!' He chuckled and puffed up a bit at this.

'Good to see you again,' he said, reaching out a hand. 'Fainting aside.'

'Yes,' I replied, shaking his hand with a rather feeble grip. By then the fever had gone but I was still feeling very weak. Every muscle in my body quivered with that queer feeling you get after having a fever, as though they had all completely atrophied during the last twenty-four hours. 'I'll admit, I'm a bit mortified,' I said. 'I hope I didn't cause a scene.'

'Well, I got some funny looks carrying you down the elevator and through the lobby, but I wouldn't worry too much about it,' Cliff said. 'Fainting's nothing to be embarrassed about, especially for a woman.'

I nodded and began to sit up. I blushed again to realise I was wearing only a slip. I glanced around the room for my clothes and spotted them on the floor near the foot of the mattress, neatly folded, with my shoes lined up next to them. I swivelled in the bed to put my feet on the floor, but as I did, I bumped into something heavy and metal.

I looked down to see a row of canned goods stacked near the head of the mattress. 'Oops. Beg your pardon. What are *those*?'

'"What are *those*"?' Cliff snorted, his eyes wide with disbelief. 'Are you pulling my leg? You were asking for those all night. I had to go to three different grocers to find some.'

Utterly baffled, I squinted to get a closer look. 'Oh!' I exclaimed once I'd riddled out the labels. Stacked in front of me were several cans of Del Monte brand peaches and pears. '*I* asked for these?'

'Over and over,' Cliff said. 'You kept mumbling, "I need canned peaches and pears. Where are my canned peaches and pears?" So finally I went out and got some.' I chuckled. He peered at me. 'What's so funny?' he asked.

'I guess I was hallucinating after all. This is what my grandmother used to feed me when I was sick,' I said, picking up a can and smiling at the familiar logo. 'When I was a little girl. I guess she figured they were soft and mushy – easy to eat when you're sick – and I'm sure I liked the sweetness of the syrup. But, honestly, I don't remember asking for them last night. I'm so sorry; I must've been really quite ill.'

'Well, anyway,' Cliff said, shrugging, 'you asked for 'em, and here they are. How's about I fix you some now?' He lifted a can from the floor and moved to the kitchenette. 'You *were* pretty sick, and you haven't eaten anything in a while.'

I suddenly felt shy. 'Well, all right.' I watched as he cleaned out a bowl and opened the can and poured the contents in. He came over to the mattress and perched on the edge beside me, then handed me the bowl and a spoon. I thanked him, accepted the bowl, and took a nervous bite. He'd picked one of the cans containing pears, and the soft, grainy texture filled my mouth and slowly dissolved like sugary sand. A bit of juice dribbled down my chin and I quickly moved to wipe it away.

'Here,' he said, reaching for a shirt – one of his – and dabbing my chin as though the shirt were a napkin. I felt a rush of heat to my cheeks. 'Say, it looks like you're getting some of your colour back,' he commented.

'Yes. I'm feeling a little better,' I said, embarrassed.

'Your hair's awfully different these days.'

I put a self-conscious hand to my short hair. 'I cut it.'

'It suits you.'

'Thanks.'

'So,' Cliff said, 'what were you doing at old Bonwright, anyhow?'

'Oh,' I said, suddenly realising. 'I guess I'd better explain about that.'

29

CLIFF

When Eden told me she'd been working for My Old Man, it kind of blew me over sideways. It wasn't that it didn't make sense because when you thought about it, she worked in publishing and so did he, and the publishing world is a small place after all, so it shouldn't have come as such a surprise. The truth of it was I had put Eden in one part of my mind and My Old Man in the other and when they came together in my head it was all very disorienting.

'In a way, I have you to thank,' Eden said, sitting there in her slip on my mattress. This statement surprised me some more, because I couldn't think of why or how I'd played any part in My Old Man hiring her. As far as I knew I'd never had any influence on the stubborn bastard.

'That day at the Minetta Tavern,' she explained, 'you told me not to give up on finding another job, and you mentioned his secretary had quit.'

'Hmm, so I did,' I said, remembering.

'I didn't plan for it to work out this way, but I'm awful glad it has,' she said.

I tried to figure out if I was glad, too. Eden working for my father . . . There were reasons to feel jealous, maybe, but it was hard to determine which way around the jealousy went. Anyway, I knew I ought to be happy for Eden, because she was a smart girl and deserved to have the job she wanted. I told her she was welcome, and as I said it I decided it was true and a self-contented feeling came over me, having done something nice for someone else.

'There's another thing I ought to tell you . . . something I rather hope we can keep between us,' Eden said. I didn't have a clue in hell what she was talking about but it sounded like she was about to confide in me and I was intrigued. She went on and told me there'd been a woman at Torchon & Lyle who'd had it out for her – I remembered some of this from the day at the Minetta when she told me about her firing – and her confession now was that she'd wound up getting hired at Bonwright under a different last name. 'I hope you don't think awful things of me,' she said. 'At Bonwright . . . I'm "Eden Collins".'

'I don't think that's anything so terrible,' I reassured her. 'You got a bum rap with that Miss Everett, and you were clever enough to do something about it. The world doesn't cater to wallflowers or patsies.'

She smiled at me and I could see she was tremendously relieved.

She had been awful sick but now she was feeling better. After she got dressed and fixed herself up, I helped her get back to the Barbizon, and as we said goodbye in the lobby an old prude painted up with enough make-up to give Carmen Miranda a run for her money glared at me and reminded Eden that male visitors were not allowed upstairs. They'd done away with the curfews at the Barbizon but to see this woman you wouldn't think so. It was plain she was keeping track and had noticed Eden hadn't come home the night before and she was mad as hell that she wasn't allowed to give Eden a lecture or fine her or throw her out or whatever it was the Barbizon used to do to women of wanton ways. Not that Eden was a woman of wanton ways, but it was clear this hypocritical hawk of an old lady thought so. When I said goodbye to Eden I kissed her hand like a gentleman and threw in an exaggerated old-timey bow just to thumb my nose at the lady at the front desk.

'See you in the Village later this week?' I asked. 'How 'bout we bump into each other again on purpose, say at the White Horse on Friday?'

'Oh,' she said, biting her lip. 'I'm supposed to meet a girlfriend of mine. Is it all right if I bring her along?'

'Of course.'

'I'll be there.' She blushed again and I knew I had her on the hook.

Later, I wondered if she didn't have me on the hook, too, because I thought about her an awful lot all the rest of that week. I recalled the picture of her sitting there in her slip, perched on the edge of my mattress. On Friday I was intent on the White Horse and not even Bobby with his plans to round up a couple of gals for us dissuaded me. He knew right away something was fishy when I turned him down, because no one ever turned Bobby down when he invited a guy to go catting with him.

'Pal could use a girl,' I pointed out.

'Sure. Problem is Pal never knows what to do once he gets one,' Bobby said. 'I've done everything but gift wrap 'em for him.'

It took some convincing to get Bobby to give up on me but when I finally got him to leave my pad, I put on a clean shirt and combed my hair and went solo over to the White Horse. It was funny to feel so nervous over a girl. I left my tenement on the east side of the Village and hurried westward towards Hudson Street. It was a warm night and groups of fellas were milling about out in front of the bar with beers in their hands, their faces looking ghoulish whenever someone struck a match to light a cigarette. Sometimes the White Horse could be a rowdy place. It was always full to the brim with hipsters hopped up on bennies and beer.

'Cliff!' I heard a voice shout as soon as I walked in the door. I looked to my left and sitting in a booth in the next room was Swish. I hadn't expected to bump into him although I don't know why I hadn't thought of this, because Swish frequently went to the White Horse and he always sat in the booth where it was rumoured Dylan Thomas had drunk his final drink. Now there was nothing to do but make my way across the creaky wooden floor and join him.

Swish and I made small talk as I glanced periodically back into the main bar, checking for Eden.

'So, it looks like old Eisenhower is on board with the bill to sign Alaska into statehood,' Swish was saying. He had developed a recent fascination with Alaska after reading somewhere that there was a place in Alaska where you could stand and look out across the Bering Strait and see the USSR in the distance on the other side. Neither of us knew if there was any truth to this, but Swish insisted we ought to take a road trip as soon as possible to see for ourselves. 'As soon as you finish that novel of yours,' he was saying now. 'We'll go up there, Cliff old boy, and it'll be grand because you'll have a pile of money from publishing your genius book and we'll learn to hunt and live like kings and take a couple of Eskimo wives to cook up all the game we'll catch.'

'Sure, sure,' I said, looking again towards the bar's entrance.

Swish was always coming up with epic adventures, but so far we had yet to go on any of them.

'Say, who do you keep looking for, anyway?'

As if on cue, in walked Eden. The sweater sets she'd worn the first time we'd met were long gone – or at least she knew enough not to wear them down to the Village and instead she looked like a real bohemian chick now with her short, slick haircut and capri pants. With her was that gal, Judy something-or-other. I recognised her from the night we'd all gone to hear Bobby do a cold reading of his buddy's play. Eden glanced around the room with that intelligent, curious way she had and spotted me and Swish sitting in the next room.

'Hullo, hullo,' Swish said, waving them over. He was energised and happy to see Eden. But after we'd all said our hellos and settled back into the booth, Swish looked at me and cocked his head as a new thought occurred to him. His eyes slid from me over to Eden and back again and I believe in that second he'd caught the truth of it.

'How're you feeling?' I asked Eden. 'Have you made a full recovery?'

'Good as new.' She smiled. She and Judy exchanged knowing glances and it was plain that Eden had told Judy the story prior to their arrival. I hoped this meant Eden had put in a good word about how I'd been so thoughtful, taking care of her and bringing her those goddamned canned fruits. The way Eden blushed whenever she looked at me and chattered away nervously with her hands made me think she probably *had* talked me up, just as I'd hoped.

But either way, it didn't matter much to Judy, who was in an ornery mood that evening. She had on a little silver bracelet of a watch and she kept touching it and looking at it and twice she even showed it to Eden while wearing a little grimace on her face and it didn't take a genius to figure out that Judy had set a time limit on how long she wanted to spend with us bohemians down at the ol' White Horse. She thought the lot of us were beatniks and up to no good and Judy was the kind of girl who was out to snare a husband – or, at the very least, some martinis at a nice restaurant and plenty of change for the powder room.

The last straw came when Bobby turned up. At first, Judy perked right up at the sight of Bobby. I thought we were in luck, because it looked like Bobby hadn't successfully picked up any girls yet that evening. He came barrelling into the White Horse with another fella who looked a little like Marlon Brando and the pair of them together made for a sight that was rather easy on the eyes, and between the two of them I thought they ought to keep Judy occupied. They sat down to join us and for a short time Judy stopped looking at her watch. But then . . . it was clear Bobby and Brando were more interested in talking to each other than anyone else. Judy looked both disgusted and a little let down as the comprehension set in and even I sighed and felt bad for her.

Meanwhile, I was having a grand time talking to Eden. She'd matriculated from a small private women's college out in good old Indiana and even though I'd never heard of her alma mater, Eden had read a lot of good books and knew an awful lot about politics and current events, so I guess it must've been a pretty okay school in the end. But even with the mutual enthusiasm of our book banter I could sense I was running into a sort of wall. The wall was Judy and it was becoming evident that in order to get to Eden I needed to earn the approval of her friend. Now Judy was gathering up her pocketbook and getting ready to go, and if she did, she would likely bring Eden away with her. I had to think of something fast.

'Say,' I said, 'I wonder if you gals would help me out with something.'

'What's that?' Eden asked. Judy just looked at me dryly.

'Well, it's for my mother, really. She's throwing a charity luncheon tomorrow afternoon at the Cedarbrook Club and some people have dropped out at the last minute. She needs to fill up tables. If you two are free, you'd be doing me a real favour if you'd come occupy a table with me.'

'*The Cedarbrook Club?*' Judy's eyes went wide, as I knew they would. 'Isn't that the famous country club out in Connecticut?'

'Lunch would be on me, of course,' I said. This was only partly true, because strictly speaking lunch would be on my mother – or at least on her membership – but I figured the less I said about that, the better. 'All you'd have to do is show up and eat a Crab Louie salad and say hello to some people.'

'But would that mean saying hello to your mother?' Eden asked. 'Sure.'

'Won't she think it's funny? After all, I work for your father.'

'Nah, c'mon . . . she's pretty oblivious to all that. She won't know if we don't tell her. She'll probably just think I finally found myself a nice date I can bring around. She'll be friendly, I promise.'

I could tell this flattered Eden. She bit her lip and exchanged a look with Judy, politely checking with her friend for permission.

'Well, yes,' Judy said finally. 'I suppose we could go. I've never been to the Cedarbrook, but I've heard plenty about it.'

'Swell,' I said. 'I'll borrow a car, and pick you gals up at the Barbizon at noon.'

Judy was still all packed up and ready to split, but at least now

I had an assurance I would see Eden the next day. They asked me a few questions about whether it was formal and what to wear, which is natural, I guess, because girls are always worrying about things like that. I answered their questions but the truth is I didn't know for sure. My mother *had* invited me but I hadn't been planning on going and now I would have to telephone her first thing tomorrow morning and tell her I'd changed my mind.

30

EDEN

'Here I am!' Judy sang out as she hurried into the lobby of the Barbizon. She was dressed very smartly in a little blue rayon-crêpe number with a full skirt and a wide cherry-coloured belt cinched around her waist. We kissed each other hello and when she wasn't looking I rubbed a bit of red lipstick from my cheek.

'Hadn't we better wait outside by the curb?' she asked.

'Let's.'

She was excited, I knew, because she was eager to be able to say she had been to the Cedarbrook. Cliff's generous invitation had warmed her to him a bit. 'If he belongs to the Cedarbrook, he can't be all bad,' she said after we'd left the White Horse. 'I still don't see why he runs around with those hooligans in the Village. But perhaps we'll meet some nice people today.' By nice people, Judy meant nice men.

'How are things at work?' I asked Judy now as we stood on the sidewalk, squinting into the sunshine.

'Oh, fine, I guess,' she replied in a bored voice.

'How is . . . Miss Everett?' I asked. I was burning with curiosity for the gossip, but in attempting to bring up Miss Everett's name, I suddenly felt very shy.

'Oh, you know.' Judy shrugged. 'Still a bitch, striking terror into the hearts of young girls.'

I laughed, oddly gratified to hear it.

'Actually, though,' Judy continued, cocking her head, 'she complained so much, they finally let her have a reader officially assigned to help her exclusively. Bitsy-something. And would you believe, Miss Everett seems to like her! Says she's the best reader the company's ever had.'

A strange pang went through me.

'She's so odd,' I said, shaking my head, attempting to keep my voice normal. 'I don't understand her. She really had it out for me, and I didn't do anything at all to her. Remember how hard I worked, staying late all those nights? Why, I wasn't even *her* secretary, technically speaking!'

'Mmm-hmm,' Judy said in a faraway, distracted voice, producing a compact from her pocketbook and powdering her nose. I could tell she was far less interested in affirming the injustice of my dismissal than she was in her reflection.

'Why do you think she did something that outrageous?' I insisted.

Judy snapped the compact shut. 'Well, I've told you my theories. Look, Eden, it's best to just forget about her. Who knows why she does anything at all, the bitter old maid.'

I couldn't help but recall all the terrible things Miss Everett had done, exploiting Mr Frederick's misconduct and ultimately Mr Turner's bigotry to get me fired. Suddenly a thought occurred to me, and I felt a small shiver of panic.

'Judy . . .' I said. 'Do you think this is the kind of country club that doesn't . . . that doesn't . . .' I tried to think of how to phrase it, but was rapidly failing '. . . allow certain *kinds* of people to join?'

Judy blinked at me, a blank expression on her face. 'Oh,' she said, comprehending my meaning. 'Oh, I wouldn't worry about that. You're "Eden Collins" now, aren't you? Besides, you're very clever. No one will even know.'

She'd said it to reassure me, but it had the effect of making me even more uncomfortable, like she'd missed the point entirely.

Just then a flashy sports car pulled to the curb, and in it we spotted Cliff. He honked and jumped out to open the door for us. 'Hullo, ladies!' he called. I had to admit, he looked rather dashing in a jacket and tie. 'Hop in.' We did, and he hustled around to the driver's seat with an athletic spring in his step.

'Where did you get the car?' Judy enquired, admiring the look of it.

'Buddy of mine from Columbia,' Cliff answered. 'Guy named Rex.' He turned over his shoulder to look at Judy in the back seat. 'Say, I oughta introduce you two sometime; you'd like him.' He winked, and we zoomed away from the curb.

The drive out to the Cedarbrook Club was pleasant. It had been some months since I had been out of the city, and I had forgotten how nice it could be to ride along in a car, watching houses and little wooded areas fly by. Judy kept the conversation going by asking Cliff a few more questions about the mystery owner of the car, but I contented myself by staring, trance-like, out the window. When we arrived at Cedarbrook, we were stopped by a guard at a little gatehouse, and Cliff produced a membership card. Then he steered the car along a little ribbon of road as it wound through what felt like miles and miles of golf greens.

'Ah, yes, here we are. The Old Lady's stomping grounds,' he announced, pulling up to an imposing Georgian building that, I assumed, served as the main clubhouse. 'I tell ya,' he said to me, 'she'll be delighted I've come, and that I've brought along such classy company.'

A young, pimply boy drove the car away, leaving us to make our way inside. Most of the clubhouse was rather old-fashioned. Marble and heavy wood, and that purposely drab variety of library furniture seemingly preferred by wealthy people everywhere. But the dining room where Cliff's mother was hosting her luncheon was newly renovated, very modern, and quite smart, panelled in blonde wood and covered in wall-to-wall pink carpeting.

Cliff was quick to get a couple of cocktails in our hands. 'What's the use of being at a country club if we can't toss back a few free martinis?' he joked. Shortly thereafter, we went looking for our place cards and found our table.

'There you are!' a tall, elegant, frosty-blonde woman said, floating over to us. She planted a kiss of air on Cliff's cheek. 'Honestly, Clifford, I'm still in a state of shock. You've never come to one of my luncheons.'

Cliff smiled, clearly embarrassed. 'I wouldn't say *never*,' he replied.

'No . . .' she said, an amused smile playing on her lips as she inspected first Judy, then me. 'Well, I shan't say it ever again.' Reading the subtle cues of her son's body language, she turned to me and held out a hand. 'Doris Nelson, how do you do?'

'Mother, this is Eden Collins,' Cliff introduced me. Upon hearing my first name, Eden, not a single flicker of recognition passed over her face. I was relieved. Cliff continued. 'And Judy . . .' He paused, realising he did not know Judy's last name.

'Wheaton,' Judy supplied.

'Wheaton, how lovely,' Doris purred. 'And such a fresh face, wholesome as the wheat itself.'

'Why, thank you,' Judy replied. She was gazing at the diamonds in Mrs Nelson's ears with stunned wonder.

I was surprised. Doris Nelson had struck me as a cold, unfriendly woman over the phone. But here she was, elegant and warm, and clearly full of philanthropic spirit; the luncheon doubled as a fundraiser for an orphanage in a nearby town.

'I'm so delighted you've come,' she said now, smiling in my direction. 'You managed to get my Clifford out to the club on a weekend!' She chatted with us for a few more minutes and floated away – purely due to obligation, she assured us – to mingle with the guests who'd bought tickets and were donating to the orphanage.

We sat at a large round table with five other guests. Either Cliff had contrived for the arrangement of our place cards or else he had gotten very lucky: immediately to the left of Judy's elbow was a handsome young law student named Chester. Five minutes into the meal, Cliff and I were left to make much of our own conversation. I got to know a great deal more about him. In particular, I admired his determination to become a writer, especially given that he had Roger Nelson for a father. I knew first-hand Roger Nelson cast a long shadow and was not an easy man to impress. And I felt Cliff and I had something important in common: we both straddled the publishing world and the grittier world of the Village.

'Thank you for coming,' Cliff said after we had gotten through soup and salad and reached the dessert course. 'Are you having any fun at all?'

'Oh, tons,' I said. 'It's so nice here, and I've really enjoyed our conversation together.' We exchanged bashful smiles and a lingering gaze.

* * *

Later that evening, once Cliff had dropped Judy off at her women's hotel and me back at the Barbizon, I telephoned Judy so that we might gossip about our day. She and Chester had already made plans to have dinner the next night, and Judy recited the laundry list of personal details she'd gleaned about him over lunch. I shyly brought up Cliff.

'He's awfully sweet on you, Eden!' she said over the line.

'Really, you think so?'

'Mmm-hmm. And you know, you could do a whole lot worse than to wind up with a fella whose parents belong to the Cedarbrook Club.'

'Oh, but the future . . . I don't see how it could work out!' I said.

'Why not? What's the problem?'

'Well, for starters, I'm his father's secretary. I doubt Mrs Nelson would like that much. I'm sure she would much prefer Cliff date a girl who's never worked a day in her life: a society girl like herself. And as for Mr Nelson . . . well, say things got serious . . .'

'Yeah?'

'Well, I probably couldn't work at Bonwright any more. How could I? And Mr Nelson would be awful mad if I quit to run off and marry his son.'

'Oh, *pshhh*!' Judy scoffed. 'It'll be a fun detail in the story of how you two met – you know, something to tell the grandkids. Roger and Doris . . . they'd both get over it as soon as the first baby turns up. Besides . . . if Cliff's father is the way Cliff says he is, well, then maybe it serves him right for not paying very much attention to his son!'

'Gosh, I hope that's not what Cliff sees in me,' I said. 'You don't think that's it, do you?'

'Are you kidding me?' Judy said. 'The way he looks at you with little stars in his eyes? Not a chance.' There was a pause, and I could tell she was fiddling around with something – perhaps a nail file – in the background, which she put down. 'Listen, Eden,' she said, her voice growing serious, 'I think it's admirable that you have your aspirations about becoming an editor, but what if that never happens? Or what if it does and you find you're not fulfilled by it? Don't you want to take out some insurance on your own happiness?'

'What are you getting at?'

'I'm just saying, you've complained a lot about how Mr Nelson doesn't seem like he ever intends to promote you. And you already know what it's like other places; I don't need to remind you about Miss Everett, and there are plenty like her out there. Maybe it's time to, you know, *cultivate* some backup options. It couldn't hurt. If you like this Clifford character, maybe that's not the worst thing you could do.'

I was quiet, thinking about this.

'All I mean to say is that I know you're a career gal, sure, but I also think every woman should live up to her potential, and you'd make a good wife if you wanted to, Eden,' Judy said. 'Honest, I mean that as a compliment. And what does Cliff want to do anyway? Be a writer, right? I don't see how being an editor is that different from being a writer's wife. Don't most writers' wives type up all their husbands' work and edit it, too?'

'I suppose so . . .'

'Anyway,' Judy said, her tone suddenly shifting. 'I hope you don't mind me speaking my mind. Listen, I'd better go soon. There's another girl who wants to use the phone.'

'All right. Goodnight, Judy.'

I hung up, but Judy's argument stayed on my mind. I was certainly attracted to Cliff, and it seemed he was attracted to me.

And he was very determined to make something of himself; perhaps it might be exciting, after all, to be a writer's wife. Judy had a point: a writer's wife *was* a first editor of sorts.

I laughed out loud when I realised I was getting ahead of myself. Cliff, after all, hadn't even asked me out on a date yet.

31

CLIFF

I proposed to Eden during the summer of '58, not long after our first date. The whole marriage business was spontaneous as hell and I hadn't ever really pictured myself married, but I liked Eden and together we liked to laugh and shake our hips in spastic ecstasy to bop and, of course, we had a dandy time in the sack. But mostly I married her because it made me heartsick to think of her marrying someone else.

There was also some business with My Old Man – not about him cutting me off but about all that Brooklyn business I mentioned – that Eden understood. I'd never told anybody about the time when I was eleven and I followed My Old Man on the train out to Bensonhurst and what I'd seen once I got there. But I told Eden about it one day when we were lying naked together in the middle of the afternoon with sunshine pouring through the bars of my studio's little window. We both had our eyes closed when I told her the story and she intuited enough about me to stroke my arm as I talked to let me know she was awake and listening and hearing all of it but she also knew enough never to bring it up again in any of our other conversations and I figured a man could do a lot worse than to marry a girl with this quality.

When I asked her to marry me Eden's eyes grew big and bright and excited, but of course Eden being Eden, she had a hell of a lot of questions about how things would work. *Would we tell our folks and should she keep working for My Old Man and what about her name and blah, blah, blah,* and before too long it became obvious that we weren't planning a wedding so much as an elopement. But if I'm being honest, an elopement suited me just fine and it suited Eden, too; I didn't want or need her to quit her job at ol' Bonwright, and she didn't want to, either. The things we liked about each other were tangled up in our ambitions, and our ambitions were tangled up in each other, too, but of course we hardly knew it at the time.

Eden felt awfully guilty about the fact she would have to miss some work but eventually I managed to convince her to give My Old Man some line about visiting her sick aunt back in Indiana and before too long we were making plans to go down to City Hall and Bobby was composing a little song for us on his guitar and Pal was writing a special poem for our day and calling it an *epithalamium*, which I was too embarrassed to admit I had to look up in the dictionary in order to find out was the Greek term for a wedding poem.

Seeing as how our folks weren't invited that day, it was just Bobby and Swish and Pal and a handful of other people from the cafe circuit, and of course Eden's friend Judy, slicked up in her red lipstick, wringing Chester's arm with excitement and jumping up and down, eager to catch the bouquet. There we were, standing around at City Hall, all of us looking a little thin and lanky in the photographs that were taken that day, as though we were all just young pups still waiting to grow into our bodies and tripping over our feet in the meantime. Swish with his madman hair and leathery face from all the hobo-ing and Bobby standing loose at the hips with that glint in his eye and his Golden Boy looks and Pal with those long, black lashes and shy smile and me and Eden and our nervous half-smiles walking wobbly-kneed like a pair of foals as if it were our first time for everything all over again.

The whole group saw us off later when Eden and I boarded the bus at Port Authority for Niagara and threw rice and called out sweet and sincere encouragements to us. As I waved goodbye to the group of them I caught Swish's eye and for the most fleeting of seconds I saw a hint of something rueful there and I knew all too well this was about how Swish felt about Eden and how I'd been a bit of a bastard to come between them. When the bus's engine roared to life I looked back and it was gone, and a week later when Eden and I returned from our honeymoon I looked for it again in Swish's gaze, but if it had ever truly been there, by then he had decided to let it go and I believe in the spirit of a true friend he had decided to occupy himself with other things and never again gave it much thought.

When we got back to New York, Eden packed up her two suitcases at the Barbizon and deposited them in my little studio in the Village. I made a jokey show of carrying my bride over the threshold and this made us both laugh and together we had ourselves a second honeymoon on the mattress on the floor.

32

Eden was very much in favour of my idea of becoming a writer and the idea was we were going to settle down together and I was going to spend my days writing while she worked at Bonwright and then in the evenings she would come home and type up everything I had written that day and we would make love and bask in the assurance that good things had been written and that we were living out the script of what was destined to become a chapter in literary history. It was a good plan except the words did not come to me right away and during the first couple days when I hadn't written anything and Eden had come home, ready to type, we had made love anyway and afterwards she stroked my hair and told me the words would come and said perhaps I was just a night-time writer and didn't know it yet. Then she would stand in front of the hot plate in the little kitchenette and boil some coffee as the light from the streetlamps glanced off her smooth-bodied nakedness and dark, liquid hair. I enjoyed balling her tremendously and afterwards I always felt light and hungry and hollow and spent in a way I'd never felt with anyone who had come before her.

I would lie there watching her boiling the coffee in the dark and feel I had done a good thing in marrying her. Eden was a small girl but nevertheless was very long in the torso and despite her slenderness her hips flared in a beautiful, generous way and in the phosphorescent light of the streetlamps she looked like something on loan to me from another planet and maybe also another era, too, and it was all very surreal. When she had finished with the hot plate she would snap the electric lights on and put the coffee in front of me and I would go to the desk to sit and stare into the dim pages of the notebook that had all day lain empty. Eden would shimmy her shoulders into the tattered silk robe she had bought on a whim one day while in Chinatown and had worn every day thereafter and then she would pick up a book or a manuscript and quietly read with the idea that we should let inspiration take its course.

Eden always reminded me I had written two stories I liked very much and if I could write two good stories, then I was capable of writing more and even better and it was just a matter of coming up with the right strategy for unblocking my creativity. Being that we ran with a bohemian crowd, naturally Eden was open to all kinds of solutions to my writer's block, but I had to draw the line when she started harping about how I ought to go see a head-shrinker. Lots of people in our circle were going to shrinks in those days and reporting back wondrous things, but if you ask me, the ones who said all the best things about being in analysis were women and queers who had sex problems. I didn't have a sex problem and didn't see how a shrink could help me be a better writer and after a few disagreements on this subject I got Eden to lay off about the whole business.

The other major theme that turned up often in our disagreements was Rusty. After Eden and I were married, it wasn't long before Rusty turned up again. Eden detested him from the first second she laid eyes on him and this was partly because when Rusty showed up on the stoop he expected me to drop whatever I was doing and take him all over the city to get some kicks on my dime, which was really *our* dime now, Eden's and mine. At one point Eden threatened me with the prospect of having to go out and take a day-job if I didn't stop blowing all our rent money on that whiney sonofabitch. That Whiney Sonofabitch was Eden's name for Rusty when Rusty was not around. When he was around she never said a bad word to his face and was just as nice to him as I was and I realised the aura of Rusty's boss had gotten to her, too, and she was afraid to ruin my prospects if she told Rusty where he could go stuff it. Neither of us could be sure whether Rusty truly planned to hand my stories over to the famous literary agent but the simple thought of it alone was enough to put us on our best behaviour.

At one point Rusty told us he had given the pages to his boss but then he said his boss had taken the train up to Westchester and had accidentally left them on the train and would we mind typing up new copies for Rusty to give him. Of course we said we didn't mind at all and Eden set about typing the new copies right away. Rusty said the agent had read and finished one of the two stories and that he had liked what he had read. I thought that this was incredible news. I asked Rusty which one but Rusty couldn't remember and then each time we saw him after that he had forgotten to check with the agent which one it was.

'He's bluffing,' Eden said one evening while we were alone. 'He hasn't given anyone anything.'

This was likely true but in the moment I hated her for saying it all the same.

'Rusty isn't lobbying for anybody but himself,' she continued.

'Well, I think that's a case of the pot calling the kettle black,' I said.

'What do you mean?'

I shrugged. '*You* work at Bonwright. It's not as if you're arguing my case to My Old Man, now, are you?'

She froze where she stood ironing a shirt with her big eyes blinking at me and I could tell the thought had never even occurred to her.

'You . . . you don't honestly think I ought to do that, do you?' she asked.

'No,' I said, but I had to think about my answer for several minutes because when I pondered it I realised maybe I *did* think she ought to. She could somehow bring my talents to his attention, say . . . somehow get him to read my story that was about to run in *The Tuning Fork*, even if she had to play dumb about our marriage or go about it anonymously.

I kept this idea to myself but it only made a certain amount of sense. Now that we were hitched she ought to understand that what was good for me was also good for her. I had helped her win the job with My Old Man by tipping her off in the first place and she had even said herself she ought to thank me for it. Besides all that, she had technically lied to My Old Man about her name and I'd kept that secret for her, too. All and all, I'd been a bang-up husband if there ever was one, and what was the harm in a wife helping out her husband, anyway?

33

MILES

'You've saved up enough money to go now, haven't you?' Janet asked in a quiet voice.

We were sitting on a bench in our usual spot: the north-easternmost end of Central Park, by the Harlem Meer, the little duck pond that bordered 110th Street. I turned to meet her gaze, but she was staring out over the water, so I observed her profile. She had a very long, regal neck. I hadn't ever taken close note of this distinctive feature before. In fact, the more I looked at her, the more I was impressed by the fact I'd never noticed how much she resembled some kind of tall, graceful variety of bird. She wore her hair slightly curled and clipped short to her head, possessed a small forehead and chin and a triangular, beak-like nose. Her eyes were large, wide, and up-tilted, like that famous bust of Nefertiti. She was, paradoxically, both meek looking and expressive at the same time.

'It's difficult to know how much will be enough,' I said. 'But I suppose, yes, I think I've got enough saved now to make the trip.'

'When will you leave?'

'I'm not sure yet. I've . . . well, I've got to give notice,' I said.

'That old man is certainly paying you a lot of money.'

'Yes. He is. I've been lucky,' I said. She shot me a look I couldn't read. 'Maybe he'll want to rehire me when I get back to New York,'

I continued, hoping to encourage her. 'And we'll have enough to get married saved up in no time at all.'

'No. There'll be other jobs,' Janet said with sombre conviction. 'I wouldn't want you to work for him again.'

I nodded. To my surprise, I agreed with her. While I'd grown to like Mister Gus, there was a strange kind of comfort in knowing my employment with him was only temporary. It was his overwhelming loneliness, perhaps, that unnerved me. I felt sorry for him, but it was almost as if I believed his loneliness to be contagious, and some primal instinct signalled to me that I ought to avoid catching it.

'You'll tell me, though, won't you?' she asked. 'When you buy your ticket to leave?'

'Of course.' Her concern was endearing. 'Of course I'll tell you,' I repeated.

'And you'll say goodbye?'

'Yes, of course; that, too. And you realise I'll be back before you know it, right?'

I reached for her hand, and she instantly folded her face into my chest. I put an arm around her and attempted to comfort her. She had the fine, thin bones of a bird, too, and her skin was perpetually cool to the touch.

'Don't you . . .' she said, in a tiny voice, muffled by my shirt, '. . . don't you want to try it . . . just once, before you go?'

She was talking about being together. I knew this was so, because she talked about being together quite a lot lately. A modest girl and a virgin to boot, she had become inexplicably fixated on the idea that we should make love before I departed for California. I wasn't sure what to make of this. It struck me as an act of girlish desperation, not that of an adult woman who was full of desire and acting on her own volition.

It worried me. I was worried the timing was wrong. I was worried we wouldn't be enough for each other. I was worried I would fail her somehow – not in any of those trite physical ways, but worse: in some way neither of us would be able to face or put a name on.

First encounters were bound to be a bit of a let-down, and I didn't want Janet's first time to be like mine. I'd lost my virginity not long after my father died. Anxious to get the act over with, I had cast my eye around and wound up going to bed with a neighbourhood friend, a big-hipped, bosomy girl named Leota who was three years my senior. Leota was the first woman I'd ever known to wear a 'fall', a sort of false-hair contraption that she daily clipped into her own short hair, which she wore brushed flat to her skull and pinned up in a tiny bun that was – more often than not – only half-concealed by the fall. The resultant effect was something of a perky, cascading ponytail with an odd nub of hair poking out from the top. Like the other neighbourhood girls, Leota had always flirted with me in that hollow, benign way, and yet while the other girls skittered away after making their bold offers, Leota gave me the impression she might be willing to take things further, if only to satisfy a bet she had with herself about me.

My overtures were brief; I invited Leota to come over to my family's apartment one summer day when I knew my mother and Wendell would be out, and bravely slipped a hand under her blouse. I found she was not only willing but enthusiastic about the matter. She was already experienced in the act of love, as girls whose bodies blossom at an early age often are, and I recall the air of absolute practicality she conveyed as she removed her fall from her hair just before we embarked upon our joint endeavour. A short time later, once the act had been completed, she stood before the bureau clipping it back in. Her eyes slid from where she worked the clips into her hair to my face as it was reflected in the mirror, and I sensed she was figuring out something about me in her mind, something she had never directly acknowledged before. At the termination of our lovemaking I had very quickly slipped my undershirt back over my head and tugged my shorts on. But now, as Leota looked at me where I sat with the rumpled sheets caught in the waistband of my shorts, my legs hanging awkwardly over the side of the bed (my socks, in an absurd comical twist, had never left my feet throughout the entire episode), I suddenly felt undressed and exposed. For a fleeting moment she narrowed her eyes at me in the mirror and it was as if she were already trying to review the session of what had just happened between us, trying to recall the phantom shape of my manhood inside her – as if in doing so she might uncover the shape of what was in my heart.

'Huh,' was finally all she said, snapping the last clip into place and picking up her purse to go.

After that, Leota seemed to understand something about me, something I'm not certain I even understood about myself at the time. Our interlude was a secret we kept between the two of us, and we remained friends, exchanging relaxed smiles and saying hello whenever we saw each other at school or around the neighbourhood. I even danced with her once or twice at the local dance hall, but our interactions were brief and polite; never again did she unclip that fall from her hair in my honour.

I'd had other encounters with women since. Women liked me, were charmed by me, but even when they were willing to go to bed they maintained another kind of distance. None of my escapades translated into anything lasting. Janet was the first woman I'd met with whom I could picture a future. She was bright and wanted to be a schoolteacher. She was sensitive to the world around her; she looked more closely and listened more carefully than most people.

And she gracefully accepted the facts of life she could not change, a skill I had never mastered but always coveted.

No, I would not disappoint Janet, I thought to myself. Not over a matter that could be remedied with simple patience.

'Darling, you know we have no place to go,' I pointed out. It was true; I didn't care to repeat the experience I'd had with Leota at my mother's apartment – nor did I think I could ensure its vacancy these days – and the apartment where Janet lived was packed to the hilt with three adults and four children.

'I know,' she said in a dull voice.

'Let's have something special to share when I get back,' I said, giving her a reassuring squeeze. 'Something to look forward to, something just for you and me.'

'All right, Miles,' she said. 'You know best.' She sniffed and stiffened her jaw and moved her face away from my chest. Two little stains from where her eyes had watered up marked my shirt, but when I looked at her, she did not appear to have been crying. Perhaps it was just the wind or the awkward angle of our embrace. Either way, her eyes were dry now and she was looking away again, out over the duck pond.

'I'm looking forward to when you get back,' she said.

'Me, too,' I replied.

I glanced at the park around us. It was beautiful, newly lit up with autumnal colour. I remember summer ended that year the way it always did in Manhattan: in an effusion of smouldering oranges and otherworldly yellows that always sent a pang to the heart.

34

If I was indeed going to make the trip to California, it meant I had to give Mister Gus my notice. I was dreading this task, for I knew he would consider it an act of betrayal. I offered to give him a full month if he liked, during which I could recommend another messenger boy who might appreciate the extra work.

'Hmph,' he said, and muttered something under his breath to the effect of 'Serves me right for overpaying you.' He refused to allow me to help him arrange for my replacement, and told me to merely finish out the week.

As my final day approached, he grew more and more quiet, and looked off into the distance more than was typically his custom. Every so often his lips would twitch and he would draw in breath as though to speak, but no words followed. He seemed perpetually on the verge of saying something, if only he could remember what it was.

Finally, on my penultimate day, a front-page headline in the *Post* gave him his opportunity. I remember it was one of those overcast, warm autumn days in Manhattan when sunny skies suddenly fill with lightning, rain, and mosquitoes. The city smelt of wet leaves, clouds pressing low overhead like a flat grey ceiling. That morning I retrieved the papers as normal and set about dusting and tidying his bedroom as he sifted through them. He was in a cantankerous mood, and he mostly ignored me at first, grumbling about the papers being wet even though I had taken care to keep them dry and had tucked them under my raincoat on my walk back from the news stand.

He asked for a towel, which I brought to him, and as he made his way through the stack of newspapers he pretended to sponge imaginary water from the pages of each one. When he got to the *Post*, he put down the towel, clucked his tongue, and harrumphed loudly. This was not a complaint about the paper being damp. I knew from a quick perusal on my way back from the news stand that he was looking at a front-page story about two men who had been found murdered near the Ramble in Central Park. It was a sensational, violent story. The men had been beaten to death, and the killer – or *killers*, as it appeared to have been a group – were still at large. The paper implied the two men had been found in an indecent state, but did not name the details – I can only assume to avoid a libel suit.

'Hmph,' Mister Gus grunted. He shook the newspaper to snap more stiffness back into the folded pages. 'Did you see this, boy?'

I nodded.

'Well?'

'Well, sir?'

'Well, what do you think?'

'I suppose it's a shame,' I said. I did not want to discuss the headline, but Mister Gus had clenched his jaw and I knew this meant the course of conversation was set. He would not be dissuaded.

'And exactly which part would you say is shameful?' he pressed. I knew I needed to proceed carefully. When it came to questions of morality, Mister Gus could be very severe. He was the type of person who needed others to agree with him, and took it as a personal affront when they did not. At the same time, I had my suspicions about Mister Gus, but he was very secretive about his past, and nothing concrete had surfaced to absolutely tip my final judgement one way or another.

'Which part would you say is shameful?' he repeated.

'All of it, I suppose,' I said, hoping this was diplomatic enough to satisfy him. 'It's a shame.' Unfortunately, now I had his full attention. Mister Gus lowered the paper to his lap, cocked his head to the side, and narrowed his eyes at me.

'And do you believe the police will apprehend the men who committed this murder?'

'I suppose they'll try,' I said.

'Oh yes,' said Mister Gus, 'they'll *try*. But will they make an arrest?'

'I don't know.'

He lifted the paper again. 'It says here there's reason to believe the victims were engaged in deviant behaviour at the time of their beating, and had communist sympathies. What do you think of that?'

I shrugged.

'It would be rather difficult, don't you think, for the authorities to know *what* these two men were doing at the time of their beating? Unless they were omniscient – which I assure you, most policemen are not – or are speculating, or else had talked to the thugs who beat these two men to death.'

I didn't answer. Instead, I turned to open the curtains and proceeded to fluff the pillows on the divan positioned beneath the giant windowsill. I was aware we were hurdling towards some sort of intersection I had hoped to avoid. Looking back now, I always knew the truth about Mister Gus's life and about the source of his bitterness.

'Central Park,' he said, 'has a funny history. Especially the Ramble. Have you ever ventured into that part of the park around evening time, boy?'

'Not on purpose,' I said, a little too quickly. He gave me a long, assessing, disappointed look. I could tell he thought – mistakenly, I might add – that I was lying.

'So you've seen what goes on in that tunnel in the park, eh?'

I nodded. He rolled his eyes at the coffered ceiling and chuckled.

'Perhaps it's a rite of passage; after all, we know as far as shepherds go, the Good Lord quite enjoys playing the occasional practical joke on his flock.' As he turned to me the bitter pinch of his smile turned my stomach. 'I saw the same thing, too, back when I was still a boy,' he continued. 'Happened upon a couple of young men in the throes of it while out taking a walk with my father. You can't begin to imagine my embarrassment.' His milky eyes focused on some invisible object upon the far wall of the bedroom. 'My father . . . my father was disgusted. "Nothing for it," he said to me. "Sodomites will always find one another in every city. You can't keep them apart; it's part of their wretched nature."' He paused. 'He was right, you know. We *will* always find one another, because – like all animals prowling this earth – we cannot bear to believe we are the only ones of our kind.'

He'd used the word *we*, and I felt a cold shock go through me as I picked up on this brazen admission. He sat up and leant forward over the bed, away from his nest of pillows. I could see the tendons straining in his neck to hold him up where his muscles failed. His beady blue-grey eyes grew very round, and his voice suddenly became a loud, pleading hiss.

'I say this to you: choose it, boy! Choose it before it chooses you. Because it will. You think there's a way it won't, that somehow there's a way to live your life so you won't ever catch its eye, but it will and you can't. So choose. Choose while you're young and you can believe in someone and can make it last a little while. That little while is the only eternity any of us mortals ever get to have. Don't let fate do the choosing for you; don't wait until you're old and desperate – and *wretched*, as my father declared, for he wasn't wrong – and you're left to fumble in terrible places and it's only your body . . . yes, only your body trying to prove to the soul that it's not alone, and failing time and time again.'

I looked at him; his bottom lip was trembling, and I understood there was love in his plea. Not for me but for someone else, someone from his past or – even likelier still – for some younger, earlier, as-yet-unspoiled version of himself. I was touched by the strength of his plea, and for a moment that seemingly bottomless wellspring of knee-jerk repulsion within me ceased to flow over. I thought, for a moment, to admit to understanding what he was talking about. I even thought, in a fleeting impulse of optimism, to promise him I would heed his words and try to do as he said.

But less than twenty seconds ticked by before my thoughts automatically and reactively shifted to my mother. My mother, who had lost first Marcus, the brave son, and then my father, the soldier she'd married in dress uniform. In my role as second son I had always attempted to fill the vacancies left behind by these two men, at times trying to be the role model to Cob I am certain Marcus would have been to me, at other times trying to hold my mother's hand when Wendell was too drunk or absent or bitter to prop her up, and ultimately proving myself a piss-poor replacement on both fronts. Now I stared into Mister Gus's eyes, thinking of my mother and of Cob, and a door within me very firmly closed.

'You'll have to forgive me, Mister Gus,' I said. 'I'm not as educated as you are in the ways of the world; I'm not sure I know what you're talking about.'

He sat there for a moment, blinking, the intelligent light that had burnt so fiercely during his speech slowly dying from his eyes.

'I see,' he said finally.

During the rest of the day he left me alone to complete my minor chores in silence. He stared out the window and watched the rain falling. When it came time to bring in his supper for the evening, he gave the tray a weary glance and pushed it to the side altogether.

'Sir? You've been quiet. Are you all right?' I asked.

'Go home, Mr Tillman,' he said. It was the first time he had called me anything other than 'boy', and it caught me off guard.

'But you'll need someone to take away the dishes. And also . . . there's still . . . your bath.'

'I said GO HOME!' he yelled. His volume was surprising; I hadn't thought him capable of shouting so loudly.

We locked eyes, and in that moment we understood each other perfectly. 'As you wish, sir,' I said finally. I put down the napkin I'd been holding out to him and moved in the direction of the door, then hesitated.

'I'm sure you'll be glad when you have a new boy to assist you,' I said. I was trying to be cheerful; it was a peace offering, but I could tell he took it the wrong way. I attempted to smile but was brought up short by the expression on Mister Gus's face. He had always looked old, but now he looked older than I'd ever seen him look; his countenance was nothing short of a death mask. It was an expression beyond sadness, as though he'd been hollowed out. I recognised him for what he was: a dying animal, helpless and full of pathos, but one that could only lash out if I got any closer.

I regarded him for a moment, then turned and walked out. We did not speak after that. On my last day, we spent the entire day in silence. On my way out the door, I found an envelope with my name scrawled on the outside and a one-hundred-dollar bill inside.

35

EDEN

All at once, Cliff had a breakthrough. I didn't know what set him off, but something had. He'd been suffering with a terrible bout of writer's block, until one day I came home from the office to find him writing furiously, sheaves of paper strewn around him as though a tiny bomb had gone off. It was like a scene out of a play or a movie: the frustrated artist suddenly finds inspiration and, looking half-mad, begins to churn out his vision as quickly as possible. I gasped and clapped my hands together.

'Shall we celebrate?' I asked.

'I'll go for it,' he said, meaning the bottle of wine. 'I want to see as much of this in type as soon as possible. Do you mind?'

'Oh.' I hesitated, comprehending. 'Sure. Here.' I pulled a five-dollar bill out of my pocketbook and handed it to him, hoping he wouldn't spend it all. He dashed out to go around the corner to the liquor store and I did my best to gather the pages strewn about the floor and put them in order.

By the time he came back I'd gotten the Smith Corona set up on the card table, all ready to go. 'Is it—?'

'A novel? You're goddamned right it is,' Cliff said, grinning. 'I knew it was just a matter of time before I started one, and here we are!' Standing over by the kitchenette, he struggled a bit with the bottle he'd bought and a loud POP! sounded as a champagne cork flew up and ricocheted off the ceiling, nearly putting the sole overhead light bulb out. He poured a generous dose of the golden bubbly liquid into a mug and I reached a hand out, assuming this was for me.

'Ah-ah,' Cliff chided, shaking his head. 'Let's get the typing done first. It's important that it's typed up in tip-top form.'

I looked at him. 'All right,' I said after a short pause, not wanting to start an argument. I understood he'd been blocked for quite a while and was likely letting his excitement get the better of him. And more than anything else I was excited *for* him. I gathered up the pages of longhand and tapped them into neat alignment on the card table. I checked to make sure the typewriter ribbon was in good shape, rolled a clean sheet of paper into place, and tapped the carriage return lever to move the roller all the way over to the right.

'And off we go!' I said, winking at Cliff. He grinned even wider and took a heavy swig from his mug.

'Eden old girl, it's too soon to say, but I really think I've done it!'

'I can't tell you how happy I am to hear it, Cliff.'

I began typing. He sat there drinking and watching as I worked. I took my time, typing with painstaking care and reading as I went along. The story was a little disjointed and I couldn't quite follow the plot. It appeared to be, I realised with a tiny cringe, a novel of self-examination narrated by a young man during his college years. A few times I checked to make sure I'd put the pages in the right order. I knew Cliff's composition was in its early stages and I didn't want to discourage him. If, down the road, he wanted my help, I would gladly give it to him. I was proud to realise my job at Bonwright and even my stint at Torchon & Lyle had already sharpened my editorial eye.

'Where did this sudden inspiration come from?' I asked, pausing to roll another sheet of paper into the typewriter.

'My lovely wife,' he said, leaning over my shoulder to kiss the nape of my neck as I resumed typing. 'She encourages me.'

'That's awfully nice of you to say.'

'I tell you, I'm on a tear, Eden! I'll have this done in a matter of weeks, and then I'm gonna get a book deal, I can taste it!'

He was getting ahead of himself but I didn't want to say so. I'd seen lots of young writers fall into this trap. Some of them had the imaginary book tour all planned out before they'd even finished the first chapter.

'Say,' Cliff continued, snapping his fingers, 'I'm going to talk to Gregg Carns about the amount of the advance he got, just to get an idea of the ballpark I'd be in.'

'Now?' I asked, slightly alarmed to think he was about to go out for the night and leave me to type his pages alone. Gregg Carns was an acquaintance of ours. He was a hipster who lived in the Village and who it was rumoured had gotten a sizable advance for a novel about a group of junkies who drive cross-country to Frisco. It had sold very well, and one reviewer called him the voice of our generation. But with every royalty check, the odds of him ever writing a second book slimmed exponentially as he fell deeper and deeper down the bottle.

'No, no,' Cliff said, smiling and kissing me on the cheek. 'Don't be silly. Tonight we're celebrating, just the two of us. And I want to be here when you finish typing so I can read it over. I'll find Gregg tomorrow and ask him.'

I typed, Cliff read, and eventually I was able to get a couple of sips of champagne before it was all gone. It was late when we finally went to bed, but we were both full of joy and made love with a voracious, exultant hunger. I woke up exhausted in the morning, looking a little wan as I dressed for the office, but I hardly cared. Cliff was writing and that made him happy, and that was all that mattered.

When I came home from work the next day, I worried the spell would be broken – that Cliff's sudden inspiration might turn out to have been a fluke. But I found him very much in the same way as the day before. And just as I had the day before, I gathered up the whirlwind of papers scattered about the floor and set about typing them up, the only difference being Cliff drank beer instead of champagne as he watched me.

After a week or so of this routine, Cliff had accrued a fairly sizable stack of manuscript pages. He was getting restless. The beer gave way to whiskey, and the main topic on Cliff's mind slipped more and more from writing to getting published.

'Listen, Eden,' he said one Sunday afternoon, 'an idea has occurred to me and you're not going to be on board with it right away, but I want you to hear me out because I think it would be beneficial to both of us, and what's a marriage about if both people don't benefit?'

'I'm not sure I understand,' I said. He sat me down and explained his proposition. His father was one of the most literary editors in all of New York, he pointed out, and who else should Cliff work with but an editor exactly like that? The problem was his father was prejudiced against him.

'I'm not sure I can fix that, Cliff,' I said as gently as possible.

'But that's where you're wrong, Eden old gal. You *can* fix it. You can slip My Old Man my manuscript and tell him it's an anonymous submission. Then, when he goes bananas for it, you can reveal who wrote it. It's genius!'

'Oh . . .' I said. I demurred. The manuscript, I knew, was not ready. Mr Nelson would not go bananas for it, but I couldn't tell Cliff this. It would devastate him, and worse: I knew it would break something between us I knew I would never be able to fix. 'I think,' I said hesitantly, 'I'd better stay out of this. It might confuse things. And things are awfully confusing as it is . . .'

'You're just being selfish.'

I blinked. 'Selfish?' I repeated, thinking to myself that a selfish girl wouldn't pay the bills while her husband stayed at home.

'After all, it was *my* tip about *my* Old Man that got you the job. I gave you a leg up on the competition; the least you could do is give me the same. It's not like I'm asking for anything immoral . . . An anonymous submission isn't a very big favour, at that! You know, you're awfully high and mighty for a girl who goes around *lying about her name.* What would My Old Man say if he knew about *that*, I wonder?'

Hearing this threat, a cold shock of betrayal went through me and my heart skipped a beat. I was speechless.

'I don't understand why you won't do this for me, Eden,' he continued. 'Do you *want* to hold me back? You and I both know you *lied* to get that job, and I haven't told a soul, have I? No, I've been a very good husband to you. I deserve this!'

I stared at him in disbelief. It was terrible, awful: we were having our first true fight. 'Let's not argue,' I started to say, but it was too late. He could see I wasn't going to do it, and that had thrown him into a state of outrage. Cliff picked up a desk lamp – the only other source of light besides the pathetically dim overheard bulb – and smashed it on the floor. Then he ran out of the apartment and slammed the door with tremendous force.

I picked up the pieces of the lamp and threw them in the rubbish pail. I spent the remainder of the evening reading manuscripts in the eerie quiet that followed in the wake of the sound of the lamp being smashed, the door being slammed. Cliff didn't come home until four o'clock in the morning. He climbed into bed stinking of booze. We both rolled on our sides and slept with our backs to each other.

36

As angry as I was with Cliff, it was awful tough to remain angry for very long. My inability to hold a grudge had something to do with my overwhelming sympathy, and my sympathy had to do with certain things Cliff had told me about his father. After we made love for the first time, he'd relayed a story from his childhood. It was the middle of the afternoon and we were lying naked on the mattress in his studio, holding each other, breathing in the scent of each other's skin. Cliff was always funny about his father and, knowing Mr Nelson, I thought I knew why. But when he told me this particular story, I understood his mixed-up feelings went much deeper than anything I'd previously assumed.

Cliff told the tale in fits and starts. It was obvious it represented a tender spot; I worried if I said anything – even just a single word out loud – he wouldn't continue. So I simply listened, and stroked his arm to reassure him. I had to piece it together in my mind later, smoothing out the rough edges when Cliff left a sentence here and there unfinished, usually because his voice broke up and he needed to collect himself.

I was ultimately able to piece together the following account:

One day in April when Cliff was eleven years old, he and his friends caught a case of spring fever and decided to play hooky. As young boys enrolled in a private school in Connecticut, playing hooky meant taking the train into Manhattan, sneaking past a doorman, and going upstairs to one of their families' empty 'city apartments' with the idea to raid the liquor cabinet.

The boys had only just arrived in Grand Central and were standing outside, pooling their change for a taxi, when Cliff looked up to see his father striding down the sidewalk. Cliff's first reaction was one of panic. His frightened brain jumped to the conclusion his father had been alerted to his absence from school and had come down to the station to find and punish him. He dashed behind a news stand to hide. But as he watched his father turn and duck down the stairs and into a subway station, he realised his father was not looking for him at all. To the contrary, it was clear his father was oblivious to Cliff's presence.

He couldn't think of where his father could possibly be going. The only appointments Cliff's father generally took outside the office were lunches, but it was well past the lunch hour, and his father was not one to take the subway when he could take a taxi. Cliff's curiosity overcame him, and he decided to pursue the mystery. Cliff's friends attempted to dissuade him, but Cliff had made up his mind.

Cliff snuck down the subway stairs after his father, hiding behind trash bins and other passengers waiting on the platform. When the train came, Cliff waited for his father to board and then darted into the car behind. He positioned himself so he could make out his father's shape through the windows between cars, but where his father would be unlikely to glimpse Cliff in return. But as the train rocked along the tracks over the Manhattan Bridge and into Brooklyn, an uneasy feeling came over him. It dawned on him that if his father had a secret, he wasn't sure he wanted to know it.

When his father finally got off at Twentieth Avenue in Brooklyn, Cliff followed him, and the mystery grew even more perplexing. Trailing at a distance, Cliff crept along as Mr Nelson made his way to a park where a Little League game was going on. He watched as his father climbed up into the bleachers, took a seat, and proceeded to cheer on the game. Cliff was stumped by this turn of events. Why on earth would his father take the train all the way out to Brooklyn to watch a Little League game? All too soon, he had his answer. The game ended and one of the players – the shortstop who had notably hit the game's one and only home run – ran off the field and directly up to Cliff's father. Cliff squinted to get a better look. The boy seemed to be close to Cliff's own age, but where Cliff was rather small, this boy was rather big. He was tall, with dark hair and olive skin. In fact, everything about the boy's origins alluded to some kind of Mediterranean tribe, save for a pair of very pale, Nordic-looking eyes.

Cliff continued to watch. Cliff's father clapped the boy on the shoulder with firm enthusiasm once, twice, and then a third time. They began to descend the bleachers, and it was clear they intended to depart together. Cliff felt nauseated. He wished he hadn't gotten on the train to Brooklyn; he was convinced his father had taken up some kind of unnatural interest in this young boy. That is, he was convinced this was the case until he drew close enough to hear his father say, 'C'mon, son, let's get you home to your mother.'

At this, Cliff was absolutely perplexed. He followed them. They left the baseball diamond and walked several blocks, turning this way and that, crossing avenues, until they came to a red-brick row house. A woman was standing on the porch, leaning in the open doorway and watching the street as she blithely smoked a cigarette. Cliff ducked behind a cluster of garbage pails left on the curb and observed the woman from afar. She had an ample figure and small waist. A prominent mole on her left breast peeped out from the low neckline of her tight blouse, and she had short black hair. Two perfectly rounded curlicues were plastered to her face, framing a pair of high cheekbones and red-painted lips. There was something beautiful about her, but also common, like an advertisement for cheap cosmetics.

Upon seeing Cliff's father and the boy from the baseball field approach, she twisted her lips into a sort of sideways smile and called out, 'See, Johnny? What'd I tell ya? I *told* ya he'd be at your game.' The tall dark-haired kid nodded, and his chin jutted out in a proud way. He held back a grin, his face straining to remain manly and stoic. The woman moved out of the doorway to let him pass, and 'Johnny' ran inside.

'Well . . . aren't you a sight for sore eyes, Dolores,' Cliff's father said. Ascending the stoop that led into the house, he gave her a kiss on the cheek. Looking bored and amused at the same time, she rolled her eyes and winked at him.

'Depends on who's doing the looking,' she replied. Then, as if remembering something she had forgotten, she straightened up and was all business.

'C'mon inside,' she said, throwing her cigarette down and stamping it out with the toe of her right pump. 'I got sauce on the stove.' Cliff's father went in the house. She followed him in and shut the door.

Cliff rose from his hiding place behind the garbage pails and stood there, bewildered. After several moments passed and no one re-emerged, he drew even closer, taking a position near a shrub directly across the street. There, Cliff waited and watched. The row house was two storeys, with a little porch and a bay window. Within the bay window was some kind of dining room and Cliff had a plain view of Dolores, Johnny, and his father all sitting around a cramped table. Dolores set the table with some kind of meal that appeared to consist of spaghetti and green beans. There was something peculiarly intimate about the scene that bothered Cliff. He watched as his father reached over and rumpled Johnny's hair just as Dolores reached to pull the curtains shut. It felt as though all the air had gone out of Cliff's lungs. Crouched in the shrubs like an alley cat, his muscles cramped; he didn't move, he barely breathed. A neighbour parked an old-model Oldsmobile onto a nearby curb and walked right past Cliff, not seeing him. Dusk crept in.

Eventually, the downstairs light was replaced by an upstairs light. Then that, too, clicked off. By that point it was quite late. Birds that had been roosting had fallen silent, disappearing to wherever it is birds go after they roost. The scanty handful of stars bold enough to show their faces in the Brooklyn night sky appeared, crickets chirped, and some distance away on the main streets horns were honking, teenagers were cruising and hollering to one another. After the light on the second floor went out, Cliff waited another hour more.

Finally, Cliff stood up on stiff knees, realising for the first time he hadn't a clue how to get all the way back home to Connecticut. With a great sense of dread he realised he would have to phone his mother. He was likely in a lot of hot water. She might even be aware he hadn't been at school. But funnily enough, at that moment, he wasn't especially worried about himself or whether he could evade punishment. He was caught in a different predicament. He was worried about his mother's feelings, about how he would explain what he was doing in Brooklyn, and about how she might react.

He stood outside a phone booth in front of a diner, dancing from one foot to the other and changing his mind several times until a middle-aged woman with a stringy neck and a smoker's voice leant out the door of the diner and yelled, 'Hey, kid, that ain't a urinal, so don't even think about it!' Cliff gave her a look and treated her to his middle finger. Then he promptly entered the booth, lifted the receiver, and placed his call.

His mother drove all the way from Greenwich to pick him up. When he mentioned Brooklyn on the phone, she hadn't sounded surprised, nor had she prodded him for an explanation. She simply asked the name of the diner and the intersection where it was located. The family employed a driver named Leonard, but she didn't mention him and Cliff understood she was making the drive herself and coming alone. Too tired at that point to be surprised any more, Cliff was merely confused and disappointed by this turn of events. All things considered, he couldn't really complain; his mother was coming to get him and she hadn't threatened a punishment for his having played hooky, and that would have to be enough of a comfort for the time being.

It took her a long time to get there. Cliff sat on the curb for hours, hungry from having not eaten all day, smelling the glorious greasy scent of grilled cheese sandwiches, realising for the first time that day that he hadn't eaten. Strange emotions overtook him. First he was angry with his father, and then, inexplicably, his anger veered off in the direction of his mother. As the minutes ticked by, he grew angrier and angrier, until eventually he was seething with fury. But his anger vanished the minute she pulled up to the curb. She was dressed in only a housecoat, her thin face drawn and pale, and it was obvious she had applied cold cream to her skin earlier that evening and then wiped it off in order to make the journey. She appeared fragile to Cliff, and for the first time he comprehended the fact of his parents' mortality in a manner that had evaded him throughout his younger years. She leant across the bench seat to lift the lock on the passenger door of the Hudson and he climbed in. Wordlessly, they drove back to Greenwich, whereupon she parked the car in the garage, went into the house, and climbed the stairs to go to bed.

'Goodnight, Clifford' was the sole sentence to escape her lips.

A letter of excuse written in his mother's impeccable penmanship was waiting for him on the breakfast table the next morning along with his usual soft-boiled egg. It read: 'Please excuse Clifford's absence. He was ill yesterday.' When his friends asked him whether he had dispelled the mystery of what his father was up to, he shrugged and, shaking his head, said, 'I lost him.' His friends poked fun at him, calling him a crummy detective. For a few days he became their lackey, until eventually some other boy made a gaffe, and their attentions were drawn to the new victim. Cliff and his mother never spoke about what had happened.

'She knew,' Cliff said to me as we lay on the mattress. 'She knew all along that he had a girl on the side. That I had a *goddamned brother*, for Chrissake . . .' He paused. We had our arms wrapped around each other; I felt his jaw clench as he swallowed. 'Once, over the breakfast table, she said to my father, "You've spent a lot of nights sleeping in the city lately, Roger. I think you ought to cut back." Just like that! Right in front of me, like we didn't both know exactly where he'd been spending his nights.'

I couldn't think of what to say, and I knew, on instinct, that Cliff would rather I say nothing at all. So I simply went on stroking his arm, letting him know I was awake and listening.

After we were married, I asked Cliff once if he wouldn't like the chance to talk to his half-brother someday. They were, after all, related. And nearly the same age. But by that point I knew Cliff well enough . . . I should've guessed already what his answer would be.

'What for?' he asked, a sneer slowly soaking into his features. 'I tell ya one thing . . . if I ever did, I would be sure to knock the bastard's block off, the lousy no-good pretender.'

37

CLIFF

I guess Eden and I were true newlyweds because we went from one day having a fight and not being able to stand each other to the next day me doing something as sweet and simple as bringing her a packet of daisies I'd bought for twenty-five cents at the news stand and suddenly the two of us couldn't keep our hands off each other. I'd had some valid points during our big argument and I didn't think I ought to give them up, but there was one thing I was awful sorry about and that was bringing up the subject of Eden's name. I could tell it had her rattled. If she knew me at all she ought to know I would never rat her out, but in any case I felt pretty lousy whenever I remembered that part of our fight and I decided I would lay off Eden for a while about the whole business of slipping my manuscript to My Old Man.

One Saturday Rusty turned up unannounced as per his usual habit while Eden and I were busy making love under a shower of rare but glorious afternoon sunshine. Of course we knew when the buzzer sounded it was Rusty and we also knew we had to stop what we were busy doing and answer it or else there would be consequences. I extracted myself and pulled my pants on begrudgingly, knowing full well there are only so many afternoons you get in life when you are young and so is your wife and you still have love between you and the sunshine pours in through the windows in such a way that the very word *generous* seems to hang in the air. But since Eden wasn't going to slip My Old Man a manuscript, I needed to get to Rusty's boss now more than ever and there were always consequences if you made Rusty cross so down I went to the stoop. It turned out there were consequences anyway, because when Rusty came trudging up the creaking wooden stairs and into the apartment he took one look at the sticky sheen of our faces and at the bedsheets that were now twined into a thick vine and dangling off the mattress a little like the braid of Rapunzel's hair and he knew exactly what had been going on just minutes prior.

Whenever someone else was making love or balling someone it put Rusty in a foul mood and a small but devastating tantrum was sure to follow. I didn't completely understand the reasons for his foul mood but it was as if he believed there was only a set amount of sex in the world and whenever someone else used some of it up they were taking away from the stash that was rightfully his. He paced around our apartment like an aggravated jungle cat. Eden made him a melted cheese sandwich on the hot plate but he refused to take a single bite of it and instead kept complaining about how his shirt had gotten wrinkled on the cab ride over because the driver had been so lousy he'd been forced to hunker down in the back seat to avoid flying out the cab window whenever the driver made one of his death-defying swerves into traffic. I almost asked how Rusty had managed to pay the taxi without someone to spot him the money but I held my tongue. Finally, Eden offered to iron it for him and he sighed and took his shirt off as though acquiescing to a great favour.

The sight of Rusty sitting at the kitchen table in his undershirt with his narrow shoulders and skinny arms and his chest so soft and saggy was enough to make me gag but I did not have to stomach it long because Eden was an efficient ironer and when the shirt was done Rusty whipped it back on and stood up and when he got up he yelled, 'Good Lord, I don't know how you people can stand it in here; it positively reeks!' Then he declared we all needed to get outside and do something. Eden and I changed our clothes and soon enough we were outside standing on the curb, helping Rusty hail a taxi. The afternoon sunshine was all gone now; twilight had set in and all the electric signs were beginning to glow like embers against the ashen sky. When a cab finally pulled over to let us in, Eden gave me a look that said: *Of course this is another thing we're going to have to pay for with money we don't really have because we both know perfectly well he's not going to offer to pay for it.* I shrugged as if to say: *What do you want me to do about it?* She sighed and I sighed and we got in. I think we were both especially compliant that evening to Rusty's demands because of the big fight we'd had about my manuscript. If Rusty ever got around to giving my work to the big important literary agent the problems between us would be solved and we would never fight again, so we figured it couldn't hurt to give him what he wanted.

It turned out Rusty didn't really want fresh air because what he really wanted was to smoke some tea, so we ended up giving the driver an address in Harlem because in those days the tea was plentiful in Harlem – so much so that if you didn't have any money to buy, sometimes you could just get out and walk the streets and breathe the air there to get good and stoned. I didn't mind so much going to Harlem, because once up there we could check out some of the jazz joints and it was always a good time to go hear the Negro musicians blow as only the Negro musicians could.

When we got to Harlem we found both the tea and the jazz in the same place. It was early still, so the nightclubs hadn't filled up yet and we had a table to ourselves. The waiter told us in order to see about the tea we'd have to ask at the bar and of course Rusty wasn't very well going to do this part and so it was all up to me. The bartender directed me to a stockroom in the back of the club just past the men's toilet and once there I stood in front of a pair of decommissioned urinals until finally a heavy-set mulatto who was all frowns abruptly pushed through the door and without a single word or twitch of expression took my money and handed over the tea and shuffled out just as directly as he had come in.

When I got back to the table Rusty and Eden were discussing something and when I sat down Rusty took the tea from me and abruptly changed the subject by asking me what did I think of the fellow sitting at the bar. After all the cloak-and-dagger with the tea I was a little annoyed to watch as Rusty started rolling a marijuana cigarette right at the table for everyone to see but I decided to ignore this and oblige his request and looked over at the bar. There were two light lemony-skinned coloured girls, one fat man so big his haunches concealed the bar stool supporting him, and one athletic-built Negro in a turtleneck and horn-rimmed glasses. I assumed Rusty meant the young athlete.

With a start, I realised the young man we were staring at was Miles.

He must've felt our eyes on him because just then he turned and looked in our direction. I waved and he gave a tight nod and smile. It was funny seeing him at that bar. I guess I knew he'd been born and raised in Harlem and all that, but even so, he spent a lot of his spare time running around the Village and when you are used to seeing a particular person in a specific setting it was jarring to encounter him someplace entirely different; it made you feel almost like the person had a second life he kept secret from you. As I looked at Miles now, I imagined his other, Harlem life.

'You two know that fella?' Rusty asked.

Eden and I nodded.

'He runs around the Village scene. Kind of funny to see him up here.'

'Bring him over here and invite him to the party at your pad,' Rusty said to me, and I realised the imperial toddler was back.

'We're not having a party at our pad,' I said, and Rusty gave me a look and suddenly I understood: we *were* having a party at our pad. I crossed the bar to where Miles sat on a bar stool and after a few niceties cajoled him into joining us at our table. I could tell Miles was uncomfortable to see us outside the Village, but it was not in his personality to be impolite so he followed me back to the table.

Eden seemed genuinely pleased to see old Miles. They smiled openly at each other and she asked him about Columbia and about graduating and about the bicycle messenger business. Rusty and I sat there scowling, me because here was my wife as chummy as can be with a fellow I wasn't aware she knew so well, and Rusty because the whole idea was that everybody should pay attention to him and most especially that Miles should pay attention to him.

'Tell him about the party you're throwing,' Rusty said, cutting into the conversation. I told Miles about the party and invited him and he looked vaguely uncomfortable.

'I don't know,' he said. 'I'm going out of town soon.'

'When are you leaving?' Rusty demanded.

Miles hesitated. 'I've still got to make sure everything's in order, but in the next week or so.'

'Well, our party is *this* week, so you can fit it in, no problem. Tell you what: we'll make it a bon voyage party,' Rusty insisted.

'Oh, don't do that,' Miles said, hesitating. 'But I suppose I can drop in,' he continued, mostly to me and to Eden.

Rusty grinned in victory and leered a bit in a drunken, stoned manner as he looked Miles over. Miles shifted uncomfortably under Rusty's stare and pretended rapt interest in the musicians on the stage despite the fact they hadn't started playing just yet.

I saw Eden give both of them a nervous glance but when she looked at me with a question in her eyes I only shrugged. Just then the first blast of the trumpet sounded and barked its way through a tongue-twisting series of very fast jazz notes and the stage lit up with coloured lights as the musicians started to play. Rusty relented and turned his attention to the stage and so did we and those musicians began to blow with an impressively urgent and limber force. The club began to fill up and soon the room was thick with smoke from cigarettes and tea and cigars and also the groggy garlicky heat of sweaty bodies standing close to one another.

I could already tell it was going to be a late night, and once again Eden and I were probably going to spend more money than we could afford, and that meant by the end of the month we would be scrambling all over again to get the rent paid. I wasn't feeling sorry for myself; these were just the facts. And now Rusty had demanded a party, which meant soon we were going to be hosting some kind of shindig at our pad and that would also be an expense. I wasn't looking forward to any of this but at that time we were both still afraid to disappoint Rusty. There was a vague indirect sprinkling of dread over my thoughts that night, like a handful of kernels that had yet to sink into the soil. But it was a nice night, or at least that's my memory of it, so instead of worrying about anything Rusty could get up to, I sat back and listened to the tremendous musicians blow. After only ten minutes or so of listening to the jazz I had managed to push those seedlings of nervous dread to the back of my mind with the hope that, once there, they would fail to take root.

38

Of course, it was only natural to invite Swish and Bobby and Pal and, even though the party was something Rusty had demanded, it was nice having all the gang back together and it wasn't long before Eden and I began to feel like the whole thing had been our own idea in the first place. The early-autumn chill had let off a bit and everyone was in good spirits that night. Pal had just had a little poetry chapbook printed and it was impossible not to smile back into his friendly blue eyes as he passed it around with a look of sheepish pride. Swish also was in fine form: he had gotten a haircut and dropped the ratty hobo attire for the evening and stood in the corner hunched over with his characteristic wiry thin-guy posture, debating politics with a freckly blonde kid dressed in glasses and a rumpled checked shirt. The blonde kid didn't so much debate back as listen and nod.

Bobby was always the last to turn up at parties and we all knew this about him and even had grown to like it. Whenever things started to slow up and get dull, Bobby would crash through the door with all his explosive energy and inject the atmosphere with new life. True to form that night, after we'd all been sitting around for a while and had gotten a few drinks into things, Bobby showed up with a couple of huge hash bricks he'd gotten off a crazy Frenchman and a trio of girls whose names he hadn't even bothered to learn but who he'd decided to call LaVerne, Maxene, and Patty after the Andrews Sisters. I didn't talk much to the girls that night as it was clear they were all in it for Bobby and were trying to outlast one another to see which one of them would finally wind up basking in Bobby's beauty for the night. I remember they giggled every time he called them by the Andrew Sisters' names despite the fact no one liked the Andrews Sisters and it was clearly a condescension and we all found their lack of dignity mildly irritating.

Overall, though, even the Andrews Sisters couldn't ruin the mood that night, which was good. We were all keyed up and ready to get our kicks. After Bobby made his entrance the room suddenly got very full and all the conversations began going a million miles a minute and nobody paid much attention to Rusty, so for a moment I thought he might get bored and go home. Of course he didn't, because he was waiting for Miles to turn up, and eventually Miles did turn up looking very clean-cut and muscular and then a little later there was some bad business that I'm ashamed to say I hadn't anticipated and so did very little to stop. The bad business started when we had all moved the party up onto the roof.

When Miles got to our apartment he poked his handsome dusky face into the room with an uncertain air and knocked timidly on the open door, despite the fact he'd obviously found us. Sonny Rollins was piping hot and loud out of the record player. Eden waved and left my side to go over to his. The two of them were joined by Swish and very shortly afterwards all three of them were locked into one of Swish's great debates. By the time I made my way across the room Swish was heavy into a diatribe about whether or not it would be better to live as a coloured man in the USA or in Russia.

'Don't get the wrong idea,' Swish was saying when I walked

up, 'I hear what you're saying about Dos Passos because I have a true affection for that cat of course and all his politics, too, and I would like nothing better than to agree but what I'm saying is a man of colour – a man such as yourself – might do better to live in a foreign nation where his people haven't already been harnessed to the government like a godforsaken capitalistic extra appendage of the state and you could start over without the burden of your people's history and maybe with the right intellectuals even make a new history of your own . . .'

Miles frowned in a friendly way and shook his head at Swish and I saw Swish's body tighten in the pleased apprehension that someone was about to disagree with him. 'You're assuming I want to forget my people's history,' Miles said. He inflected the words *my people* in a kind of wry way and I think this was meant to imply Swish was using an expression he had no right to use. The point was lost on Swish, because Swish had always been of the opinion that simply being born had entitled him to all rights of every kind and most especially the right to talk about anything he wanted to with whatever expressions suited him best.

'Well, why wouldn't you?' Swish asked. 'It's a beggars' history, cobbled together by the very people who have made you beggars. The Negro will never be equal to the white man until he sheds his history as a slave and gets everybody to forget all about the shame of letting himself be enslaved.'

'It's a history of adversity,' Miles said, suddenly very quiet and serious. 'And adversity is what makes a people strong in their own conviction of themselves as a people.'

'Well, you're hanging on to your own noose is what I say, and in the larger order of things this is why your people have stayed exactly where they have stayed.'

It was almost imperceptible but I saw Miles flinch at Swish's words. Very coolly he collected himself and cleared his throat and I could see then that Miles had probably had more than one conversation with the kind of intense white guy Swish was and had learnt long ago not to rise too passionately to the bait because that was exactly what these guys always wanted. 'I see,' Miles said. 'And would you have the Jews forget their persecution during the war, too?'

'You bet I would,' Swish said. 'The war of course was awful for the Jews, but the survivors only make themselves into victims by sitting around talking about how awful it was for them.'

This time it was Eden's turn to flinch. Most of the time I forgot that Eden was Jewish and now as I saw her flinch I remembered her true name again. But before I had much of a chance to reflect on this fact I felt the short, stingy, hovering presence of Rusty at my elbow.

'Tell your friend to stop being a drip,' Rusty said in a low voice into my ear, meaning Swish. I hated that he knew I would do what he told me to do, but he did have one thing right and that was how gloomy the conversation was getting. Swish meant well but he liked to stir up controversy – he saw it as his way of upholding American democracy – and conversations that started off in an unassuming tone could sometimes turn sour and poison the night and cause everyone's mood to take a turn for the worse.

'How about we all go up to the roof,' I said, and everyone but Swish shot me a smile of relief. The great political debate was dropped as we headed in the direction of where Bobby and the Andrews Sisters had disappeared minutes earlier by climbing out the open window and up the fire escape.

The roof was really the only place for the party to go. Over the first few months following our honeymoon we had discovered the apartment was tolerable for two people, but only by a slim margin. Certainly it was much too small to host a full party, so one by one people crawled out the fire escape and climbed up the rusted iron ladder that led to the roof.

When I got to the top of the ladder I inhaled a lungful of thick sickly sweet air and I knew Bobby had decided to try the hashish. As a group we mostly smoked tea and not hash, because sometimes hash gave you bad returns at the end of the night, but it's also true that whatever Bobby did we were all likely to follow suit and so it wasn't long before everyone on the roof was smoking the hash and it turned out to be okay stuff. The temperature was pleasant and the night sky seemed wide open and almost ghostly as it glowed with the dim buzz of a million refracted city lights. Pal called up to us from the fire escape to lower the bucket and rope that we kept on the roof. When we lowered it he filled the bucket up with bottles of beer and whiskey and vodka and we hauled it all up and after that the party had officially moved to the roof for good.

Once we'd settled into our new location, some of us stood holding drinks and talking, some of us jazzed about to the music floating up from the windows below, and some of us spread old blankets on the tarred ground and lay down to smoke and look up at the sky. Eden and I found a dark corner and got to talking. I took her small, fine-boned hand in mine and thought again of how wise I'd been to marry her.

I didn't notice when Rusty and Miles disappeared from the party and neither did anyone else, but later when we tried to figure it out we guessed it must've been an hour or so after we all adjourned to the roof that Rusty was bold enough to slip the Amytal into Miles's drink.

I heard that, just like the bennies, Rusty had gotten the Amytal off his old aunt with all the health problems. In any case, wherever Rusty got the stuff he gave Miles that night he must've underestimated Miles's body weight and tolerance, because when we heard the ruckus coming from the little antechamber of a shack that enclosed the air shaft over the building's main stairwell, we opened the door and there was Miles thrashing around with a discombobulated groggy sort of violence, giving Rusty a real ring-dinger of a black eye as his arms and legs flailed out in all directions and he fought against the effects of the drug.

It took us a while to react. We were all still very stoned on the hash, which had turned out to be smooth enough but very strong. We stood staring at the two struggling figures in a state of shock as they thrashed about and before long Rusty had a bloody nose to go along with his black eye. Blood and snot poured down in a pattering dribble as Rusty bent over to pull up his trousers, which were still around his ankles. The motion of it set off a new wave of terror in Miles afresh and his muscular back jerked against the stairwell door inside the rooftop antechamber. He thrashed about, and then all at once the rusted chain that had likely kept that door sealed for the better part of two decades broke loose and the door flew open. Miles staggered through it and stumbled wildly down the stairs in a horrible, sickening way that made my stomach lurch; it was like watching a confused animal fight for its life.

We stood there listening to the sounds of Miles thump and tumble his way down the stairs. I didn't move until I heard the familiar clatter of the building's front door. At that point Eden and I dashed to the other side of the roof to peer over. Far down below, Miles limped blindly out into oncoming traffic. Although it was difficult to tell from his body language, I think in his confused state he was trying to hail a cab. Several taxi drivers avoided him until finally one pulled over. Seeing too late his passenger was a crazed coloured man in torn clothing, the driver tried to pull away from the curb but was ultimately saddled with Miles as his fare.

With shock and shame we all turned to look at Rusty.

The party was more or less over after that. People trickled down from the roof and out the front door of our apartment talking in private rumbling voices about where to go next. I took Rusty downstairs to the bathroom down the hall from our apartment and gave him some towels and told him to clean himself up. I shut the door. I didn't want to watch him fix up his cuts and scrapes and I sure as hell didn't want to help him. When Rusty emerged forty-five minutes later, he limped quietly down the hallway without so much as glancing back into the apartment at us and we watched him make his pathetic journey to the stairs, looking a little like a pirate hobbling along on a peg leg. Just like that, he disappeared without another word.

The mere fact I had helped him with the towels meant Eden wouldn't look me in the eye for the rest of the evening. When we finally switched out the lights and lay down on the mattress on the floor that night, she turned the cold moonlit expanse of her back to me and in a voice so soft it was barely audible murmured: *We led him to the fucking slaughter.*

I reached for her hand but she pulled it away.

39

MILES

I slept for days. The occasional sound of Wendell yelling in the living room drifted into my bedroom, and even further, into my dreams, but I could not care. At regular intervals, my mother bustled in and out, depositing plates of food and later, seeing them untouched, clearing them away. She washed in and out like the tide. Cob materialised at my bedside, pushing his Coke bottles up the bridge of his nose, holding up a glass jar, showing off a cicada in the process of moulting. The grotesque sight of it entered my nightmares, slowly bursting out of its own body like a monster in a horror movie, leaving behind a dead, brittle sculpture of itself still gripping a broken branch.

On the third day, I got up and looked at myself in the mirror.

Even in its worst state, the cicada was more attractive by a long shot.

Janet could not understand why I insisted on saying goodbye over the telephone as opposed to meeting her, as we had planned, in our usual spot in the park. But it was time to go. As soon as I could stand upright without seeing purple spots, I packed a small suitcase and made my way to Port Authority, where I purchased a ticket for a Greyhound. I sat in the back. The engine rumbled to life. We plunged into the Lincoln Tunnel and came up into the light. Marshland and factories. Pitch pine and birch flashing by in chaotic rows, soldiers breaking ranks on the battlefield. Hour by hour, mile by mile, the earth began to flatten. The driver braked at hamburger stands, rest stops. The bus shuddered each time the engine was cut. I imagined the death rattle of a dinosaur. Faces changed, a revolving cast of characters. Smells of grease, of garlic, of cigarettes, of body odour. A tuba was lugged on and carried off. A little girl threw her doll out the window and was spanked very horribly and publicly for all the passengers on the bus to witness.

Woods gave way to corn, corn to wheat, wheat to desert, desert to mountains. A bizarre feeling of disbelief each time the scenery matched expectation: red barn over the cornfield, cartoonish cactus standing in one-armed salute amidst sand, tumbleweed. Everything as different as you could want from New York, everything exactly as promised. The final leg, craggy granite melting into a valley, into foothills and oaks, folds of land opening at last upon the nickel-coloured bay. Soaring over the bridge and into the heart of San Francisco, tinge of salt in the air.

Later that night, under the dim bulb in the cramped bathroom of my hotel room, my face in the mirror revealed a map of healing: faint traces of yellows, purples, and indigo dying out under the canvas of my skin. A scab like a thick leathery patch on my cheek, beginning to fall off. An exo-skeleton to leave behind.

'What happened to you?' a nosy woman in the bus seat next to me had asked, meaning my face.

'An accident,' I said.

I should have answered, *I am moulting*.

I climbed into bed, muscles sore from disuse, bones still vibrating from the rumble of a phantom engine. Images flashed against the black screen of my closed eyelids. Those last nights in Manhattan. Rusty. Cob and his cicada. Trees flashing by, tick-tick-tick, until they transformed into steel bridge girders and petered out at the end of the earth. The task still before me. Always the thought of my father.

40

Rusty had, for better or worse, pushed me forward on my mission. It's strange to think, but the journey is so linked in my mind to my healing bruises, I cannot imagine it otherwise.

It was already late morning when I finally rose the next day but I didn't know it at first; the hour was masked by the grey fog out my window. I was soon to discover what a curious place San Francisco was. The fog collected on tree leaves in the park, dribbled from eaves in the neighbourhoods, and made sentimental tears on the stone facades downtown. I gazed in wonder at the white wedding cake of buildings that made up its skyline and the gingerbread shapes of its funny, colourfully painted houses. Cable cars clattered up hills and thundered down them, the brakeman straining at his lever. Honeymooners wandered hand-in-hand along Fisherman's Wharf, where a saxophonist duelled with an organ-grinder for attention. Hipsters with unwashed hair read poetry on the lawn in Washington Square while leathery-faced Italians played loud, intense card games on folding tables beside the church where Joe DiMaggio and Marilyn Monroe famously posed for wedding photographs.

The city struck a stark contrast to everything I'd known growing up in New York. Manhattan is concrete and ambition, steam rising from a manhole in winter, a hot blast from a subway grate in summer. Its inner workings grind away at all hours, purring in the name of commerce. New York streets are distinctly sultry – especially in Harlem. The defining sights and smells are those that humans make. The eye-catching colours of shop signs, of awnings, of advertisements. The scent of meat being grilled, of ladies' powdery perfumes, of sour body odour – all this mixing with the cabbagey smell of garbage hovering on the street curbs.

I found that in San Francisco the vibrancy of life was not so much evinced by the enormity of man-made ambitions as it was embedded in the nature that surrounded the city; its brilliance was cached in the cypress trees that leant romantically against the hills, the glitter of the bay, the startling patches of blue sky that occasionally broke through the fog. *This* was what inspired and enlivened the young people and artists in the city, what called to starry-eyed couples and nostalgic bohemians. I took a walk in Golden Gate Park. It had a peculiar tang about it that took some getting used to at first – some sort of herbaceous pungency that at times smelt incredibly fresh and clean, and at other times sharp and feral, not unlike cat piss. It seemed to emanate from the wet bark of the eucalyptus trees, intensified by the cool, crisp breeze of the Pacific.

Just before I'd left for Port Authority, Cob had armed me with a handful of tiny glass jars. Now I sat down on a large tree stump at the top of a hill in the middle of Stow Lake and made a haphazard attempt to collect a few insects that might interest him. I caught a beetle with an iridescent blackish-green shell that struck me as exotic. I dropped it in the jar and admired it in the light, a rainbow of colours hidden in the green.

The truth was: I was stalling.

I'd come all the way across the country but couldn't face the next step, and there was safety in failure. I had never truly believed my father had been a hero in the First World War, and I certainly didn't believe he'd been a hero in the Second. If I never found my father's locker, I could never be disappointed by anything he'd written in his journal. Moreover, I could never be disappointed if the locker turned out to be empty altogether. I was preventing one tragedy by ensuring another.

But then I pictured coming home, having spent my savings, having spent my *mother's* one hundred dollars. My mother, who worked so hard. There would be questions about my trip when I got home, a demand that I tell the tale of my efforts. Lying was out of the question. It was in my personality to omit – I was adept in the art of omission – but I could not tell outright lies. Not to my mother. An hour passed as I sat nursing that paralysed feeling in the park, until finally the thought of reporting back to my mother empty-handed sickened me more than the thought of making an attempt to locate my father's locker. When the balance finally tipped, I stood up, pocketed Cob's jars, and brushed the dust from my slacks.

Where to begin? I hadn't imagined actually *arriving* in San Francisco; for months it had remained so safely, so thoroughly far away. I was at a loss at what to do next. I decided the most sensible tactic would be to retrace my father's footsteps. My father's regiment had deployed from the wharves down at Fort Mason; I decided that was where I would begin.

It was sunny by the time I walked down to the gatehouse near the marina. I could see several enormous dull-grey ships at the docks and the navy bay glittering in the distance beyond. A couple of military trucks were lined up at the checkpoint while men in uniforms flashed their identification to a man who stood by a doorway and made note of their comings and goings. I hesitated. The official nature of the scene was intimidating. I hadn't quite thought this part through. Here I was, three thousand miles from home, and I hadn't planned for one more step. I approached the gatehouse cautiously.

'Where's your uniform, soldier?' the man asked, frowning at me and clutching a clipboard.

'I . . .' I stammered. 'I'm a civilian.'

He frowned at my bruises. 'What's your business here?'

I explained to him about my father, the key, the locker. He seemed less than enthralled by my story, wearing a distracted expression as he nodded several men in uniform through the gate while I talked.

'No footlockers on the premises here, buddy,' he said once I'd finished explaining. 'But even if there were, I couldn't let you come on base and rummage around. This ain't a public amusement park, you know; it's a military base, property of the United States army.'

I realised I was being turned away, and sudden panic clamped down on my throat. I coughed. 'Maybe you could just tell me—'

'Like I said, this ain't a tourist office. Move it along; we got a job to do here,' the man said with an air of finality. Scornful, he waved me off, but I remained frozen, blinking at him with dismay. 'Look, buddy, we got a bunch of boys coming back from Korea who never expected to stay there half so long, so if you don't mind, we're a little busy around here.' His wave transformed into a shooing gesture and his attention turned to a truck waiting to be cleared for entry.

If there had been a way to slam a literal door in my face and continue to man his post, I'm sure he would have. Either way, the effect was the same. Bewildered, I walked away from the marina, following Van Ness as it sloped uphill in the general direction of my hotel. I wanted to lie down, think, regroup. I was staggered by the foolishness of the cowardice I'd been struggling with earlier that day in the park, putting off trying for fear of succeeding; now it dawned on me there was a very real chance success may not even be possible. For the first time, it struck me what a naïve undertaking this was: my mother had handed me a key and sent me on a quest, and here I was following this singular clue, like an idiotic character in a fairy tale. What had I expected? The world suddenly felt very vast, and I felt very small. I was coloured, in a strange city, and worst of all for my purposes: a civilian searching for a footlocker on a military base.

Back at my hotel I rested on the rickety springs of my bed, staring up at the ceiling, thinking of what to do. I would keep trying, I supposed. There was nothing else I *could* do, and there were other army installations to try. I would make a list, take the logical steps. One at a time; one foot after the other. I would try until I ran out of money. No one could blame me if I tried until I ran out of money.

41

The next day, I tried the Presidio. The day after that, I took the ferry across the bay to try Fort Baker, in Sausalito. I even took a bus out to Treasure Island, on the off-chance my father had passed through the naval base, and that I might be admitted there. Each time, I met the same result. Thwarted and frustrated, I found myself beginning to while away my remaining afternoons at the main branch of the library. It was located near the plaza that contained the opera house, ballet, and courthouses, in that oddly Parisian yet somewhat derelict civic heart of the city. I walked among the aisles of heavily pruned plane trees, listening to the sharp flap of bird wings, eyeing the dust of pigeon feathers. I found my way into the library, and always returned to the same sections: the periodicals, the microfiche room. I was searching, I realised, for evidence to support – or disprove – Clarence's claim. I scanned every headline that contained any mention of the 369th Regiment. I started by focusing on 1943 to 1945 but soon after expanded my search. The only thing I discovered was how little news coverage the 369th Regiment had received during the Second World War. It was possible, too, I realised, that a murder overseas might not be reported by the army, as military investigations were not required to abide by civilian rules.

In the evenings I took walks, often winding up in a bar or coffee shop. One evening, my wanderings led me into the heart of North Beach. As I strolled up Columbus Avenue, the thin wails of live jazz floated out from the buildings here and there and drifted across my path on the sidewalk until I found myself finally lured into a club. I pushed through an upholstered leather door to a dark, humid cave filled with people bobbing their heads and tapping their feet to some very lively bebop. Everyone's face shone with sweat and smiles, from the single girl at the corner of the bar all the way to the elevated space where the band played. The musicians onstage possessed solid talent; I could tell they were immigrants to the West, bringing with them the voice and attitude of the opposite coast, and here was a vestige of Harlem that warmed me as I heard it. I perched on a stool at the bar and soon enough the bartender came over to take my order.

After two beers, when I had thoroughly soaked in the mood of the room and was feeling good, I thought it best to go back to my hotel before it got too late and the spell wore off.

Outside on the street the famous San Francisco fog had rolled back in. I walked leisurely in the direction of my hotel, listening to the foghorns blow somewhere out on the water I knew lay some distance behind me as the gentle slope of North Beach gave way to Fisherman's Wharf. There were three of them and it seemed to me they blew in syncopation with one another, but perhaps my impression of this was influenced by all the jazz I'd just heard. It was funny . . . every once in a while I'd hear, see, or smell some little thing and it would hit me how far I'd travelled from home. I would hear a sea lion barking in the distance and it would dawn on me that I had come all the way across a continent and was now in California. I felt this way now as I strolled along the city streets listening to the foghorns.

I had made it about five blocks up Columbus Avenue when I reached into my coat pocket and felt the unfamiliar shape of something square and metallic. I pulled it out and found myself staring at a brass Zippo lighter. As my coat caught the light of a nearby streetlamp, I inspected its fabric a little more closely and a sudden realisation seized me. I felt in the other pocket and was greeted with a small stack of greenbacks folded in half and held together by a silver money clip engraved with the initials *J. A. B.* A small shiver of dread passed over me, and I turned and instantly took off in a near run back in the direction of the jazz club. As I hurried along, I prayed I would be able to switch the coats without having to explain my mistake to anyone. I hoped I was not wearing a white man's coat, as that could complicate the transaction.

Both of my prayers went unanswered. Immediately when I pushed my way back through the red upholstered door of the club's entrance I glimpsed a man hovering in the front alcove, scratching his head and holding the coat I now recognised was mine. He was white; a young man, close in age to myself. As I drew closer I observed he was of medium height and build, with a vaguely olive complexion and genteel Roman features. A lock of hair fell over his furrowed brow and he frowned as he leant his face down nearer to the coat, turning the garment over and over.

'Aha!' he said as soon as he caught sight of me and – moreover – the coat I was wearing. 'And just in time! I couldn't puzzle it out. Here I was, about to question whether I'd had too much drink.'

He smiled at me. His young face glowed in an open, easy manner. There was a curious sense of familiar warmth in it, and for a brief moment I lost my words.

'I'm terribly sorry,' I said, recovering. I shrugged out of his coat as quickly and delicately as possible, annoyed at myself for not thinking to remove it before I'd walked through the club door.

'You ought to be,' he said, still grinning. I noticed a faint trace of a southern accent. 'It'd probably be healthy for my liver if I *did* do some questioning on that subject.'

'I mean, for the mix-up,' I said. 'It was an honest mistake.' I handed over his coat. He accepted it but made no immediate move to return my coat. Instead, he held both of them up to the meagre lightbulb overhead.

'Would you look at that,' he said, squinting. 'They're remarkably similar. Except for the tiniest difference in the nap, eh?' I concurred, relieved as he finally released my coat to me. 'What alerted you to the switcheroo?'

'I put my hands in the pockets,' I admitted.

'Oh yeah!' The young man snapped his fingers and abruptly plunged his hand into one of the pockets. As he produced the money clip, I felt a sudden sense of chagrin.

'Hey,' I said, unable to keep a harsh, defensive note from creeping into my voice. 'It's all there. You can count it.'

He chuckled. 'No, no, no,' he said. 'Take it easy! No one's accusing you. I told the fellas I've been drinking with – see those guys over there? – that I'd pay for the next round. That's why I came looking for my coat in the first place.'

'Oh.' I smiled, sheepish and relieved.

He looked at me, an expression of amusement lingering on his lips. He had the eyes of a brooding puppy; his irises were a deep, lush brown, while his eyelashes were very black and very long. I glanced away on gut instinct, as though I had looked at the sun.

'Say, I suppose I owe you a reward,' he said.

'Beg pardon?'

'A reward – you know, for bringing the coat back. When you

lose something and someone takes the trouble to bring it back to you, it's customary to give a reward.' His smile widened devilishly into a grin. 'Will you accept payment in the form of a drink?'

'You don't have to do that.'

'Sure I do.'

I hesitated. I glanced over to where his friends were sitting. Three men sat hunched over in a booth. The sight of them made me uneasy, and an image of Rusty flashed through my mind.

'That wouldn't make sense,' I said. 'I'm the reason for the mix-up in the first place.' I gestured to the coat in the crook of my arm. 'And besides, if I've returned your coat to *you*, it's fair to say you've also returned my coat to me.'

'You make an excellent point,' he said. He took his coat, hung it back up on a coat-peg, and threw his arm around me. 'In that case we both owe each other a reward; we'll have to make it two drinks apiece.' He winked. 'C'mon, you can help carry.' He propelled me in the direction of the bar. 'I'm Joey,' he added.

Behind me I could hear the sounds of another jazz ensemble taking the stage and tuning up.

'Miles,' I answered.

'Where're you from, Miles?'

'New York.'

We ordered a round of whiskey neat and carried the drinks over to the booth. His friends peered curiously in my direction. They were arranged – completely by accident, I suppose – in a sort of chromatic-gradation scale according to their respective colouring: on the far right sat a freckly tow-head, the man in the middle was sandy-haired, and on the left was a brunette wearing glasses.

'Fellas, I'd like you to meet Miles, joining us all the way from New York. Fate, by way of a wool coat, has brought him to us tonight.'

We slid into the left side of the booth, where Joey perpetuated their colour wheel with his olive skin and dark locks, and I completed it in a way I'm sure they had not anticipated. They whistled upon his pronouncement.

'Long way from home, ain't ya?' said the sandy-haired man. It wasn't rude, but it wasn't altogether welcoming, either. He begrudgingly scooted over to make room in the booth and the seat trembled with the force of it. He was not quite fat, but there was an unapologetic stoutness about him that suggested he was once an overweight child and that he had managed to channel his sizable mass into a role as a playground bully.

'I suppose,' I said.

'Over there is my buddy Eddie,' Joey said, pointing to the tow-head and working counter-clockwise. 'And Eddie and I have just met Bill and Donald here.'

'How do you do?' I said.

They nodded politely. There was a funny atmosphere around the table, as though I had interrupted something already in progress. I took a swallow of whiskey, the amber liquid catching the glow of the flickering candle that sat in the middle of the table. Joey watched the light on my face closely as I drank, smiling at me as though we were old acquaintances and he'd just remembered some of the reasons behind his great fondness for me.

He was, I realised, an extremely handsome young man. I looked around the table at the others. There was more of an age difference between them than was detectable at first glance. I'd guessed Joey to be twenty-five or thereabouts, and only Eddie, the tow-head, appeared to be similar in age. As my eyes readjusted to the dim light of the darkened booth, I saw there were bags under Bill's eyes and a certain puffy looseness to his jaw line that suggested he was closer to forty. Donald, too, seemed older. The initial impression of youth he gave off was the product of a certain kind of fastidiousness, for he was trim, his dark hair was combed with precision, and his turtleneck and glasses had been selected with great care. His complexion was also smooth and well kept, but there were a number of minute telltale signs that gave him away: the tiniest crinkling at the outside corners of his eyes, a handful of silver threads woven into the dark brown around his temples.

'So, Miles,' Joey said, turning to me and carrying on our conversation as though we were alone in the booth. 'Are you going to tell me why you're carrying around jars of strange-looking bugs in your coat pockets?'

I felt my face flush. It hadn't dawned on me that, while I'd discovered the contents of his pockets, he'd likely discovered the same in return. 'My kid brother collects insects,' I said. 'They're for him.'

'Sounds like you're a good big brother,' he said, smiling. Then he frowned. 'Say, does that mean you kill the bugs, or do you let 'em live?'

'Cob – that's my kid brother – when he finds an insect that's already dead, he pins them to a board, but only if they're already dead. There are tiny holes in the lids of those jars; I was going to try to bring them back to New York alive. He builds terrariums for them.'

The frown disappeared and Joey smiled again, evidently pleased by this answer. It was oddly touching that he should care about the lives of a few insects. There was something about Joey's slouchy confidence and ease of manner that reminded me of Bobby. Yet, at the same time, there was an air of kindness and sensitivity about Joey that Bobby lacked.

Across the booth, the conversation was getting rowdy. We paused to listen for a few moments, and I inferred that Donald had been teaching Eddie to say something in French, a turn of events that had stout, far-from-francophone Bill incensed.

'Don't listen to him!' he hollered at Eddie and pointed to Donald. 'He can't talk a lick of French; he only wants you to think he can. It's all gibberish. Who knows what he's saying? Go to Paris and repeat that to any Frenchman on the street and they'll punch you in the nose.' Donald's trim, compact body stiffened.

'Perhaps they might,' Donald said, smiling condescendingly at Bill and giving Eddie a wicked, lascivious wink. 'But not because it's gibberish.'

'Anyway, who needs Paris? Travel's a waste of dough, if you ask me,' Bill said. 'You come home with nothing to show for it. Unless you count automobiles – I just bought myself a cherry of a Ford,' he said, his mouth twisting into a boastful smirk. It was clear he'd been thinking of how to segue to this very fact for the better part of the evening. 'It's parked right out front.'

'Hold on, now; you have a car here?' Joey asked. Joey's renewed interest in their conversation made Bill smile. He puffed out his chest with fresh optimism.

'Sure do,' he said.

'Well, why didn't you say so?' Joey said. 'What're we doing, sitting here, when we could be out taking a spin?'

And just like that, with Joey's charming white smile shining like a lighthouse beacon around the booth, it was decided. We finished our drinks and Joey cajoled the group into action. I racked my brain for a way to remain behind, for as much as I had taken a genuine liking to Joey, I didn't care for the rest of them and I didn't want to go along. The idea of getting into Bill's car filled me with dread. I worried about being taken to a part of the city where I wouldn't be able to handle myself. Everyone rose from the table and shuffled out the door. I followed reluctantly, drifting behind until Joey doubled back and threw an arm around me, herding me along.

'Ain't she a beaut?' Bill said as we approached a very shiny four-door, two-tone red-and-white Ford Fairlane parked at the curb.

I composed a few excuses and tested them out silently in my head, but I cringed when I pictured delivering any of them to Joey, flashing back to the expression of betrayed disappointment I'd glimpsed on the young man's face at the Hamilton Lodge Ball. I had only just met Joey, but for reasons I didn't quite understand, I couldn't stand the thought of seeing that same expression appear on his face. I would go along, I decided – for now.

I climbed into Bill's shiny Ford, Joey on my heels and the whiskey and jazz from the club swirling in my head. The engine growled to life and we rolled down the windows to breathe in the cool, fog-laden night air.

We drove all over the city that night. It was a kind of alcohol-fuelled informal tour, and the reason when I think of San Francisco now, I feel instantly light-headed and see a ghostly blur of neon from the all lights on Broadway and Geary. Someone – I can't remember which of those boys now – cooked up the crazy idea that we should take the car down Lombard Street. It was one o'clock in the morning and the tourists who usually swarmed all over Lombard were absent, the unusual stretch of street looking like an abandoned playground. I can recall us hooting and hollering with terror as we crested the hill and dropped down into the stretch of red-brick switchbacks that are known to make up 'the Crookedest Street in America'.

'Let's do it again,' Joey cheered, once we had reached the bottom of the street. 'Loop around, and let's take turns. We'll each try to go as fast as we can, and we can see who drives it best.' Had anyone else suggested it, I am certain Bill would've frowned and denied the request. But as I watched him turn to face Joey, proud of the excitement he had instilled in the beautiful boy that Joey was, it was plain that Bill was hungry to do anything that would produce more of that effect, and soon enough we were at the top of the hill again. Someone called out, 'Chinese fire drill!' and we all jumped out, ran around the car clockwise, and jumped back in, this time with Joey behind the wheel.

Joey piloted us down the hill without incident, save for one little bump of the right front tyre to the curb as he turned down the second switchback. He hadn't driven it any faster than Bill had, but we all cheered him at the bottom; very likely our motivations were more invested in seeing his radiant face illuminate again than to congratulate him on his mediocre driving skills. After Joey, Eddie was given a turn, and then Donald. Donald took his watch off and the four of them passed it around in order to time one another, each of them trying to top one another's speed. Eddie turned out to be an expert driver; Donald was not. I'm fairly certain there was a potted plant in some kind of Grecian-looking urn in front of one of those elaborate Victorian homes that didn't wholly survive our misadventure that night. At one point a police car came trolling around, the officers peering into our automobile with disapproving eyes, debating whether to pull us over for cruising. It was clear they had their suspicions about a car full of men. We drove away for a little while, until Joey insisted we go back.

Bill's interest in the activity dwindled along with his enthusiasm for each successive driver, and by the time Donald had completed his descent and returned us to the top of the hill, Bill was done with the business of letting other men put minor dings and dents on the great shiny body of his treasured Fairlane.

'Awright,' he said. 'Enough's enough. Let's go see about a li'l house party I heard about over in the Mission.'

'Wait a minute,' Joey said. 'Miles hasn't had his turn.'

'*Miles* doesn't need a turn, do you, *Miles*?' Bill said, not turning around to look at me where I sat in the back seat.

'Suppose not,' I said. In truth, I hadn't wanted one.

'See? Miles forfeits his turn. Now let's get to that party.'

'He can't forfeit,' Joey insisted. He was sitting next to me and reached over to squeeze my hand. I felt a strange jolt of electricity. 'I want to see him drive it. Let's just go down one more time.'

Bill sighed, and this time he *did* turn around. He gave me a good once-over, glaring at me from the front seat. His eyes found the place where Joey's hand remained on my own, and then rested there. He pursed his lips in bitterness. I tried my best to signal my innocence, that he was mistaken about me, but he took little notice.

'Does he even know how to drive a car?' Bill asked aloud, as if I weren't present.

'Only one way to find out,' Joey said, turning to me and winking.

'Jesus, Mary, and Joseph,' Bill said. 'Fine. Let's get this over with. I can't believe I'm putting up with this cockamamie idea.'

'Why don't you want to let him drive?' Joey pursued.

'I think you know why.'

'What's the big deal, Bill?' Donald asked. 'Negros have been driving us around in cars for ages. One more night isn't going to hurt any.'

Bill was pleased by the demeaning comment, for he guffawed loudly. 'Hah. All right, fine; I give. Everybody out!'

We got out and switched places. But by then the atmosphere had changed. There was no giddy dashing about the car and joyous slamming of doors. We simply got out and marched in a sombre circle. I climbed into the driver's seat, aware of Bill sliding into the back seat directly behind me. The car doors clicked shut and Bill leant over my shoulder, his hot breath spilling over my neck.

'You'd better damn well know how to drive, boy,' he growled.

'Look, fellas, I really don't have to do this,' I said. I tried to make my voice as relaxed and friendly as I could manage.

'Yes, you do,' said Joey. 'I've got my money riding on you being the best driver here.'

'Oh yeah? Is that so?' Bill turned to where Joey sat next to me in the front passenger seat. 'You want to put something on it in earnest?'

'Sure,' Joey said. 'Why not?' His grin masked what I took to be a belligerent note in his voice.

'What d'ya say to a hunnerd bucks?'

'I say swell. Got yourself a bet,' Joey replied. I had watched Joey count the dollars in his money clip only a couple of hours ago, and then watched him spend most of that amount. It was clear everyone in the car was also privy to this fact, and it occurred to me that Bill was somehow depending upon it. I shuddered to imagine how Bill might try to collect a substitute payment. But Joey only winked at me. I widened my eyes back in return. What did he think I could do, and why?

I wrapped my hands around the cold lacquered plastic of the steering wheel. We'd had the whole zig-zag stretch of Lombard to ourselves for the better part of the evening, but now a family of tourists had turned up to have a go at it. I decided it was best to wait until they had cleared the steep switchbacks entirely before embarking.

'Day trippers,' Donald declared disdainfully. He squinted to get a better look at the dilapidated car. 'Oh, Lord help us. Probably from the Central Valley. It's almost two o'clock in the morning, and they're too cheap to stay overnight in the city, so they're cramming all the sights into one day.' The car reached the bottom of the hill and hesitated, finally turning off onto Leavenworth.

I took a breath. The truth was, this was only my seventh time behind the wheel of a car in the course of my entire life. My family had neither the money nor the need for a car. The subway took us everywhere we could hope to go. In fact, it was only by virtue of an uncle who fulfilled his promise to my dying father by once a year making the long road trip into the city from Detroit to check on our family in New York that I'd been taught how to drive at all. I closed my eyes and said a prayer. I'd decided the best I could hope for was that I would not cause any major damage to an automobile I could not afford to repair. I had a sudden flash of Marcus, the brother I'd never met, whose photograph I'd nearly bored holes into with my eyes growing up.

All at once, as though it were not connected to me, my foot abruptly lifted from the brake pedal and slammed on the gas. A terrified silence fell over the car as we flew forward and plunged downward, first this way, then that. At some point I was dimly aware of my feet riding both the gas and brake at the same time. Joey's hand gripped my upper arm; this time it was less a gesture of support and more the brute vice grip of fear. The car moved like a skier slaloming down a slope without incident, and although the endeavour was filled with enough anxiety to last a year, in truth the whole thing took mere seconds. When I reached the bottom I felt my foot slam down the brake only, and I reached behind the steering wheel to wrench the car into park. The car rocked roughly on its tyres and came to a standstill.

It was silent, save for the sound of the men gasping as they caught their breath.

'Ho-leee shit!' Eddie exclaimed. He reached over the seat, gave a quick clap upon my back, then squeezed Joey's shoulder. 'Holy shit, man! I think you just won yourself a hundred bucks!'

'I'd say so,' Donald said. I caught a glance of Bill in the rear-view mirror. His mouth had rolled into a firm line, and he seemed less than pleased with the result of my efforts. At that moment I understood I had been a fool not to realise that putting a dent in his Fairlane was not the worst thing I could've done.

'We never shook on it, and you know that means it ain't really a deal, but I'll give you your money anyway,' he said.

Still exhilarated, Joey took no notice of Bill's sneer. 'Did I *tell* you or did I tell you?' he grinned, talking to everyone and no one in particular. He turned to me, awkwardly squeezing my shoulder in happiness. 'Say, I ought to split my winnings with you.'

The thought of my collecting fifty of the begrudged one hundred dollars proved too much for Bill. I noticed his eye beginning to twitch with angry irritation. His temples bulged as his jaw worked.

'All right, everybody back out! Time to gimme back my rightful seat,' he said. He opened the car door and the rest of us automatically followed suit. 'Quick, quick!' he commanded, and everyone stepped faster, double-timing it around the Fairlane for one last ridiculous Chinese fire drill. During all the previous intervals when we had scurried around the car like a tiny colony of confused ants, I had been the last to climb back into the vehicle, not wanting to take a seat until I could be sure I wasn't getting in anybody's way. This time was no exception. One by one, car doors slammed shut as I belaboured my steps slightly more than the others and looked for the single remaining seat. I saw my place was now in the back seat and I reached for the door handle. But before I was able to depress the button, Bill stuck his head out the driver's-side window.

'Too bad you can't run as fast as you drive, darkie!' he yelled. Suddenly I heard the engine of the Fairlane give a tremendous roar. The tyres squealed, and as the car peeled out I tried to release and pull my hand away but I was not quick enough. I felt it nearly rip at the wrist.

I cried out involuntarily from the pain, reactively tucking my injured hand in my opposite armpit and squeezing it tightly there in some sort of gesture meant to stave off the excruciating discomfort as it radiated up and down my nerves. I watched the tail lights of Bill's Fairlane recede. They moved off like a pair of glowing red eyes floating into the dark, foggy night as the automobile sped away. The air immediately around me was thick with the sickening scent of burnt rubber, and I glanced down to observe two distinct black streaks on the pavement that had been left behind by Bill's tyres. I stood there blinking, partly from surprise and partly from the involuntary tears that had sprung to my eyes as a result of my injured hand.

So, I thought. They had left me. My heart still thudding hot in my chest, I inhaled a deep lungful of cool, wet air. Somewhere in the distance a dog barked, and somewhere else a mourning dove hooted its haunting, owl-like cry. I hurried homeward, hoping not to cross paths with the police cruiser again before I made it back to my hotel.

42

About a week or so passed. I put the automobile incident behind me and refocused my energies on hunting down my father's locker. Try as I might, I was still hard-pressed to get on base. The guards were unfriendly, consistently meeting my enquiries with a brusque, firm indifference. The money I'd saved was dwindling; I began to brace myself with the thought of returning to New York empty-handed after all.

Then one morning I rose, shaved, dressed myself, and ambled down the hotel stairs, passing by the man who tended the front desk. He was a burly man with a heavy moustache and I felt vaguely sorry for him whenever I saw him, for he was obliged to sit in a bizarre little windowed enclosure, the kind that resembled a movie theatre ticket booth. It had been painted burgundy and framed up with gilded woodwork, as though to distract from the fact it had obviously been put in place by a wary manager worried about robbery. I usually gave the morning clerk an impersonal, apologetic nod and continued on my way, but that morning as I made my way to the front door he startled me as he rapped on the glass with his knuckles.

'Mr Tillman,' he called in a gruff voice through the circular speaking hole in the window. I turned and doubled back upon hearing my name.

'Yes?'

'Message for ya,' he grunted. He slid a slip of paper under the window; then took a deep sip from a dirty-looking mug and reached up to wipe a few beads of coffee from his moustache with his thumb and forefinger. I picked up the paper and read it.

Aha! Found you.
Meet me at the coffee shop around the corner when you're ready.
– Joey

I blinked and reread the message.

'When did my friend leave this?' I asked.

''Bout an hour ago.' The clerk shrugged.

'Thanks.' I hurried out the door and half-stumbled around the corner. There was Joey, sitting in the window of the coffee shop. I slowed down as I drew near, hesitated, then knocked on the glass. He looked up, surprised. All at once, his face broke out in a wide, familiar grin and another jolt of electricity went through me. He waved at me to come inside, and I walked to the coffee shop's entrance, crossed the room, and slid into the seat opposite him.

'You weren't an easy man to find,' he said once I'd settled into the booth. 'I only had a first name to go on. And your description, of course. Thankfully, your – ahem – hotel doesn't seem too concerned about the privacy of its guests.'

'You looked for me?'

'All over the city,' he said. 'Listen,' he said, suddenly turning serious and glancing at the bandage around my injured hand as he leant over the table. 'It weighed heavy on me. I want to apologise for the fellas' behaviour the other night . . . You know, for driving off. That kind of business wasn't my idea, and I really had it out with

Bill after that. I convinced him to go back for you, but by the time we did, you were long gone.'

I ought to have been leery of seeing him again. The night in Bill's Fairlane had reminded me of Cliff's party and of Rusty. The bruises from the latter incident had finally vanished only a few days ago. I knew at that point I should simply thank Joey for the apology and go, but for some reason I felt tethered to the booth.

'I'd like to make it up to you,' Joey said.

'Not necessary.'

'Well, I'd like to buy you breakfast, at least. Would you stay for breakfast?'

I tried to form the words *No, thank you* but they felt thick in my throat. I'd been walking around the city, passing entire days without exchanging more than five words with anybody, and I realised it felt good to talk to someone. My nostrils were already full of the rich smells of a good diner breakfast: eggs, bacon, pancakes, maple syrup. My mouth watered in spite of me.

'I suppose breakfast wouldn't hurt,' I relented.

A woman with tobacco-tinted skin and a pencil tucked behind one ear eventually wandered over to refill Joey's coffee and we ordered.

'What brings you all the way from New York to San Francisco?' Joey asked once she had gone. 'Besides your infamous insect safari, of course.'

I smiled and thought of how to answer. Before I knew it, I was explaining about my father, about his locker and the alleged journal it contained, and about my frustrations getting on base. 'I just don't know what to do,' I said, shaking my head.

'But there's something else, too,' he said once I'd finished explaining my mission. 'Isn't there?'

'What do you mean?'

'About this business with your father's locker. Holding you back. You seem' – he searched for the right word – 'like you're of two minds. Like you're frustrated, sure, but also a tiny bit relieved.'

I stared at him. I had never considered myself half so transparent; he hardly knew me. 'Well . . .' I began to answer. Out came the rest of it. I told him about Clarence, and about the doubt Clarence had managed to plant in my mind. Joey sat at the diner table, sopping up eggs over easy with the crusts of mildly burnt toast, while I talked more in forty minutes than I had in weeks. There was something in the way he posed a question and followed it up with a generous pause, I think, that drew me out. I had never noticed all the pauses that were missing from most people's conversations. Years later, I wondered if Joey's beautiful pauses had something to do with his being from the south and the slower pace of southern life, but I realise now this was an oversimplification. It was not only that Joey paused but that he paused *for me*, with a kind smile on his lips, sincerely waiting for my answers.

By the time Joey had sopped up the last bit of egg yolk with a final bit of toast, I had relayed every detail I'd ever known about my father, laying it all out in a jumble as though dumping a box of jigsaw puzzle pieces on the table.

'I'll help you,' he said, pulling a dollar bill from his wallet and settling the check. 'It's pretty clear this is a moment you'll regret for the rest of your life if you don't try a little harder. What you need is a good, swift kick in the ass.' He looked at me and dropped the comedy routine. Gone was the mischievous flirt from the night at the jazz club one week ago, the impulsive kid who wanted to drive down that tiny, treacherous block of Lombard Street at top speed. 'I'd like to help you look,' he repeated, this time in a more serious tone. 'If you'll let me.'

I stared at him. 'I'm certain you have better things to do,' I said. I smiled, hoping to signal that he was off the hook, that this gesture wasn't necessary.

'Honestly, I haven't,' he said. He grinned. 'I just got out of the army and I'm killing time, waiting around to hear about a job with the State Department.'

I blinked.

'Don't you see? That's the best part: I've got all the time in the world, and to top it off, I can help you get on base, maybe poke around and ask a few questions to see if anyone remembers your old man or has any records. If you're smart, you'll take me up on my offer.' He winked. I thought about it. It was true he was offering an advantage in that he was an ex-soldier: he would be able to get on base, which I, so far, had been unable to do.

I clenched my jaw and swallowed, unsure.

'All right,' was all I finally said. We shook hands as though to seal the deal and made our way out of the diner and onto the street, where the sun beat down brilliantly on the bright, chalk-coloured sidewalk. It was funny: you always held your breath in the mornings in that city, waiting to find out whether the sun would finally break through the fog, and when.

43

Joey turned out to be a good ally to have as I mustered the energy for a fresh effort to hunt for my father's journal. His charm went a long way to grease the wheels. As promised, he got us onto all the local army facilities, of which there were many. But as I suspected, getting on base was only the first hurdle. The staff that manned the administrative offices was hardly friendlier than the guards at the gatehouses, and all of them insisted a footlocker like the one my mother had described to me didn't exist.

Finally, when I was on the verge of attempting to convince Joey not to waste any more of his time, a clerk at one of the offices in the Presidio pointed to the key in the palm of my hand and declared, 'Why, you ain't looking for no footlocker on a military base. Sure as I'm born, that there's the kind of key they use for the lockers down at the Y.'

'The Y?' I repeated.

'You know: the Y. Young Men's Christian Association. Military boys use the Y for all sorts of things; it's a regular home away from home,' the clerk said. 'I tell ya, that looks like the kinda key they have for locking your things up at night at the big Y on Golden Gate and Leavenworth.'

Joey and I exchanged a surprised look. Here was a development that should have been obvious but that had never occurred to me.

'How did I not think of that?' Joey said. 'The Y. Of course!'

We found San Francisco's main YMCA at the intersection the clerk scribbled down on a slip of paper. The sun was beginning to go down by then, making long shadows on everything, and the entrance to the Y sported a pair of Roman columns that lent the building a rather tired, sombre, bank-like air. Inside, it was humid and a bit rundown – but I suppose that's to be expected of any building subject to constant use. We approached the large reception desk that loomed in the entryway, but it was unattended. There was a thick, heavy boys' dormitory scent that permeated the place; it smelt like a concoction of equal parts fried chicken, gym socks, and cigarette smoke. Men roamed about in every state of dress. From somewhere in a hallway a telephone rang while a television played in a large room nearby. I thought to wait at the reception desk for someone to come, but Joey motioned me on.

'C'mon.'

As he walked nonchalantly through the maze of hallways and staircases I realised there was a certain ease of familiarity in his step. He knew his way around. I shouldn't have been surprised Joey had been here before, but I found myself wondering with whom. But before I could work up the nerve to ask him, we came to a hallway between a gymnasium and some kind of Turkish bath. I looked and saw it was lined with metal lockers. I held up my key and saw that it was likely the right size for one of these.

'Aha.' Joey grinned. 'Thought so!'

I couldn't help but grin back at him. My heart gave a heavy pump and I realised I was beginning to feel excited. I searched for the locker that matched the tiny number embossed on my father's key. I took a breath, lifted the key to insert it, and hesitated, my hand hovering before the locker's blank metal face.

'Go on,' Joey urged after several seconds ticked by. 'What are you waiting for?' This was rhetorical. He knew, of course. In matters like this one, there were only two states: *before* and *after*. I was holding on to one more second of *before*.

But I got myself worked up over nothing. The locker door did not swing open to reveal an empty dark space or even a locker full of my father's things, for the locker door did not swing open *at all*. Once I finally put the key in the lock, it slipped in easily enough, but it did not turn. I tried it again, this time more forcefully. Nothing. I inserted it upside down and tried again, but to no avail. I was baffled. Certainly it was the right type of key, in the right type of lock. I checked the number on the key, and the number on the locker: 273. There were no sixes or nines to confuse things . . . They certainly matched.

'I don't understand,' I murmured.

'Let me try it,' Joey said, taking the key from my hand. He tried to turn it with the same result. Suddenly we became aware of a presence standing behind us.

'Excuse me,' came a gruff voice. We turned around to see a thick-necked young man in gym attire, his hair dripping with what smelt to be sweat. 'That's my locker.' We simply stared at him. He took a closer look at the two of us, glanced at his locker, and frowned. 'Say, what kind of monkey business are you up to, anyhow?'

'This is *your* locker?' Joey asked. 'It can't be.'

'Sure it is,' the man replied. 'Why wouldn't it be?'

I held up my key for him to inspect.

'Hmph. Well, that's funny,' the man said, squinting at the number on the key. He produced a key of his own and held it up to mine. 'But they're not the same where it counts.' He pointed at the teeth of the two keys, and it was true: the size of the key and the style of the embossed numbers were identical, but the jagged ridges were cut differently.

'Say, I'm starting to get the feeling you wise guys are up to no good,' the man warned. Joey didn't answer, lost in his observation of the pair of keys now shining in the palm of his hand. I detected a slight pinkish hue creep into the man's face and tried to surreptitiously elbow Joey, but to no effect. 'Look,' said the man, growing impatient, 'I don't know what kind of con you're trying to put over on me, but I think I've had enough. I'll take my key back now.'

'Whoa, buddy,' Joey said. 'It's no con. We're just trying to figure something out.' It was the first time I saw Joey's charm fall flat.

'I'll give *you* something to figure out,' he said. He lifted a fist, and it was clear what was bound to happen next.

'We've upset you,' I blurted, 'and we're very sorry.' The man turned to look at me. 'It's all an honest mistake,' I continued. I smiled my most ingratiating smile – the one that was all white teeth and dark skin and usually made me detest myself whenever I used it. 'Let's go talk to the manager, shall we?' My hands, during the course of this plea, remained clasped behind my back, as I had learnt was the necessary position to defuse a fight among men, especially if you are a young Negro with what people describe as an athletic build. Just then another young man came into the hallway of lockers and so I added, 'Please, that's reasonable, isn't it, sir?' for good measure. There was nothing like begging a man in front of an uninitiated bystander to make him less interested in hitting you.

It worked. He gave a glance to the young fellow who had

just entered the hallway and dropped his half-formed fist. He grunted. 'Fine. Follow me.'

Luckily, this time the manager – who had not been present when Joey and I had entered the Y – was there when the three of us arrived at the front desk. He was puffing anxiously at a cigarette and wore a second unlit one tucked over his ear, all while trying to jimmy open a drawer under the reception desk with a ladies' nail file. He looked up, glimpsed the three of us approaching, and instantly frowned, accurately perceiving that along with us came extra work for him.

'Having some kind of beef, boys?' he asked. He gave up on the drawer and put the nail file down.

'I found these two operators trying to break into my locker,' our escort replied.

'They any good at it?' the man joked, holding up the nail file and pointing to the locked drawer, but no one laughed. 'Hmm.' The manager made a closer inspection of us; first of me, then of Joey. 'Haven't I seen you here before?' he said to Joey.

'There's been a mix-up,' Joey said, not answering the question.

'What kind of mix-up?' the manager asked.

We explained our situation and showed him the key.

'Hmm,' the manager said, taking his cigarette out of his mouth and squinting one eye at the key. 'These fellas might be telling the truth, Floyd,' he said to the thick-necked young man. With one mighty push of his feet, the manager scooted his rolling chair to the far end of the reception desk. He opened a drawer and produced a very weathered-looking logbook.

'Two seventy-three, you say?'

I nodded. Everyone watched with intrigue as his finger slid down the page. Finally it stopped and he tapped a single line of entry.

'Yep. Had a whole slew of these after the boys started shipping out to the South Pacific. Everyone comin' and goin' every which way. Problem is, half of 'em never came back! Marked as abandoned. We had to change the locks.' He rubbed out his current cigarette in an ashtray and retrieved the cigarette tucked over his ear. 'That explains why they were fooling with your locker, Floyd,' he said. Floyd looked disappointed. I knew he had been hoping to deliver a sound pounding. But he wasn't alone in his disappointment. I was feeling pretty crestfallen myself; we'd finally found the correct locker, only to discover it had been classed as 'abandoned' and turned over to a meathead named Floyd.

'Got some ID on you, fella?' the manager asked me. He did not ask Joey. I hesitated, unsure if he meant to harass me.

'Sure I do,' I said, shrugging.

'Well, if you can prove you're kin, that's all we need.'

'All you need for what?'

'Why, to claim the contents, of course.'

My eyes went wide and I almost fell over. 'Excuse me?'

'That's all we need,' the manager repeated. 'Unless you're not here to claim the contents?'

'Oh, he's here to claim the contents,' Joey answered for me. 'You betcha he is.' Everyone except the manager appeared excited by this turn of events. Even Floyd looked slightly less peeved. Curious about what these mysterious 'contents' could be that previously occupied his locker, he lingered a bit before finally losing interest and lumbering away.

A basement storage room was searched and a paper carton labelled TILLMAN – 273 was produced. After showing my identification card and signing five typewritten forms (all of which immediately went into another carton in the dusty storage room, where I'm sure they have never been seen again by another living human being since), I was the proud owner of a large, leather-bound journal full of slightly water-damaged, curling, yellowed pages, all loaded to the hilt with my father's barely legible handwriting. It was a rather pathetic-looking prize. If Floyd had stuck around, I'm certain he would have been immensely disappointed. But I was grinning like a fool. Joey grinned, too.

44

EDEN

After our disastrous party, Cliff and I began spending more and more time apart. In the evenings, he went out drinking with Swish while I comforted myself with stacks of manuscripts. In the mornings, I laid out breakfast while Cliff slept in. I quietly set the table with coffee, toast, tomato juice, a grapefruit sliced in half, a couple of hard-boiled eggs. Then I tiptoed out the door to go to work. During the rare times we ate breakfast together, neither of us brought up the subject of what had happened to Miles. Our guilt was an elephant in the room, a heavy weight on both of us that neither of us was willing to directly acknowledge.

One evening, however, I came home to see Cliff getting dressed in a sports jacket. It was the same jacket he'd worn the day he'd taken Judy and me to the Cedarbrook Club.

'Where are you going?' I asked.

'Dinner with my folks,' he replied, inspecting the jacket for lint and not making eye contact with me.

'Oh,' I said, bewildered. 'That's a surprise. There wasn't anything pencilled in on your father's calendar.'

'Well, you don't need to know *everything* that goes on in *my* family,' Cliff snapped. 'You're a secretary, for Chrissake.'

I was taken aback. 'What . . .' I stammered, 'what is that supposed to mean?'

'Nothing,' Cliff said. 'I'm sorry. Look, I gotta split.'

'Cliff . . .' I said, dismayed.

'What?' He turned around. 'I gotta put in some time with the Old Man and the Old Lady. It's not like I can invite you along, now, can I?'

He checked his pocket for his key and shuffled out the door, pecking me on the cheek in a rote manner as he went. I stood there looking at the closed door, still slightly stunned by his reaction. He had emphasised certain words. My *family. You don't need to know. You're a* secretary.

I began to wonder if our elopement wasn't all a big mistake. The picture I'd had in my head that day after coming home from Cedarbrook and talking to Judy on the telephone was fading away. It had been a strange journey from being Eden Katz to being Eden Collins – a journey that didn't really feel complete, to be honest – and it dawned on me that I hadn't the faintest idea how to be Eden Nelson.

I was restless after Cliff hurried out. I'd been working so hard lately, there wasn't even very much to read; I was down to the dregs of the slush pile, and I feared the manuscripts there weren't enough to hold my attention that night. I thought of popping out to the bar around the corner and using their phone to call Judy, but I knew she had a date with Chester.

It occurred to me that I knew of a book launch that was happening that evening, and perhaps I ought to go.

For a good while after starting my new job at Bonwright I'd been afraid to go to the publishing parties as I had done when I worked at Torchon & Lyle. At first, I was afraid I might run into Miss Everett. I imagined she might cause a scene or else cut me in some terrible way in front of a group of people. But then I remembered how unsociable she could be and how she never went to any of the publishing parties. Nonetheless, I'd gone to an awful lot of parties back in my Torchon & Lyle days, and even if I was safe from Miss Everett, there was still reason to be cautious about bumping into an acquaintance who knew me as Eden Katz. If someone who knew me as Eden Collins rubbed elbows with someone who knew me as Eden Katz and my name happened to come up, there would be confusion, and that confusion might spell embarrassing disaster for me.

But it was also true I had a new look now . . . a new haircut and style . . . I might not be immediately recognisable. I mulled it over. The prospect of staying in that night was absolutely dismal. The allure of the publishing parties began to beckon again, and I decided to take a chance and go. I changed into a nice blouse and skirt and took the subway over to a modern-looking ballroom in a five-storey building near Columbus Circle.

I was right about the haircut making a difference. I was relieved – and perhaps, later, a little disappointed – to realise how truly anonymous I was among the guests at the publishing party. Once inside, I strolled the room, recognising people to whom I had once made a conscientious effort to be introduced, but they floated right on by me, vacant looks in their eyes and placid smiles on their lips. I'm sure if I approached them directly and reminded them of my name, they would've shaken my hand enthusiastically and remembered me – or at least pretended to remember me. But I had a second option at my disposal now: I could also introduce myself all over again, and no one would suspect a thing.

At one point during the evening, I found myself standing near a cluster of men, all of whom were deeply engaged in animated debate. Ayn Rand's new book, *Atlas Shrugged*, had been published the previous year, and it seemed no two critics could agree on the book's merits; you either loved it or you hated it.

'It's every bit as good as *The Fountainhead*,' one man was in the middle of arguing as I joined their circle.

'Exactly,' replied a thin, older gentleman in a sarcastic voice. 'Every bit as *good*.'

'Well, say what you will about *The Fountainhead*,' the first man sniffed, obviously offended. 'But *I* certainly wouldn't scoff at those sales figures. And did you hear? The print run for *Atlas Shrugged* was a hundred thousand! The masses have spoken. People want to read her books.'

'I can't see why,' a third man chimed in. 'All that dreadful harping! You'd get preached at less in church.'

'She harps because she's a woman; that's what they all do,' grunted a swarthy, snub-nosed man.

'I don't see much about her to prove she truly *is* a woman,' the older gentleman said. 'She's all hard edges and brass.'

'But she's part of their sorority nonetheless, I'd wager. You there,' the first man said, turning to me. I froze. 'Young lady. You're a woman. Surely you like Ayn Rand?'

I bit my lip, feeling put on the spot. I cleared my throat. 'No,' I said coolly. 'Actually, I don't.' I hoped I wasn't skating out onto thin ice. 'I don't care for her prose style, and I'm not especially in favour of her ideas. She's a woman, sure, but in my opinion she doesn't seem to know how to write women characters. At least, not any I'd ever recognise from real life. They might be tough as nails, but they certainly aren't very modern or liberated when it comes down to it.' I hesitated and reflected a moment. 'To tell the truth, I don't love her or hate her; I suppose I simply find her strange,' I said. 'Her ideas are so inflexible and so absolute, and yet I can't see how she – Ayn Rand, a woman – could possibly fit into the selfsame philosophical world she herself has set out to create.' I stopped. They were all staring at me by this point, and I felt my cheeks flush.

'That's very astutely put,' a female voice said. I looked to where the voice had emanated and saw a woman; I don't know why I hadn't noticed her before. She was very diminutive – which, in my case, is really the pot calling the kettle black, I must admit – but she was perhaps even a bit shorter and more slender than myself. Yet despite her small stature there was something striking about her, something that suggested she could fill up a room, too, if she wanted to. Part of this impression came from the manner in which she put herself together. She wore an impeccably tailored green suit, and standing among the men at a publishing party she was a dot of rich emerald colour in a sea of grey flannel suits.

'And what is your opinion of the book we've come here to celebrate today?' she asked. I thought I detected a note of testing in her voice.

'Oh, no one ever discusses the book at the launch. Isn't that bad form?'

'Good girl,' she said, and gave a hint of a smile. She touched my elbow and steered me a small distance away from the men. The men resumed their debate about Ayn Rand without us. I put out my hand to introduce myself.

'I'm—'

'Eden Katz, I know.'

I blinked, dumbstruck and suddenly frightened.

'No, we haven't been introduced,' she confirmed, reading my mind. 'But, you see, I've gone to quite a lot of these, and I make it my business to listen to everything going on around me. I've been told I have a very good memory for faces and names.

'Mavis Singer,' she said. She reached into her pocketbook and politely produced a card. 'Farbman & Company.'

'Oh, you're an editor!' I said, encouraged to see the title embossed on her card. 'Gosh, I'm awfully surprised you remember seeing me.' I nodded over my shoulder to the rest of the room and shrugged. 'I thought I'd gone to a lot of trouble to make an impression, but nobody else seems to think so.'

'I remember your name was Katz. And I remember that you worked for Bob Turner at Torchon & Lyle,' she said, and paused as though considering her next sentence carefully. 'Given those two facts, I wondered how you might make out. Are you still there?'

I swallowed, sensing I was cornered. I didn't want to get caught, but there was a wonderful dignity about Ms Singer, and I felt compelled to tell her the truth – in whatever form I could manage it. 'I'm at Bonwright now,' I answered. 'With Roger Nelson.'

'Hmm,' she said. 'That's a rather interesting place for you to wind up, too.'

I didn't know what she meant by this, but it made me nervous, so I waited for her to continue.

'You know, Eden, I remember how difficult it was when I started in this business. There can be quite a lot of . . . *pitfalls* to navigate, especially for a woman. If you like, I can come over to Bonwright and check in on you sometime, take you to lunch and offer some advice if you want it.'

'Oh – uh, no,' I said hurriedly. 'It's a lovely offer, but I wouldn't want to take up your time.'

The last thing I wanted was for her to turn up at Bonwright looking for Eden Katz and find Eden Collins instead. Ms Singer looked me up and down as if trying to puzzle me out. She raised an eyebrow at me.

'Or you could drop in on me at my office, if you prefer.'

I bit my lip. 'Well,' I said, 'that might be nice.' Frightened as I was of being exposed, I was tempted.

'You're welcome anytime,' Mavis said, still trying to read my face. I knew I hadn't made it easy. She smiled pleasantly and we shook hands. I slipped her card into the little clutch I was carrying, and we both returned our attention to the rest of the party. I thought of her again later that evening, back at the apartment, when I emptied the clutch out and sorted through all the cards I'd collected. Usually, I wrote little notes on the backs to remind me of people's personalities and tastes, and then I put them all in a big manila envelope for safekeeping.

That night, when I got to Ms Singer's, I simply held the card and gazed at it, pondering. She had certainly seemed smart and kind, and it appeared she was encouraging, willing to be a kind of mentor to a young person like myself. But then, Miss Everett had seemed that way, too, at first. I went back and forth several times over, debating whether or not to call Ms Singer and accept her kind offer.

Eventually, after staring at it for several minutes, I tucked Ms Singer's card away with the others in the envelope, with a solitary question mark written on the back. I didn't quite know yet what to make of Ms Singer and her interest in my career.

45

CLIFF

I was off to have dinner with my folks at the '21' Club. It was true what I'd said to Eden about having to put in some time with My Old Man and My Old Lady. I'd spent less and less time with them ever since I'd dropped out of Columbia, mostly because whenever I did see them they only sang one tune, and that was to harp on me about getting a job. It was not a song and dance anyone wanted to hear, much less one I wanted to hear, but they were my family after all and I nonetheless felt obligated to see them from time to time.

But if I'm being totally honest I will tell you I was the one who initiated our dinner arrangements that night. I'd phoned my mother and gave her some line about how much I missed both her and My Old Man and that I was feeling too distant, and would she come into the city and have dinner? I even offered to make the reservation, which I thought was a nice touch. Throughout my childhood, my mother was often more preoccupied with her charities than she was with child-rearing, but she was always susceptible to a good guilt trip. Of course she called my father just as soon as we hung up and demanded we all have dinner together as a family.

I felt bad when Eden came home and saw me getting dressed to go out, because I'd set up the dinner at the last minute and of course I hadn't told her about it. It wasn't as though I could invite her anyway and I hadn't expected she would get so bent out of shape about it. But as soon as I looked at her face it was plain to see how hurt she was. We'd been fighting – or not really fighting so much as silently warring, because when we fought Eden had this trick of being absolutely small and quiet and terrible – ever since the bad business that had happened at our party. For a little while before all that party business, just after we'd eloped, we'd been truly happy but I wasn't sure any more that we were a match made in heaven. She had seemed like she was all for my becoming a writer at first, but when you really got down to it, she was very limited about what she was willing to do to help me achieve this goal. She was happy enough to type up my work and all that jazz but she wouldn't help me when it really mattered, and that was when it was time to get it into someone else's hands and get it published.

Earlier that day, Gene had stopped by the apartment. He had finally printed the first volume of *The Tuning Fork* and he'd dropped by my pad to give me a couple of contributor's copies. I was pretty happy to see it; if there's one thing a writer loves, it's to see his name in print. Usually whenever I looked at my name I looked right through it, but when you see it in print in a magazine or a book you get to see it the way other people see it and suddenly it becomes a solid thing like it never was before. Gene and I knocked back a few beers together and admired the slick look of the magazine and by the time he left to go lay copies out around all the Village cafes I'd gotten pretty high on myself. That was when I'd gotten the idea to phone my mother and set up dinner.

Now I was on my way to the restaurant, wearing a jacket that itched and was a little too tight in the shoulders but was the one I knew my mother thought was most respectable. The pair of them were already at the restaurant when I arrived, which turned out to be bad news, because once the maître d' showed me through the dark barroom with all kinds of bric-a-brac hanging from the ceiling to their table and I saw them, both of them sitting with their hands folded together on top of the red-and-white-checked tablecloth, I realised my impromptu demand to have dinner together had alarmed them.

'Are you all right, Clifford?' my mother asked as soon as I sat down.

'Is this about money, son?' my father huffed. 'Do you need money?'

I looked from one anxious face to the next. It was a helluva first reaction to a son wanting to have dinner with you, and very telling, too. I was disappointed they thought so little of me, but then they had always thought exactly that little of me and why should this change now? I reasoned. I cleared my throat and told them I was fine and didn't need any money, which, strictly speaking, was mostly true; the first part was more true than the second.

'Why the urgency, Clifford?' My Old Man pressed.

I shrugged. 'Can't a fella want to have dinner with his parents?' I said. It could be exasperating to be in their company and I had somehow forgotten this fact in the time I'd spent away from them. I remembered it now in spades.

'The boy misses us, Roger,' my mother said, patting My Old Man's hand where it lay on the table. 'Let's not question it too much lest the sentiment fall to pieces.'

The waiter came over and took our order.

'Want to order a bottle of Montrachet, Pops?' I asked My Old Man. It was what he ordered when we went to '21' and had something to celebrate. I felt like we did have something to celebrate but of course I hadn't told him about *The Tuning Fork* yet, so he couldn't know.

'Why would I do that?' he snapped. 'And I've asked you before, Clifford, *not* to call me "Pops".'

He was irritable and impatient. It was plain that he wanted to be somewhere else and once again I'd gone and miscalculated the best way to approach him. Our dinner went on like that. My mother was charmed I'd wanted to see her so badly and was full of chatter, while My Old Man was ornery and kept looking at his watch. The pristine copy of *The Tuning Fork* I'd brought was tucked away in my old college attaché case, which was leaning against the leg of the chair I sat in. I glanced down and imagined the pages filed away in the dark down there and it felt like I was harbouring something combustible that might go off at any time like a bomb. I wanted to wait for the right time but it was becoming increasingly clear to me that I would have to make my own moment. Finally, when our dishes had been cleared and my mother had ordered dessert, I took the issue out and slid it across the table to my father.

'What's this?' He frowned.

'A literary magazine,' I said.

He was silent as he gazed down at the table with a wary look in his eye.

'The *Tuning Fork*? Never heard of it,' he said finally.

'It's new,' I said. 'A friend of mine just started it up. Gene – my friend – is pretty savvy. He's going to do big things on the literary scene.'

My Old Man raised an eyebrow before he could stop himself. He had been drinking Scotch through the whole meal and now he put up his finger to signal the waiter to order some more but couldn't seem to get the waiter's attention. 'Yes. Well. I suppose down in the Village all kinds of people are printing things up and calling it literature these days.'

'It's a good magazine,' I said, and immediately hated myself for saying it. My voice had taken on that goddamn whiney quality of defensiveness, which I knew would not go unnoticed by My Old Man. My voice was all froggy and I cleared my throat. 'As a matter of fact, I have a story in this issue,' I said more loudly. 'It really is a good magazine,' I repeated stupidly.

'I'm sure it is, and it's very nice that your friend is so fond of you,' he said in a patronising voice. Unaccustomed to being ignored, My Old Man gave up on the waiter, puckering his lips in agitation.

'That's not why he took my story: he asked me for it,' I said. 'I didn't even know him before all this jazz. It was a *solicited* submission.'

'Of course,' My Old Man said. I hated the inflection he could put into the simple words *Of course*.

'Clifford, darling,' my mother cut in, sensing the discord and uncomfortable with it. 'I'm sure your story is marvellous. I'd bet money on it. Wouldn't you, Roger? Wouldn't you bet money on it?' She elbowed him.

'Yes, yes,' My Old Man said. It was the affirmation my mother wanted but there was no dignity in it for me because his tone of voice was dismissive as hell.

'Easy for him to say,' I grunted under my breath, suddenly angry. 'It's not his money.' I was referring to my mother's fortune. Hearing me mutter, My Old Man's head snapped to attention, a dark storm cloud hovering in the vicinity of his brow.

'What was that, dear?' my mother asked.

'Nothing.'

'Look,' My Old Man continued, suddenly changing tacks now that he'd given up on acquiring a final round of booze, 'I've just realised I have some business to attend to back at the office. I'm afraid I'd better run back there now and take care of it. Doris – the business might keep me quite late; I think I'll sleep in the office tonight. Will you be all right driving back on your own?'

'Certainly, dear,' my mother replied.

I was good and steamed. My Old Man couldn't have been any more vague – *some business to attend to?* – but it didn't matter how vague he was, because my mother wasn't going to try to pin him down to specifics and he knew she wasn't and that was just the way it was. They had struck some sort of accord years ago, most likely without ever even talking about it, and this dynamic was well established and by now it had become the bedrock on which they had built their marriage. He stood up and straightened his tie. He wasn't even going to stick around to be polite as my mother ate her dessert, the lousy bastard. He made his farewells, kissing my mother on the cheek and shaking my hand, and sailed across the room to retrieve his coat.

I knew perfectly well where he was going next and it wasn't back to the office. I looked at the table and there was the issue of *The Tuning Fork* with my story in it, still sitting in the space where the busboys had cleared my father's plate.

'Did you want your father to have that copy, dear?' my mother asked me, following my gaze to where the magazine lay forgotten on the table. 'I can bring it home and put it on his nightstand.'

It took everything in me not to guffaw rudely and say something about My Old Man rarely sleeping next to the nightstand she meant, but I looked at my mother and I knew how badly it would hurt her.

'Nah,' I said. 'No big deal.'

I sat with her as she ate her profiteroles but excused myself soon after. I kissed my mother goodbye and made my way to the coat check. I didn't have any cash and I had stupidly forgotten to ask Eden for some and now the coat check man was smiling at me expectantly.

'Here,' I said, slapping the issue of *The Tuning Fork* on the coat check counter. 'You can use it for toilet paper.'

I left it sitting there and walked out into the chilly autumn evening.

46

MILES

After we left the Y, I went back to my hotel room alone. I spent the evening handling the journal, gazing at it in amazement and nervously turning it over in my hands, but not opening it. I wasted away the better part of the night and the next morning engaged in this bizarre, devoted ritual. I forgot to eat. I have always regarded people who claimed they've forgotten to eat as melodramatic, but once the journal entered my life, I understood better: it is difficult to think about consuming anything when you yourself are being consumed. At one point I dozed off for a blessed, relieving spell, my arms hugging the journal to my chest, its musty scent greeting me upon my awakening, reminding me of the stern business at hand. As vaguely suicidal as it sounds, I was aware of wishing, for the briefest of moments, that I could've remained asleep. There was something about the journal that brought me back to earth as I woke up and came to; the fact of its existence soaked into my body like ink bleeding into a page. Looking back on things now, I realise I was trying to brace myself for the journal to somehow rewrite my memories of my father – or, worse, delete them altogether – and one can never be ready for such a thing.

Around noon, there was a knock at my hotel room door. I jumped and froze.

'Miles?' came a muffled voice.

'Joey?' I shook myself into motion.

'Hey,' he said in a familiar friendly voice once I'd taken the chain off the door and opened it. His eyes scanned the room and rested upon the unopened journal lying on the bed. Down the hall, a baby started crying, reminding me to feel a shiver of shame for my seedy surroundings.

'Come in,' I offered, then hesitated. 'If you want.'

'Sure.'

Joey moved into the room, and I closed the door behind him. The baby's shrieks filtered into the room at half-volume.

'So, good reading? What did your father write about?' he asked, sitting down on the bed and glancing at the journal. It had been almost twenty-four hours since I'd reclaimed the contents of my father's old locker at the Y.

'I don't know.'

'What do you mean, you don't know?'

I heard him gasp slightly as I shook my head.

'You mean you haven't opened it?'

'It's not that simple,' I said.

At this, he snorted. 'Hah, okay, fine. But show me someone who says his family is simple, and I'll show you a liar,' he said.

I realised, in that moment, we had spent all this time searching for my father's locker, but that I had never asked Joey very much about his own history. I knew he hailed from hill country in Kentucky, that his family owned a bourbon distillery and were reasonably well off, or so I assumed from Joey's vague descriptions of things.

'What is *your* family like?' I asked now.

He shrugged. 'Rich. Stupid. But I have some nice memories of my mother. She was bright, full of life, very patient with me when I was a child.'

'I see,' I said, recognising all too well the familiar phrasing of his words. 'How old were you when she died?'

'Seven. No one ever told me she was sick. I suppose I was a little bit of an angry kid after that. Looking back on it now, I guess that's why my father packed me off to boarding school for a time. Well, that, and his new wife . . . half his age and dumb as dirt, but still conniving enough to get a diamond on her finger and me enrolled in boarding school within the same week.'

'I'm sorry,' I said awkwardly.

'Don't be,' he replied. 'Boarding school wasn't so bad. Plenty of poor little rich boys and you start to look around and realise a lot of guys have it worse than you do.' He paused and smiled at me. 'Besides,' he added, 'I fell for my first love in boarding school.'

He was very comfortable saying this. I wondered, privately, how many there had been.

'No . . . boarding school certainly wasn't the worst part of my childhood,' he said. 'The worst part was when my uncle came to stay with us. He was the one who decided to take me out of boarding school and bring me back home.' He shook his head. 'I wish he hadn't.'

'What happened?' I asked.

'Nah,' Joey said, refusing. He stood up. 'Let's not talk about that now. Right now I want to celebrate. What do you say? You're clearly going to hold off opening that thing like it's some holy shrine,' he said, gesturing to the journal. 'Let's do something fun in the meantime. Maybe a good distraction will loosen you up.'

'What do you have in mind?'

'My friend Sally Ann is throwing a party,' he said. 'She's got this rickety old house up on Potrero Hill and throws the best parties.'

Part of me dreaded the thought of going to a party, but Joey had a point about needing a distraction: ever since I'd brought the journal back to the hotel with me, I'd been in a state of arrested development, unable to push myself forward.

Joey offered to pay for a taxi. We flagged one down and rode along, talking excitedly and blowing cigarette smoke out the windows. Once across town, the taxi climbed to the top of a steep hill and dropped us off in front of an elaborate, sagging, dilapidated Victorian with lots of frilly, fussy scrollwork like icing on the eaves and gables. At one time the house must've been charming, but now it was an eyesore. Someone had painted the house a garish combination of red, purple, and yellow while painting the trim a glossy black, the colour of an oil slick. There were spots where the paint was already peeling and a number of places where the paint's fidelity to the contours of the scrollwork was imprecise.

A long staircase led up to the front porch. At the top of the stairs, we pushed a buzzer, but this formality was pointless, for the party was raging so loudly it swallowed up the sound of the buzzer. Joey shrugged again and turned the doorknob, and we poked our way shyly into a crowded room. A few partygoers nodded at us in a vague, indifferent way as we brushed past them. They were dressed in a sort of unintended uniform, in black turtlenecks or striped sailor shirts, all punctuated with a sprinkling of black berets and red scarves. Everyone looked self-consciously artistic and off-kilter, and I recognised an echo of Greenwich Village in this scene. In a far corner, a group of people gathered around a young art student who was reading a poem aloud as an RCA projector cast sporadic images of nude men and pregnant women juxtaposed with ripe fruit and the mushroom cloud of an atom bomb exploding onto a whitewashed wall. Jazz trumpeted from a record player in the next room.

'Let's find Sally Ann,' Joey shouted over the noise.

He grabbed my arm and steered me through the party. We moved down a series of hallways until we came to the centre of a large back-parlour where a woman sprang up from where she had been on a blue velvet sofa, leaning on the shoulder of a clean-shaven man and smoking a hookah pipe.

'Darling!' she said, tossing away the hookah hose upon seeing Joey and throwing her arms wide for theatrical effect. 'My very *own* darling! I'm positively overjoyed!'

'Sally Ann!' Joey called back, throwing his arms wide in return. They fell into a hug.

Sally Ann was a honey blonde with satiny-looking curls cut short to her shoulders. Her lipstick had been drawn on in a painstakingly careful manner, successfully carving out a bow tie where God himself had declined to craft one. She wore a full tulle skirt the colour of cotton candy and a pair of pale pink slippers. A smart black sash had been cinched about her waist with the clear aim of emphasising her hourglass silhouette. And although it was doubtful she had set foot outside of her apartment during the course of the evening, a superfluous white pill hat crowned her head, complete with a rather absurd, billowing ostrich quill that first shot upward, then eventually drooped down to nearly brush the tip of her nose, hovering directly in the space between her bright blue eyes.

As I took her in, her clothing and countenance appeared like the direct product of some women's magazine's article on how to be a good hostess – but so much so that there seemed to be an air of costume about her, as though her get-up was mocking the very idea.

'What on earth *is* this thing?' Joey asked, picking up the

mouthpiece from where she had dropped it on the carpet and following the hookah's hose back to where it was attached to its coloured glass vase.

'Isn't it exotic, darling? Dick brought it back from the Middle East to amuse me.' She leant towards us in a confidential way but did not lower her voice. 'I think he's got it in his head this Arabia nonsense will inspire me to join his little harem,' she said, elbowing Joey in the ribs and tilting her head to direct our attention towards a man across the room. Dick stood leaning over a petite doe-eyed girl, brushing her neatly trimmed bangs out of her eyes and cooing something into her ear.

'You're not cut out for harem life, Sally Ann,' Joey commented. 'You're a class act at centre stage but I don't know how well you'd do in the chorus.'

'Frankly, my darling, neither do I,' she replied. Sally Ann turned to me, took a closer look, and flourished a hand in my direction. 'But I see you brought your own fine specimen!' As I bristled at this condescending appraisal Joey shot me a look of apology, but Sally Ann seemed not to notice. 'Who is this maddeningly handsome and muscular young fellow?'

'This is my friend Miles. Miles? Sally Ann. Sally Ann, Miles.'

'Oh, but you don't *have* friends, darling,' she said. She suddenly whirled about in my direction. Later, Joey explained that Sally Ann was incapable of addressing more than one person at a time. It was how she had cultivated that breathless, confiding charm of hers. As a result she had a perpetual habit of referring to whomever she wasn't addressing in the third person, as though they weren't present. 'Honest,' she continued, blinking her blue saucer-like eyes at me. The conversation was now a private one between the two of us. 'Ask him! He doesn't have friends. Not one.' She leant in. 'Do you want to know why? Because all of his friends fall in love with him,' she answered. 'It's true! They *all* do! Every last one.'

'Aren't *you* his friend?' I asked.

'Well, now; you've got me there, you clever devil.' She laughed and reached out for Joey's faintly stubbled, lightly clefted chin, pinching it between her fingers and tipping his face in my direction. 'But I swear to you, it's true. And can you blame them?'

I was too embarrassed to answer. Joey blushed and Sally Ann laughed again. She released Joey's chin and turned again to me.

'I haven't seen you around before,' she said, making a quick study of my person. 'And I know *everyone* in the city.'

'It's true,' Joey said. 'She does.'

'You aren't from here, are you?'

'No,' I said. 'New York.'

'My, that's quite a distance. How long do you plan to stay?'

The question caught Joey's attention, as though it dawned on him that *he* hadn't asked how much longer I planned to stay. My only mission had been to find my father's journal, and now it was accomplished. Sally Ann, I noticed, was watching Joey's face from the corner of her eye and registered his uptick of interest.

'I suppose . . .' I faltered, glancing nervously at Joey, 'I'll probably catch the Greyhound back in the next day or two.'

'Why so soon? Don't you like Frisco?' Sally Ann asked in a stagey, pouting voice, as though I had just insulted her favourite cousin.

'I do,' I reassured her. 'I'm afraid it's a question of money. I've run through too much already; my hotel room is a daily expense I can't afford indefinitely.'

She was still watching Joey out of the corner of her eye as I announced my imminent departure. Reading his reaction, her mouth twisted and her eyes narrowed, and I realised with a shock that she was jealous.

'Isn't that a shame?' she remarked, turning to Joey. 'Won't you be sad to see Miles here leave so soon?' It was plain she already knew the answer.

'As a matter of fact,' Joey said, fixing me now with a steady gaze, 'I will.'

We exchanged a sombre stare as Sally Ann shifted on her feet, annoyed to find herself so easily ignored.

'Well!' Sally Ann exclaimed, breaking the weighty tension of this exchange. 'This calls for a drink! It isn't proper to send someone off without a toast to wish him *bon voyage*.'

She ushered us to a little wet-bar in her living room, her cotton-candy tulle skirt swishing absurdly as she moved. We made our way through the bodies at her direction. She cleared her throat and a handful of party guests who were poking around the bar's stash of booze tittered and politely moved off to the side.

'You know . . .' she said, ducking behind the bar and rummaging around, 'I think I may have just the thing . . . Now, if I can only lay my hands on it . . . Aha! Here it is!' She resurfaced, proudly holding up a bottle of champagne by its shiny-foiled neck. I looked at the iconic shield-shaped label and made out the words *Dom Perignon*.

'Wouldn't you like to save that for a special occasion?' I asked. In the ten or so minutes since we'd met, I had been able to work out for myself how little Sally Ann liked me. She shot me a look now that said I was not to interfere with her performance of magnanimous delight.

'Nonsense. We should drink to your visit and send you off in style! And besides, why drink tomorrow what you can drink today?' she replied. 'That's my motto.' She winked. 'Now,' she continued, offering the bottle in our direction, 'who would like to do the honours? Joey?'

Joey accepted the bottle and proceeded to unwrap the foil and remove the wire cage. The cork came out with a loud *POP!* and the mouth of the bottle smoked a little like the barrel of a gun. Most of Sally Ann's glassware was already engaged, and we wound up pouring the champagne into three Dixie cups. Sally Ann ordered Joey to fill them up to the brim.

'Now,' she said, taking on an imperious tone, 'give Miles a proper toast.' She raised her paper cup high in the air.

Joey looked at me. 'I don't know if I can do it justice,' he said, shaking his head.

'May I say something?' I interjected.

'Of course,' said Sally Ann. 'Go right ahead.'

'I don't believe I would've found my father's journal without you, Joey,' I said. 'I was very lucky, that night, when I picked up the wrong coat by mistake.' I raised my glass.

Not yet privy to the context, Sally Ann appeared vaguely intrigued.

Joey raised his cup. 'I'm happy for you, Miles, that you found what you were looking for. I'm happy that I got to help, if only a little bit. I wish . . .' He trailed off and looked at the carpet. All around us, the party raged on, but I was so focused on Joey in that moment, it was as if someone had turned the sound down. Joey cleared his throat and looked back up. 'It's a shame you can't stay here longer.'

'To Miles,' Sally Ann chimed in, taking over, 'who is no doubt a true charmer, for he has evidently managed to beguile the infamously impossible Joey.' She winked again, glancing back and forth between our faces and smiling to herself upon seeing our mutual discomfort.

No one said anything further. We clinked paper cups, the sound of waxed paper tapping together, and all of us took a sip. It was warm and a bit foamy; the bottle should have been put on ice.

'I've just had the most brilliant idea,' Sally Ann blurted, breaking the lull. 'Maybe Miles *doesn't* have to leave town so soon after all. I mean . . . if it's only a question of hotel expense.'

I should have known what was coming next. Sally Ann was the type of girl who expressed her jealousy by pushing her unrequited love closer to his object of desire. I had seen girls do this to other girls, pretending mad glee at the prospect of playing matchmaker and madam for the boy who got away. But I had never seen a woman do this to two men. Given the perils of the day, it struck me as cruel-spirited on her part.

'What are you talking about, Sally Ann?' Joey asked.

'I happen to own an old houseboat,' she replied. 'Across the bay in Sausalito. My grandfather left it to me, and I don't really do much with it. Mainly I've kept it in order to hold parties on it; you know, little bohemian affairs in the summertime.

'I throw a mean campout,' she added, giving Joey a little knowing smile and nudge. 'In any case, it's not exactly the Ritz, but it's got all the necessities . . . plumbing and electricity and all that.'

She turned to me.

'I don't see why you couldn't stay on it, if you wanted to.' She smiled, a wicked gleam creeping into her eye.

'Say . . . that might not be a bad idea . . . What do you think, Miles?' Joey asked with a sudden wave of fresh energy. 'You could stay on a little longer, see the sights. After all . . . three thousand miles is an awful long way. Who knows when you'll ever make it out here again?'

I considered. 'That's true,' I said. I still hesitated.

'C'mon, what do you have waiting for you back in New York, anyhow?' Joey prodded.

I shrugged. I realised I *did* want to spend more time in San Francisco. With Joey.

'And of course Joey will keep you company,' Sally Ann added, as though reading my mind. We both turned to look at her, unsure how she meant this comment. 'You'll stay with him on the houseboat, won't you, dear?' she said to Joey in a glib, casual voice.

Joey blinked.

'I've only just met Miles,' she explained, 'and I would be more comfortable loaning the houseboat out to a stranger if I knew someone I trusted would also be there.'

Her red lips twisted into a tight, closed-mouth smile. It was a challenge, a dare. Sally Ann had offered Joey something she knew he wanted. She was daring him to accept.

'I . . . suppose I could do that,' Joey replied hesitantly. He studied my face for some signal of approval or rejection, but there was nothing there for him to see; I was as still as a stone, frozen on the surface while my heart beat wildly within my chest. I could feel it pumping so hard as to rise into my throat. 'If Miles doesn't mind the arrangement.'

Joey had told me he and Eddie were crashing with a buddy of Eddie's. I supposed one free place was as good as another, but of course there was more to Sally Ann's proposal than just that. Standing there, sipping our champagne, we all knew it, but nobody was willing to say so – not even Sally Ann, who clearly delighted in our awkwardness. I wondered what Joey would tell Eddie, and Eddie's buddy.

'Good!' she exclaimed now. 'Then it's settled. I'll give you the key,' she said to Joey, 'and Miles can check out of his hotel first thing tomorrow morning.'

'Great,' Joey murmured.

'Great,' I echoed. I turned to Sally Ann and thanked her in a rote voice as she smirked at me, smug and knowing.

Sally Ann drank the rest of the champagne with us and handed over a key with a rabbit's foot key chain that was worn through to the shiny tendons. Then she released us back into the thrumming energy of the party, an expert fisherman throwing back her catch. She smiled over her shoulder as she swished away. Joey and I bumped around the room, making small talk with other party guests as if terrified to be alone together, manic and jumpy and excited and thoroughly discomfited.

The same question repeated over and over in my mind . . . What had I agreed to? The answer was something that both Joey and I would decide together, and at the same time I knew it had already been decided. I knew one thing: I would not have made the same decision back home in New York. There was something permissive about this faraway city, barely hanging on to the edge of the western hemisphere. I was a different person here. I, too, was hanging on to an edge of sorts, but for the first time in my life was willing to let go.

It wasn't until a full day or two later that I realised when Joey had asked me *What do you have waiting for you back in New York, anyhow?* I had missed my chance to say: *Janet. I have Janet waiting for me.*

47

It was dawn by the time we left Sally Ann's party. We went to my hotel. It was clear the man in the reception booth recognised Joey from the day before. He watched us out of the corner of his eye, his lips faintly twisted in an expression of disgust, so Joey waited downstairs while I went upstairs to quickly pack up my things.

'Here is my forwarding address,' I said upon checking out. I pushed a slip of paper under the window. On it I'd scribbled the number of the Sausalito PO box Sally Ann had given us. The clerk accepted the slip of paper with a grunt. He looked me over with a flat, stoic gaze and spat the sunflower seed he'd been chewing into a cup. I found myself feeling sceptical that I'd ever see any forwarded messages.

'Ready?' Joey asked.

As we walked down to the pier to catch the ferry, I took off my coat and carried it folded awkwardly over my arm. The weather in San Francisco, I had decided, had something of the coquette about it. It was impossible to dress for it. One minute you might find yourself basking in the blinding sunshine and sweating under the heavy weight of your winter coat, while the next you might be shivering in the kind of grey, bitter cold usually reserved for Gothic novels.

The ferry ride was pleasant. Once in Sausalito, we followed the shoreline past the marina to a group of eccentric-looking structures. Joey later told me the history behind the houseboat, as it had clearly been cobbled together over the years. Sally Ann's grandfather had purchased the houseboat, as well as a small fishing boat, back when Sausalito was still a fishing village. With no Golden Gate Bridge at that time, San Francisco was a faraway place, a glowing orb across the bay that meant a lot to the yachtsmen who made port and talked loudly about their holdings in El Dorado gold mines, but was little more to the local fishermen than a glorified lighthouse. When both her grandfather and father had died and this meagre legacy passed on to Sally Ann, she sold the fishing boat but retained the houseboat, mostly – as she had told us – as a secondary location for the infamous parties she threw.

The day we moved in, we picked our way around the deck and past the plants in their chipped terracotta planters, and turned the key for the first time. Right away, nothing was how I'd pictured it. When I had first heard the word *houseboat*, I expected lots of white and navy paint, and for everything to be airy and lightweight and able to float on water. Contrary to my expectations, the front door was a heavy piece of redwood. Joey pushed it open and we were met with a rush of cool, sombre, wet air. It smelt of silt and marine salt and of fragrant herbs and at the same time of a cold, mouldy basement.

Like the front door, the walls of the houseboat were made out of redwood. But unlike the front door, which had lost most of its natural red pigment to the elements, the wood of the walls was alive with colour. The panelling inside the houseboat was a marbled combination of crimson, amber, and gold. There was a tinge of shiny gloss to the walls – not from any owner's attempt to seal them with a gloss, but from the simple passage of time rubbing them smooth with human contact. In a far corner sat a wood-burning stove made out of black iron. This was by far the most unexpected item in the room as far as I was concerned. I don't know what I had imagined should keep the boat warm, but certainly not this. Its heaviness alarmed me; it seemed to me the boat might sink under its weight. And the idea that one should heat the boat by burning the very thing that kept it afloat – wood! Nonetheless, there it sat, belching heat into the room once it had been properly fed.

The interior of the houseboat bore the evidence of several curious attempts to fix it up. Someone had laid down felt as a sort of makeshift wall-to-wall carpeting. It was billiard green and wet to the touch during my entire stay on the houseboat. If you walked over it in socks, your soles were wet for the rest of the evening. When I think about it now, it makes sense that perhaps the green felt accounted for a good portion of the cold, mouldy basement odour that seemed to permeate everything.

The houseboat was sparsely furnished, yet somehow felt stuffed with bric-a-brac. Various tools and fishing accouterments hung from nails hammered all over the walls of the boat's one main room. Magazines and newspapers were stacked waist-high, and the windowsills were littered with scraps of paper and receipts. A pair of outdoor deck chairs sat in the middle of the room, surrounding a small wooden table too high for the chairs. It was a height difference that rendered all three items somewhat useless; this observation was verified when I sat in one of the deck chairs and promptly found the table came to my chin. The only other major piece of furniture on the houseboat was a captain's bed built into the far corner. It was an unusual size: ostensibly it was a double bed, but was a good six inches shorter than one might ordinarily expect. I'll admit I had quite a bit of trouble with that bed. The nights I slept there, my feet dangled over the edge, and I often woke up only to discover they had gone numb due to the night's chill and poor circulation.

Joey and I took two very different attitudes towards the houseboat. We both saw it for the dingy dump that it was, but we responded to its dull sheen and drab environment in opposite ways. Joey made changes. He began with the windows, wiping clean the crust of white haze some previous occupant had purposely applied with soap. He dragged what little furniture we had around the room, seeking their ideal arrangement. He lifted whole stacks of newspapers and magazines and dumped them into the bay. 'The fish can catch up on the headlines,' he said.

It was obvious Joey was in the mood to create some kind of true home on that houseboat. I did not notice or understand this at the time, but I see it now. I had a very different reaction to the houseboat. I moved around the space like a stranger, careful not to leave my mark. If I needed something that might require that I hunt in the cabinets or in the trunks, I waited until Joey came home. Or, even more often, I went without. I touched nothing, I opened nothing, I dusted nothing.

It was not that I was leery of Sally Ann, worried that she might turn up unannounced. It was more nebulous than that. It was the houseboat itself I didn't want to disturb, as though it might swallow me up if I opened the wrong drawer or stirred the wrong cobweb. The truth is I was afraid.

Up until the moment I packed my suitcase and checked out of my hotel, Joey was merely a helpful stranger who had developed a vested interest in helping me look for my father's journal. This is the lie I told myself. And this is the lie that kept me comfortable in his presence and allowed me to continue inching closer to him without feeling the space between us diminishing. But the day we moved onto the houseboat, this lie evaporated, carried off by some more substantial breeze. I was well aware that as soon as we unlocked the door and let ourselves in, I should have turned and left. There was only one bed and no sofa; I'm certain Sally Ann was conscious of this fact when she offered the houseboat in the first place.

We didn't speak about sleeping arrangements as Joey and I began to nervously unpack our things. The banter between us was too easy, and too difficult, all at the same time. I knew I should get out of there and never look back. But by then the lie had delivered me into the hands of the truth, so to speak, and there *was* no going back. I was, for the first wonderful, terrible time, exactly where I belonged. Together we put our things away with a shared sense of solemn, frightened dignity. When our suitcases were empty, we turned to face each other in the middle of the room and, with a soldier's bravery, Joey reached out to hold the back of my skull, very gently, in his hand.

We were lost to each other after that.

48

Settling into life on the houseboat, Joey puttered around, whistling like a happy canary and making his improvements. He was, I soon learnt, a minor master when it came to the art of jerry-rigging things. When we discovered the heavy iron door of the wood-burning stove fell off its hinges whenever we opened it to stoke the fire, Joey managed to replace the pin in the hinge with a bent coat hanger and a stray railroad spike he found near the tracks in town. He polished a hubcap and hung it in the shower to serve as a shaving mirror, for the bathroom had no mirror. Upon opening up a weathered trunk, he discovered some old fishing traps, so he cleaned them up and put them out in the water around the houseboat. He caught a pair of Dungeness crabs and boiled them that night until their shells were perfectly laced at the edges with a rusty flame-orange colour.

Occasionally we took the ferry across the bay to San Francisco. Other times we took walks in the wooded hills around Sausalito. When it came to running errands in town, to avoid unwanted attention, we decided it was best for Joey to go by himself.

Whenever he ran errands, I found myself sitting alone, staring at the journal I still had yet to open.

* * *

The object itself was intimidating. It was thick, heavy, and bound in hard leather. The pages were crinkled with weather and age; from the side it looked like a book stuffed with a pile of stiff yellow ruffles. I got the sense that, had the journal been any less substantial, it may not have endured its long journey. The cover was scratched and worn, stained with mud, coffee, and – in one suspicious spot – what appeared to be blood. That stain in particular drove something home for me: *this object had been to war.* War, an abstract place far removed from my existence, now made real through the brownish-maroon residue of someone's blood . . . my father's, or someone else's, entirely unknown. I'd regarded my father's stories about the First World War with so much doubt, and now I realised with a sense of shame this doubt was the privilege of a spoilt, oblivious child.

Finally, one morning while Joey was out and the fog lay thick over the entire bay, I tipped open the cover. Just like that. I'd done this once or twice before, studying my father's handwriting in the abstract, but not reading the words. This time, however, I allowed my eyes to linger. I began to read. If there were any clues or hints that might support or debunk Clarence's story, they were likely towards the very end, during the Second World War, when my father had run out of pages just before shipping out to the Pacific front. But I decided to start at the beginning. If I was going to learn the truth about my father, I was going to learn all of it.

It began with my father's enlistment. My grandfather had given his son the blank journal in 1917, the day my father decided to sign up for the army, and urged him to record his experiences. In his first entry, my father wrote about standing on line at a dance studio on 125th Street and adding two fictional years to his age in order to enlist, nervous and excited, proud to serve his country. The entries continued as my father reported the events that eventually led him from training camp to the battlefield. I use the word *training* loosely, for compared to the white regiments the Hellfighters' training was a joke. While the white regiments trained for months, the 369th trained for mere weeks in their civilian clothes and were handed broomsticks to practise with instead of rifles. They were treated even worse when they were sent to finish their training in South Carolina, the locals making an effort to ensure the coloured boys from the north understood they were subject to Jim Crow and everything that came with it. At the front, they were put on labour service duties for months, until finally it was decided they would be sent to the trenches as part of a French division.

I recalled during my childhood how my father displayed what can only be described as a kind of emotional patriotism for France – second only to his patriotism for America – and as I read the pages of his diary the reason for his sentiment towards the French finally clicked: the French cared far less about the colour of his skin than the fact he was a loyal and able-bodied man. He wrote about how staggering it was to suddenly be treated with a sense of dignity. He and the others in his regiment were issued French helmets and sent to the front lines, where, impressively, the 369th never lost a single trench or foot of soil.

In a less overtly complimentary way, perhaps it could be argued the Germans were nearly as egalitarian as the French, for the nickname 'the Harlem Hellfighters' had been bestowed upon my father's regiment by the Germans. I chuckled a bit when I read that, imagining a German staring goggle-eyed at a black man charging into his trench and concluding that such a terrifying force of nature could only come from the mouth of hell itself.

I also began to understand why my father had been so tolerant of

Clarence, letting him overstay his welcome in our house. According to one of my father's entries, he credited Clarence with saving his life, pushing my father out of the way of a sniper's bullet as they sat stand to at late dusk during the regiment's first few days in the trenches. The bullet had whizzed so close it had nicked Clarence's ear, inflicting a superficial wound that bled profusely. Grateful, my father turned over his day's wine ration to Clarence, and thus their friendship was cemented.

Once I began reading, momentum carried me along and I quickly got lost in more and more pages. My father was hardly a wordsmith, but there were so many descriptions in his journal that, to my mind, verged on poetry. He wrote about the careful way he checked the seals of his gas mask. About the yellow haze that sat heavy in the trenches. About being the first regiment to reach the Rhine and what it had been like to stand on its shores and look out over the landscape. I felt a balloon of pride filling in my chest, not only for the things he had seen but also for the tender way he paid attention to the world around him. He wrote about his homecoming to New York, and about marching in a parade – I can only assume this was the same event Clarence had mentioned – and about trying to repress a grin the whole way up Fifth Avenue, turning at 110th Street, then Lenox, and marching into the familiar heart of Harlem.

When Joey returned from his errands he looked at me twice, flinching with surprise when he caught sight of what I was reading.

'You're reading it,' he stammered. 'How – how is it?'

'Good,' I said. This was honest, in fact. 'His accounts of the trenches in the First World War are really something . . . and to think, he saw all this when was only sixteen . . .'

'Sixteen?' Joey repeated.

'He was so eager to enlist, he was one of those who lied about his age.'

Joey waited. I could tell he wanted to ask more questions, but out of polite consideration he didn't. He puttered around, putting things away, but consciously remaining within earshot just in case I felt like sharing. We spent most of the day like that: me on the bed, reading with intense concentration, as Joey buzzed quietly nearby. Hours passed, the daylight waned, and Joey thoughtfully switched on the electric light bulb that hung over the head of the bed.

'Huh,' I guffawed sometime later, reading one entry in particular. The entries trailed off after the war ended and my father left Europe and came back to America. He remained in the National Guard, but during weekdays apprenticed himself to a small radio repair business in Harlem.

'Listen to this,' I said. Joey came over and sat on the foot of the bed. I proceeded to read from the journal:

Young woman came in today to pick up her daddy's radio . . . told her I had to replace one of the vacuum tubes . . . she act like I was making something up, made me damn near take the whole radio apart to how her what I done . . . wasn't satisfied until I let her hold one of the tubes for herself, saying, 'This it? This all that need fixing? This look like a whole lot of nothing. Don't look like that much sound could come out of little old this.' I explained the science of radios to her best I could, pack her up with that Marconi and send her along, back to her daddy. Pain in the backside, sure as I born! But got a funny little way about her. Couldn't help but think of her for the rest of the day . . .

'What's so funny?' Joey asked.

'That,' I said, still chuckling, 'had to be my mother.'

'Oh,' he said, smiling and laughing along with me. He waited for me to say more, but when I didn't, he politely went back to puttering. I greedily read all the details of my parents' first date, a story that, in my mother's retelling of it, had been much more chaste.

The hour grew late. Eventually Joey climbed into bed next to me and occupied himself with a paperback novel as I continued to read. The minutes ticked on well past midnight and into the wee hours, but I could not stop reading.

'Listen to this,' I said softly, my chest heavy as I read:

My boy passed on today. I seen a lot of things in the war, but I didn't recognise him when they pull his body out of the river. Like my eyes and brain weren't working no more. Mae had to give the confirmation, she nod at the officer and the officer write 'Marcus Tillman' in the report. Mae always been stronger than me. Now she saddled with more burden than ever, because I feel like some part of me no longer working. Can't say a man is ever whole again after losing his first son.

Joey looked at me, waiting for me to explain.

'My older brother,' I said. 'Marcus. He died the year I was born.'

Joey gave a solemn nod. There was a tender, compassionate look in his eyes, and in that moment I believed he understood the conflicted, intricate feelings I had on the subject, the anxiety I'd always felt about the ill-timing of my birth, the way I suspected I was a poor replacement for the brother who had come before me.

'May I?' Joey said, reaching a gentle hand for the journal. I let him take it. He turned a few pages. The entries had, understandably, become infrequent in the time that followed Marcus's death, but then eventually picked up again. Joey did not have to flip many pages until coming upon what he was looking for. He looked up at me and smiled.

'"I don't know what I done to have a son half so smart as Miles,"' Joey read aloud. He continued to read my father's words – as my father praised my intelligence and potential, laying claim to me as his 'best and brightest creation' – and compassionately ignored the glassy look in my eyes as I blinked away my reaction.

'And, on that note,' Joey said, smiling affectionately at me, 'I think you need some rest. Let's go to sleep.' He closed the journal and leant over me to slip it onto the little nightstand beside the bed. 'Don't worry,' he added, noticing my face. 'I know you want to, but you can't read the whole thing in one sitting. It'll keep.'

49

Two days later, I found myself on the ferry, watching the fat brown bodies of sea lions slip off piles of harbour rocks and into the water as the ship pulled out of the dock in Sausalito. The ferry was San Francisco-bound. I had read through the entirety of my father's journal and, with a specific mission in mind, decided to return to the main branch of the city library.

For the majority of its pages, reading the journal had been heartening. My father's account of the trenches in the First World War struck me as heroic and honest, a young man's first test of his mettle. His anecdotes of life between the wars, of meeting my mother and starting a family, had brought me closer to him, allowing me a rare glimpse of my childhood through his eyes. It was the final spate of entries – the entries leading up to his aborted tour of duty during the Second World War, just as I'd suspected – that had given me cause to once again recall Clarence's damning words and question my father.

In 1941, the US army was still segregated, and while many of my father's peers were replaced by newly enlisted men, the Harlem Hellfighters more or less remained intact as a division of the National Guard. But after the Japanese bombing of Pearl Harbour, my father's regiment was reorganised and reactivated for duty. They were sent upstate for training, stationed briefly in Massachusetts, then shipped out west, eventually destined for Hawaii and Okinawa. By that time my father was thirty-nine, although his original white lie to the army when he enlisted put his age as two years older. Either way, he was an anomaly among the eighteen-year-olds who enlisted and who made up most of the regiment around him. Young privates poked fun at my father and Clarence behind their backs, scoffing at the pair of 'old' men who didn't have the common sense to bow out of the National Guard when they were expected to. According to my father's journal entries, these jibes weren't very subtle, but he managed to let most of them roll off his back.

There was one exception to the rule of my father's tolerance, however. My father's commanding officer, Captain Julian Harris, was a cocky young bully. As a sergeant, my father was meant to serve as Julian's right-hand man. Furthermore, as a veteran with a good amount of experience, my father took it upon himself to offer Julian advice. This proposal was not happily met. Insecure about being undermined by 'an old geezer who thinks he's a war hero', Julian responded by treating my father like a lackey. He put my father through his paces during training camp, singling him out at every turn, pushing my father's mental and physical capabilities to the limit in the hopes that he might break. While my father seemed able to ignore the other men's rude treatment, Julian managed to push my father's buttons. Reading his journal, I realised with a chill that my father's anger and resentment were very real. This was a side of him I had never known.

Things went from bad to worse between the two men when it came to light that someone in the regiment was stealing radio parts, very likely selling them on the black market. Julian instantly accused my father. Given that my father had spent time working in a radio repair shop, he made a good suspect. He had knowledge of which parts were valuable and where to sell them undetected. It unnerved me that my father never denied the accusations in any of his entries. Perhaps, though, this is not so strange; journals are documents we write for ourselves, under the assumption of privacy. If my father was innocent, it is logical that he may not have felt the need to defend himself *to* himself. Nonetheless, I found myself longing for a denial, for proof of his innocence. Instead, my father's journal entries chronicled a record of Julian's offences to my father's dignity, until eventually my father ran out of pages. He stashed the journal in a locker, with a final note that he was worried he'd written too much about his dislike for Julian. 'Best to leave my grievances behind,' he wrote. 'Don't want no one using them against me.'

It was that final note that unnerved me the most and reawakened Clarence's accusations. I tried to picture it. There my father was, still under suspicion of having stolen radio parts, sailing across the Pacific with a man he detested more than any other human being on earth. Clarence's voice echoed back to me: *he murdered a man just so's they wouldn't have no proof o' his thievery* . . . It didn't seem possible. The man I knew didn't have the act in him – not the theft, and certainly not the other. But both my father's uncharacteristic anger and the circumstances were unsettling. I wanted more.

Once the ferry pulled into the city, I walked down Market Street, finding my way back to the Civic Centre and, more specifically, to the library. I had only been in San Francisco for three and a half weeks, but it felt like aeons since those first days I'd spent rattling around the microfiche room and requesting backlogged periodicals from the circulation desk. This time I was helped by an elderly male librarian who – partly out of need and partly out of curious, nostalgic affectation – used an antique ear trumpet. 'Doesn't do to ask patrons to speak up when you work in a library,' he explained when he caught me looking at the whimsically shaped brass trumpet. 'Beethoven himself used one of these,' he added in a slightly defensive, huffy tone. When I described what I was looking for, taking care to politely speak into the ear trumpet, the librarian led me through the reference shelves, to a section of hardbound volumes of *The New York Times Obituaries Index*.

'If the feller was from New York like you say, I'd start here. You know how to check the index, don't you?' He looked at me sceptically. I nodded. 'Wish all papers would put these out; very helpful,' he sighed, patting the spines. He turned and left me to my search. I pulled down a few volumes, from around the time of my father's embarkation to his eventual discharge. There was only one man my father had truly hated. Ironically, I prayed now that particular man had made it through the war.

I scanned the alphabetical list in the back. My stomach sank when I saw the name.

Harris, Julian Owen.

I flipped to the corresponding page. Sure enough, Julian had been murdered, only two weeks prior to my father's discharge. 'The victim of a terrible act of violence, Captain Harris was stabbed to death walking back to his barracks while stationed overseas . . .' I felt the life go out of my body. I needed to sit down, and I crawled into one of the stiff wooden chairs at a nearby reading table. Holding the book in my lap, I stared at the table.

Minutes passed as I sat with my brow furrowed, staring into the wood grain but not seeing it. Even now, I am hard-pressed to describe the feelings that went through me as I sat there, absorbing the fact of Julian's murder. Clarence had insisted a murder had occurred, and indeed it had.

But then my eyes returned to the newsprint, and my attention fell on one line in particular. 'Military police believe the killing was motivated by robbery. In addition to cash and a wristwatch, the thief notably removed Captain Harris's rank insignia. Captain Harris's silver bars were missing from his uniform, and to date, have not been recovered.'

A bell went off in my brain. During that final fight with Clarence, my father had repeated over and over again, 'Explain to me what these bars doin' in yo' things!' It had been cryptic at the time. *Bars* didn't mean anything to me, and I couldn't understand why my father was so worked up, his eyes instantly bloodshot with some kind of unnamed anguish. Now it made sense.

Clarence.

Both the riddle and the answer had been staring me in the face the whole time. I idly wondered why, if my father had found the captain's bars in Clarence's things and he had reached the same conclusion I did now . . . why he didn't turn Clarence into the authorities. But then I put myself in my father's shoes and imagined what I would have done, given the chance. Clarence never admitted to it, not in the conversation I'd overheard. My father believed Clarence had saved his life. Other than the bars, there was no proof. And even with the bars, it was my father's word against Clarence's. It wasn't clear the authorities – white or coloured – particularly wanted to solve the murder nearly as much as they wanted to keep it out of sight and forget it.

Well, then, I thought. I had my answer. Or as much of one as I was ever liable to get.

When I returned to the houseboat that evening, I told Joey the story of Julian's obituary, of the missing captain's bars, and of the final argument between Clarence and my father. I lay down on the bed, exhausted.

'You think Clarence kept the insignia as a kind of souvenir?'

I shrugged.

'A creepy thought.'

'Yes,' I agreed.

'I'll bet you feel relieved,' he said, smiling.

I thought about this but shook my head.

'Why not?' he asked.

'All those years . . .' I said, 'I doubted him. I doubted he had done anything very heroic in the first war – it was such a distant thing, you see . . . and then I doubted he had acted honourably when he shipped out for the second. What kind of son does that make me?'

'Ah,' said Joey, crawling into bed next to me. 'That's the funny thing about doubt.'

'What do you mean?'

'It makes you feel rotten as hell. But if anyone bothered to think about it, it's a symptom of love. It means it matters to you. It's the brain questioning the wisdom of the heart. It doesn't mean the heart doesn't know better all along, it only means the brain doesn't understand how.'

Later, it struck me as uncanny that Joey had said these words, but at the time they were simply a comfort, a suggestion that my love and doubt came from the same pure place.

50

CLIFF

I was fed up with writing, for a little while, at least. My big plan had been to casually drop a copy of *The Tuning Fork* on My Old Man and then, when he read my story and liked it, naturally he would ask me did I have anything else and I would surprise him with the novel manuscript I was working on. But when things didn't happen like that it took the wind out of my sails and I found myself stalled again.

Being a writer was fine and dandy, but punching a typewriter was not much for exercise and it occurred to me one day that between writing all day and drinking all night I was getting soft, so I started doing some boxing over at the Y. All the other guys who boxed at the Y each had about ten years and fifty pounds on me. They were big oafy guys who shared a thirst for contact sports and hadn't seen enough action in the war. Some of them were clean-cut and some of them were tattooed all over with pin-ups and anchors but clean-cut or not, they were all really the same guy and I was the only truly different one.

I was aware of the differences that made me stand apart and especially of the fact I'd read books they had not. They were not intellectuals and they did not care that Hemingway had boxed and that he had claimed that understanding the rhythms of the boxing ring had helped him write better dialogue and better scenes. They did not care about reading or about Hemingway or about writing, full stop. They only cared about throwing the next punch, and how. I liked them for this. There was something simple and clean and pure about their limited minds that made them almost noble in a way.

Of course the feeling was not mutual at first and I had to earn their respect. I did this by throwing a mean right hook while managing not to blow out my shoulder. Plenty of guys could throw a good right hook, and if a guy was especially big he could put his weight into it and really lay someone out. But most of the guys who had a strong hook eventually threw out their shoulders and then they had to go to the doctor and occasionally even the surgeon and after that they were out of commission for a good long while and sometimes they never recovered well enough to properly box again. This was due to bad technique. If you threw a good right hook using the proper technique there was no risk of injury, but most guys had not been taught proper technique, only that they ought to throw as hard as they could.

Luckily for me, I had a buddy at Columbia who had boxed for Oxford and he had taught me the secret to a proper hook. The guy who taught me was a graduate student called Richard – always Richard, never Dick or Ricky or any of that business. I met him at a bar up near Morningside Heights and quickly discovered one of his favourite pastimes was to drink beer and talk a lot about Schopenhauer until he was good and buzzed and then he always wanted to go out to an alley and explain how Schopenhauer and boxing were related. He'd land a lot of blows and they hurt plenty, but he was also very gracious about showing you how he'd landed each one and so the experience of it ended up being kind of a cross between a sparring match and a professor's lecture.

In any case, I showed a few of the guys at the Y the trick of throwing a right hook while still preserving your shoulder, and when they could see it worked and feel it worked, the rest of them all wanted to be taught how.

Among themselves, they held local matches and worked out a scheme for everyone to bet and for the winner to walk away with a little bit of prize money. They didn't really bet as a means of making an income so much as a means of funding the prize and taking turns winning it. The more of a long shot you were, the larger percentage of the overall pot you got to take home, so there was a great excitement to an underdog winning one of these matches. As the smallest guy at the Y, I was the biggest of the underdogs. When I pressed them to give me the odds and tell me what my take of the prize money would be, it was quite a decent sum and too difficult to resist. I thought of everything the money could do for Eden and myself, and about how it would be nice to be the breadwinner for a change. I could really make things up to her.

I imagined myself winning and taking Eden to a fancy French dinner and buying her a swell hat. She was dotty for hats; don't ask me why, because in those days hats had fallen out of favour with the hip crowd and none of the chicks down in the Village wore hats unless of course you counted berets, which were all over the place below Fourteenth Street. Formal hats were strictly for squares. But Eden still salivated and stared in the windows every time we passed a milliner. It was one of her conservative tastes left over from Indiana, where I pictured her mother hosting the weekly bridge club and her father strolling the golf links in argyle socks pulled to his knees, and whatever else people in the great Midwestern suburbs do when they are trying to imitate the things they see in magazines and on television. Eden liked hats but she never bought them for herself because she said they were too expensive and anyway she didn't have any place to wear them. I agreed but I still wanted her to have a nice hat all the same, and I wanted to be the one to provide it.

In any case, I signed up for a fight and the guys set a date. They all assumed I would fight this Spanish kid Carlos, because he was the closest to my size but I surprised them all by insisting on fighting a big Polish guy named Jozef. I had watched both of them fight and Carlos was small and quick while Jozef was large and slow. I decided slow was better even though Jozef was a heavyweight while I was a welterweight at most and – if I am being brutally honest – probably more of a lightweight when I really trained and trimmed all the beer and whiskey off my gut. Of course we were nuts to be mixing weight classes like this; I was confident I was the better boxer pound for pound, but nonetheless there were still an awful lot of pounds separating me from Jozef. I was expecting to lose but was excited all the same.

The week leading up to the fight I was very disciplined about not going out so much and doing as much extra training as I could stand. Eden noticed the difference in me and I couldn't hide some of the bruises. When I explained I'd been boxing I could tell she disapproved. I told her I was doing the boxing because it helped me get my writing juices flowing again but I could see she still didn't like it. She probably would've rather had a husband who knitted in order to get a second writing wind but this was foolish of her because that was not at all who she had married. I figured she would take back her disapproving frown once I'd won the prize-fight money and taken her to dinner and bought her that hat.

On the day of the fight I arrived feeling calm and ready to give it my all. Perhaps it's simply a question of feeling you have nothing to lose. I looked around the gym that afternoon and saw that nobody in the room was expecting me to win and suddenly this made me feel very free. To them, I was the kid who had been born with a silver spoon in his mouth and gone to fancy prep schools and I was supposed to get the stuffing knocked out of me. In the worst-case scenario I could lose and this would gratify the expectations of every man in the room and there would be nothing terrible in simply giving these men the satisfaction of their expectations being fulfilled. I could see they had already put me through the humiliation of a knockout in their heads, so the most unpleasant part of it was over.

Jozef was already there and was dancing on his toes, doing warm-ups when I arrived, only he didn't ever really step very lightly so it was less like dancing and more like shuffling around flat-footed in that slow, stupid, thumping way he had while a couple of other guys wrapped his fists and laced his gloves. As I looked at him I began to feel slightly guilty for having picked him to fight. I didn't know him that well but some of the guys at the Y had commented that Jozef might even be a bona fide simpleton, and they argued that if this was true then it might not be fair to fight him the same way you would fight a guy who was not a simpleton. They had a point but the fact remained Jozef was enormous and no one had officially declared him a simpleton and so I had no reason not to give it my all.

I peered across the gym and watched him work up a sweat. Between callisthenic manoeuvres, a couple of guys came over to him with a bucket to sop his face with a wet cloth. The fight was on and it was clear, even with Jozef being as dull-witted as he was, everyone was expecting me to lose. Jozef was huge and when it came down to it, you kinda had to put your money on any guy who was that huge. The fellas attending to him were snickering and I realised they were eager to watch Jozef and his heavy fists show me just how little a proper prep school education mattered in the boxing ring.

They draped a towel around his neck and rubbed his shoulders with their callused fingers and as I gazed across the room I regretted not telling Swish and Pal and even Bobby about the prize-fight, because they would've been perfect guys to have along to do these things, and they would have cheered me on and made plenty of wisecracks to keep me entertained along the way. But I had to settle for two of the guys from the Y who had been nice enough to step forward when Tony, the makeshift referee, asked for volunteers. Robert and Arturo were decent guys and equal to the task but there was a dull, obligatory air about their service. They didn't believe I stood a chance against Jozef and tended to me while at the same time making it plain they wished I would just save everyone the trouble and have the common sense not to get into the ring in the first place.

I got good and ready and before I knew it, the bell rang for round one. Right away Jozef came at me like a bulldozer and pinned me in the corner. I felt two terrible body shots hit their marks and shortly afterwards he had me bulled on the ropes. From some far-off place, I heard Tony blow his whistle and warn Jozef to keep his punches up. By the second round I got wise and started feinting and this really seemed to take Jozef off the offensive, for a little while at least. A good boxer knows you should spend the first part of a fight studying your opponent and once you have done that only *then* really lay in your best blows, and I was buying time so I could study him. We danced around each other trading jabs and in this way I got to know where and how he was at his slowest. This went on for a while, with me buzzing around Jozef like a mosquito and darting in to land the occasional jab.

Jozef, meanwhile, was getting impatient and started heckling me to fight his way and try to land some big wallops. I largely resisted his taunting invitation but it was difficult; I looked at his stupid, thick-cheeked face and the bubbles of saliva running down his chin and I sorely wanted to land one square on the broken bridge of his nose. I knew better than to give in to this impulse and instead just kept jabbing away at the sides of Jozef's head, hoping to get him off balance more gradually. By round six his patience had finally expired altogether and he began throwing huge, wild punches. And this is when I knew I had him. I'd always been good at bobbing and weaving and all I had to do was steer clear and let him tire himself out. Over and over again, I ducked as he swung and missed.

At that point the boys who'd been politely cheering us on grew notably more rowdy. They had been fairly sedate up until then. I don't think anyone had expected me to last longer than a couple of rounds but I had turned everything topsy-turvy with my ability to dodge Jozef's punches and get in all those jabs. I was aware of side bets being made between several of the fellas as they hooted and hollered at each other and I became increasingly conscious of the fact that my surprise performance was shaping up to be the stuff from which legends are born.

There were mirrors on two of the walls in the boxing room at the Y and at one point I caught sight of the spectacle we made. It was like something out of the Bible: Jozef, the big Goliath, staggering around the ring with all the precision of a drunken sailor, and me, the spry David, zipping here and there with my lightning-fast jabs in lieu of a slingshot. I shouldn't have been so taken with the picture this made, though, because the distraction of it meant I was glancing at the mirror during a crucial moment. Jozef was finally able to land one of his blows and he got me right on the left side of my head. The sheer force of it had me seeing stars and I realised if I let him land one more blow like that one, I'd be knocked out cold. I could lose the whole match in a matter of seconds if I allowed my vanity to get the better of me.

I gathered my wits and focused once again on ducking and jabbing, and won the next round. Each time they rang the bell and called the round, Jozef's face got redder and redder until at last he looked less like a person and more like a stop sign. I decided to see if I couldn't make the most of this. Every time I landed a jab on Jozef, I grinned at him as I danced away and his anger mounted. Little by little, he began to go bonkers, bulling me on the ropes and swinging away. But he couldn't land anything properly. He was desperate and his punches went flying all over the place, glancing my sides.

'Say, what're you trying to do, buddy – give me a rubdown?' I taunted him. He roared and lunged at me like a crazed animal. Tony had to blow his whistle several times over, and eventually scolded Jozef for using his head.

'Using his head?' I scoffed, unable to resist. 'Well, I suppose there's a first time for everything.' It took Jozef a full minute to comprehend the insult but when he did, he went ape-shit. I knew we were reaching a crucial point in the fight. Until that point, the match was solely about stepping out of the way, not unlike the way a matador flares his cape and moves, catlike, off to the side. Some of the fellas began booing – at me, I suppose – for avoiding so many punches, but I wasn't a bit sorry. I wasn't there to prove I was sturdy enough to be Jozef's punching bag, I was there to win, and boxing is one part brawn and two parts brain, that's what I always say. Now as Jozef rushed at me I stepped to one side and allowed him to reel past, then I spun around and drove my fist directly into his kidney. I heard him groan as I made contact and I knew – just as David had reached that sweet moment of realisation before me – that Goliath was destined to fall. I got in several more shots like that one, with some variations, and after the twelfth round it was an undeniable victory. Tony raised my glove in the air and called it, albeit with some reluctance. The room erupted into cacophony of sound, some guys cheering, some guys booing. Everybody, it seemed, had an opinion.

'Randy! Go an' fetch the winnings,' Tony shouted into the din of noise once he had dropped my hand. Robert and Arturo came over and helped me off with my gloves while Randy dashed out of the room and came back carrying a rolled-up wad of greenbacks secured with a rubber band. 'Awright, Cliff, here you are,' Tony said, handing it over. 'The whole pot. Cungradulations.' He stepped between the ropes and down from the ring. Other guys were coming up now, climbing into the ring and clapping me and Jozef on the back.

'Good going!' some of them shouted. 'Atta boy! Who'da thought?'

'Boo! What'd you wanna do a thing like that for?' others jeered. 'That ain't a fight.'

They felt cheated, I realised, out of the bloody pounding they had thought I was sure to receive. Without a referee, Jozef would've laid me out cold for sure, they pointed out. This was true, but I didn't care. The bottom line was there *had* been a referee and I had boxed my way to a victory, fair and square. I was happy about my win and as I looked at the wad of cash clutched in my hand I realised I wanted to lose myself in the celebration of it.

'Who wants to have a victory drink with me?' I shouted around the room.

51

Of course they all wanted to have a victory drink, because the guys at the Y figured I was buying and people are always in a hurry to spend money when it is not coming out of their own pockets. Guys who had cheered me on came out to toast me and guys who had booed me and been clearly disappointed when Jozef failed to knock my block off came out to freeload and to razz me some more. We started at a little bar around the corner from the Y but at some point somebody got the big idea that we should get a hotel room with my winnings and throw a real party with girls and everything. Of course by 'girls' the fellas meant prostitutes and before too long I did a little calculation and realised the night was shaping up to be a bigger expense than even my winnings would cover.

But the thing about parties is once in motion they are near impossible to stop and I'll admit I did very little to slow this one down. I figured the fellas couldn't possibly expect me to pay for everything and I was sure when the time came to settle up at the end of the night each fella would be decent about things and foot his share of the bill for the girls and the booze and, if I was lucky, maybe even part of the room bill. My idea about taking Eden to dinner and buying her a hat was out of the question at that point, but at least I'd had the good intention and anyway I could win other fights and take home more money in the future. This was my first real prize-fight and I'd won and I was entitled to a true celebration.

I celebrated a little too hard, however, because sometime around three or four o'clock in the morning I'd gotten so rip-roaring drunk that my ears began to ring and my vision began to blur and then I blacked out. I don't remember anything after that.

I woke up alone in the hotel room, late the next afternoon. Well, not *alone* exactly, because in fact the hotel manager and two of his beefier bellhops were standing over me. The room was in shambles. As I sat up I heard the tinkle of broken glass and thought I recognised tiny pieces of what used to be a lovely blue vase. Cigarettes were mashed into the carpet. The window was wide open and feathers from a ripped pillow swirled about in various nervous corners of the room. A pair of women's stockings hung from the lamp next to the sofa.

'Time to check out, sir,' the hotel manager said. 'These gentlemen will help see you on your way, but I'm afraid you'll have to pay the damages first.' His voice suggested this was going to be a very businesslike transaction. 'Naturally,' he added with a smile.

I gave him what remained of the crumpled bills in my pocket. 'I'll have to call my banker for the rest,' I said, imitating his obnoxious demeanour. He dropped the smile and did not appear amused.

Private telephone lines were very expensive in those days and Eden and I still didn't have one in our apartment. But there was a bar around the corner where Swish and I often drank and they liked me there and I knew if I could get the bartender on the phone I could get him to send someone to go around the corner to fetch Eden and tell her about my predicament. It was a workday so Eden didn't arrive home until after five o'clock but after a few attempts sure enough it worked and she got the message and then all I could do was sit and wait and hope she'd come and bring the money. I sent along the amount of my bill in the message and I didn't know where she could possibly get that kind of money, but Eden was smart and I knew she would think of something.

Over an hour passed before she finally turned up. Then the sun went down and I was under a sort of informal house arrest. The hotel manager went off to take care of other business and I was forced to sit and wait on the sofa in the busted-up hotel room while the two muscle-headed porters stood over me like a pair of buzzards sizing up a dying wildebeest.

I thought I was feeling pretty bad, what with being all banged up from the boxing match and hungover, but I didn't know what bad was until I saw Eden walk into the room. She had probably wondered where I was when I'd never come home the night before, and here she had her disappointing answer. Her face was pale and she looked very tired.

'Mr Nelson,' the manager called out to me as he crossed the room with Eden at his elbow. 'You'll be happy to know your wife here has been kind enough to settle the bill for you.' He dropped the businessman routine and shot me a spiteful grin. I sorely wanted to punch the sonofabitch. He knew perfectly well he could have sent a bellhop up to get me while Eden waited downstairs in the hotel lobby but instead he'd purposely dragged her up to the room so she could have a look at things for herself. I could tell from the way she came in she wanted no part of this scene but now she had been dragged into it. I watched her stepping carefully in her black ballet flats, cautiously picking over the broken glass on the carpet. And I suddenly became acutely conscious of exactly what she must be taking in: empty bottles and broken glass on the floor, lipstick on my collar, and the whole room lousy with cheap perfume. In my mind I cursed the phony sonofabitch manager again; it amused him to watch her find me like this, of course.

'I brought your coat, just in case,' Eden said, holding it out to me. I thanked her and pulled it on over my shirt and rumpled pants, happy to hide the wretched state of my clothes.

Of course the manager asked the two porters to escort us out of the hotel. He reverted back to that phony hospitable tone of his as though he were doing us a great kindness when really he was just making sure we got the boot good and hard and when he said it I almost lost it and hit him. But then I thought of Eden and knew the best thing I could do was to steady my trembling fists for her sake. It was bad enough she was going to have to endure the humiliation of being thrown out; I figured the least I could do was to make this last part as civil as possible.

I took Eden by the hand and allowed them to hustle us out and before we knew it we were standing on Fifty-Second Street. By then it was well after seven o'clock and I felt like an entire day was missing from my life. It was a cool, breezy night, the kind of night in Manhattan where you remember the city is an island and where it seems like the wind is blowing in from both rivers at the same time. I moved in the direction of the subway but Eden allowed my hand to drop.

'I'd like to walk,' she said in a faraway voice.

'It's an awful lot of blocks.'

'I'm aware.'

'All right,' I agreed. 'We'll walk.' We turned south and set off in the general direction of the Village.

'What happened?' she asked. There was no complaint in it but it unnerved me nonetheless because her voice was strange, distant.

'There was a prize-fight.' We took a few more strides in silence. 'I won,' I added.

'Oh,' she said. 'Congratulations.' She smiled a little wan smile for my benefit. I was astounded. Even when I had gone and done the terrible things I'd done, she could still find a way to be goddamn encouraging.

'I guess we got a little carried away celebrating. I didn't mean for things to get out of hand like that. I'm sorry you had to come to the hotel. Someone . . . one of the fellas must've stolen my wallet. They slipped me some kind of Mickey or something and left me there to rot, the slobs. You know how boys can be when they get rowdy. I bet they're somewhere having a good laugh about it now.'

She sighed. I knew she did not believe me, or at least that she only partially believed me, because Eden was too smart to ever fall for the whole thing hook, line, and sinker. I always *mostly* told the truth, but Eden knew I tended to leave a fact or two out.

'Say, where did you dig up the bail money?' I asked, trying to keep things light-hearted.

'I'd been saving a little bit,' she replied. 'I used to call it "Rusty money" – emergency money, in case things got out of hand. Anyway, it's all gone now.'

At first, I was angry and hurt that she had been saving money on the side and not telling me about it, but the very instant I thought this, a second thought came to me that sobered me right up. She wouldn't need to save money on the side if it weren't for me in the first place and anyway the fact that she did squirrel away cash had come in very handy just now and it was the reason I was walking home to my apartment and not riding in a squad car to a midtown jail.

We passed a milliner. It was closed but the lights were on. In the window someone had erected a large iron hat rack made to look like a tree. I know nothing about hats but these hats were very colourful and engineered like spaceships and struck me as being quite chic. Just as Eden had been too tired to question me further about the circumstances that had led to my debacle at the hotel, she was too tired now to perk up and look at all the hats in the window as she would have ordinarily done. It damn near broke my heart to see it.

I thought about telling her all about my plan to use the winnings to buy her a beauty of a hat and to take her out to a swell dinner, but I knew she would only hate me more for telling her about my good intentions as though those counted for anything. Instead, I simply walked beside her the rest of the way home in silence. It was the best and most considerate thing I could do.

52

EDEN

Curiosity finally got the better of me. Well, curiosity and also a kind of frustrated malaise, I suppose. Malaise in my marriage, malaise when it came to my prospects for advancement at Bonwright.

I reached for my typewriter's vinyl dustcover and slipped it over the machine.

'Where are you off to, Eden?' a girl named Donna asked in a curious tone. It was an hour too early for our usual lunchtime.

'I've got a doctor's appointment,' I said, feeling bad for the lie. You would think, with all the deception that had cropped up in my life over the past year, I'd be comfortable stretching the truth by now, but I wasn't.

'I hope it's nothing serious,' Donna said, looking hungry for something to gossip about.

'It's not,' I said, disappointing her. 'Only a check-up.' I gathered up my pocketbook and crossed the typing pool to where my coat hung on a rack in the corner of the room. 'Mr Nelson knows I'm leaving now. I just checked on him, and he shouldn't need anything until after he comes back from lunch.'

'All right,' Donna said, turning back to her own work with disinterest. 'Hope you don't have to sit around too long in the waiting room listening to the sound of that terrible drill. I hate that!'

'Me, too. See you later!'

I took the elevator down and left the building. It was cold outside, but sunny and bright. Most of the leaves had fallen from their branches; the wind blew them into the dry gutters, where they rustled about listlessly as though they were antsy for the eventual rain, the sleet, the snow.

It wasn't very far, so I made my way on foot over to Madison and Fiftieth Street. The building was different than I'd expected; it was a former mansion of some variety, carved up so each wing was devoted to a different small enterprise. Between Torchon & Lyle and Bonwright, I'd come to associate publishing houses with cold steel high-rises, not former residences – albeit grand – like this one. In the black-and-white-tiled lobby, I found the little gold plaque that indicated which wing housed Farbman & Company. There was a very small birdcage of an elevator, and a set of marble stairs. I took the stairs.

Once at the top, a friendly receptionist led me to Mavis Singer's office. Most of the office doors were open as we walked along the hallway, and I peeked in here and there. It was heartening to see that, despite being a woman, Ms Singer had been assigned an office of equal size as her male peers, instead of being tucked away in a smaller office on a different floor, as Miss Everett had been, and as most female editors were accustomed.

'Hello, Ms Singer,' the receptionist called in a friendly voice, rapping lightly on the inside of the open doorframe. 'Eden Katz here to see you.'

How strange it was, I realised, to hear the sound again of my true name.

'Oh yes, Miss Katz!' she said, looking up from her desk and smiling pleasantly. 'Come in, come in. I'm just wrapping up a few things here and then we can go to lunch.' She offered me a seat. Just as she had been at the book party, she was very neatly put together, this time in a navy wool women's suit. Her office was library-green, with large windows that let in the light.

'Minor bureaucratic items,' she explained as she arranged things on her desk. 'Let me put them in order so I can hand them over to Betty on our way out.'

'Certainly,' I said. 'Take your time.'

There was a brisk, clean efficiency about her. We chatted as she organised the documents on her desk and on her credenza.

'What are your ambitions in the publishing industry, if I may ask, Eden?'

'I want to become an editor someday.'

'I thought as much,' she said. 'Very good. At the parties, I noticed you've been paying attention and have your head in the business.'

'Yes.' I hesitated. 'I'm starting to wonder, however . . .'

'How badly you want it?' Ms Singer supplied, glancing up at me. She gave a terse shrug. 'Well, it's not for everybody.'

'No, it's not that,' I replied. 'I still want it. Awfully bad, as a matter of fact. It's just . . . well, most people seem to think I'm being unrealistic, that I ought to have other goals to fall back on.'

'Like a husband and children?'

'I suppose so.' I shifted in my chair. 'Wanting to be an editor . . . do you think I'm being unrealistic?'

Ms Singer paused in her organising and stopped to look me square in the eye. 'Put aside the fact I hardly know you and can't say what is or isn't realistic for you in particular . . . Rule number one in publishing, Eden: know your audience. I'm a woman and I'm an editor. Two guesses what my opinion is on the matter.'

I felt sheepish. I didn't have a clue why I'd blurted out that ridiculous question to Ms Singer, of all people.

'It's all right, Eden,' she continued, as though she had read my mind. 'You asked the question because you're still trying to decide for yourself, and there's nothing wrong with that. But' – she held up a finger – 'when you blurt out that question in front of different people, you are going to get back very different answers.' She leant in. 'For instance, if you blurt out that question in front of Roger Nelson, I'd be willing to bet you'll get a very different answer than the one I just gave you. I figure it couldn't hurt to offer you an earful from the other side.'

She stood up and carefully loaded her arms with different stacks containing contracts, sales reports, and manuscripts. I offered to help.

'No need,' she said, 'I'm quite capable.' Truer words were never spoken, I thought. 'Now, shall we?'

Over lunch we talked some more about publishing and editing. I recounted what I'd done at Torchon & Lyle and the duties I'd been assigned now that I was at Bonwright. To my relief, she didn't enquire what had prompted my move from one publishing house to the other. I skirted delicately around the subject of Miss Everett, hinting lightly that there had been some discord between us but never saying anything outright. Ms Singer seemed to know the personalities of everyone who was anyone in publishing very well. I wondered if she didn't already know about Miss Everett, or about Mr Turner and his alleged biases.

There was something refreshing and forthright about Ms Singer. She was friendly enough but at the same time very professional. She didn't gossip or disparage her colleagues. She invited my confidence and at the same time she didn't ask any question that might pry into my personal life. The biggest personal revelation we shared was that we were both originally from the suburbs of much smaller cities: her hometown was in New Jersey and mine was in Indiana.

'At the risk of making a banal observation, Manhattan can be a shock, can't it?' she said over lunch.

'Yes,' I admitted. 'I never knew how . . . how much I depended on suburban life to sort of . . . include me, but also *erase* me . . . if that makes any sense.'

'Don't try so hard to be invisible, Eden,' she advised with a knowing tone. 'There aren't any accolades for that. Just be yourself.'

At one point I was tempted to come clean and tell her the truth about Torchon & Lyle and how I'd had to get the job at Bonwright as 'Eden Collins', not 'Eden Katz'. But then I pictured telling her – a woman named *Singer*, working at a company named *Farbman* – and I felt a deep sense of shame. It could also backfire and go terribly wrong: though I didn't think she would, there was always the possibility Ms Singer might feel it was her duty to pass along the illegalities of the situation to Mr Nelson out of a sense of professional courtesy. I'd had enough of things backfiring and decided to keep my confession to myself.

I was glad I did, too, because shortly after I ruled out telling Ms Singer about my name, she said something that reminded me – for a fleeting moment – of Miss Everett.

'One thing, Eden . . .' she said.

'Yes?'

'It's none of my business, but if you really want to make it as an editor, I would advise against marriage or a family.'

I blinked, surprised by the abrupt unsolicited opinion.

'You are quite young and perhaps the world will change someday, but as it stands, it's near impossible for us women to have our cake and eat it, too. I'm nicer about it than others, but even I've had a tough time keeping a girl on after she's decided to become pregnant. Some girls can marshal their mothers or an elderly aunt to babysit during the days, but the prevailing expectation is that she'd rather be at home and if she wouldn't there's something wrong with her that ought to be fixed. It is likely that at some point you will have to choose between a career or a family, and it's good to know in advance which one you want most.'

She did not say *more*, she said *most*, implying that it wasn't a question of a slight tip in the balance – more like a necessary landslide. What would she have said if I told her I was already married, that I'd gone and secretly eloped with the boss's son? The sense of shame came over me again. It was like something soggy seeping into my physical body, bringing me down. How had my life gotten so tangled?

'Okay, I've done my duty and said my peace about that,' Ms Singer said in a cheerful voice. 'Now let's move on to something else.'

We finished our lunch in a punctual manner – no extra martinis or cigars after lunch for Ms Singer – and I hurried back to the office. I can't say why I felt so blue, but I did. I liked my job working for Mr Nelson just fine, and yet a tiny part of me couldn't help but wish I could go back and do it all over again: moving to New York and hunting for a job and all of it. It would've been nice if I could've met Ms Singer first instead of last.

Later that evening I came home to an unexpected sight. I turned my key in the lock and opened the door to find Cliff addressing an envelope and stuffing a stack of manuscript pages into it. I drew closer, and recognised the manuscript as the pages I'd been typing up for him.

'Eden old girl!' he called out. He smiled, and I saw that he was in an upbeat, cheerful mood. 'Come, sit down.' He shepherded me over to a folding chair beside the card table.

'Now,' he continued, 'I know I've put you through a lot these past few weeks.' I assumed he was referring to the disaster with Rusty and Miles at our party, the wrecked hotel room and corresponding bill I'd had to pay after he'd won a prize-fight at the Y. I eyed the manila envelope warily, hoping he wasn't about to ask me – yet again – to slip the manuscript to his father as an anonymous submission.

'Don't worry,' he said, following my gaze and reading my mind. 'My point is I'm sorry, and my apology is to leave you out of things, just as you requested. You know, I've hit upon the crux of the problem: all this time I've been dancing around the subject with My Old Man. I've never once come out and asked him to plain read my work! Can you believe? So, after chewing it over pretty good, I've decided to approach my father once and for all, man-to-man.'

I was shocked. It was, I thought, perhaps the first time I'd ever heard Cliff use the term *my father* instead of *My Old Man.* I wasn't quite sure what to make of this.

'I'm submitting my manuscript myself,' he said proudly, 'the good, old-fashioned way. I'm going to make this strictly business: a real bona fide submission, from me to him. Going to mail it and everything!'

'Wow,' I said, slightly impressed, slightly horrified. My mind flashed immediately forward to what Mr Nelson would say, if he in fact took the trouble to read Cliff's manuscript in its present state.

53

MILES

Without consciously intending it, I had begun writing a memoir of sorts. On a whim, I'd picked up a composition book at a stationer in San Francisco, and before I knew it I was filling up the pages. I began to write down every childhood memory of my father I could recall. Other times, I rewrote the anecdotes in my father's journal. I alternated between my memories and his, strategically folding two halves together – the war hero and the old man in his armchair – so that they made a whole. It was a curious sort of call-and-response memoir. For me, it was also cathartic: a way to reconcile the avalanche of information I'd gained about my father upon recovering his journal with the thoughts and questions I'd had about him as a child.

'Listen to this,' I would sometimes say to Joey, reading a passage from my father's journal I had rewritten, or sometimes – when I was feeling especially brave – a passage written in my own voice, constructed out of my own memories. He would stop his happy whistling and put down whatever he was tinkering with and listen carefully, nodding along as though impressed.

Most of the time I knew his quiet demeanour and sober, attentive expression were donned purposely for my benefit, as Joey's natural state was a chatty and merry one. But one day, as I was reading one of these passages aloud, a shadow passed over Joey's face that struck me as far more personal, and slightly anguished.

'Something wrong, Joey?' I asked.

'No,' he said, but the shadow was still there. I closed my composition book and looked at him more carefully.

'You mentioned your uncle once,' I said, blindly guessing at the source. 'That he was the one who took you out of boarding school.'

'Yes.'

'What happened after that?'

Joey shrugged. 'It's not important.'

'Please, I want to know. From what you've said, he didn't always live with you. Why did that change?' We were outside on the narrow deck that wrapped around the entire perimeter of the houseboat, and Joey was crouched over a broken electric toaster he'd found, trying to repair the contraption just for the hell of it. 'Was he your father's brother?'

Joey shook his head. 'My mother's. Her family did very well breeding horses – really impressive ones that ran in the Derby – but the truth is my uncle lost most of the family money betting. Around the time I was sixteen, he had to come live with us because he was flat broke.

'That wasn't what he told people, of course. He needed an excuse, so he decided I was it.'

'What do you mean?' I asked.

'He said he'd come to live with us to do right by his sister's memory and "correct" his nephew's development.' Joey caught the expression flickering over my face. 'He said I was too soft,' he explained, 'that boarding school was turning me into a pansy. Of course, it wasn't. But he'd visited me a year or two earlier at school, and I think he'd caught on to the way of things for me.'

Joey did not say what he meant by *the way of things for me*, but he didn't need to: I knew. I wondered if Joey's uncle was what had come between him and his first love.

'The loaded insinuation was all he needed to get my father to allow him to dole out whatever corrective measures he deemed necessary. When it came to his progeny, my father was always happiest when other people were put in charge of doing all the real work. He has no spine and knows it. So . . . all this is to say, after my uncle made his veiled accusation and offered to step in, he pretty much had free rein. Drunk, unemployed, and in debt, he made a full-time job out of bullying me under the pretences of "home-schooling". I suppose it *was* an education of sorts, after all.' Joey shrugged again.

I thought of Wendell, grateful that while my mother didn't exactly stand up to him, she nonetheless did her best to keep me and Wendell separated from each other, and she never put Wendell in charge of my conduct in any way.

'At least I knew what I was in for,' Joey continued. 'My uncle had come to stay with us once before, just for a week or so, a few months after my mother died. It was the first time I'd ever met him, and with my mother passed on, I remember being excited. I thought he might look like my mother, he might have her laugh, he might hold his fork the way she did . . . He didn't look anything like her. I just remember noticing how *red* he was. His complexion looked perpetually sunburned, his hair was strawberry – his eyes, even, were bloodshot. His neck sweated a great deal; there were stains around all his collars. I was only seven. That time, too, he declared I was too soft. He took it out on me by teaching me how to hunt.

'I'd told him about a little ritual my mother and I had of taking a walk around the property in the evenings and feeding the deer dried sweetcorn. My mother had a special way about her; she could get the deer to eat out of her hand.

'The first thing my uncle did was make me build a hunting blind with him. That was the kind of hunter he was, you see: the kind to stack the deck by sitting in a blind and putting out feed. It wasn't terrible right away. I thought we were building a tree house at first. It may sound naïve, but I'd never killed anything in my life – not even a squirrel. I'd only ever shot BB guns at empty cans.'

I was inclined to believe Joey on this score. I thought of the concern he'd shown for Cob's insects that first night we'd met. Since settling into life on the houseboat, Joey was more often the one to feed and care for the insects in their little glass jars. He'd gone so far as to check a book on entomology out from the library.

'We were up in that hunting blind when it happened,' he continued now. 'It could be that I was just a kid, that it was only my imagination, but that first deer that walked into the clearing . . . I swore it was this one doe in particular, one that used to come around and eat directly out of my mother's hand. We must've made a noise, or else she caught wind of us, because she looked up to regard us with her wet brown eyes, and she and I found ourselves locked in a stare. She was a beautiful doe, something regal about her, and gazing at her – for a moment at least – it seemed like I had somehow fallen out of time, that I was back with my mother, feeding the deer at dusk the way we always had.

'But then my uncle dumped the rifle in my arms and shouted at me to shoot. I did as I was told. I said a silent prayer she'd get spooked and run away, but she froze.'

'What . . . was the outcome?' I ventured.

'Bullet caught her in the foreleg and tore through her knee. She staggered and fell, but then she tried to get up again. She ran a few yards, and fell . . . ran and fell, ran and fell . . . The sight of it made me sick. My uncle raged at me, complaining that I'd only wounded her and caused her a slower, more painful death.

'Those words were what put me to shame. He beat me with the butt of the rifle until I was bloody, but I hardly remember the pain of that. It was the pain of that doe, out there in the woods, sprinting and falling, sprinting and falling, flailing and on the losing side of life, that hurt the most.'

He looked at me.

'That's the part I still remember the most.'

I didn't know what to say. I felt bad for having brought it up, for having pressed him to talk. At the same time I was glad to know him better, to understand what made him tick.

We made lunch. The dark shadow dissipated from his features. Joey appeared to have shaken it off. For the remainder of the afternoon and evening, he was as happy as ever, puttering around the houseboat and whistling again like a canary.

It wasn't until later that night, after we'd gone to bed and slept for a few hours, that he hollered at the top of his lungs and sat up under the covers, dripping with sweat. I knew immediately he'd had a nightmare, and I knew, too, what the nightmare was likely about. I wasn't sure how to help, other than to soak a washrag in cold water and hold him while pressing the cool rag to his forehead.

It was unexpected and new to me, this vulnerability of his. It was the first time I saw it, and I didn't quite know what to make of it. It's true to say it made me love him more. But if I am being honest, it also made me more afraid of everything we were, everything we were doing to each other, and, most especially, everything we would do to each other in the future.

54

I began to experience the kind of growing pains that all lovers experience whenever they move in together and begin to play house. Which is to say, Joey's way of doing things was not my way of doing things, and vice versa. The major difference in our habits was, I believe, one that had its roots in class and race. In many ways, the colour of my skin dictated mine, Columbia education be damned. I was aware of what little advantage life had afforded me; I was careful not to bring unwanted attention on myself. I had mastered the art of invisibility.

Joey, on the other hand, was privileged, and white, and had mastered the art of being seen. His uncle's beatings had only made him more determined to do as he pleased with his life, and he was only careful when it came to avoiding detection from official sources. From his tales, I deduced he had toed a fine line in the army. These were tales that made me nervous.

One of his favourite habits on the houseboat was to lie on the deck sunning himself, naked as the day he was born, eating cherries and spitting the pits into the water.

'We don't want to attract attention,' I often reminded him.

'I'm getting a suntan, not robbing a bank,' Joey would reply, waving me off.

He refused to take things seriously, even when the Coast Guard made a turn of the harbour, patrolling. I tried to shoo him off the deck and back inside, but of course I'd have been better off herding cats. Instead, I wound up ducking inside while he grinned at the officers and made a jokey salute as they passed. This happened more than once. I was shocked and vaguely terrified – and, in all honesty, also a little amused in spite of myself – when one day Joey managed to invite them to come aboard our deck and have a beer.

Joey's charm produced that effect – such scenarios as you could hardly believe. His charm was, without a doubt, his greatest strength and most attractive quality. So it unnerved me one day to realise how profoundly it also bothered me. I remembered his casual familiarity with the YMCA and felt a terrible, deeply annoyed jealousy. I'm afraid to admit, I judged him: he was too brazen, too comfortable, too easy with himself, and I wanted him to understand how dearly we might pay for this.

My irritation with Joey took on a strange form: I found myself hiding behind Janet.

'You ought to know,' I said to him one day, 'I'm not like you.'

Naturally, he wanted to know what I meant. I told him I had a girl back home whom I planned to marry.

'Sure,' Joey said, shrugging good-naturedly. 'But that's nothing very serious.'

I blinked at him. 'What do you mean, "nothing serious"?'

'I mean, of course you have a girl.' I searched his face for sarcasm but found none. He asked me a few questions about Janet – mere details, really. How did she dress, where did she live, what kinds of movies did we go to see, et cetera. He seemed idly curious, the way a kid might ask questions about life in China from a returning tourist.

'You don't seem bothered by all this,' I said.

'Why should I be?' Joey replied, shrugging. 'She sounds fine – very down-to-earth and all that – but you can't have the same kind of feelings for each other as we do. It's not the same thing.'

'We're expected to marry. I wish you'd take this more seriously.'

'Nah,' he said, slipping his arm around me. 'You just wish I was more like you: a grumpy old bastard in a young man's body.' He winked, and I sighed in resignation.

One afternoon I was alone on the houseboat, transcribing pages from my father's journal, as had become my routine, when Joey's friend Eddie came looking for him. It was a pleasant day, and I had thrown all the windows and doors open to let in the fresh air. It was very quiet, and I had lost myself entirely to the stillness when an abrupt rap sounded on the open redwood door and Eddie poked his head in. I wasn't expecting anyone, and the brilliant flash of sunshine on his white-blonde hair nearly startled me out of my chair.

'Whoa, fella,' he said, holding his hands up in surrender. 'Sorry about that, chief.' I hadn't seen him since our late-night cruise down Lombard Street in Bill's Fairlane, but I recognised him easily. As he stood in the doorway he cut a distinctly lanky figure against the bright sunlight pouring in behind him. He looked like a boy who had just run in from a cornfield in Iowa or a wheat field in Nebraska. You almost expected to find a few stray pieces of straw in that white-blonde hair.

'I guess we don't have a lot of folks dropping in unexpectedly,' I said, pulling my nerves back together and giving a good-natured chuckle. I had liked Eddie that first night I met him; he seemed straightforward, gentle.

'"We"?' He grinned and arched an eyebrow, making me slightly uncomfortable.

'He stepped out,' I said, meaning Joey. 'There's some beer, I think.'

'That'd be swell,' he said, nodding, and I went out onto the deck to fetch up two bottles. We didn't have an ice-box on the houseboat and Joey had solved this lack of a modern appliance by putting the sealed bottles of beer in a crab trap and lowering it into the chilly water. Eddie came outside and watched as I hauled up the rope and opened the trap.

'Looks like one of Joey's bright ideas,' he said, pointing to the crab trap with a faint smile playing on his lips. There was a twang to his Kentucky accent that Joey did not have. I opened one of the beers on the deck railing and handed it to him, then opened one for myself. Despite the fact the beers were sealed, there was always a faint odour of motor oil and just the tiniest hint of brackish seawater about them. We went back inside and sat awkwardly on the two deck chairs in the middle of the room. The breeze wafted in from the open door and the sound of water softly slapping the moorings drifted up to us.

'What do you think of Frisco?' Eddie asked, making polite conversation. I was grateful he had not brought up the night of our car ride.

'I like it out here,' I replied. 'It's . . .' I struggled to find the right words, but they wouldn't come '. . . so different from New York.'

He laughed and made that particular pronouncement that all people who are not from New York make: 'Yeah, New York's a nice enough place to visit, but I don't know how anybody can ever live there.' He shook his head. 'It's certainly not for me.'

'I don't know when Joey will be back,' I said. I noticed he was already more than halfway through his beer. Eddie, for all his cornfield patina, appeared to be a fast-drinker.

'Well, that's all right. I just came to tell him I checked my PO box, and I got my letter today. Wanted to see if he did, too.'

'Your letter?'

'From the Department of Labour,' he said. 'I got the job. Just wanted to thank Joey.'

'Thank him for what?' I was confused. Joey had mentioned both he and Eddie were applying for government jobs, but until that moment I hadn't paid much attention to this fact, caught up as I was with my father's journal and my new life on the houseboat.

'It's an administrative position – I'll be working as the secretary to some kind of mining engineer – but I ain't ever worked in an office before. Now I gotta learn how to type before the end of the month. Me, typing, hah! I'm pretty sure Joey's old man pulled some strings, and I'm grateful.'

'Oh,' I said, taking all this in.

'Yep, Joey's old man is a cold fish, that's for sure, but he still does Joey a good turn from time to time.'

'I guess congratulations are in order,' I said, offering him my hand.

'Say, thanks,' he said. 'I just came around because I figured Joey might've gotten his letter, too. I'm itching to find out if we'll be in DC together like we planned.'

Something about the way Eddie had said those words, *like we planned*, suddenly had me feeling hostile and irritated. I stood up, and – not very gracefully – snatched the empty beer bottle out of Eddie's hand. I gave a little grimace that was meant to be a smile.

'Well, I've got to get back to work,' I said, moving as though to clear the bottles away and get back to business. Eddie cocked his head at me and I could tell what he was thinking. What had changed between us, he was wondering. And what could I possibly have to do so urgently?

'All right,' he said, as though giving up on the answer. He rose and smoothed down his T-shirt and blue jeans. 'Well, I just came to tell Joey my news and see about that letter. You tell him I stopped by?'

'I will,' I promised. Eddie nodded and I felt embarrassed, aware of myself as a bratty child who had just thrown a tantrum. 'I will,' I repeated stupidly, and tried to smile. 'Thank you for coming by, Eddie.'

He smiled back easily. His blue eyes seemed kind, his white-blonde hair angelic. I was a fool; my suspicions had been entirely my own. He turned to go and took a few strides towards the door, then paused.

'Miles? You'll look out for him, won't you?'

I froze. 'What do you mean?'

He smiled sheepishly and shrugged. 'Oh, I don't know . . . Joey's reckless. Letting guys like Bill and Donald buy him drinks . . . Anyway, two men, well, sometimes that attracts attention. And a white man and a Negro, well, people have a habit of *remembering* that pair, you understand? But he's seemed to calm down some since he met you, and I'm glad. I hope you can . . . just' – Eddie shook his head – 'keep it that way, and take good care of him.'

He turned and walked out the door. I watched him disappear, a black silhouette cutting through the bright light of afternoon.

Joey came back an hour later, carrying two bags from the little grocery store in town. I got up to help him but froze when I saw clutched in his hand was an open envelope.

'Eddie stopped by,' I dutifully reported. 'He was granted a position at the Department of Labour and he wanted to thank you for your father's influence.'

Joey's face lit up. 'Oh, that's swell!'

'Eddie also wanted to find out whether you'd received *your* letter,' I added. He looked down at the envelope he'd been carrying as though he had forgotten it was there.

'I did!' he said. 'I got the job!'

'Congratulations,' I said. I smiled and we embraced, but the truth was I wasn't sure what any of this meant, and my heart was only halfway in it.

55

'Your job with the State Department . . . what will you be doing there, anyhow?'

We had slept in, whiling away the morning in bed. Or rather, Joey had slept in. I had lain awake, listening to the sound of his soft snoring, restless, trying to picture Joey's life after me. The life he would now have *without* me. Now he was awake. I got up to put on my pants, while Joey followed suit with considerable reluctance.

'I'll be writing up armament reports for the Political-Military office,' he answered. 'It's only a paper-pusher job, really, but some of the information is classified: the quantities of munitions we supply to other countries and such.' Suddenly he laughed. 'Actually, when you think about it, it's not altogether different from what I was doing before.'

'What do you mean? From what you were doing in the army?'

I asked him what guys actually did in the army when there wasn't a war on. He shrugged and said as far as he could tell it wasn't all that different from working in any other industry because mostly it was all about supplies: you either counted supplies or audited the use of supplies or moved supplies from one place to another. I asked him wasn't there more to it than that and he shrugged again and said: 'Maybe for the officers. But the enlisted men . . . it's like running one big national warehouse. Sometimes we pretend there's a war on and we do training exercises. Then a couple of guys write up a report on how much supplies that would take.'

In spite of myself, I laughed.

It was difficult to stay mad at Joey. But ever since he'd gotten his letter from the State Department, a little ball of resentment had been rolling around in the pit of my stomach, growing bigger and bigger. I had no reason to feel betrayed. From the first moment I agreed to join him on the houseboat, we had never discussed the terms of our relationship, not once. And it wasn't as if I hadn't seen Joey flirt with others or observed his familiarity with the YMCA. Nonetheless, I was angry to think I could be one of a number, a transition point as he moved back to one coast from another.

Joey noticed the shift in my disposition almost immediately.

'What's eating you, Miles?' he asked. He came over and put his hands on my shoulders. 'Ever since I got my good news yesterday, you've been acting funny.'

I opened my mouth to deny it, but stopped. I would not be dishonest with him.

'I suppose I'm not ready – just yet – to part ways.' He cocked his head and searched my face.

'What are you talking about?' he said, laughing. 'The job's in DC – that's the beauty of it. When you go back to New York, we'll be on the same coast.' He released his grip on my shoulders and let his arms slide down around my waist. 'It's possible we can go on seeing each other!' he said with a triumphant, matter-of-fact smile, as though he had solved a difficult math equation that he'd been working on.

'Oh,' I said, stunned. I felt the back of my neck bristle with a sudden cold sweat. 'I hadn't . . . thought of that.'

'Of course, the weekdays will have to be all work and no play, but on weekends I can take the train up to see you and get a hotel room for us.' He dropped his arms from my waist and picked up the letter he'd left lying on the table, looking it over and thinking aloud. 'You know, the pay isn't a heck of a lot, but it isn't terrible, either. Maybe if I scrimp a bit in DC we can eventually get a little place of our own somewhere in Manhattan.' He put his arms back around me and tucked his face into my neck. Suddenly he started. 'Gosh. What's a matter with you? Your heart is beating a million miles an hour!'

'I'm all right,' I said. 'I'm just excited, I suppose. This is news to me. I'm taking it all in.' I *was* excited. And more than a little frightened.

'You want that, don't you?' he asked. 'To go on seeing each other?'

'Sure I do.'

'Well, then,' he said. He gave my body a squeeze and released me. 'We ought to celebrate.'

'All right,' I agreed, still dazed. Everything had changed in the blink of an eye.

'I'm happy. Aren't we happy?' he asked.

I shook myself from my trance, trying to register the question he'd asked. *Aren't we happy?* 'Of course.'

'Look, you finish up what you're doing here.' He gestured to where my composition book and my father's journal lay open on the table. 'I'll go back into town and see if I can't get us some champagne.' His eyes sparkled and he grinned, and I found myself grinning back. He started to leave, then paused and spun back around. 'Oh!' he said, and pulled an envelope from his pocket. 'Oh, yeah – this came for you. In my excitement yesterday, I put this in my pocket and forgot about it.'

Joey handed me the envelope and leant over to kiss me. I kissed him back in a perfunctory way.

'Be right back.'

'Okay,' I agreed, and watched him go.

When I looked down at the letter, I froze. My heart stopped and I felt the blood drain from my face. It was from Janet. I opened it. Her letters had come back to her in the mail, she wrote, marked *RETURN TO SENDER* and, alarmed, she'd tried to telephone my hotel room. What was this post office box address the hotel clerk had given her? Where was I sleeping if not the hotel?

It didn't take me long to figure out that the clerk at my former hotel in San Francisco had opted to return my mail while at the same time bewildering Janet with news of the PO box address when she'd called. I wondered if this had been done out of malicious intent; he had certainly glared at Joey and me with hatred and disgust.

I folded the letter back up and slipped it into its envelope, wishing dearly that it didn't exist. The small tremor of panic I'd felt when Joey suggested we go on seeing each other once we were both back on the East Coast had been amplified by the abrupt materialisation of Janet's letter, Janet's handwriting, Janet's words. What was I doing? I was suddenly terrified.

In less than ten minutes I had all of my things packed and had walked down the road – in the opposite direction Joey had taken – to telephone for a taxi to take me across the bridge to the bus station in downtown San Francisco. I wrote a note – a painfully casual note, for I was trying harder to convince myself than I was trying to convince him that I was indifferent to this affair – to say I was headed back to New York. My family needed me, I wrote (without giving specific details I knew he would never have believed anyway), so I was going back east and anyway it was time for me to be moving on. I cannot imagine what it was like for Joey to come home and find that note. I feel pretty low whenever I think of it, to have written it, for it was full of cowardice and lies.

56

The ride back to New York was dull, grey, seemingly endless. The roads were slick with early-winter rain, causing the bus's brakes to squeal from time to time as the driver attempted to wrangle the great lumbering steel beast steady as we zoomed over the pavement. Newcomers getting on the bus struggled out of their dripping coats and allowed the rainwater to soak into the upholstery, releasing the humid odours of wet, dirty wool. Morale among the passengers was low, befitting my own mood.

I made it back to New York and came home in a surreal daze, back to my old bedroom in my mother's apartment. Technically speaking, I was a Columbia graduate now – no longer a student – and my prospects ought to have been bright. But I felt neither here nor there. I was free to go forth as a man with a diploma, an adult who could proudly put the words *summa cum laude* on his résumé, yet I felt distinctly dispirited and unambitious. My life had not really begun. I had thought that it was actually beginning during my time in San Francisco. Or, more specifically, in Sausalito, on that houseboat. Those rare days had felt more like the start of something than anything else I'd experienced. But it had been a false start; I was sure of that now I met with Janet to tell her I was back in town and explained things to her as best I could. I mentioned Joey, but said that we were merely friends and that he'd put me up for a spell as a matter of financial practicality. Money was likewise the reason I gave Janet for seeing her less often.

'I can't afford to take you out as much,' I said to her.

'I like the park,' she said. 'The park is free.'

'It's getting much too cold out now,' I said. 'I promise I'll get some work soon, and then I can take you out properly.'

'All right,' she agreed.

But this was a false promise, too. I wallowed about and didn't go looking for work, not right away. My mother and Cob were puzzled by my depression. From their vantage, they only knew I had gone away on an adventure and returned victorious with my father's keepsake, his words, his journal, his war stories.

'I'm proud of you, son,' my mother said, holding the journal when I first showed it to her and gazing at it in wonder. 'You done it.' She opened it to a random page and her face screwed up with emotion as her eyes ran over the familiar shapes of my father's handwriting. Then the sound of Wendell snoring in the living room broke her reverie and she hurriedly handed the journal back to me, then wiped her eyes. 'Here,' she said in a low voice, 'I hope you read eve'y word, and it makes you proud.'

'It already has,' I said, hoping to reassure her.

'Then why you look so sad?'

There was an answer to her question, but not one I could speak aloud.

During my first week back, I barely got out of bed. At first she was perplexed, but soon enough puzzlement gave way to impatience, and eventually, my mother – a woman who could only tolerate inactivity for so long – roused me.

'I don't know what cause you got to feel so sorry for yo'self, but

I didn't raise no lazybones!' she scolded, creating a small tornado of force as she pretended to tidy my room. It was impressive; she managed to rip the sheets off the bed and stuff them in her laundry basket before I was entirely out of it.

I took the subway down to the messenger dispatch in midtown and was given my old job back. I did not attempt to contact Mister Gus or resume my duties for him, figuring it was best to leave well enough alone. My days were spent peddling around the city, making deliveries for the messenger service, and my evenings were spent sidestepping Wendell. Whenever we bumped into each other in the living room or in the hallway, we squared off and stalked around my mother's apartment, leering at each other with the hateful eyes of two jungle cats.

My greatest pleasure during that dreary time was the delight in Cob's face when I read entries from our father's journal aloud to him in the evening. But other than the happy, golden half hour or so I spent doing this, I was left with a profound sense of being idle after Cob went to bed. I told myself this was a result of no longer having my studies to occupy me, but I knew things were more complicated than that.

I had felt the first pangs of regret before I'd even signed the note and left the houseboat, but I didn't know how much these feelings would intensify until I came home one day and found my mother waiting anxiously in the living room, pacing in circles.

'He wouldn't say what he come for,' she announced in a plaintive voice when I entered the apartment.

'Who?' I asked.

'The white boy who rang the bell. He asked for you by name, but he wouldn't say what he come for.'

My heart leapt.

'Did he say he was coming back?' I asked.

'No,' she said with certainty.

'Oh.'

'He *say* he wait for you at the coffee shop around the corner.'

'What?'

'He *say* he wait for you at the coffee shop around the corner,' she repeated, and gave her foot an impatient stamp. 'Hurry now. You go an' see about it. I don't know *what* on God's green earth he want, but he trouble, an' this family ain't fixin' for no trouble.'

With my messenger bag still slung over my shoulder, I dashed for the door. Enthusiasm carried me down the stairs, along the street, and around the corner.

I was feeling a bit high and dazed when I neared the coffee shop . . . and then, peering in the large plate-glass window, I saw him. Suddenly everything came crashing down around me as I surveyed the situation and the dim buzz of comprehension began to seep into my core. The white boy waiting for me in a booth at the coffee shop was *not* Joey as I had hoped and expected it would be, but it *was* someone I knew. I blinked at his familiar sandy-blonde hair and pert retroussé nose, and as I did so, he looked up and noticed me, too.

It was Cliff, from the Village. I had not seen him since the terrible night of his house party. What he wanted from me now, I couldn't say, but he had seen me and there was no going back. Saturated with the soggy weight of disappointment, I took a deep breath and pushed through the coffee shop door.

57

CLIFF

I guess I surprised everybody pretty good by going up to Harlem. It was all part of my new policy of goodwill. I'd decided to turn over a new leaf. I knew I'd been a lousy husband to Eden lately, what with all that prize-fight business and the hotel room. I'd gotten into a pretty destructive state, and when you got down to it even I had to admit the truth behind this had to do with my frustrations about my writing and My Old Man. I had resolved the issue by grabbing the bull by the horns and approaching him directly and making an official submission. Eden was mostly staying out of it but she *did* mention it had arrived in the mail and that she had spotted the envelope on My Old Man's desk. I had addressed it directly to him and marked it 'Private and Confidential' and a week later I received back a date-card in the mail, making an appointment for us to have lunch at Keen's. 'We will discuss your pages,' he'd written in his cramped chicken-scratch handwriting at the bottom. It was a little funny he hadn't commissioned Eden to send the date-card out because according to her he rarely did that sort of thing personally, but then again I was his son and it was only natural that I get better treatment. I knew the pages I sent him were good and he was likely to think so, too, and I tried not to read too much between the lines. Now there was nothing left to do but wait.

I spent some time contemplating things while I waited for our lunch-date to roll around and in particular I spent some time thinking about how I could be a better man and a better husband to Eden. It occurred to me that we both still felt bad about what had happened to Miles the night of our party and if I wanted to make things better all around, one thing I could do was to go up to Harlem and look him in the eye and apologise, man-to-man. It was the decent thing to do, and as soon as I made up my mind to do it I began to feel very benevolent just for having the idea.

Deciding to apologise to Miles was easy, but tracking him down was another question. He'd been absent from the Village scene ever since that bad night on our roof. He had talked about going out of town but surely he had to be back by now and this meant he was staying away intentionally. I thought I remembered Miles's surname as being Tillman. I checked the Columbia directory but came up with nothing. He was not in the book, either, but there *was* a Tillman listed and it gave an address that was not far from the jazz club where Eden and Rusty and I had run into him. I figured it was a sign I was on the right track.

I took the train uptown and walked around Harlem until I found the address. Some Negro kids were rough-housing on the stoop and when I asked them did they know Miles Tillman they said 'Sho' 'nuff,' they *did* know Miles Tillman, and that I could find the Tillman family on the fourth floor. Once I got upstairs, a middle-aged woman answered the door. I asked for Miles and she looked at me in alarm and it dawned on me that I had on a collared shirt and a nice pair of trousers and to her I probably looked like the taxman.

'He's not in any kind of trouble,' I explained. 'I'm just here to tell him something about a mutual friend of ours.' This wasn't entirely true, because Rusty was hardly my friend, let alone Miles's, and the only thing I wanted to tell Miles was how mistaken I'd been to allow Rusty into our group and into the party, but I didn't want to explain about all that to the woman standing at the door. I could tell she did not believe in the existence of a mutual friend but she wasn't about to say so. Instead she nodded politely but still looked a little jumpy. Miles was out but would be home soon, she said, and invited me to come inside and wait in the living room. I peered over her shoulder into the apartment and saw that it was nice enough but decided to decline her offer to go inside on account of the fact I had made her uneasy. I was right to think this, because when I told her I would wait at the coffee shop around the corner on 125th Street she looked relieved. I asked her would she be so kind as to send Miles over when he came home? She said yes and off I went.

I wasn't waiting very long before Miles turned up, which was good, because I'd had to order some coffee just to sit there and I didn't have a lot of money and wanted to avoid ordering anything else. I don't know who Miles was expecting but it certainly wasn't me. I was sitting in a booth by the window and staring out into the street when he cut around the corner. His face was dark and shining with sweat and he had an eager air about him, but when he saw me he froze and the smile vanished from his face. I tried not to take this personally because I knew it was mostly on account of Rusty and the horrible thing he had done to Miles. I saw the tight frown creep into Miles's face and I understood he had not forgotten one second of it. There was nothing I could say to make it better but I had come to apologise anyhow. When you really get down to it most apologies are useless but it's nice to make them anyway and for some reason – like I said, because of Eden and because of my new leaf – I was really hot on making this one.

Miles entered the coffee shop and walked right up to my table with a pinched look on his face. He was standing before me and the time for my apology was at hand. We stared at each other. 'My mother said you came calling at the house for me,' he said.

'Yes,' I said. The formality of his tone shook my confidence. He stood hovering over my table, looking uncomfortable. 'Sit down,' I said. He set down the satchel he was carrying and sank into the seat opposite me. He was graceful in the way he did it and as I looked him over I remembered how lean and muscular he was, and how good-looking. The glasses added something, too. Miles cleared his throat and I knew he was waiting for me to speak.

'You weren't expecting me,' I said.

'No.'

'But you were expecting someone,' I observed. He didn't answer. 'Who were you expecting?' I asked. I had no right to ask but I was curious and couldn't help myself. Miles narrowed his eyes and looked at me with that same distrustful expression he'd worn that time I'd approached him in the jazz club, and hesitated.

'Just a friend. Someone from San Francisco,' he finally said.

'A friend from Frisco?' I echoed. I hadn't pictured Miles existing outside of Harlem or the Village, let alone outside of New York, and Frisco was a place I had always meant to go but had never been. Evidently before me sat a worldly Negro who got around. I was impressed. 'You been there much?' I asked.

'Just got back.'

'Hey, cool, man,' I said, hoping he would catch on to my approving tone and understand that we were natural friends. 'Frisco's a madman's town,' I added. I had not meant to sound authoritative but it came out that way. Miles nodded. He started to say something but just as he did the bell over the door of the coffee shop jingled and a young Negro boy ran in.

'Miles!' The little boy grinned and launched himself into Miles's arms. Miles caught him and settled him into his lap but did not grin back. 'Mama said you came home and lef' again.' The boy turned and grinned in my direction. He was a free, easy boy, a kid with the kind of primitive spirit people often talked about when they admired the Negro race. I had never seen a child smile in such a pure-hearted way and it was a marvel to see, but in the very next moment Miles dampened that smile so that it still glowed but a little less brightly.

'I have some business to attend to, little man,' Miles said. 'You run along now and tell Mama I'll be sure to be home in time for supper.'

'You promise you gonna read to me some more about Pa?'

'As soon as I get home. Now go on, Cob. I mean it.'

The boy shuffled his feet and slumped his shoulders. 'Well, anyway,' he turned again to me, 'nice to meet you, mister.'

I was tickled by this and so I put out my hand and the little boy shook it with a tremendous solemnity and introduced himself as 'Mister Malcolm "Cob" Tillman.'

'All right, then, that's enough,' Miles said. 'Go on, Cob; get.' A stiffness had crept into Miles's voice and Cob and I exchanged a look that meant we both knew we would do well to heed him. The boy spun on his feet and dashed out the same way he had come in.

'My kid brother,' Miles explained.

'Cute,' I said. He seemed squirrely about this and stiffened.

'Look,' Miles said, 'I don't mean to be rude, but what do you want?'

'I came here to tell you my feelings on things,' I said. My voice was getting all funny in my throat. I was suddenly nervous as hell. 'And you know,' I continued, 'you know . . . to tell you that I'm no longer friends with Rusty.'

'Congratulations,' he said.

'I mean, I don't know if I'd have even called him a friend in the first place. If you want to know the truth, he was shamming us all. Me included. Boy oh boy, did I let him pull the old wool over my eyes. He turned out to be a real lousy rat. But you know that already.'

Miles only nodded and I could see his jaw clench.

'So I just came here, like I said, to tell you that I wish I would've punched him when I had the chance. You know, before all that nonsense started. Really I do, honest.' I had almost said *before all that nonsense on the roof* but I sensed Miles did not need a more specific reminder to know what I meant.

Miles nodded. 'I guess that makes two of us,' he said finally.

'I mean, I really wish I had,' I repeated. 'I would've felt bad whaling on such a weenie of a guy, but I would've laid him out cold if we ever went toe to toe.'

'Yes, well,' Miles said, 'I better be going.' He rose from the booth before I could say anything. 'Nice to see you again,' he said, shouldering his satchel and reaching out to shake hands. I really had to give it to him, he had a polite way with people. I could tell it had not been a pleasure to see me again but he wasn't about to let it show.

'Cliff.' He nodded.

'Miles.' I nodded in return.

We shook. He stepped quickly for the door. I wasn't quite satisfied with the result of our meeting; something was still missing.

'I really do wish I'd laid that bastard out cold when I had the chance,' I called after him. I don't know why I kept repeating this. I guess it was the closest thing I had to an apology and anyway it let Miles know that I was really on his side and that was the important thing. He nodded and slipped through the door, then gave me a terse wave of his hand as he passed by the window.

I watched him as he disappeared around the corner and then I sat in the booth alone and drained the rest of my coffee. I'd pictured the whole thing differently: me making my apology to Miles and him being grateful and the two of us getting all chummy. I'd also pictured going home to Eden and telling her all about it and having her smile in that way she had when she was proud of me and glad to be my wife. Maybe we'd even get Miles to rejoin the group down in the Village again and he'd come and we'd show him how nice and generous we could be towards a Negro. Sitting there in that booth, I realised how foolish this idea had been.

I looked out the window at the traffic and the people bustling by. It had been dry all day but now an early winter rain had begun to fall and there were big ugly blotches all over the sidewalk. The walk back to the train was going to be very wet and even with my nice trousers pegged up high I was probably going to end up with wet pant legs, which I hated.

I figured it was no good putting off the inevitable soggy walk, so I slid out of the booth. But as I stood up I happened to glance into the other side where Miles had been sitting and caught sight of something. Lying on the seat was a composition book stuffed with papers and bound shut with a rubber band. It must have fallen out of Miles's satchel while he was sitting down and then when he'd gotten up he'd been in too much of a hurry to notice it had fallen out.

I picked it up. I had already been to his family's apartment and so I knew where he lived and I knew I ought to return it to him, but for some reason I didn't do this. In retrospect, knowing everything I know now, I honestly wish I had. But that's like saying I wish I had punched Rusty the minute I met him or that I'd never gone to that hotel room after my fight at the Y. All of these things were true enough but the past was the past and what happened, happened. Instead of bringing Miles's composition book back to him I found myself burning with a tremendous curiosity.

I undid the rubber band and peeked inside and saw the composition book was full of what looked like some kind of makeshift manuscript. I stared at the pages, remembering our day together writing in the cafe. I wondered if the manuscript was any good. It would be interesting, at least, to read a little before returning it.

58

At first I only read Miles's pages in small doses. I think I put it off a little because I didn't know if it was his diary or what and if it turned out to be terrible stuff I knew I would feel awkward about that when I went to return the composition book. But the stuff Miles had written in the cafe that day had been all right and it just so happened these pages were pretty decent, too. Right away I saw the stuff had merit. Some of it needed small adjustments here and there and as I read I marked those places for Miles's benefit, trying to be helpful. Criticism is a form of true help even though not everybody can see his way clear to this all the time. It occurred to me that by doing Miles this favour and marking down my suggestions for improvement I might have a second shot at an apology.

If I am being honest, then I will tell you I had a second motivation in reading and marking up Miles's pages and that was to distract myself from my impending lunch-date with My Old Man. I was confident in the novel manuscript I had mailed to him at Bonwright but there was just something about the old bastard that always got my hands to turn all clammy.

This meeting at Keen's would determine my future – everything had been building towards it – and to think about that fact alone was a little like trying to stare directly into the sun. You had to look away and I found that focusing my attention on Miles's composition book was a good way of doing this.

It was tricky marking down my criticism at first because I wasn't entirely sure what I was reading. It seemed like a memoir at times and at other times it seemed like war fiction. A lot of it was about being in the war and I was surprised at the vivid portrayal of various battles. At first I thought Miles had a strange and unruly imagination, but then I recalled what his little brother had said when he had run into the coffee shop and asked if Miles was going to read to him some more about their father, and I understood better what it was I was likely reading and I respected the writing all the more for its authenticity. I'm all for imagination but if you ask me Hemingway had it right when he said there is no substitution for true-life experience and that you should write what you know. I don't want to hear about the war from some phony who never went to the front lines and I don't know why anybody else would, either. Anyway, I knew that wasn't the case with this manuscript after I pieced together that the war bits were probably Miles rewriting his father's stories.

Overall, there was a real narrative in it, too, and that excited me. The story was twofold, because some of it consisted of his father's anecdotes from the trenches – about what it was like to be hungry and tired and not have any socks, all the while ducking mortar shells and carrying guys whose legs had been blown off through a veritable rat-maze and that sort of thing – and the other part of the story was about Miles and about what it had been like to grow up thinking your father was a kind but doddering and decrepit old man, only to find out later he had been noble and brave and a war hero. The first part was gripping in its retelling of dramatic events but the latter part had a kind of unflinching honesty about it and this was where

Miles's writing was at its truest and strongest. He wove together the father's war scenes and the son's scenes at home with his cripple of a father very well and you could see a sort of modern portrait of a father and son emerge. Naturally, there was a sense of sadness and culpability in discovering he had underestimated his father, and Miles had a graceful way of diffusing the sentimentality of the story that served him very well.

In any case, I had a good time reading Miles's pages and it even got so I looked forward to the part of my day where I sat down to read his work. One thing about reading the pages of another novice writer is that you can learn a lot by studying the parts they get right and the parts they get wrong. Having grown up with an editor for a father I could easily spot the flaws in Miles's writing but at the same time his work was often very good and in a lot of ways he had developed strengths that were opposite my own. I don't remember when I started copying passages from his pages over into my own notebook, but at some point I began to do this as a way of dissecting what was good about Miles's technique as a means to learn these qualities and adopt them for myself. I would copy out a few of Miles's passages by hand and then I would type them up on the typewriter.

When I reached the typewriter stage, I made little edits to improve the plot and I changed this-or-that detail to make the story more personal to me. For instance, I changed the young man and his father from being Negroes to being white, because it seemed more authentic and more in keeping with what Hemingway said about writing what you know and I was wise enough to understand at that phase in my career I was too green to write from my imagination of what it was like to be a Negro. In any case, all of this rewriting was very good practice. When I reread the pages I'd typed up and saw how nicely Miles's story was shaping up under my expert eye I felt my confidence return and I began to feel hopeful again about what My Old Man was going to make of the manuscript I'd sent him.

'Have you been using the typewriter?' Eden asked me one day when she noticed the typewriter ribbon looked pretty beat up. I told her I had but that it was no big deal.

'You know I'm willing to type for you,' she reminded me.

'That's all right,' I said. 'I'm working on something new and I think typing it up myself is helping things along. And besides, it's good exercise for me: I wouldn't want to forget how to punch the old typewriter anyhow. You know, some guys compose on the typewriter. Their sentences just come straight out their heads and into type-print and soon enough that'll be me.'

I couldn't tell her about what I was typing because I didn't want to explain about how I'd gone up to Harlem to see Miles. I was still disappointed that it hadn't gone as I'd pictured it would and that things with Miles were still tense. In any case, for now she knew nothing about any of that Miles business and she smiled at me from across the room, happy I was feeling creative again and that I'd gone back to writing while I waited to hear back from My Old Man about the novel I'd sent him.

'All right,' she said. 'Let me know if you need me to get a new ribbon.'

'I will,' I said.

59

Finally the day for my lunch with My Old Man arrived. The weather was beginning to turn cold in earnest just then and as I roamed the streets of midtown on my way to Keen's, half the people I passed looked chilled and stiff in their fall jackets and the other half looked warm and stuffed, bundled into their bulky winter overcoats. The city was electric with the energy of late fall. Cold bluish light filled the narrow triangle of Herald Square and pigeons stalked around in jerky, pointless circles pecking at bits of discarded paper. The air was laced with the peculiar sweet yet burnt smell of roasted chestnuts.

I was the first to arrive at Keen's and the maître d' walked me through the dark wood-panelled dining room to my father's usual table under a grim portrait of a man in a wig who must have been important to New York in some way back in the day and who looked like George Washington but was not George Washington. I'd woken up with a strong case of nerves that morning so I'd decided to walk the whole way up from the Village and I'd smoked a bit of tea during my walk and now that I was sitting down it really started to hit me. The tea was doing a number on my head and I sat there lost in the beautiful blankness of the white tablecloth until I looked up and saw My Old Man crossing the room towards me.

'I've never known you to be early.'

'Ah, yes. Well, no one's perfect,' I said. I don't know why I said that, but it seemed like a witty thing to say at the time, but as soon as I said it, I could tell neither of us knew how I had meant it. I was beginning to think maybe I'd gone a little overboard on the tea, which started to panic me because I thought my father would see it in my eyes and I'd be busted for sure. I had doubted he would smell it because Keen's was very famous as a place where men went to smoke pipes and all around us men who had finished with their lunches were lighting up. I realised I was getting paranoid and needed to calm down. I reasoned with myself that there was nothing I could do about it now except to play it cool and anyway My Old Man seemed significantly less interested in my eyes than he was in the menu. He put on his reading glasses and disappeared behind the enormous rectangle of oversized card stock.

'Don't you have that thing memorised by now?' I asked. 'And anyway, isn't the point that everyone orders steak here?' I was trying to be jolly and I'd said it in a jokey way and meant it as a friendly comment, but for some reason My Old Man wasn't in a very good humour that day.

'They have different cuts,' he said. 'And don't be insolent, Clifford. If I'm looking at the menu, it's for a reason. Trust me, with all the reading I do for a living, I don't go around looking to read things for no reason.'

I hadn't expected him to snap at me like that and I could see no source for it, but it shut me up pretty good for the next few minutes. I wondered if I wasn't going to be getting bad news about the draft I'd given him. But I told myself this was just my paranoia talking and that I needed to calm down and let the lunch unfold. I was dying to cut to the chase, but after our exchange about the menu it would've been terrible to bring the subject of my pages up.

And I knew enough about My Old Man to let him be the one to bring it up first. Besides, it was better to get to him after he'd had two or three martinis and not a second earlier.

I waited patiently while our lunch dragged on. At that point the tea really *had* made me lose all sense of time and it seemed like ages before our steak came and then another century before the creamed spinach we'd ordered finally showed up, but luckily the waiter was very attentive with the martinis and they came one after another in generous-sized glasses with lots of green olives. By the time the dessert cart rolled around, the tea had all but worn off and had been thoroughly replaced with a gin buzz. I ordered bananas Foster. They brought out the bananas and we looked on while a waiter poured rum over the top and lit it on fire and then dumped the whole thing over vanilla ice cream. I don't know why I ordered it. I usually don't like bananas; I think I just wanted to see the fire. Besides, I had a sweet tooth from all the marijuana I'd smoked and I didn't want to be sitting there nervous with nothing in front of me while My Old Man smoked.

As a general rule, My Old Man never ordered dessert at Keen's. Instead he handed over his little membership card and the waiter sent someone up to fetch down his pipe. They were funny when they brought out people's pipes. They always put it on a silver platter and draped a purple napkin over it, and then when they got to the table they whipped the napkin off like they were performing some kind of magic trick. This made me laugh a bit because it wasn't like the guy being presented with the pipe was ever surprised by what was under the napkin; he owned the damned thing, for crying out loud. I wondered if they had ever brought someone the wrong pipe, because then it really *would* be a surprise.

In any case, they brought out My Old Man's pipe and pulled

off the purple cloth and he picked it up and proceeded to light up.

'About your pages,' he said, leaning back and puffing on the pipe.

'My submission. The novel draft,' I said, not so much to correct him as to remind him how big my ambitions were and how seriously I was taking things.

'Yes,' he said. I waited while he puffed some more. 'I'll be frank . . . it's half-baked at best.'

'Well, of course,' I said. 'It's not finished yet.'

'Hmmm.'

'The point is the potential.'

'I agree,' My Old Man said. 'The point is the potential. And I have to tell you, Clifford, I'm not entirely convinced it has that.'

My mouth fell open. 'No potential?'

He shook his head. 'I don't see it.'

I blinked at him or at least I think I blinked at him but the combination of having smoked a lot of tea and having been unexpectedly ambushed probably meant I only sat there wide-eyed and staring.

'There,' he said affably. 'Now I've gone and said it and we can get on with our afternoon. You know, I'm just as uncomfortable about this as you are, Clifford – perhaps even more so. Fathers don't like to have to be the bearer of such news.'

'No potential?' I repeated.

'I can tell you're disappointed, but it's time you took it on the chin like a man.'

'You're . . . you're jealous,' I said with sudden revelation. 'You wanted to be a writer when you were my age but you didn't cut it and now you can see I've got the balls you haven't. *I'm* the one who's a writer!'

All at once his hand struck the table with a violent slap and his voice turned mean as hell. 'Insult me all you want, Clifford, but I've built a successful career on being able to tell a writer from a beatnik, and I'm sorry to be the one to say it, but no, Clifford, you're *not* a writer, and you should face the very real possibility you never will be.'

'Well, gee, Pops. Don't beat around the bush because you're worried you might hurt my feelings.'

He said nothing and instead smoothed the tablecloth and began glancing furtively around the restaurant and I could tell he was trying to determine whether anyone he knew had witnessed our argument.

'Thanks for the swell lunch,' I said, and put my napkin on the table and walked out. I had tried to deliver the line with dignity and disdain but it came out sounding like the kind of sarcastic comeback a spoilt brat would dish out.

I'd been looking forward to Keen's for the better part of a week and now things had gone completely pear-shaped but that wasn't even the worst of it, if you can believe it. After I left My Old Man, I went straight down to the Cedar Tavern and ordered up some godawful Wild Turkey and once Mitch, the bartender, had poured it for me I told him he might as well leave the bottle. He shot me a look of pity but didn't say anything, only left the bottle on the bar and I promptly took it over to a booth in the corner and hunkered down, ready to drown my sorrows.

The funny thing about the Village back in those days was everyone was always bar-hopping and if you were a Village kid and you sat around the same bar long enough you would eventually see all the other Village kids as they made their rounds. Sure enough, after I'd been drinking for a while, in walked Bobby and Pal and with them I noticed Gene and another fella. It was a gloomy day and I was kind of hunched up low in a booth, and they sat in another booth right behind me and never saw me.

I was in a foul mood of course and already drunk to boot so I wasn't exactly eager for company and I took a minute before getting up to say hello. I heard Gene's friend ask him about how Gene was making out with *The Tuning Fork*. My ears perked up. My father had belittled my novel draft, but there was still the story that had run in *The Tuning Fork* and I figured I had that to my credit, at least.

'It's difficult to say,' Gene answered the other fella. 'The copies I put out around the Village were all snapped up but part of the point in creating the journal was to get the attention of the publishing houses and see if I couldn't influence their taste here and there.'

'It was a very nice-looking issue,' Pal said, in typical Pal fashion.

'Yeah, it was nice-looking, and the content was top-shelf,' the friend said. 'Except for that terrible piece by that one fella.'

'Which one?' Gene asked.

'The Hemingway imitator. Some sort of terrible prep school drivel about a guy and his girl at a baseball game. I don't know why you took it.'

'I know . . . but there was a reason for that,' Gene said. 'The guy who wrote it is Roger Nelson's kid.'

'You mean Roger Nelson, the editor at Bonwright? His son?'

'Cliff,' Bobby chimed in. 'His name is Cliff.'

'Oh, that's right,' Gene said, nodding to Bobby and Pal. 'You two are buddies of his.'

'Yeah,' Bobby said. I waited for him to really give it to old Gene, but when he continued all he said was, 'But, say, you were wasting your time if you wanted to get to Roger Nelson through his son. Cliff and his old man are like cats and dogs.'

'I didn't know that when I took the piece,' Gene said, 'or I wouldn't have taken it. I thought if I printed Cliff's story his father would be sure to read it, and even if his son was a hack he might see some of the other fellas' work and they'd get exposure that way.'

I waited a few minutes for Bobby – or even Pal, though Pal was not known for confrontation – to really lay into Gene and tell him where he could go, but as the conversation moved on to other subjects I realised I was waiting for nothing. Bobby wasn't going to defend me and neither was Pal and maybe this was because all the while when they were telling me what a swell guy I was and how they believed I would someday be a writer if I kept at it, they hadn't believed in me after all.

Talk about kicking a fella while he's down. I sat there not moving and barely breathing as they talked and drank until finally they pushed off to the next place.

60

EDEN

Cliff was in a state. It wasn't difficult to figure out what had happened. At work, Mr Nelson had handled Cliff's manuscript submission privately. After I spotted it on Mr Nelson's desk, I never saw it again. But between the two of them, I had my ear to the ground well enough to know they'd been scheduled for lunch that afternoon. Having typed the manuscript myself, and knowing that Cliff brought out his father's harsh streak, I could only imagine what Mr Nelson had said.

So I was hardly surprised to come home from work that day to an empty apartment. I assumed Cliff was likely out drowning his sorrows, raising a ruckus with Swish or else Bobby and Pal, running around the Village like a madman. I didn't care for Cliff's destructive tendencies – which were becoming more and more a dominant part of his personality these days – but in this case I at least understood and felt sympathy for the impulse. I hoped, whatever he was up to, he could get it out of his system, lick his wounds, and carry on. It turned out my hopes were misguided, or at the very least terribly naïve, for his father's rejection sent Cliff into a blind rage more terrible than any I'd previously witnessed. I had a very dim premonition of what was to come. I went through my usual routine of fixing a little snack for dinner, reading, and cleaning. The radiators were on too hot that night, I remember. I had just opened the window to air out the room and was getting ready for bed when Cliff suddenly came thundering through the door, even more rip-roaring drunk than I'd expected.

'To hell w'th 'em!' he hollered in a slurred voice. 'To hell w'th 'em ALL!'

'Clifford!' I screamed as he dropped an empty bottle and glass flew everywhere.

'And YOU,' he said, as though, upon hearing my scream, he'd suddenly noticed my presence in the room. He lifted a finger and pointed it in my face. 'To hell with you most of all!' He lurched, his head swayed, and his attention fell upon the little card table where the Smith Corona sat. He suddenly seized the typewriter and, in one gut-muscled heave, threw it out the open window. I watched it fly with wide eyes, too surprised to make a peep, and heard the strange crunch and clatter of the typewriter as it hit the pavement outside. Cliff wasn't quite done yet, however. Next he pulled open a dresser drawer and reached for the stacks of pages within. Page after page, everything he'd ever written and everything I'd ever typed up for him, went into the metal bucket we kept as a wastebasket.

'There!' he shouted. 'Now everything's 'xactly where it should be!' He flopped down on the mattress. 'To hell w'th 'em. To hell w'th 'em all,' he muttered into the pillow. Several minutes later I heard the telltale guttural growl of a snore.

I unfroze and went to the window. Poking my head out, I saw that the typewriter was beyond salvaging. Luckily, the window looked down onto a small alleyway between our building and the next; therefore no one had been maimed as a result of his tantrum. I swept the broken glass into a dustpan. Then I crossed the room to the wastebasket, sighed, and began pulling Cliff's pages out.

I was in the midst of sorting and stacking Cliff's manuscripts back into neat piles, when I got the second surprise of the night. One of the manuscripts caught my eye. I didn't recognise it. It was significantly longer than most of the other things Cliff had written, a body of work that – except for the aborted novel manuscript his father had likely rejected earlier that afternoon – mostly consisted of half-finished short stories and the occasional poem.

I began to read, right there, transfixed while in the middle of cleaning the floor, and soon couldn't put it down.

I don't know where or how the story had come to him. The last thing I'd ever expected him to be able to write about and portray with such eloquence was the story of a father and a son. I knew there were sometimes writers who had rich inner lives, who could write out of a keen sense of imagined empathy; now, for the first time, it was clear Cliff possessed that gift. I reread the pages several times, startled, and increasingly convinced that here was the novel we had all been waiting for, a novel that wasn't only about the war but about the next generation – *our* generation – picking up the pieces afterwards. It was truthful, it was poetic, and most important . . . it was *publishable*.

The next morning I got up per my usual routine. Cliff was still snoring. By that point the scent of bourbon had begun to sweat through his pores. I didn't envy him the headache he would have, but I knew of at least one thing I could do that might make it better. I tiptoed about, laying out breakfast, and then left for work with the manuscript tucked neatly in my bag.

61

MILES

I was frantic, but had no clue what to do about it. There was no way to know where or when my composition book had gone missing. Common wisdom dictates that, when you lose something, it's best to retrace your steps. Unfortunately, being a bicycle messenger meant these steps stretched over the entire length of Manhattan, from the top of the island to the bottom, not to mention from the East River to the Hudson. It could have slipped out of my bag at any time, perhaps as I carelessly deposited and extracted packages and envelopes throughout the course of the day.

I thought, too, perhaps it had fallen out at the coffee shop where I had met Cliff. But when I went back the next morning to enquire about it, the man behind the soda counter only shrugged and said, 'Sorry, pal, no one's seen anything like that.' If Cliff had picked it up, he would have returned it to me, I reasoned – wouldn't he? I wasn't entirely sure of this conclusion. He had seemed friendly enough, but I didn't trust him. His cagey behaviour unnerved me, and our conversation had amounted to little more than a superficial exchange. I couldn't understand why he had come all the way up to Harlem to see me, unless it was to assuage a conscience I wasn't entirely convinced he possessed. I went down to the Village and tried ringing his buzzer, then made a half-hearted search of all the regular bars he haunted, but couldn't find him. Swish, Bobby, and Pal hadn't seen him, either.

In the bigger scheme of things, I suppose I ought to have been grateful: I hadn't lost my father's journal, only my composition book. I brought the composition book along with me sometimes, just in case I had a spare moment between deliveries and remembered something from my childhood about my father that I felt like jotting down.

I understood my father's words weren't replaceable and mine were. If I really wanted to begin my project again, I could. But there was something terrible about the thought of starting over again; it set off a riot of feelings in me, it made my body feel limp with despair. I wasn't sure exactly what it was I had lost, in losing the composition book. I didn't dare allow myself to believe I was writing a memoir I might some day try to publish – I never admitted to ambitions so grand – but some part of me understood it was the first draft of *something* I had loved, and something I had needed to finish.

I wanted badly to tell someone about my loss, and I wanted that someone to be Joey. Joey would hold me, understand me. But of course Joey was out of reach now. I had seen to that myself.

Of course, there was still Janet. It was Janet's letter that had summoned me home, away from Joey and the houseboat and everything we'd shared on it. I knew I ought to take better care of Janet and that I had Janet's feelings to consider. Since getting back into town, I had put off seeing her again, but now I asked her out to a movie, knowing the theatres were always a treat for her. She was excited and immediately said yes, and then shortly thereafter we met up at the box office. I let her pick the picture. She chose – seemingly at random – a Fellini film, *Nights of Cabiria*, which had come out the year before and was now playing at a discount at the Paris.

The movie was a mistake. It was gloomy and stark, the story of a prostitute looking for love and only being met with the cruelty of other peoples' indifference. There I was, fidgety and distracted throughout the entire film, and I couldn't concentrate. We'd gotten popcorn but I didn't feel like eating it; it stuck in my throat each time I attempted to swallow some. Something was causing me terrible discomfort, like a kind of indigestion, only more nebulous than that, and it affected me all over. I reached for Janet's hand in the dark and realised – with a shiver of disgust – that muscle memory had me expecting the familiar shape of Joey's. When the film finally ended, we stepped outside to find it was already dark. We had gone to a matinee, and the sun had not yet set when we had gone in. This, too, made me anxious and sad, and it was as if we had missed out on something important in not witnessing the end of the day's light.

'Wasn't that awfully depressing?' Janet said. Janet always liked to discuss whatever it was we had just seen. Her tone of voice suggested she was trying to make polite conversation, not complain, but for some reason I found myself incredibly irritated with her.

'Well, love is like that,' I said with impatience. She widened her eyes, both puzzled and a little afraid of my sudden anger.

'You don't really think love is like that, do you?' she asked. 'Not *all* love.'

'A hell of a lot of it,' I said, just to be petulant. She took my arm and attempted a sweet smile. Janet's perfume, which I had found pleasantly floral back when we first met, suddenly struck me as rancid and treacly.

'Not *our* love, though,' she said, leaning into me and peering up into my face. She patted my upper arm. 'Look at us: we're just fine. We're happy together.' There was a pause, and I knew this was my cue to say something in return, but I didn't feel up to it. 'Aren't we happy?' she prompted. I had a flash of Joey asking me the same question, back on the houseboat. It was bizarre the way time was like an accordion, and distinct moments that felt so disparate sometimes folded together with a callous symmetry.

'Sure,' I said, leading her in the direction of the subway. The pain of the lie shot through my body. 'Sure we are. We're the picture of happiness. That's why no one will ever make a movie about us.'

I saw Janet home and then headed back to my mother's apartment. Once inside, I stood in the kitchen, staring at the mute beige shape of the telephone. I lifted the receiver, then set it back in its cradle, then lifted it again. Finally, I made up my mind. I watched my finger dial, and the rotary wheel spin back into place.

'Information. May I help you?'

'Yes. I'm looking for a listing in Washington, DC,' I said. 'Edward C. Jenkins.'

'One moment, please . . . The number is Hamilton 5-6240. Would you like to be connected?'

I hesitated. This was my chance to back out. I hadn't thought about the long-distance charge that was sure to show up on my mother's bill. Finally, I asked the operator to put the call through, hoping I would think of a reasonable explanation when the time came for it. The line began to ring. I felt a cold trickle of sweat stirring beneath my shirt.

'Hello?'

'Eddie?'

'Who is this?'

'It's Miles,' I said. 'Miles, from . . . San Francisco,' I added when Eddie did not respond right away.

'I know from where.' His usually cheerful southern twang sounded flat, sober, laced with anger.

'I guess I'm calling because . . .' I didn't know what to say. 'I wanted to ask how Joey is doing,' I choked out.

'Ask 'im yourself,' Eddie said. I was quiet. Finally Eddie sighed and relented. 'Look, if you really want to know, he's holding up at his new job all right, but he's gone back to his old ways, Miles. Staying out all night, running around with seedy types. He's new in town. Too new to be so careless, if you know what I mean.'

He declined to recount the specifics, and I understood why. We both knew the telephone was not the most private of instruments.

'Does he talk about me, Eddie?'

'Oh, he talks about you, all right. He's awful mad at you, Miles.'

'I'd like to apologise to him.'

'Well, that might take some doing,' Eddie grunted.

'I know. Will you help me, Eddie? If I go down there?'

There was a long pause. Without realising it, I was holding my breath. The clock on the wall in the kitchen seemed to suddenly tick more loudly.

'There's a bar,' Eddie finally said. 'Most nights you can find him there. The kind of place no one will look twice at a Negro walking in, even in DC . . . if you're really serious about fixing things with him.'

Eddie gave me the address and I scribbled it down.

'To be honest, I don't know what business you have together,' he said, and hung up.

*   *   *

The next day I found myself on yet another Greyhound. This time I was headed south. The bus was heated but I steadily perspired a cold sweat throughout the entire ride. My hands were like ice, as though the blood couldn't quite reach them.

It was evening and a cold drizzle was falling when the bus pulled into DC. I hadn't brought an umbrella. I stepped off the bus at Union Station and made my way through the long waiting hall. In the short time it took for me to make it outside, the rain had escalated from drizzle to downpour. Now the water was coming down in sheets, and there was no way to avoid getting drenched. I switched to a local bus and made my way across town, eventually finding my way to the bar Eddie had described over the phone. It was a dive, the kind frequented by a specific clientele. I was nervous but not surprised.

I pushed through the door and, once inside, let my eyes adjust as I surveyed the room, looking for any sign of Joey. Before I knew it, someone was hollering at me, trying to catch my attention.

'Say, fella, you gonna order a drink or what?'

I looked over to see the bartender frowning at me and realised I was hovering in the doorway. Truth be told, I had always harboured a private terror of bars just like this one. Old queens and men wearing rouge and the married stiffs in suits who, at the stroke of midnight, would turn tail and run back home to their unsuspecting wives. It ought to have reminded me of the Hamilton Lodge Ball, I suppose, but it didn't. Although chaotic and grotesque, the Hamilton Lodge Ball had also been whimsical and infused with glee. This bar was teeming with a deadly combination of angst and malaise. The air was bitter and lonely.

'I'm looking for a friend,' I replied to the bartender.

'We don't take kindly to people who come here just to look,' he said. I nodded but continued on past the bar to a little room in the back, searching for Joey.

My heart almost stopped when I found him there. A group of men were hooting and howling over a game of darts, two of them very burly, one of them old, and one of them dressed in drag. And there was Joey: staggering around, a heavy five o'clock shadow on his cheeks, his beautiful face lopsided, distorted with drink. As Joey completed his turn at the dartboard, one of the burly men tried to pull him into his lap, and Joey gave an angry laugh while trying to spit in the man's face. They were playing, but not in the spirit of true playfulness; it was the kind of play born of hate, hate for each other, but more than anything hate for themselves. My stomach twisted and I thought for a minute I might be sick. I gathered myself.

'Joey,' I called gently.

His brow furrowed and I watched him peer around the room in drunken confusion until, finally, his eyes landed on me. For a fleeting second his eyes lit up in recognition. But then an even darker shadow passed over his stubbled face.

'Joey,' I repeated. 'I came from New York. I came all the way to find you.'

'Oh yeah? And exactly how did you know where to find me?' I didn't answer, but as Joey glared at me, I saw that he guessed the truth: Eddie.

'Say, who's your friend?' the man who had been wrestling with Joey asked.

'Nobody,' Joey replied. He stood on one side of the cramped back room and I on the other. He looked away, not making eye contact.

'Joey, please,' I said again, keeping my voice low. 'Please let me speak with you. In private.'

I prayed the others wouldn't get involved and continued to look at him until finally he looked at me and returned my stare.

'Please,' I repeated. I realised I was begging. I didn't care.

He held my gaze for several seconds, an acid look in his eyes. I never felt hated so much as I did in that moment. Then, all at once, something snapped in him and he moved for the exit.

'Fine,' he said, striding quickly out of the back room and through the bar. 'Let's go.' Immediately, I followed him.

'Hey! *Wait a minute!*' his companions called after him. But we were already out the front entrance.

It was still pouring. He led the way, swerving on the sidewalk ever so slightly as he marched drunkenly along.

'Where are we going?'

He didn't answer me. After two blocks or so, he turned and stopped in front of a narrow red-brick row house, four storeys tall and crowned with a steeply pitched roof. Joey pushed open the gate, walked up the stoop, and paused in front of the door. He reached in his pocket for a key.

Unseen tenants coming home from work had abandoned their wet umbrellas in the front chamber, leaving them to leak small puddles of water all over the tiled floor. The hallways smelt musty, with a tinge of wet dog. The stairs groaned as we climbed them, wooden stairs covered with carpet that was nearly worn through. Finally we reached the fourth floor and walked to the end of the hallway, and Joey unlocked and opened the door to his apartment. I followed him in and stood in the darkness, listening to the sound of the door latching shut again behind me.

He switched on a light. We stood there unmoving, staring at each other as the dripping accumulated on the carpet until it made a tiny splashing noise with every drop.

'Joey,' I said, 'I'm sorry.'

I stepped towards him, opening my arms. All of a sudden he punched me square across the jaw. My head spun to one side. Pain shot through my face from my teeth to my ear, but I continued to reach out blindly and tried to grab him anyway, hoping to hold him and calm him down. He fought back, and we fell to grappling with each other until we were wrestling on the ground and he was punching me again. We knocked over a lamp and I felt it break over my back. Joey had the upper hand now. He got on top of me and I felt blows landing all over my body as I tried to fight him off. We were slick with the rainwater we'd carried in on our skin and clothes, and hot with exertion. I tasted blood and realised my lip was cut.

'Joey!' I cried.

We went on struggling. My heart began racing as – for a split second – I was able to read his mind: he was seriously considering killing me. Finally I got a hold of his face and kissed him. He kissed me back, then punched me savagely, then kissed me again. We went on like this until the punches dwindled and finally ceased and our hungry mouths took over everything. I felt his hands under my clothes. He ripped my shirt and I reached for his belt.

Afterwards, we lay together on the floor next to his bed, holding each other. The hateful rage that had enveloped us not more than twenty minutes earlier had now fallen away from us in a shift that was both exotic and perfunctory, like a woman shedding a silk kimono. I lifted my head to kiss him very gently on the temple.

'For a minute there, I thought you might murder me,' I commented.

'For a minute there, I did, too,' Joey said in a quiet, serious voice, and as he said it I understood he absolutely meant every word. We fell into silence again.

'Miles,' he said finally, 'don't you ever fucking leave me like that again.' He shuddered and squeezed me tighter to him. I reached a hand to smooth his cheek, the back of his neck.

'I won't,' I said. It was a promise, but already I wasn't sure I could keep it. I was already terrified of what I had reignited in both of us.

62

EDEN

'This,' Mr Nelson said after calling me into his office, 'is quite good, Eden.' He patted the stack of typed pages I'd rescued from the wastebasket in the wake of Cliff's nervous breakdown. It had been a week or so since I left the manuscript on his desk, and without a peep from Mr Nelson, I had worried my judgement was off-kilter, the pages weren't as good as I'd thought, and Cliff had struck out yet again. But now I smiled, gratified.

'Is it?'

'Yes, very good. And you say the author submitted it to our offices anonymously?'

I bit my lip. A tiny trill of nervous energy went through me. 'Yes,' I said, proceeding carefully. 'But I know the identity of the author.'

'Oh?' Mr Nelson raised an eyebrow. 'Well?'

'I can tell you . . .' I said.

'Yes, out with it,' Mr Nelson replied in a friendly tone.

'I can tell you,' I repeated, 'but I'd also like to talk,' I ventured, 'about officially being made a reader.'

The Santa Claus twinkle vanished from Mr Nelson's blue eyes, his brow instantly furrowed, and the corners of his mouth twitched in anger. 'I hope you're not proposing to hold this manuscript hostage,' he said.

'Oh! No, sir,' I said. 'I only thought we could revisit the subject, as we discussed some months back.'

Mr Nelson looked at me and cocked his head, scrutinising the details of my person. He pursed his lips off to one side, as though trying to decide something. Suddenly the cloud of anger that had darkened his face lifted and he brightened.

'What time is it?' he asked.

I glanced at my watch. 'Quarter to noon,' I answered.

'All right. We will discuss this further over lunch, then,' he said. It wasn't really a question. He shuffled some papers on his desk and stood up and straightened his tie. It was obvious he expected me to fetch my coat.

'But . . . you already have a lunch appointment on your calendar,' I reminded him. 'With Mr Morris.'

'Phone him up and cancel,' Mr Nelson commanded in a matter-of-fact tone.

I was flustered. The last time I had been to lunch with Mr Nelson – the *only* time I had been to lunch with Mr Nelson – was directly after my job interview, when I'd been made to pass along the news to a very lovesick Barbara that her services as a temp were no longer needed. I could only imagine what Mr Nelson had in store for me now.

'As I've said before, Eden, I don't pretend to understand you modern gals these days. But if you're going to play hardball like a man, then we'd damn well better have this discussion over martinis.'

We went to Sardi's and sat among the caricatures with their exaggerated ski-slope noses, clownish eyelashes, and wide, maniacal grins. We began with martinis and some small talk. When our food arrived, Mr Nelson ordered a second round of drinks.

'I was here with Ring Lardner once,' he remarked. 'He knew just about everything a man can know about baseball. There's his portrait right over there.' He pointed to a rather unflattering profile of Mr Lardner hanging on a far wall.

The waiter set a fresh martini glass on the table before me, filled to the brim with crystal-clear gin. As a general rule, Mr Nelson preferred gin, and he was the one doing the ordering.

'Cheers,' Mr Nelson said, and I carefully raised my glass to clink with his. The glass was too full; the tiniest wobble of my hand sent cold rivulets of gin and vermouth dribbling over my fingers. I lifted the toothpick that was balanced on the rim and slid one of the olives off with my teeth, then set the toothpick on my bread plate.

'All right, Eden,' Mr Nelson said in a voice that was perplexingly stern and merry at the same time. The Santa Claus twinkle had come back to his pale blue eyes, and I realised this was likely Mr Nelson's usual procedure: two martinis, a little business, and a third to seal the deal. I wasn't sure I could keep up, but I knew it was imperative that I try. 'Name your terms,' he said.

'Reader, for now,' I said. 'And then, in another six months, I want to be considered for assistant editor, based on the number of manuscripts you acquire on the recommendation of my reader's reports.'

He cocked an eyebrow at me. 'Well, you've certainly proven you know how to manoeuvre,' Mr Nelson said.

'You told me yourself manoeuvring is part of the job.'

'Yes . . .' he mused. 'Fine, then. I'll agree to make you a reader.' He straightened up. 'Now, about the manuscript. I'd like to get this matter squared away. Is anyone else reading?'

By *anyone else*, he meant other editors at other houses. 'No,' I said.

'Well, why the shroud of mystery in that case? Surely this fellow wants to be published.'

'Yes.'

'And published by Bonwright?'

'Oh, very much so. I can vouch for that first-hand.'

'So, let's have it, then. Who is the author?'

Under the table, I crossed my fingers. Then I took a breath. *Here goes nothing.*

'The author . . . is your son.'

Mr Nelson's eyes widened and he very nearly choked on his martini. Coughing, he carefully set the glass down and dabbed his chin with his napkin.

'I don't understand. Clifford wrote this? *My* Clifford?'

'Yes.'

'Well,' he said, shaking his head. 'That's rather difficult to believe . . .' He stared down at his hands on the table and began to drum his fingers, lost in thought. 'You know, he submitted a different manuscript to me a week or so ago. I dealt with it privately. It was . . . well, not at all like this.'

I know, I thought silently to myself.

'Is there any chance . . .' He hesitated. I had a funny feeling I knew what he was getting ready to say. 'Is there any chance . . . this originated elsewhere?' he finished. I understood why he posed the question, but I was glad Cliff was not present to hear it. As his wife, I even felt a little punched in the gut on Cliff's behalf.

'Well, I saw the original pages written out in longhand,' I offered. 'In his handwriting. And then he must've transcribed them with the typewriter.'

Suddenly, Mr Nelson's gaze came back into focus and landed squarely on me. He squinted.

'You seem awfully familiar with my son, Eden. I wasn't aware the two of you had met.'

'Oh,' I said, flustered once again. 'I know him through a group of mutual friends.'

This was true: I *had* met Cliff through a group of mutual friends. But I wasn't ready to divulge any of the rest of it, not without talking to Cliff. Looking back on it now, I see it was rather foolish of me, but I had an idealised notion in my head of how everything would work out. I'd get my promotion, Cliff would become a famous author, and Mr Nelson would get to publish the novel he'd been after ever since the war ended. Then, I imagined, Cliff and I would reveal our marriage at a strategic moment. Judy was right: it was a story to tell our grandchildren someday. A secret, romantic elopement; I would be the one who managed to bring Clifford Nelson's talent to the attention of his illustrious editor father.

I am rather ashamed to say, I pictured all of this coming to pass: my grand role in the publishing world, part of a great literary family.

'Well,' said Mr Nelson. 'I'll admit I'm a bit overwhelmed . . .' He shook his head again. 'I have to say, I wasn't very kind to Clifford last week. I thought it was for his own good and that he needed a dose of tough medicine. But if he can write like this, perhaps I was wrong. I hope he'll forgive me.'

'If you're offering to publish his work, I believe that's all the apology he'll need.'

Mr Nelson smiled, looking relieved. I knew then: Cliff had never been very good at apologies, and I assume this trait had been passed down from father to son.

'Yes. Now, let's discuss *how* we'll publish . . .' Mr Nelson said, and we went on making plans through the rest of our lunch. I was surprised to see how excited he was; he wanted to rush things along as quickly as possible. 'It seems to me it needs only the lightest of edits, do you agree?'

I did agree. I was flattered he'd asked my opinion. Between that and the martinis, I had quite a buzz. A question occurred to me, and the gin made me bold enough to ask it. 'Do you think you would've liked the manuscript just as much if you had known ahead of time it was Cliff's?' Mr Nelson hesitated.

'I don't know. I see your point, and perhaps I *have* been too hard on him over the years. But the most important thing is I see the merit of this manuscript very clearly at present, and I'm very proud of him.'

His eyes watered slightly, I couldn't tell whether it was due to the gin or because his paternal spirit had moved him. By that point the bill had already been paid and there was only one swallow left in each of our martinis. Abruptly, Mr Nelson lifted his napkin from his lap and threw it upon the table.

'Let's go tell Clifford the good news, shall we?'

63

MILES

For a brief, blissful spell, I forgot all about my composition book. Recovering Joey was like recovering a part of myself. Our lives began to braid themselves together again, and at first I was happy. Joey, just as he had proposed on the houseboat in Sausalito, took the train from Washington to New York and we spent our weekends together. By then the city had entered the full throes of winter, and we strolled the city streets bundled into heavy overcoats, chuckling about it as we occasionally bumped shoulders, rounded and armless as a pair of fat *matryoshka* dolls knocking into each other. Sometimes we warmed ourselves by popping into a bookshop, the smell of newsprint and wet wool filling the air. Other times we watched the ice-skaters in Rockefeller Centre or wandered down quieter, brownstone-lined streets, the tree branches above us white and bare, the dry brown remains of their leaves slowly crunching into dust underfoot.

But, more than anything else, we spent a great deal of time alone together in Joey's hotel room. As it is with all lovers during the winter season, the dark and cold jointly provided adequate excuse for us to linger about in a tangle of warm bedsheets, gazing at the dull grey windowpane and disdaining the fools willing to venture out and leave such coziness behind. We spent hours loving each other, but we also spent hours lying about doing nothing, too. We held each other with lank arms, sharing our private musings about the world, our skin smelling of sweat and of the cheap white soap inexplicably preferred by most hotels.

I always made time to see him. My weekends were his. I made excuses and, I'm ashamed to say, I lied to a great many people. I told Janet my mother was sick and needed me to help around the house, and I told my mother I was sleeping at Janet's; my mother grumbled her disapproval but accepted this based on the dual facts that Janet and I were engaged and Wendell was growing more and more irritated with my continued presence in what he considered 'his' apartment.

Those were the most remorseless lies I have ever told, for together Joey and I made our own world, a place where I needed no reprieve; it was a temporary life – made up of only two days that bracketed the week – but one that absorbed me even more fully than our time together on the houseboat. We became one human being. Everything we did during those weekends, we did together. On Sunday mornings we bought a single newspaper and exchanged the different sections until the entire hotel bed crinkled with paper and the sheets were smudged with newsprint, at which point we would do the crossword together, laughing and kissing.

Weekends weren't enough, and we began sneaking in weekdays, too. After several visits to the city wherein we hardly left the room, Joey became preoccupied with the idea we would grow bored of each other if we did not make an effort to get out of the hotel room and go somewhere from time to time. This, as far as I was concerned, was ridiculous. I could never get enough of Joey's company, indoors or out. But I had to agree that, if nothing else, the hotel room could be quite stuffy and hot, and it would do our lungs good to take the air.

'Where do you want to go?' I asked one Friday when he'd come into town a day early.

'The park,' he said, meaning Central Park. 'And then the Metropolitan Museum of Art.'

'All right,' I agreed, realising I had been a terrible tour guide. I loved New York, and all at once I wanted Joey to love it, too.

We took the Lexington line to Seventy-Ninth Street on the east side and trekked into the park from there. It had just snowed, and we followed the footpath that led past the small, manicured pond of the conservatory and deeper into the park, towards the Boathouse and the lake. We crossed through the terraced brick clearing that contained Bethesda Fountain, that winged angel of the waters forever taking one ethereal step forward and dutifully blessing the pool below her. The fountain was turned off for the season, and the empty pool was laid thick with a layer of ice. As we neared the fountain, Joey began to laugh and trot towards it, faster and faster. He climbed in, and me after him. There was something slightly childish and giddy in our play. We touched the four cherubs, something a visitor might never do in summer. Once we'd climbed out of the fountain, we followed the footpath over Bow Bridge, and then followed the paths that wound into the Ramble. The ground grew more hilly, the trees more dense, and the path more winding. We laughed and began to chase each other in the snow. The snow was clean and white and gave that satisfying squeak with every step we took.

Suddenly, Mister Gus flashed into my mind, that newspaper article, and everything he had said during my last week working in his mansion.

'Joey,' I called out. 'Let's go to the museum now.'

'Sure,' he agreed. I doubled back and we retraced our steps, staying in the park's more civilised areas and proceeding into the Ramble no farther. Having been born in New York and having lived in Manhattan all my life, I knew there was a way to cross through the Ramble, a way that would eventually take us back to the museum, but my memories of Mister Gus's words had me spooked.

We left the park and followed Fifth Avenue up to the neoclassical facade of the museum and climbed the steps. There was a special kind of busy, enthusiastic energy in the air near the entrance to the Met. We pushed through the great glass doors and tumbled into the large marble double-winged foyer and found our way first to the coat check. Despite the cavernous space, it was humid and warm with all those bodies clustered together, the great hall echoing with the squeak of rubber galoshes. The woman in front of us spoke only in Japanese and handed over a beautiful silk overcoat to the man behind the coat check counter. He looked at it and harrumphed to himself as he hung it up, muttering something under his breath about the war.

'What's your favourite spot in this place?' Joey asked once we were free of the coat check and we had paid our entry.

'There are two,' I said. 'One is the hall leading into the Impressionist gallery upstairs, and the other is in the Egyptian wing, where they keep the mummies.'

Joey raised his eyebrows. 'An Egyptian mummy? Here, inside this building?'

'Yes,' I said. 'A few of them.'

'Let's go see that.'

We set off in the direction of the mummies and strolled leisurely, like idiots, into the Egyptian wing.

There was a school group there, and a sea of excited, bobbing heads shifted around us as children scurried from this exhibit to that, a few harried teachers trying to herd them back into order. They were second- or third-graders, I'd have guessed – somewhere around Cob's age – and almost all of them coloured, making me think this was a public school outing. My eyes fell on a little boy standing slightly apart from the group, staring into a glass case. As we drew nearer, I got a look at what he was staring at. It was a case full of jewellery made out of the iridescent carapaces of some kind of scarab beetle. The little boy wore an expression of fierce concentration, as though trying to memorise every detail of the beetles' shells. He looked an awful lot like Cob, I thought to myself, until I realised with a start that it *was* Cob. In that very moment the spell of his concentration was broken and his gaze flicked in my direction.

'Miles!' he called out, his eyes going wide. He ran over to me.

'Cob,' I said weakly, still stunned. 'What are you doing here?'

'It's our field trip day, remember?'

A faint memory from the previous week of Cob babbling on about some kind of field trip came back to me. How could I have been so careless, so foolish? 'Of course,' I said. Joey was standing next to me, slightly puzzled, and now Cob's focus turned to this mystery figure.

'This is my friend Joey,' I said to Cob. Cob nodded and put out his hand.

'How do you do?'

Joey shook it and smiled with genuine affection, deducing that before him stood the great insect collector he'd heard so much about. Cob smiled back at Joey, then frowned at me.

'Ain't you supposed to be at work, Miles?' Cob asked.

'They gave me the day off,' I said. Cob looked at me suspiciously.

He was seven, but not stupid. 'You'd better get back over there with your classmates,' I said. One of the teachers was glancing in our direction, obviously concerned by the sight of two strange men talking to one of her young pupils. 'We were just going,' I said, giving Cob a quick pat on the head and moving away. 'I'll see you at home.'

We left, Joey picking up on my cue and following closely on my heels. I looked over my shoulder just once and saw Cob still standing where we had left him, frowning.

We didn't talk as we stood in line for our coats. Joey could tell I was disturbed. Once outside, he finally asked, 'That was your kid brother?'

'Yes.' I realised I was panting; panic had crushed the very air out of my lungs. I stood there thinking of what to say to Cob the next time I saw him, whether to explain or act cool and casual.

'Quite a smart little man,' Joey grinned, an encouraging, upbeat note in his voice.

'I need a drink,' I said.

'All right,' Joey said, catching on to my mood and looking at his watch. 'But it's only three o'clock. Where should we go?'

'Let's . . . go down to the Village,' I said. There was a certain stiffness to the Upper East Side that unnerved me. I was desperate for anonymity and the Village seemed like a safe bet. Artists and bohemians; nobody looked at you twice. Even when you knew people, they didn't act as though they cared what hour you'd started drinking or who you were with, so long as you were being authentic, whatever *that* meant.

'Hey, Miles, don't worry over it,' Joey said as we walked in the direction the subway. 'He thinks you're playing hooky but he doesn't think anything else. He's too young for that.'

I didn't say anything to this.

'He seemed like a nice kid,' Joey said in an encouraging tone. 'Kind.'

'Leave it alone, Joey,' I said. 'Let's just go have a drink and forget about it.' The rest of the way down to the Village, we were silent.

64

CLIFF

One person I hadn't run into since the night of our party was Rusty. It was true Rusty had behaved like a pretty big villain, and everyone – Swish, Bobby, and Pal included – had agreed that if we ever ran into him again he'd get the cold shoulder. Of course, I wasn't much for talking to Bobby and Pal just then. I wasn't much for talking to Swish, either, even though he hadn't been there to join in when old Gene began stabbing me in the back. He was part of their gang and I figured they could all go to hell – the whole pack of 'em – which was why I was at the White Horse drinking alone when I ran into Rusty and why I temporarily forgot all that business about giving him the cold shoulder.

'Heya, Cliff,' he said to me when he spotted me. His voice was casual and normal and I knew he had made it sound like that on purpose and this meant Rusty wanted to pretend like nothing had ever happened. 'Brought you this,' he said, setting a full glass of beer on the table. 'Looked like you were running on empty.'

It was true my glass had nothing left in it but a thin film of suds at the bottom. I thought about making some crack about Rusty putting something in the drink but then I changed my mind because it was useless to bring up a sore subject. Rusty was a coward at heart and he might pull that crap on someone like Miles, but he wouldn't pull it on me.

'You drinking alone?'

I nodded.

'Want some company?'

I shrugged. He sat down and we shot some bull. Rusty was one of those guys who loved to hear bad things about other people, so we both tried to come up with everything we could about guys we both knew. But then the subject of Bobby came up because with Rusty the subject of Bobby always came up. I didn't want to talk about Bobby, or about Swish or Pal just then, and I said so. Rusty raised an eyebrow and smirked as though he was in the know and this was our little secret and that really irked me. He changed the topic and we sat there rubbernecking all the people who came in the door.

'How's the writing going?' he asked me now, and obviously this was his other old tactic to get on my good side. But I'd stopped hoping Rusty would exert any influence on my behalf. I shrugged again.

'I don't know,' I said, and I realised I was being honest. I hadn't been tinkering around with my writing much any more. After I'd come home drunk that night and thrown everything away, Eden had rescued it all from the wastebasket and sorted the pages and stacked them up real nice. When I saw what she had done, I felt bad, but I hadn't poked around with any of it. The truth was, I was pretty close to giving up for good. As lousy as it was to think, I knew it was only a matter of time before I went out and got the kind of job my folks had been harping about all along.

'Tell you what,' Rusty said now, 'I'll buy us another round.'

He got up and went to the bar and I watched him go, thinking about how the tables had really turned. It used to be I paid for every drop he drank when we were out. I knew better than to ever expect an apology for what had happened on the roof at our party but Rusty buying beers was about as close to it as anyone was ever bound to get from that rat.

It was funny that I had thought of Miles because just then he walked in the door. He didn't see me. The way the White Horse is laid out there is one entrance but three rooms, one after the other running along Hudson Street. The table where I sat was tucked all the way back in the third room. I could see the bar at a distance from where I sat but unless the people turned on their stools and purposely peered through the doorway they weren't likely to notice the folks in the other rooms.

Now I watched the bar to see what would happen once Rusty and Miles got an eyeful of each other. Miles was with a guy I'd never seen before who had the good looks of a movie star and who reminded me a little of Errol Flynn. They ordered a couple of whiskeys neat and started right away talking to each other with serious, confidential expressions on their faces. It was clear that whoever the other man was, the two of them were very close. I considered going over there and saying hello to Miles and telling him I had picked up the composition book he'd dropped in the diner in Harlem, but then he would see the company I was keeping and catch on to the fact I was friendly with Rusty again and the last time we'd talked I'd sworn I was through with Rusty for good. The fact that Rusty had come over – uninvited, but even so – was bound to make a liar out of me and I slouched a little lower in my seat and hoped Miles wouldn't look through the doorway.

But just then Miles caught sight of Rusty and flinched. I held my breath. I was sure Rusty was going to do something rude, make some sort of snide gesture or remark, but to my surprise Rusty merely approached Miles and the young man and shook hands politely. Miles recoiled but shook Rusty's hand anyway and I could see mostly he just didn't want trouble. Rusty proceeded to chat it up for a few minutes, making what looked like small talk, as calm and as indifferent as ever. Then he left the bar and came back over to me.

I was surprised by this, because Rusty always struck me as one of those stingy bullies and I figured he would really have it in for Miles. I expected a few petty remarks at the very least and as Rusty put down the beers and slid back into the bench now I considered perhaps I'd misjudged him.

'It was swell of you to keep your cool,' I said.

'I'm a swell guy,' Rusty said.

'I would've thought you'd try for some kind of revenge.'

'Nah. I don't pick on my inferiors,' Rusty said, all tough and proud, like he was the kind of guy who lived by a goddamned code or something. 'Besides,' he added, 'if I really wanted to get revenge, I could, you know.'

This sounded more like the Rusty I knew. 'How?'

'That fella he's with? Got his first and last name and a few little titbits. Turns out he works for the good old State Department – how 'bout that for some comedy? That ol' sonofabitch Joe McCarthy might've croaked, but his way of doing business hasn't. All it would take is one phone call. It just so happens, I know some fellas who work for the State Department. You know: anonymous tip, that sort of jazz. It would bust up their cosy little knitting circle.'

I asked him what he meant but I already knew. It was a malicious idea. Once you knew Rusty you knew exactly how he thought. Rusty elaborated and as he talked I began to wonder if he wasn't going to make that phone call simply out of spite. The more he talked about it the more he seemed excited by the idea. I tried to sneak another look at Miles, wondering what terrible thing he must've done in a past life to merit having caught the attention of a villain like Rusty, but Miles and his friend had gone.

Before I could think about it any more, Eden sailed through the door. It was funny, because we'd been awfully sore at each other lately and you wouldn't think I'd be happy to see her. But there was something about the way she walked into the room and smiled when she saw me that reminded me of how it had been that first time I'd waited for her to turn up at the White Horse.

When she saw Rusty sitting with me, her smile flickered and faded a bit but did not vanish altogether.

'Cliff!' she said in a happy, breathless voice, ignoring Rusty. 'I have some wonderful news.'

65

MILES

I told Joey I wanted to go home.

'Home?' he asked. I could tell by his voice he was hoping I meant the hotel.

'To my mother's apartment,' I clarified. Our chance encounter with Rusty at the White Horse Tavern had left me supremely uncomfortable and I was still worried about what Cob might be thinking, having seen us at the museum. 'I'd like to go home,' I repeated. 'Now.' My brain ticked through the list of possessions still in Joey's hotel room. There wasn't much, only a change of underpants, an old razor, and a fresh shirt; I didn't need to go back for any of it, not right away.

'All right,' Joey said, baffled and clearly hurt. 'Will you come back to the hotel later?'

'I'll phone you,' I replied, and said goodbye. We were standing on the sidewalk on Hudson Street, and didn't embrace. I walked away quickly and didn't look back.

When I got to the apartment it seemed empty at first. I heard a faint stirring from the back of the apartment and I was surprised to find Cob in his room picking up fragments of shattered glass and smashed insects.

'Cob – get away from that glass!' I commanded, kneeling down to take his place. 'Let me do this.' He stood up and stared at me glumly as I took the broom and dustpan from his hands.

'What happened?' I asked.

'Wendell got mad,' he said. His child's voice sounded old and weary. I prodded him a little more as we continued to clean up, and was able to piece together, more or less, what had happened.

My mother was out running errands and Cob had arrived home from his field trip. Excited about the beetles he'd seen in the Egyptian wing, he had chattered away about them to Wendell, who – as habit often found him – was seven beers deep into his afternoon. At some point Wendell grew irritated with Cob and got into one of his ornery moods, until finally he went on a rampage around the house, shouting at Cob and calling him 'an inconsiderate bug-crazy little shit'. That's when he'd flown off the handle altogether and charged into Cob's room, smashing the jars of live bugs Cob collected and cared for, stomping the insects underfoot. Now Wendell was gone – out for another beer around the corner, surely – and Cob was trying to clean up everything before my mother came home.

'Wait! Save that, please,' Cob called out as I brushed up what appeared to be some kind of carrion beetle. Cob had made a small terrarium for the beetle, and had been feeding it tiny pieces of hamburger meat. Now the life had been knocked out of it, but somehow its hard outer shell had remained intact. I carefully extracted it from the broken glass and handed it to Cob. With an expression of deep sadness, he pinned it to one of his felt boards, where he kept and catalogued his non-living insects.

'I guess it can go here now,' he said in a dull voice. Out of the corner of my eye I became aware of a tiny movement somewhere on the floor by the window. It was a swallowtail butterfly, injured, but trying to come back to life in jittery fits and starts. I remembered Cob had caught the butterfly as a caterpillar and nurtured her as she spun her cocoon. I went over to the window, scooped her up, and brought her to Cob.

And then he did something that broke my heart.

He picked up the swallowtail and looked at her for a moment. With a cold, mechanical movement, he placed her against the felt board and swiftly pushed a pin through her. Her wings pulsed twice slowly and stopped moving.

'I might as well get to her before Wendell does,' Cob said.

As we finished putting the room back in order, I made up my mind. I would have to make the call quickly, before my mother got home. I walked to the kitchen.

'I won't be back to see you this weekend, Joey,' I said once the hotel clerk had put me through to his room. 'I've got some things to do.' I could tell from Joey's voice on the other end of the line that he was disappointed, and also frightened.

Having cancelled my plans with Joey, I spent the rest of the evening thinking about Cob, and soon enough the thought of my lost composition book returned to gnaw at me. I had, over time, increasingly come to the conclusion that I'd lost the book when I'd gone to the coffee shop to meet Cliff. If he *had* picked it up, I couldn't imagine why he would want to keep it instead of returning it. I hoped he was just too lazy.

Either way, there was only one thing to do: track him down and ask him about it once and for all. I made my way over to his East Village apartment. I stood on the stoop, but as I was about to press the buzzer, the door flew open.

'Oh! Pardon me,' a woman's voice said. To my surprise, I found myself staring at Eden. She froze when she caught sight of me. 'Miles?' she said in disbelief. I explained to her, in very abstract terms, about Cliff's visit to Harlem and that I'd come looking for him now because I'd dropped something and it was possible he'd picked it up. Her brow furrowed.

'He's upstairs, all right,' she said. 'But I'm afraid he's in a bit of a state: he's going on nearly two days of celebration.'

'Is it all right if I go up?'

'Of course,' she said. Then she hesitated. 'But, Miles . . . you should know . . . well, Rusty is there. That's why I'm stepping out to run some errands. I couldn't stand to be around him any more. I'm still . . .' She paused as though searching for the right words '. . . very sorry about what happened to you that night.'

I nodded. I didn't want to talk about it. I also didn't want to see Rusty again – it was bad enough Joey and I had run into him only the night before – but if I truly wanted to determine the whereabouts of my composition book, I had no choice. Remembering the night before, a thought occurred to me: Cliff had likely been *there*, somewhere in the White Horse Tavern, lurking in a corner. The two of them running around together had never brought about anything good for me in the past.

'You said Cliff is celebrating?' I asked, wondering what awaited me upstairs.

'Oh yes,' Eden said. 'Cliff is just over the moon. He's written a novel – a very good one, as a matter of fact – and his father is going to publish it at Bonwright.'

'A book?' I asked, my stomach suddenly dropping.

'Oh yes. It's amazing . . . I'm so proud of him,' she said. 'Cliff is much deeper than I ever imagined. You know, he hasn't the easiest relationship with his father, and yet he wrote an incredibly detailed, subtle, touching story about a father and a son. The son grows up with a disabled father, you see, and doubts the father as a role model, but what he doesn't know is that the father was actually a war hero of great integrity . . .'

I went numb as she prattled on. Nothing could've prepared me for the shock as I listened to Eden describe the details of Cliff's literary victory, the dim comprehension of exactly what he'd done with my notebook slowly sinking into my bones.

66

CLIFF

Rusty and I were in my dump of an apartment, singing drunken medleys to each other. We were celebrating my book deal. The sun had just gone down and an eerie glow was radiating through the window like an atom bomb. Once the simile came to me it bothered me something awful, so I got up to turn on the overhead light to break up the violet light of the glow. No sooner had my finger left the switch than I heard a loud noise at the door and a man came crashing into the room. It was a tall Negro man and at first I thought we were being burgled but then I made out the familiar shape of Miles.

'Whoa, whoa, whoa!' I hollered, and waved my arms.

'You dirty son of a bitch,' he spat at me, and when I saw the look on his face I knew somehow he had found out the truth of everything. Ordinarily Miles was the type of guy who looked civilised in every situation, with his glasses and posture and polite manners, but his entire being had shifted now and a deep guttural roar started somewhere in his throat. I knew he was going to lunge at me and I considered various evasive manoeuvres. Rusty was still on the ground over by the mattress and he sat up and crawled farther into the corner and I could see if I decided to take Miles on I would have to do it on my own. When he had slipped someone

Amytal, Rusty was very brave and keen to get in on the action, but when he hadn't he was much more the spectating type.

'YOU SON OF A BITCH THIEF!' Miles roared, and came at me with everything he had. Any other time, I would've laid him out flat, but hey I was exceptionally drunk that night, and besides, I more or less understood why the guy was angry and even though I didn't sympathise, I figured maybe it was best to let an angry guy get it out of his system. Let him get in a few licks and send him on his way. I felt Miles's hands grip my shoulders and drag me to the ground and soon enough he'd thrown a punch and caught me square in the left eye. I scrambled away and he caught me again and I scrambled away again.

'Truce! Truce!' I yelled, because now I was really worried Miles had lost it and might truly injure me if he didn't regain some sense. He stopped hitting me but pinned me all the same, until I was lying face-up on the floor and he was on top of me with his forearm bracing my chest and throat.

'*Who the hell do you think you are?*' he yelled, sweat and tears and spit dripping off of him and onto my face. 'You have no right.'

I could just make out Rusty in the corner looking on.

'If you think I'll be quiet about this, you've got another thing coming,' Miles warned. 'You may have my composition book, but I have my father's journal, and it doesn't lie. All those stories – his life! What do you think, Cliff, you think everyone is going to believe it's a coincidence?' he said in a bitter, mocking voice.

All at once an idea occurred to me and it was like the time I was fighting with Eden and I suddenly knew if I really wanted to shut her up what I ought to say. I wasn't proud of that fight I'd had with her but my tactics had proved effective and anyway Miles was hardly Eden. I didn't owe Miles anything.

'Say, Rusty,' I called from the floor where Miles had me pinned. 'What'd you say was the name of that fella Miles was running around with last night?'

This startled Miles. Freshly alert, he turned his head to look over at Rusty, and Rusty looked at us with that smirk of his and got a glint in his eye because he knew exactly where this was going. He opened his mouth to respond but before he did Miles cut him off and this meant Rusty and I had him on the hook.

'See, we know a few things about you, Miles. About you and your friend,' I said.

'You don't know what you're talking about,' Miles said. But as he said it, Miles's body went all stiff and I knew I'd hit the jackpot. 'He's nobody,' he said.

'You weren't looking at him like he was nobody, Miles,' I said. He let up on the pressure of his forearm across my chest and I squirmed away and sat up. I was still drunk but I had started to sober up and as I looked around the room the walls had stopped spinning and Miles's face came into focus.

I stared at old Miles, watching him shake now that I had called his bluff. 'Rusty here says your friend works for the State Department,' I continued. 'Lots of *you boys* work for the State Department, don't ya? Seems like every time I pick up a paper, I read about them kicking out yet another homosexual commie.'

I paused for emphasis. I wanted to make sure Miles heard my next point loud and clear.

'Sure would be a shame if someone were to make a phone call and report your friend – what was his name again?' I turned to Rusty. 'You remember the fella's name, don't you?'

Miles's face went slack. He took his hands off me as though my skin were hot and burnt him, and in that moment I believe we both realised he was defeated. He stood up, looked around the room, and took a few staggering steps, first towards the window, then away. Finally, without another word, he went out the apartment door.

'You don't really plan on making that telephone call, do you?' Rusty asked after Miles had gone. Rusty was clearly delighted with the situation.

'Of course not,' I said. 'I only meant to put old Miles in his place.'

'Say, what did he mean?' Rusty asked with that sly expression on his face. 'What did he mean with that business about you being a thief?'

67

MILES

That's when things turned ugly. Looking back on things now, I realise I was carrying around something combustible in me, only there was no way to know it at the time; I was too blinded by wild-eyed fear. A bitter winter had settled into the cold concrete bones of New York, and suddenly it felt as though the dark clouds overhead were laced with constant threat.

'What happened to your cheek?' Joey asked the next time he saw me.

I knew I had a cut there, a souvenir from my confrontation at Cliff's apartment. I had put a Band-Aid over it, hoping to pass it off as a shaving accident, but when I told Joey this lie his mouth twitched.

'Awfully high up,' he commented, as the cut was on my cheekbone just under my eye, nowhere near my beard line.

'Cob bumped me,' I said.

Joey did not press further. We had plenty to do that day, as we were moving our things to a new hotel. No sooner had Joey checked in and called me over than he became convinced we should check out and leave. This was a defensive measure: the clerk at our regular hotel had begun to eye us with suspicion. We knew it was impossible to go completely unnoticed, but there was generally a comfort in the apathetic dispositions of New Yorkers, who noticed but more often than not decided it was none of their business. The clerk had seemed reassuringly indifferent to us the first few times we'd stayed at the hotel, but over the course of our visits his demeanour had somehow soured, and now he was distinctly unfriendly and full of snide insinuations and veiled threats. It was only a matter of time, we both felt, until the clerk began dropping hints to the police.

To me, it felt like danger was suddenly all around us, ready to pounce from all sides, but of course Joey couldn't know why I felt this way. I hadn't uttered a word to Joey about losing my composition book, hadn't told him about my confrontation with Cliff, or that Joey and his job at the State Department had been the main target of Cliff's threats. I would like to be able to say I kept this information from Joey to protect him, but that wouldn't be truthful. The truth was I felt too angry, too short-changed, and too powerless to put any of this into words.

'I don't understand,' I said now. I could hear the anger in my own voice, but I could do nothing to stop it. 'Why did you bother to check in if you had a bad feeling about the clerk in the first place?'

'I don't know, Miles,' Joey said, tired. 'I didn't think it was as bad as it is but you should've seen him just now. He was either on a telephone call or pretending to be, going on about reporting a guest to the police. He was looking at me over the desk the whole time he was talking.'

'You ought to have changed hotels a few visits ago, Joey. You're reckless and pig-headed.'

Joey snapped to attention at my impatience. I was being irritable and nasty; I couldn't help it. I was frustrated with the whole situation, which in my mind was somehow linked to the injustice of Cliff stealing what amounted to my father's life story. Inexplicably, I decided to take my anger out on the person for whom I felt the most passionate feelings.

We went downstairs to check out. I agreed to wait outside on the street, so as not to raise the clerk's ire any further. After a few minutes Joey came hustling out.

'Made me pay in full for tonight. Knew I wouldn't argue. You should've seen him,' Joey said. 'I don't think I've ever seen anyone look so smug.'

'Let's hurry,' I said.

We took a taxi across town, farther west, nearer to the docks, where the hotels grew incrementally seedier every block you drew nearer to the Hudson. These were the hotels that played host to temporary 'assignations', as they were often dubbed by law enforcement and courts. The hotel where we finally stopped was not so bad as all that, but I was ready to complain about anything and everything.

'If these hotels get any seedier, next thing you know, we'll be sleeping in the Brooklyn Navy Yard,' I said, referring to the notorious homosexual haunt as we stepped onto the curb.

'What's that supposed to mean?' Joey replied.

Ah, I thought, *so now you've grown a spine and are going to fight back, are you?* 'It means I have the feeling you've been through all this before.' Joey's mouth dropped open. He didn't reply.

'Don't tell me you don't already know where to find the YMCA in Washington, or that you haven't learnt which hotels specialise in *discretion.* I'm surprised we're not lousy with bedbugs already.'

'Why are you like this, Miles?' Joey asked in a quiet voice. 'That cut . . . did someone beat you up? Were you jumped?'

'I told you,' I said. 'Shaving accident.'

I could tell he thought I'd been attacked, that he was sorry for me, even worried. All at once, it broke my heart to read the intensity of concern inscribed in his face.

'Fine,' he said, sighing and avoiding a bigger argument. He turned towards the hotel entrance. 'Let me go first. I'll check us in, then you can follow.'

Joey checked in, and we found our way upstairs to our room without incident. We set down our suitcases and lay down on the bed, not touching, both of us mentally exhausted. Minutes ticked by. The faucet in the bathroom sink was suffering from a minor but noticeable leak. We stared up at the ceiling and listened.

I reached for him first. I don't know why I did it; perhaps to get things over with. There was a certain gravity about our bodies coming together, just as there had been that first time on the houseboat, only this time it was much darker and more terrible and rote. We were rough, not tender. It was mechanical, and as we went through the motions I felt those first poisonous drops of hate mixed into our love.

When it was over, we wound up lying on our sides with our backs to each other. I waited for sleep to come, feeling the great and burdensome expense of Joey. He was – I was irrationally convinced – the reason I'd lost my composition book, or, at the very least, the number one obstacle that prevented me from getting it back. It galled me to think of what Cliff might've done with it and how he was going to stamp his name on it as if it had always been his. A tremor of true hate passed through me. Unable to direct it at Cliff, I directed it at the man lying next to me. Just before I fell unconscious, Joey rolled over and slipped his arm around me, pulling me close again.

It was as if he could feel the tide turning.

68

I called Joey at home the following Thursday and cancelled our plans to see each other the next weekend.

'Something wrong?' he asked.

'I wish you would stop asking that.'

'I wish I would stop feeling like I ought to.' He sighed. 'C'mon. It was one bad weekend; let it pass. You promised you wouldn't do this to me again.'

'I'm not. It's just . . . we don't have to see each other *every* weekend, Joey,' I said. 'I've got a life to live. I'm sure you do, too.'

'What's that supposed to mean?'

'I haven't been paying much attention to Janet. This isn't fair to her.'

He laughed. 'This isn't fair to anyone,' he said. 'But it's the world we live in.'

'I've got plans to be with her this weekend,' I said. I knew this was a knife of sorts. I felt it pierce his skin, but instead of pulling it back, I decided to push it in further. 'Janet and I have things to discuss. We'll be looking for an apartment of our own soon.'

'Miles . . .'

'I'm sure you'll find someone else to amuse you this weekend – and other weekends, too, perhaps.'

'Is that really what you think of me?' he asked.

'I don't know,' I said, and sighed. 'Look, I'm sorry.' I *was* sorry, but the truth was, ever since Cliff had made his threat, I had grown frightened for – and intolerant of – Joey. Where I had once smiled pleasantly, now I squirmed whenever I thought of him, and felt my throat constrict. 'I'd better go before my mother comes in and asks me who I'm talking to.'

He was quiet for a long moment, and I was tempted to hang up the phone.

'Do you love her?' he finally said.

'Who?'

'This silly girl of yours. Janet.'

I hesitated. 'I don't know,' I said finally.

'Do you love me?'

The line was silent for several seconds. 'I don't know,' I repeated. It was the truth, I realised. Joey's only response was to hang up.

It is clear to me now that what I did next I did out of fear and a desperate desire to distance myself from Joey, though I wouldn't have acknowledged this simple truth at the time.

I was out with Janet one evening when I impulsively reached for her hand and said, 'Let's get a room.' We were walking through the park, and as the sun was setting it was clear we were both chilled to the bone and would need to go somewhere to warm up. I couldn't stand the thought of another diner with bad lighting, sitting across from Janet and making small talk.

Janet looked at me now, vaguely alarmed to be so easily offered the one thing she had requested for so long. 'Let's get a nice one,' I continued. 'I've been saving up some money for our apartment, but we've done enough waiting.'

'All right,' she agreed. I could hear the nerves in her voice. She had wanted us to be together, but now that it was truly happening she was anxious, timid to follow through on her offer. We were at the south end of the park, and we left the park to stroll the streets nearby, looking for a hotel that felt right.

'How about this one?' I said. It was an old historical hotel, small – nothing so grand as the Pierre or the Plaza – but with a dignified entrance and plush red carpet leading to a revolving door.

Once inside, we garnered some looks from the reception staff. It was not likely they received many coloured couples for guests. They frowned but said nothing. I paid the deposit, and soon enough we were signing the hotel register. Janet's hand was shaking, I noticed, as she scrawled the unfamiliar combination of words *Janet Tillman*, next to the line where I had written *Miles Tillman*. A bellhop came over to take our luggage to the room, and there was some embarrassment when we admitted we didn't have any, for our sole purpose in taking the room was revealed. The clerk behind the desk gave a disapproving *tsk*, and I waited for him to throw us out or remind us they weren't the sort of establishment that rented rooms by the hour, but he let it go. Without the bellhop to show us, we took the elevator up three flights and found our way to the room on our own, which was just as well, for we were both growing increasingly nervous.

I fumbled with the key in the door, and Janet tripped ever so slightly over the threshold. The room looked out into an air shaft – I felt certain the clerk had assigned us this room on purpose – but it was well furnished, the walls and the upholstery an elegant buttery-yellow colour. I switched on a few lamps; then, remembering why we had come, I switched all of them off again, save one. Once Janet and I had taken our coats off, we stood there a moment, not knowing quite where to begin. The tension between us was excruciating.

'Let's just hold each other awhile,' Janet suggested.

'Is that what you would like?' I asked stupidly.

'It would help.'

We lay down on the bed together, and I took Janet into my arms. Her body, I realised, was completely unfamiliar to me; our petting in the park had done nothing to help me memorise the ridges and curves one might expect a fiancé to know by heart. She was a thin woman, but as I touched her now, she seemed strangely soft and doughy, and I felt slightly nauseated. Several minutes passed. I was anxious to get things over with and began to run my hands more aggressively over Janet's body, feeling under her shirt and toying with buttons. She warmed to me shyly at first, and began doing the same, until she was in the lead and I was nearly undressed. I reached over to the nightstand to click off the light of the remaining lamp, and our bodies became shadow shapes in the dark, moving and writhing as we laboured. Janet winced a bit when we finally began in earnest, and I felt all the more sorry for her, and all the more responsibility to uphold my end of the deal. Our undertaking was a task, I realised, one at which I could not afford to fail. I understood I possessed some monstrous component within my personality to do this to Janet, to treat her so; but we were moving forward now, and forward was the only direction I wanted to go. I wanted to move out onto the horizon, far past Joey, and leave him behind.

Janet began to moan softly, and I began to sweat, thwarted by the sound. I felt as though I were climbing a mountain that was forever getting taller.

Afterwards, when it was over, we lay side-by-side for the better part of an hour, our sticky skin cooling. We both knew Janet had to go home to her aunt and uncle's apartment, or else telephone and make some excuse they weren't likely to believe. She got up to put her clothes on, and I got up to follow her, assuming I would escort her home.

'That's all right,' Janet said, stopping me. 'You ought to stay and enjoy the room. It cost a lot. And, well, I'd like to be alone. I feel . . . different.'

My heart convulsed. 'About me?' I asked.

'No, no,' she reassured me. 'Just different in the way a girl feels after.'

I hadn't given Janet's virginity much thought, but now it was clear she had, and she was presently experiencing all the feelings of farewell and nostalgia that came with it.

'Are you sure you don't want me to take you home?'

'I'm sure.'

I walked her to the door.

'Thank you, Miles,' she said. I felt terrible she was thanking me, and said nothing. But then she smiled with the pleased air of a smug child, and I realised part of her felt as though she had finally won some sort of battle; that, self-sacrificial as she was, she was also claiming victory for herself.

'I love you,' she told me, and kissed me goodnight.

Alone in the room, I felt more monstrous than ever. I switched on the lamps and looked around, wondering what to do with myself. I found a small spot of blood in the sheets, and it occurred to me that a great act of violence had just taken place.

I thought about Joey and wondered what he was doing. He would've enjoyed the room I was in now, and suddenly I was sorry he wasn't there with me, sleeping next to me through the night. I picked up the telephone receiver from its cradle but thought better of it, and set it back down.

69

EDEN

Cliff's novel was being hurried into print with what was, for publishing, breakneck speed. Mr Nelson had made good on his word to make me a reader, Cliff was finally getting the recognition he so needed, and we even had less trouble with money, thanks to the $15,000 advance Cliff had received.

Cliff and I had even made plans to reveal the secret of our marriage, once and for all, to his family. (We would, we decided, eventually make a trip to Indiana to relay the same tidings to my parents in person.) The idea was – according to Cliff – we'd come out with the news during the book launch party, when his father was likely to be full of gin and happy about the novel they'd just published together.

'He'll be in one of his mercurial moods,' Cliff said. 'We can tell him just about anything then.'

This was actually a decent plan, for I'd witnessed Roger Nelson's good moods when one of his authors turned out to be the talk of the town. He usually puffed up, happy to take credit for the book's success. There was every reason to believe Cliff's novel would be the toast of New York, and if this happened, there would be no better time to reveal the secret of our marriage. Mr Nelson had given strict instructions to limit the number of galleys and to keep the publishing of Cliff's novel somewhat secretive in order to build anticipation, but those few critics who'd received an advance copy were already praising the manuscript. It was touching – albeit perhaps a little egomaniacal – to see Mr Nelson strutting around the office whenever someone paid the book a compliment.

'Good to know the boy soaked up something from his old man,' Mr Nelson would say, taking credit for Cliff's writing talent in his usual bombastic-yet-charismatic manner.

Once we'd hatched our plan to reveal our marriage to his parents, it suddenly felt more real. I was excited to finally be able to announce our union and be inducted as a real member of the Nelson family, but I was nervous, too, I suppose. Cliff and I decided to celebrate. I came home that day to find an atypically polite note from Cliff on the card table, saying he had gone to run some errands (I inferred this meant have a beer with Swish), but that he promised to be home for dinner no later than seven o'clock. *Excellent!* I thought. *I'll dash out to pick up some groceries and make a real, bona fide meal!* It would be just the thing to show Cliff how much I cared.

I made a quick round of the shops and returned home in a little less than half an hour. I'd gotten steak – Cliff's favourite – and had designs to sear it in a pan over the hot plate, something my *Modern Gal's Cookbook* promised me was possible. The trick was to get the timing right so the steak would be nice and hot around the time Cliff walked in the door. So I set about boiling the potatoes and mashing them, and then boiled up some spinach, too. Just as I finished the spinach, it dawned on me that part of a meal was the ambience, and that the apartment could do with a good scrub.

I tidied up our clothes; Cliff's were generally strewn all over the floor. I found a clean floral sheet and draped it over the card table.

We had a few empty wine bottles with candles melted into their necks (leftover from a brief period when Cliff and I had gotten into a tight spot and failed to pay the electric bill) and I put those out on the table, planning to light them right before Cliff was expected home. I looked at the clock and saw I still had an awful lot of time on my hands, so I thought to quickly scrub the floor. Once that was done, I would fix myself up and set the table.

The floor of our apartment was made of ancient wood, badly in need of refinishing. The porous wood attracted dirt into every tiny groove in its grain, and it took a great deal of elbow grease to get it even remotely clean. I put on my rubber dish-gloves, and got down on my hands and knees. Just as I was making headway with a particularly grimy plank, it suddenly sprang up, completely free. Stunned, I lifted it to find a hollow cavity just below.

In the dim light of the overhead bulb, I could see there was something down there. Carefully, I reached in and felt around. My hand hit something – something paper – and I pulled it out.

It was a composition book. When I opened it up, I recognised the sentences instantly; I had been intimately familiar with these sentences over the last few weeks. They were handwritten, not typed, and the handwriting was definitely not Cliff's. I flipped to the inside cover of the notebook and saw the owner had printed his name in the top left-hand corner: MILES TILLMAN.

My heart sank with the cold chill of dread.

I sat there, not moving, just taking in the sight of my absurd rubber-gloved hands holding the composition book. Its existence repelled me, I realised, but it didn't surprise me. That was the worst part: realising I wasn't the least bit surprised. Subconsciously, I had always known. I had known the day Miles had stopped by the apartment; I'd read the look on Miles's face. I had seen Cliff's black eye when I came home later that night. I had known and I had chosen not to know.

Very slowly, I put the notebook back into its hiding spot, and slid the floorboard back into place. Then I sat there for several minutes, frozen, just staring at the wooden floor, my brain unable to come up with a single thought. I looked at the clock, then I got up, changed my clothes, brushed my bangs, slicked on some lipstick, and lit the candles on the card table. I used the flame to light a cigarette, and then smoked a second one after that. My hand trembled as I smoked. It was abnormally silent in the apartment as I sat and waited for Cliff to come home.

70

CLIFF

Things were going along more swimmingly than ever until, all at once, there was a Great Unravelling. The Great Unravelling started one afternoon when Eden came home from work in the middle of a Tuesday. I knew something was wrong when I heard her key turn in the lock of the apartment door.

'Are you sick again?' I asked her as she came in, because to look at her you might think this was the case. She was so pale her skin bordered on blue, like watered-down milk. I couldn't figure out why she would come home in the middle of a Tuesday afternoon – except, to tell the truth, I *could* figure out why, and there were only two options: either she was sick or else she had very bad news. She looked at me now with her big, dark eyes and shook her head at my question.

'No,' she said. 'Not sick. Mr Nelson – I mean, your father – he gave me the afternoon off. He . . .' She hesitated. 'He asked me to have you telephone him as soon as possible.'

I must've shot her a hell of a surprised look, because we hadn't told My Old Man yet about the precise details of our relationship together, much less that we'd eloped months ago. She rushed to put my mind at ease – at least, on this score.

'He figured, since I mentioned I knew you through some

mutual acquaintances, I could find you to deliver the message.'

'Oh,' I said. 'But where's the fire? I'm supposed to meet with him down at ol' Bonwright in two days. What does he want to talk about that's so urgent?'

'He didn't say,' Eden replied. She looked at me and I looked at her and all of a sudden my stomach gave a deep and terrible lurch. I was possessed with the thought that this wasn't going to be good news. If it was bad news . . . I knew exactly what it was My Old Man must've found out and why he might want to talk to me. I wasn't ready to face whatever was bound to come next and I certainly wasn't ready to ask Eden about what she did or didn't know. If I thought she knew more than she was letting on, well, then I wouldn't be able to look at her face. It would kill me. Eden was a nice enough gal but she was a little like my goddamned conscience, too, and I couldn't bear to think of the way she would look at me if she knew.

'All right,' I said, forcing a casual voice. I'd been sitting around the apartment in my boxer shorts and now I reached for a pair of pants. 'I'll just run around the corner to McSorley's.'

Eden frowned. She did not like McSorley's. There were two joints – both Irish bars – within walking distance that sometimes let us use the telephone and even occasionally took down messages for us, but of the two, Eden infinitely preferred the other one. This was because, strictly speaking, she had never been to McSorley's; the bar still held a long-standing tradition of not allowing women on the premises.

I would be lying if I didn't say that's why I chose it now. My pulse was racing and I was feeling that godawful sense of manic terror. I was in *some* kind of state, and I didn't want Eden to be able to come with me to make the phone call or follow me and listen in or any of that nonsense, and by going to McSorley's at least I could be sure she would have to stay away.

But despite her frown she didn't protest my proposal and that got under my skin even more. She had no intention of following me, which meant she knew the news was bad. Her reaction only revealed the fact she'd been lying when I'd asked her what My Old Man wanted to talk about and she told me: *He didn't say.* It was plain he *did* say and that she was goddamned lying about it and playing dumb.

In less than three minutes I had my shoes on and was stamping down the stairs of the tenement, shouting goodbye to Eden over my shoulder.

Maybe it's nothing, I tried to tell myself as I pushed through the front door and stumbled out onto the sidewalk in the direction of McSorley's. *Maybe he wants to change the pub date, or the crummy typeface or the jacket or something. Lord knows the book has become awful important to him and maybe the Old Man just wants to go over this-or-that detail of the publishing process.* There was no way in hell the Old Man was going to pull it, I told myself. That simply wouldn't make any sense. We had all come too far and galleys had already been printed besides.

The thing about McSorley's was that somewhere early on in its establishment someone had gotten the genius idea that the bar should never change. I walked past the sagging barrels that lined the sidewalk outside and through the saloon doors that had seen more coats of paint than a battle-weary navy ship, and asked for the telephone at the bar. The bartender, Woody, recognised me. He nodded, reached under the counter, and slid the telephone across the ancient bar.

'Better make that collect if it ain't local,' he warned. 'We ain't in the business of making charitable donations to Ma Bell, you know . . .'

'It's local.'

He left me alone and I dialled.

'Hello?' my father answered after the fourth ring.

'It's Cliff,' I said. 'Eden told me you wanted to talk to me.' I shifted nervously. It was perpetually dim and gritty in old McSorley's. There were peanut shells on the floor and I could feel some of them pressing into the worn-out leather soles of my shoes. I heard My Old Man sigh on the other end of the line and thought I heard the clink of the crystal decanter from his bar set touch the rim of a glass.

'You should know, Clifford, we're cancelling the contract.'

A surge of acid filled my throat. I didn't say anything and neither did My Old Man and for a moment I thought maybe he'd gone and hung up.

'Clifford?' his voice came through the wire finally. 'Well? What do you have to say for yourself?'

'About what?' I blurted out. While I had been filled with dread on the walk over to the bar, nonetheless it had shocked me to hear it aloud. I could not have been more short of breath if someone had sucker-punched me in the gut and knocked all the wind out of me. As though from a far distance, I heard My Old Man let out another sigh over the tinny wire of the telephone.

'Fine,' he said. 'You're going to play dumb. And why should I expect anything else from you?'

'Play dumb about what, Pops?' I needed to hear him say it.

'We received a letter yesterday. An anonymous tip. It took me all afternoon yesterday and all evening to figure out what to do about this information. But when I woke up this morning, Clifford, I knew exactly what I needed to do. And before you blame me, it turns out I haven't any choice, anyway: the tipper sent a copy of the letter to Harry, so even if I wanted to protect you – which, quite frankly, I don't – it's out of my hands.'

I knew 'Harry' meant Harrison Tanley, the publisher who sat at the top of the pecking order at Bonwright, and My Old Man's boss.

'You're lucky, Clifford, that no one is bringing a lawsuit against you. At least, I haven't heard of any yet.'

'But . . . but . . .' I started to say. All of my sentences were only half-formed and I couldn't get my lousy brain to work.

'But what?'

'But . . . just like that? Some anonymous chump sends a letter and makes a claim against me, and you cancel the book? It's crazy. I haven't done anything wrong! What did this tipper say I did, and what proof did he have?'

'I think, Clifford, you already know what I'm going to tell you. *He said the book isn't yours*, that you didn't write it, and that he can produce a copy of the manuscript written out in longhand if he needs to! The fucking humiliation of it all . . .'

Miles, I thought, recalling the intense look of hatred on Miles's face when he burst into my apartment and roughed me up. What a lousy, rotten, jealous bastard. I'd let him get his licks in, and hadn't even struggled, but evidently that wasn't enough to satisfy him. He was after blood. No, scratch that. He was after my family, my *reputation*. My brain raced to the thought of Miles's journal, and where I had stashed it in my studio. If that was the longhand copy he meant to threaten me with, he certainly wasn't getting his hands on it anytime soon. If he meant his father's journal, well . . . it would be my word against a Negro's.

'Say, that's awfully flimsy stuff,' I countered. 'Anyone could write out a copy of the manuscript in longhand and go around pretending it's his!'

Again, that terrible sigh came over the line. 'I don't think so, Clifford,' My Old Man said, sounding tired. 'I was quite guarded about that manuscript . . . Eden was guarded . . . Very few people have ever seen it . . . Galleys only went to print last week.'

'How do we even know this copy exists? You don't sound as though you even want to look into it,' I said. There was no use beating around the bush and I figured I might as well make the accusation plain. My Old Man had always been lousy when it came to looking out for my best interests, and this instance was shaping up to be no exception.

'I don't need to look into it, Clifford.' His voice was stern and solemn and maybe a little drunk, too; when you listened closely you could hear the vague undertow of gin.

I don't need to look into it, Clifford. There, he had done it again: knocked the wind out of me, cold. It wasn't as though I could honestly claim I was surprised to hear those words . . . it was only that he was so firm in delivering them. His lack of belief in me was a foregone conclusion and I'd been an idiot to think he could ever be proud of me and behave like the true father I'd always wanted.

I started to bring up Brooklyn. It was time to tell My Old Man I'd known all along what a lousy crook he'd been to me and to my mother. I'd suffered in silence all this time and said *nothing*. Now it was time to tell My Old Man and let it blow him over sideways, as it damn well should. But before I could figure out how to really stick it to him, he took the upper hand and ended the call.

'Our lawyers will mail you the paperwork, Clifford,' he said, just before hanging up. 'I recommend we handle this as quietly as possible, for everyone's sake.' And then I heard a *click*.

* * *

'Everything fine?' Woody asked, seeing me holding the phone in front of my face, staring at the mouthpiece like some kind of goddamned cryptic puzzle covered in hieroglyphics.

'Just dandy,' I answered, after I'd had a chance to shake myself and pull it together. I put the receiver back in its cradle and slid the phone back across the bar. 'Say, though . . . I'll take a whiskey – I don't care; whatever you got in the well – neat.'

Woody tucked the telephone back under the counter and poured me the drink. 'Looks like you need this pretty bad,' he said. 'On the house. But don't go using us as your regular phone booth, hear?'

It was a hollow warning and I'd hardly heard what he said but I nodded anyway. I was hopped up on a rush of emotions and higher than if I'd swallowed a whole handful of bennies and chased them with a bucket of Swish's cowboy coffee. My legs were quivering and my armpits were cold as hell with an icy, ticklish sweat. I couldn't believe My Old Man had found me out and I couldn't think of any way out of the whole mess. It would only be a matter of time before Eden knew, too, if she didn't know already, and the thought of this made my stomach turn sour all over again.

I was finally able to calm myself down with one thought – one question, really: *what had I done that was so terrible, after all?*

It was true that the original inspiration for my novel came from Miles and his stories about his old man, but that didn't mean it wasn't really *my* manuscript, because after all I'd made some pretty significant changes and what is writing anyway but art imitating life and you have to start with *some* kind of original seed. It's what you do with it after that that matters. That's what Miles's composition book was: a seedling that I had the good eye to know could be nursed into something greater.

I could only think Miles had written that letter, even after the threat I'd hinted at about phoning in a tip of my own to the State Department about his lover. I was good and steamed. At first I thought there was nothing I wanted to do more than charge over to his house as he had charged over to mine and rough him up something awful.

But then another thought occurred to me, and I decided to go looking for Rusty instead.

71

MILES

I successfully avoided Joey for the better part of three weeks. I had come to the conclusion that I'd been right to leave well enough alone in San Francisco, and that the biggest error of my life was taking that Greyhound down to Washington, only to reignite our folly of a tryst. Now the plan – if it can be called anything remotely resembling an organised set of strategic ideas, that is – was to pretend remote indifference and watch his interest die a slow but permanent death. But Joey's phone calls to me had grown increasingly strange. He was jumpy and paranoid, but refused to tell me why this was so over the telephone. I had my suspicions what it could be, of course, but was not eager to have these suspicions confirmed.

Yet I found it difficult, one Friday in particular, to refuse his plea for me to see him. He had already come up to New York on the train, he said. He had checked into the hotel where we'd stayed on his last visit, and desperately needed to see me. Something in his voice unnerved me. There was a frayed quality to it, something I'd never heard in Joey's voice before. I found myself rankled, worried.

'It'll take me a little while,' I said. 'But I'll be there in a bit.'

'Hurry,' was all he replied, and hung up.

I had been spending some time with Cob, reading to him from our father's journal before putting him to bed. It was well after ten o'clock by the time I left my mother's apartment and hurried to the subway.

'Where have you been?' Joey demanded as soon as I stepped into the hotel room. I was startled by the paleness of his face. Dressed in only his shorts and an undershirt, he rushed at me as if he were some kind of apparition from a nightmare. I caught his shoulders in my hands – he was moving about erratically and I looked at him. He was cold to the touch and shaking; his skin was coated in a slick sheen of sweat.

'What's wrong?' Hoping it might help his trembling, I steered him over to the bed and sat him down. 'What's gotten into you?'

'Miles,' he said. 'Miles, this is very important . . . Do you think you might've been followed here?'

'Followed?' I said, not comprehending. 'Followed by who?'

'Does anyone know you're here?' he continued, not answering my question. 'Does anyone know you came here, or that you regularly meet . . . meet . . . a *friend*?' His eyes were wide and round. He leant closer and I smelt the sweetish malt of cheap whiskey on his breath.

'Did you drink all that on the train on the way in?' I asked, looking at a half-empty bottle on the dresser.

'Of course not,' he said. 'I only drank it here. I wouldn't dare drink in public; at this point it would only give them another reason to give me trouble.'

'Give you trouble? Who, Joey? Who?' I repeated, my terrible suspicions growing. His eyes slid over my face as though searching for something just beyond my shoulder, not quite seeing me.

'They questioned me,' he said. 'At work. I didn't believe they were there for me at first. I went to work like normal, and there they were. They were rifling through my desk like they owned the place! Then they took me into a room I'd never seen before. They asked me all kinds of questions, Miles.'

'*Who* did?'

'Two investigators,' Joey replied. 'From the FBI.'

I blinked. A peal of laughter unexpectedly burst forth from me. It was so terrible as to be the stuff of comedies. The picture of FBI agents interrogating Joey was grotesque, absurd.

'FBI? They've got to be kidding,' I said, more to myself than to Joey.

'This is serious,' Joey said. 'You remember the papers, don't you? All those headlines when Joe McCarthy went after a bunch of boys in the army and in the State Department?'

I remembered.

'All right. I'm listening,' I said, swallowing with sudden difficulty. 'Tell me everything.'

It had started off an ordinary morning. Joey went into the office in Foggy Bottom and as he'd passed by his secretary's desk he asked her to fetch him a cup of coffee. Before she could bring it to him, however, he had a surprise encounter with two men standing over his desk, opening drawers and going through the contents.

'Can I help you?' he asked. Yes, he could, they affirmed. He *could* help them, if he didn't mind sparing a few moments of his time. One of the men showed Joey a badge and he nodded at it in a daze. They led him through the building to a room he had never seen before. It was not an office. It was not a conference room. It was an interview room of sorts, a small, windowless space with a wooden table and three chairs.

'Have a seat,' one of the men invited. Joey did as instructed.

'Gosh, fellas, I'm confused. Did I apply for a promotion I've gone and forgotten about?' Joey joked. The men did not laugh. They were there for security reasons, they said. They both took their hats off and put them on the table, but neither sat down right away. Instead, they hovered over Joey and appraised him, looming tall and broad-shouldered in their grey double-breasted suits. His appearance there today was voluntary, they reminded him, and they thanked him for it. If he didn't mind answering a few questions, then they were certain they could get everything cleared up in no time. 'Sure,' Joey said, eager to be helpful. 'No problem.'

Joey's apprehension doubled when they asked him to take a legal oath, but he could see little way to refuse, so he took it. The two men continued to stand over him as they went about swearing him in. Joey remembered noticing his hand left behind a sweaty palm print on the leather cover of the Bible.

One of the men – Joey couldn't remember their names; he'd been so nervous, the whole experience was now a blur – finally sat down and took out a notebook. He marked down a few idle observations about Joey's dress and demeanour.

'Now, hold on just a minute, fellas,' Joey protested, conscious of his southern accent as his temper flared. 'What's *that* got to do with anything?'

The man didn't answer. He just looked up at Joey with a dull expression. His tie was soup-stained and he had steely eyes and a sallow, unpleasant face, Joey recalled as he told me his story. The other man had a well-worn countenance for a man around the cusp of thirty, probably on account of his badly pockmarked complexion.

'God only knows where they find these goons,' Joey commented as he shivered before me in the hotel room now.

They began to question him, he said. They reminded him he'd taken an oath; all this showmanship was meant to scare him, he was certain, but Joey was too nervous to puzzle out why. They asked him a few idle questions – how long he had been at his post, the name of his supervisor, that sort of thing – and then they dropped their bombshell. The US Civil Service Commission had encountered information that suggested he was an admitted homosexual, they said. Did he care to comment?

Joey's heart stopped. He couldn't think why they were asking him that; he was so careful. He also knew his answer was crucial. If he lied, it might be considered perjury and come back to haunt him, but he couldn't very well tell the truth, for obvious reasons: he would lose his job.

'Whoa, whoa, whoa, boys,' Joey said, chuckling and trying to keep a light note in his voice. 'Who told you that? Where is this coming from?'

Neither of the men answered. Instead, they pressed on. Had he ever gone to the Derby Room for the purposes of meeting other gentlemen? Did he frequent the Redskin Lounge? Did he know another State Department employee by the last name Wentworth who was known to dress in women's clothing and threw parties for other men who liked to do the same? Did he regularly associate with other homosexuals? Were there others he could name within the State Department?

Joey was blind with panic. He found himself giving half-answers to the two men, which somehow made things worse. He didn't see how bad it could be to admit to going to certain clubs and restaurants – where was the harm in that? – but his partial admissions only caused the men to redouble their efforts in trying to lure him into admitting something much more damning, and the specifics were growing more lurid by the minute.

'Hold on a minute, fellas,' Joey said, pretending to keep his calm. 'The conversation is getting . . . well . . . rather *blue* here.'

'Oh, of course . . . *pardon us*,' one of the men said in a jeering voice. 'You know, we didn't mean to offend your delicate sensibilities.'

Joey rejoined the man's comment with a stony stare. 'It occurs to me,' he finally said, finding a last-ditch shred of courage deep within his own indignation, 'if I've taken an oath, I ought to get a lawyer involved in this business.'

'Sure, fella,' the second man replied. 'I suppose you know your rights and all of that. But you know, we're only asking a few harmless questions here. You wouldn't need a lawyer if you had nothing to hide.'

Joey stood up on quivering knees, and the two men reached for their hats. 'We'll be in touch again real soon,' one of the men said. 'This matter is hardly closed.'

'Once I challenged them, they gave up pretty quickly,' Joey said as I squeezed his hand. 'Nothing about it was right,' he murmured. 'They seemed to know it. They seemed to know it was not quite right. You should've seen the look in their eyes. They *hated* me. They don't even know me, and they hate me.'

'Well,' I said, coughing to clear my throat. During the course of Joey's story a lump had lodged itself in my throat and refused to move. 'It's a good thing you finally stood up to them, then.' As soon as the sentence was out of my mouth, I knew it was a foolish thing to say, and I instantly regretted it. Joey turned to me with wild eyes.

'What are we going to do, Miles?'

I shook my head, and he looked down at his hands.

'I'm sure they'll leave you alone now,' I said.

Joey looked at me with a mixture of disbelief and disdain.

Minutes ticked by. In the bathroom, the faucet continued its annoying *plink, plink, plinkity-plink-plink,* like a clock that had forgotten its obligation to keep even-handed time. All I could feel was shock and – I'm ashamed to admit – a seedling of doubt that things had happened exactly as Joey had said. Surely he was exaggerating. As if sensing this, Joey put his face in his hands and began to cry.

'I just . . . I just don't understand,' I said stupidly. 'The FBI . . . is really taking this seriously? How did this happen?'

Joey lifted his face from his hands. He looked up at me with reddened eyes. 'That's what I found out today,' he said. His lips twisted in a sick smile. 'Somebody telephoned in an anonymous tip. That's all it takes,' he said in a defeated voice near my chest. 'You know as well as I do, that's all it takes.'

72

Joey's paranoia grew quickly. The FBI questioned him twice more, and each time they did, more and more of his easygoing personality chipped off and crumbled away, leaving both of us increasingly frightened: he, frightened of the FBI. Me, frightened of him. I ought to have been there for him, to comfort him, to reassure him. Instead, I inched further away. He had become a man disfigured by neediness in my eyes. We were two men clinging to a life raft, and Joey was the one who threatened to swamp both of us.

I told myself none of it was my fault. It was one thing if someone had phoned in a tip to menace Joey, but it was something else if the FBI kept after Joey, interviewing him more than once and investigating the details of his life further. It meant that Joey – with all his careless, jovial indiscretion – had given them cause. I could not be held accountable for that. At least, this is how my thinking went at the time.

And so, as Joey became increasingly desperate to see me, I became increasingly desperate to put some distance between us. Meanwhile, I devoted more and more of my time to Janet. In perhaps the more despicable, cowardly parts of my mind, I figured no one could accuse *me* of impropriety if it was clear to the world I was happily preoccupied with my lovely fiancée.

These two facts – my avoidance of Joey and the increased amount of time I spent with Janet – reached a crossroads one day, quite literally, on the sidewalk outside my mother's apartment building. I was walking down the street with Janet on my arm. We had spent that Sunday afternoon at the lunch counter around the corner and, knowing that Wendell was not home, I had suggested we drop in on my mother to say hello. If Janet and I were truly going to wind up as husband and wife, I thought it wouldn't be a terrible idea to bring Janet around more often.

'Shouldn't we telephone first?' Janet asked nervously as we neared our destination.

'No, no,' I reassured her, patting her hand where it curled around the inner crook of my arm. 'My mother doesn't like formalities anyway,' I said, politely burying the truth behind this, which was that my mother thought formalities were only for uppity people, and had used the word *uppity* to describe Janet once or twice in the past already. I looked at Janet's earnest, concerned expression, and smiled. It was plain to see how much she loved me and how much she wanted this to work. I was touched.

But just then, out of the corner of my eye, I caught a glimpse of something else: a familiar figure, sitting on the stoop right outside the entrance to my mother's apartment building. A jolt of cold shock went through me.

It was Joey.

I supposed I shouldn't have been surprised. There had been something ragged in his voice the last time we talked, which was also the last time I cancelled on him, fobbing him off with a flimsy reason. If he had any dignity at all, I figured, he would read between the lines and leave me well enough alone.

I had thought he sounded like a crazy man as he pleaded with me, and now here was proof that I wasn't off the mark. He was sitting, as bold as day, to the left side of the top stair. A rush of panic came over me as I wondered: how long had he been here? What was his purpose? Had he been upstairs to see my mother? He was wearing his overcoat – the one that looked very much like my own – and his knees were drawn up to his chest, giving him the air of a sullen child. Even out the corner of my eye, I could see him regarding Janet intensely, scrutinising her attractive wide eyes, the shabby faux fur of her collar, her middle-class shoes. I got a flash of Janet through Joey's jealous, assessing eyes and found myself suddenly angry.

The stoop was not very wide. My heart was thundering in my chest. I stiffened. Janet and I would have to walk right past Joey, within a few inches. And I would have to pretend not to know him.

We began our ascent. I could feel Joey's presence like a palpable barrier, as though he were radiating some sort of energy or negative radio wave. Whatever else he'd come for, he was here now because he wanted to frighten me, to punish me, I realised.

We reached the top step.

'Nice day out,' Joey commented in an idle, conversational tone. It wasn't. The winter had come to stay, and despite the occasional patch of sun breaking through the clouds, the air was full of a wet, icy chill.

'Yes,' Janet replied, to be polite. She seemed puzzled as to what a young white man was doing loitering on the stoop of a Harlem apartment building, but she didn't say so aloud, not even once we'd gotten inside the hallway and were climbing the stairs. Instead, she squeezed my arm and asked, 'Are you all right, Miles? You're not nervous for me to spend some time with your mother, are you?'

'No,' I said. 'Why?'

'Your arm. It's trembling.'

'Oh.'

Later, when I went to walk Janet to her home on the other side of Harlem, Joey was no longer there. I kept throwing little glances over my shoulder as we walked, half-expecting to see him lurking at a distance, following us. But he wasn't.

Before I made it back to my mother's apartment, I stopped at a payphone. I had a hunch where I might reach him.

'Hello?' he answered, after I dialled the hotel where we'd stayed during his last visit.

'Just what in the hell do you think you're doing?' I realised I was yelling. I didn't care.

'I needed to see you,' he replied. 'You weren't making it very easy.'

'SO YOU CAME TO MY MOTHER'S HOUSE?'

'It's not like I rang the bell and introduced myself.'

'You can't come around like that, Joey. You just can't. Don't you get it? People are asking you questions. I don't need them asking *me* questions, too.'

There was a pause, during which Joey gave out a small, sick noise that sounded like a cross between a nervous laugh and a frantic sob. 'You think I don't know that?' he said. 'Please . . . I only came up to New York to see you because . . . because I'm losing it, Miles. They're picking apart my life. My family . . . It's only a matter of time until . . . I need a friend. I need someone to help me keep it all together.'

'You have Eddie,' I said.

He was silent. Part of me wanted to give in and comfort him. But another part of me – the cruel-hearted animal that could sense Joey's terrible weakness – decided to snap its jaws shut.

'Don't come around here any more, Joey. I mean it. I have a fiancée. I told you before: I'm not like you.'

'You're not like me?'

'I'm not . . . the way you are.' Again silence. 'I'm marrying Janet,' I said with an air of finality. 'I'm sorry for your trouble, but I'm done. I want you to leave us alone.'

'Miles . . . You promised you wouldn't do this again.'

I could think of nothing to say. My throat was too thick, and my stomach was already beginning to turn inside out. There was nothing *to* say. Joey was one hundred per cent right. I hung up.

73

An unexpected event occurred around that time. I was tiptoeing around the apartment one morning, getting dressed and making breakfast as quietly as I could so as to not wake Wendell, when the telephone's shrill ring nearly caused me to drop the glass into which I was pouring orange juice. I hurried to pick it up before it could ring a second time.

'Mr Tillman?' came a man's unfamiliar voice over the line. His words were articulated with that type of stiff jaw particular to businessmen and lawyers, and I couldn't imagine why someone like that would be calling. I wondered if by *Mr Tillman* the stranger on the line meant my father.

'Mr Miles Tillman?' he clarified, as though reading my mind.

'Yes?'

'I presume you're acquainted with a gentleman named Augustus Minton?'

My mind swirled. *Mister Gus.* The voice on the phone meant Mister Gus, I realised as my brain dredged up Mister Gus's full name from some forgotten place. But why was someone calling about Mister Gus? My armpits were suddenly cold with sweat.

'I'm sorry to be the one to inform you that Mr Minton passed away today,' the man continued.

'Oh,' I said. I paused, trying to find the right words, ashamed at my relief. 'Oh,' I said stupidly again.

'Yes,' the man said. 'My name is Jim Arkle, and I'm Mr Minton's attorney.'

'All right,' I said, not certain what to make of this information.

'I see Mr Minton has your name written down here.'

My heart pounded. My mother came into the kitchen, frowning, and looked at me askance.

'The notation he's made here indicates he'd like you to have a hand in facilitating his arrangements. It says you were once his assistant and that you will know how he'd like things done.'

I was silent, hesitating.

'There's also an envelope of cash with your name on it,' the lawyer added, as though he sensed I needed persuasion.

'No, it's not that,' I said.

'Beg pardon?'

'I just . . . This is a surprise. I'll need to call my current job and notify them of my absence today, but I'll be there as soon as I can.'

'Good,' the lawyer said in a tone that insinuated he firmly believed his mention of the envelope of cash had convinced me. 'See you soon.'

I hung up.

'Miles?' my mother prodded.

'Remember the old man who paid me to run errands?'

She *tsked* and shook her head. 'That him, demanding you do somethin' for him?' My mother, with that sixth sense of hers, had always been leery of Mister Gus, an older white man who – *she* felt – was unnaturally interested in me. 'You tell him: you got enough to do without him callin' you at all hours in the morning, expecting you to drop everything and come over.'

She paused, and her frown deepened.

'Why you look like that?'

'He died today,' I said.

Her mouth opened, then closed again.

I called in sick to my messenger job. When I got to the town house, I walked so as to go around to the side and use the servants' entrance, as was my habit, but I realised I no longer had the key, so I went to the front door and rang the bell, a small copper button inside a lion's mouth. The door sprang open to reveal a short bearded-and-bespectacled man within.

'Yes?'

'Are you Mr Arkle, the lawyer I spoke to on the phone?'

'Spoke to on the phone . . . ?' he echoed.

'I'm Miles Tillman.'

'Oh – oh yes! Pardon my surprise. But of course you're a Negro! I don't know why I hadn't thought of that.'

'Why would you?' I blurted, puzzled.

'Exactly, my son, why would I, *exactly*. Well, come on in! There's so much to do,' he said, gesturing. I followed. 'I was going to get this unpleasant business under way – you know, call the coroner and such, but Ada, the cook who was hired recently – have you met? She's the one who found him – stopped me and directed my attention to these papers and told me I ought to read them first.' We had made our way into the kitchen and he scooped up a series of what appeared to be folded letters.

'Here you are,' he said, handing one folded sheaf of paper to me. I opened it and read it. In Mister Gus's tight, stingy handwriting was an enumerated list. At the top was written *MR MILES TILLMAN*

TO ADMINISTER THIS LIST. 'So that's you, hey?' The lawyer pointed.

'Yes.'

'Shall we start with the telephone calls?'

We worked our way down the list Mister Gus had written, telephoning one person at a time. We called Mister Gus's personal physician first, and he came over about an hour later to check the body and write up a certificate of death. The notary, a scarecrow-like fussy man with glasses, was second. He seemed irritated by our request to notarise the certificate, and barely looked it over before putting his seal on it and leaving. A mortician and a funeral home were called, as well as a church Mister Gus had long ago stopped attending – or so we deduced, for the name of the minister he had written down corresponded to a man the church said had made his eternal migration from the pulpit to the churchyard several years prior.

Once we had telephoned everyone, we were left to wait, and I moved to the items lower down the list. These were more like the chores I had performed in service of Mister Gus while he was alive, but with an obvious difference. For instance, Mister Gus wanted a particular suit to be laundered and pressed for his burial, and a specific pair of dress shoes polished. There were also the contents of a safe to be emptied; Mr Arkle stood over my shoulder and watched me open it. Once he saw it contained nothing but letters and photographs, he lost interest and left me to my own devices. According to Mister Gus's instructions, I was to burn these things in the downstairs fireplace, watching over them until I was certain all had been reduced to ash. I built a fire, lit the kindling, and stoked it. I put the letters in gently and watched them curl. I didn't open or read them first. I thought perhaps Mister Gus would not have wanted anyone to read them, and that was why I had been selected for this particular task. At one point, one of the photographs slipped out of its sleeve and landed on the hearth. It was an aged, sepia-tone portrait depicting a young man with his hair parted neatly down the centre and a smile turning the corners of his mouth. The words *Charlie, April 3, 1902* were scrawled in ink on the bottom right-hand corner. I had the strange feeling of being watched as I moved to lift the photograph and ease Charlie back into the flames, and for a brief moment I thought I understood exactly who Charlie was and my heart filled with a profound regret.

Eventually a newspaperman turned up, and I was even more certain as to why I, of all people, had been named by Mister Gus to assist in sorting his final affairs. As the reporter probed my recollections of Mister Gus's private life, I treated each gossipy question with the practiced evasion it deserved. When the reporter thanked me (with ironic intonation) and departed, the blackened photograph flashed again in my mind.

Towards the dinner hour the hearse from the funeral home finally pulled up to the town house. 'Well,' Mr Arkle said, sighing with exhaustion, 'I think we're mostly done here. If you have any last respects to pay, son, now's the time to pay 'em.' Seeing Mister Gus in the flesh had never occurred to me, and I looked now at the lawyer in surprise. I'd spent the whole day in the house but hadn't gone upstairs, much less into the bedroom. In this manner, Mister Gus's body had been a sort of offstage actor in our scene, setting everything into motion but remaining far away and out of sight. 'It's up to you,' the lawyer said, 'but here's your big chance.' By now it was clear Mr Arkle was under the impression Mister Gus and I had been lovers, the money-hungry apprentice and his lonely master. I didn't bother to correct him; his opinion hardly mattered to me.

I went upstairs with reluctance and poked my head cautiously into Mister Gus's bedroom. Everything was as jewel-toned and opulent as I remembered. I walked towards the foot of the bed but stayed several feet away, unable to draw nearer. With the life gone from his frame, Mister Gus looked even smaller than I remembered. The bedcovers had been folded back – for the doctor's examination, I expect – and he lay there atop the sheets clad in burgundy silk pyjamas, so slight as to barely disturb the bed. He looked so brittle, so white, almost like a shell you'd find on the beach, the curves of his gnarled fingers and cheekbones so deep as to be scalloped.

I stood there for the better part of ten minutes, my feet rooted to the floor, my eyes unblinking. I couldn't think of anything to do or say. I thought about his last words to me, uttered months earlier. One fragment in particular of what Mister Gus had said kept returning to me as I stood there . . . *and you're left to fumble in terrible places and it's only your body . . . yes, only your body trying to prove to the soul that it's not alone, and failing time and time again.* The photograph burning in the fireplace flashed in my mind for the third time that day, and I thought of San Francisco and of Joey, not wanting to believe there could ever be a part of Mister Gus's life that had ever resembled my own. There were parts of Mister Gus's life during which he had likely been happy and felt alive. And there were years that had inevitably come after 1902, in the wake of 'Charlie' – whoever he was; years driven by loneliness that had prompted Mister Gus's speech to me that I realised I'd never wanted to know about. Not then and not now. I continued to stand there, gazing upon Mister Gus's frail shell of a body.

When I finally spoke, my voice barely croaked out of my

throat. 'I'm sorry,' I said, and walked out of the room.

Downstairs, Mr Arkle was waiting for me with an envelope. Inside was a crisp one-hundred-dollar bill.

That evening, I went to a payphone and dialled the number for Joey's apartment in Washington, DC.

'I'm sorry, Joey,' I said once he picked up. 'I need to talk to you. I'd like to see you this weekend. If you still want to.'

He was quiet.

'Joey? Are you there?'

'Did they put you up to this?' he demanded. 'Look, I don't know who this is, but I don't want any trouble. This is a private line.'

I blinked, uncomprehending at first. *Did they put you up to this* . . . The words went through me with a cruel jolt. He was pretending not to know me. He was acting out of fear and suspicion, I realised. During the time we'd been apart – the time I'd abandoned him and sworn him off – his paranoia had gotten the upper hand. I felt a terrible pang of sympathy for him.

'It's just me, Joey. Something happened today that made me realise how sorry I am . . . how much I need to tell you I'm sorry. I need to tell you everything.'

'What was that?' he demanded. 'What was that clicking sound?' There was a pause. 'Where are you calling me from?' he asked in a low, suspicious tone.

'A payphone,' I answered.

He was quiet again; I could sense his tortured mind working. Finally, he sighed.

'It's a pretty sure thing I'm going to lose my job, Miles,' Joey said. The tone of frenzy had left his voice, replaced by one of slow, defeated sorrow. 'My family will know why. And you . . . I can't stand it when you change your mind about me. You can't do that any more, Miles. You can't. I can't take it.'

'I won't,' I said. I remember it came out forceful and clear, as though this time I truly meant it. And I believe I did.

74

A sudden spate of last-minute deliveries had me detained. The weather conditions were terrible that day; I recall sliding all over the frozen streets on my bicycle, my gloved hands gripping the handlebars so tightly my knuckles throbbed. A light rain had seeped into the snow that had fallen a few days earlier, rendering them soggy lumps that later refroze into treacherous, glass-like ice. Joey was scheduled to come in early on the train; it was likely he'd already checked in and was waiting for me. I knew he would worry when I didn't show up at the hotel on time, and I tried my best to hurry through my deliveries without breaking my neck, steering in and out of the throngs of taxicabs that knotted the streets. I had a sort of unofficial saying in those days: if the taxi drivers of Manhattan are driving more cautiously than you are, you are doing something wrong. Twice I caught myself speeding up to a reckless pace and had to remind myself to slow down.

Before I hopped on my bicycle and left the dispatch office I considered telephoning the hotel to warn Joey I was going to be late, but doing so might spook him, I reasoned. I remembered his paranoia over the telephone line when I called him a few days earlier, and I imagined him now, eyeing the phone with terror as the front desk connected the call to his room. So far, the clerk at the front desk at this new hotel had yet to make his opinion of us known. He didn't show signs of openly disapproving, but he could hardly be counted as an ally.

After four deliveries, I was already over an hour and a half late, but was finally on my fifth and last one. I was told the heavy stack of papers wrapped in brown parchment that I was delivering were editorial notes, and the recipient was an elderly historian producing his latest volume on the life of Abraham Lincoln. The person who answered the door of the Upper East Side town house was a little grey mouse of a woman, and – I deduced – the historian's wife.

'Ah!' she said, upon opening the heavy door of a sombre brownstone. 'There you are! Thank you for making the trip so late in the day. He'll be very glad to have those.' She reached for the parcel, but it was quite large and heavy, and I could see she was going to struggle with it. I felt a small tickle of guilt.

'Where would you like it?' I asked, knowing this meant I would be carrying it inside.

'Oh,' she said, smiling. 'He'll be needing those in his study.' She ushered me inside and I followed her down a hallway past a staircase and into a little parlour where a fireplace was sputtering and crackling with happy flames.

'Over here, boy,' an elderly man called, waving to me from behind a mahogany desk. He patted the leather ink blotter before him, and I set the parcel where he indicated. 'Thank you, boy,' he said in a wheezing voice as he reached into a desk drawer to extract a letter opener with which to cut the parcel strings.

'You're welcome, sir,' I said. I turned to go out the way I had come in, but as I whirled about I came face-to-face again with his wife, who was now holding a tea tray.

'You must be a block of ice, riding that bicycle about in this weather!' she said. 'Here, have some tea and biscuits to warm you up.' I attempted to decline. 'Please,' she said, squeezing my arm in a surprisingly vice-like grip. 'I insist.' She peered at me with a pair of large, kind-seeming eyes, and smiled. There was something sweet and fragile in her small face.

'Thank you,' I said, relenting.

It was sweltering in the room and I could feel trickles of sweat forming in my armpits, buried deep beneath my thick sweater and coat. I helped myself to two dry, crumbly biscuits and an almond cookie that wasn't half-bad, which I washed down with a cup of weak yet piping-hot tea. I tried to conceal my hurry so as not to offend the historian or his wife. Finally after a decent interval had passed, I gave a tiny, apologetic bow to my hosts and pointed to the front door. 'I'd better get back to my bicycle. I left it leaning by the gate on the front stoop.'

The old man grunted indifferently.

'Of course,' his wife said. 'But please take some for later.' She held out the plate again. I hesitated. It occurred to me Joey might like some. I took a few and stuffed them into my pockets.

Once outside, I looked at my watch. A tremor of fretful panic shook my body. By the time I finally made it to the hotel, I was going to be well over two hours late. I stood on the stoop of the brownstone, thinking about what to do. Under ordinary circumstances, I would ride back to the depot at the end of my shift and lock my bicycle in one of the little sheds in the basement beneath the publishing house, but I didn't want to take the time today. I decided to bike straight to the hotel instead.

The December sun had set hours earlier and it was treacherously dark as I pedalled through the streets, furiously weaving in and out of automobile headlights, praying not to be hit by a car. Twice I heard the squeal and screech of brakes behind me followed by a tremendous amount of honking, but I did not look back to see whether these noises were aimed at me.

When I neared the hotel, there was some kind of commotion out front. A small cluster of people was gathered around the entrance, and the large front door – it was a small hotel, and there was no revolving door – was propped open. I dismounted my bicycle and wheeled it closer, but then froze when I caught a glimpse of several policemen milling about inside. Someone had called them to the hotel, I realised with a start. Joey must be hiding in his room, distressed to suddenly find the hotel halls and lobby full of officers who might want to ask him questions, officers who might – for reasons that might make sense to Joey's paranoid mind – report Joey's presence in New York back to the State Department.

It was rotten luck to have all this happen now, especially given how rattled Joey had been lately. I needed to get to Joey, but the question was *how?* If I walked in now with the intention of going upstairs, I was sure to be asked a lot of questions.

As I made my way through the small crowd I deduced that the people gathered outside were curious spectators, people who had been walking by and caught a whiff of scandal and lingered to see what the fuss was about. I didn't know what to do with my bicycle. I spotted a middle-aged woman with a tiny dog on a leash squinting into the lobby, her thin lips pursed stubbornly off to one side. Something about her prim, disapproving expression suggested to me that she was not going anywhere anytime soon.

'Excuse me, ma'am,' I said, leaning the bicycle against the outer wall of the building next to her. 'Would you mind if I left this here for a moment?' She frowned and gave me a critical once-over but finally shook her head.

'I can't stop you,' she said. I knew better than to ask her to mind the bicycle for me; she would say no. I also knew no one would dare interfere with a bicycle that didn't belong to them with a woman like her standing nearby. I left the bicycle where it was and hurried into the lobby.

Inside, the lobby was chaotic. A handful of young officers shuffled around the room looking busy doing nothing, while a more senior-looking policeman barked something into the front desk telephone. Newspapermen in their telltale trench coats scribbled on notepads. The elevator cage went up and down, steadily reshuffling the men in the lobby, dropping some off while bringing others up. To my relief, no one took notice of me right away, and the regular hotel clerk was nowhere to be found.

There had to be an emergency stairwell. With the elevator in constant use, there was no easy way to get upstairs to Joey. I watched a group of men crowd into the cage and disappear upwards, the heavy brick-shaped counterweights and slack cables sliding down and arriving smoothly in their place. The brass needle above the elevator entrance moved counterclockwise, ticking off the floors until it stopped. Suddenly, with a jolt, I noticed the floor. It was the fourth floor. I knew that was the floor Joey was on. He'd said over the phone that he'd returned to the same room in which we'd previously taken refuge on the day we'd changed hotels. For all his wild ways, Joey liked consistency.

'Yeah, yeah, that's right,' the officer on the phone was saying, 'you heard me: cancel the ambulance.' Pause. 'No.' Pause. 'No, no, no. Like I said, no need; won't do him any good. Be a waste of time. He's a goner for sure.' Long pause. 'Well, that's what I told 'em. I already phoned over and I says, "You boys need to get the coroner over here right away," that's what I says. I told him we all got wives to get home to who've been waiting around all day to go out and do some holiday shopping.'

My stomach turned over. Whatever the commotion was about, it was worse than I thought. I looked around and tapped one of the newspaper reporters on the shoulder.

'Excuse me,' I said. 'Can you tell me what's happened here?'

'They found a man dead in his room,' the reporter said, and resumed his scribbling. 'Got some complaints from the room below that water was dripping from their ceiling, and when the maid went to investigate she found the guy had turned on the bath tap and never turned it off. Killed himself, evidently. Some fella in town from DC,' he continued.

'What room number was it?' I demanded. Before I could stop myself, the question leapt from my mouth a second time. 'WHAT ROOM WAS IT?'

'Say, what's it to you, anyway?' The reporter frowned and scrutinised me more closely. 'You here to rubberneck?' A few of the other men in the lobby glanced at us. I made an effort to regain my composure.

'All these reporters are here to report . . . the death of one man?' I stammered. My voice sounded far away. 'Seems to me there's an awful lot of people here.'

'Yeah, well, the fella who died worked for the State Department,' he said. I thought for a moment I might vomit. 'Somebody phoned in a tip he was making all these trips to New York because he was secretly meeting with the Communist League.'

'That isn't true,' I snapped. The reporter blinked at me, startled.

'Say, buddy, you're awfully cagey for a nosy bystander. What's your business here again?' By then we had gotten the attention of one of the more senior cops in the room.

'What's your business here, boy?' the cop chimed in to repeat the question, spitting the word *boy* at me.

'I'm a bicycle messenger,' I murmured, but it was too low for him to fully hear me.

'You're a what?'

'A messenger boy,' I repeated with more effort. My brain was spinning; I couldn't tell the truth – not the whole truth. 'For a news bureau. There's a reporter here . . .' I said. 'I'm to bring him extra notepads.' I held up the messenger bag that was slung over my shoulder and hoped they wouldn't want to look inside it lest they find out my whole story was a bald-faced lie.

'Yeah? Well, do you see him?'

I pretended to look about the room. 'No,' I said.

'In that case, if he needs you, he'll have to find you outside. We can't have you wandering about in here.'

'Yes, sir,' I said.

'Well? Get.'

I nodded. My body had gone numb. I willed my legs to take me to the open door, but I moved very slowly; it was as though the lobby had filled with sand. I was dimly aware of someone answering a telephone and shouting to the officer who had just interviewed me.

'Sarge? It's the dead fella's uncle on the horn. Dunno how news got to him so quickly, but you'd better take this. Calling all the way from Kentucky. He's some kind of bigwig in the bourbon business. Sounds like he's gonna throw his weight around.'

I froze mid-step. For a minute I felt like I might faint. The sergeant snapped his fingers in my face as he crossed the room to the telephone.

'What's taking you so long, boy? Step to it!'

'How did he . . . how did he die?' I asked, shaking. It was all I could do not to race up to the room.

'Cut his wrists in the bathtub,' the sergeant said in a bored voice, reaching for the receiver. 'What's it to you?'

I said nothing. As though floating in a trance, I walked the remaining distance to the open door, down the steps, and over to my bicycle.

'I hear somebody was murdered in there,' said the pinched-faced woman, more friendly now that I had been inside. I nodded at her and she looked impressed. 'Get a look at the body?'

I wheeled my bicycle away without answering her.

I walked my bicycle for a long time. Without knowing exactly how I got there, I ended up downtown, along the Hudson near the ragged pylons that jutted out from the Village shore. Once there, I dropped the bicycle on its side and sat near the icy rocks, watching the factories across the river in New Jersey belch brown steam. I imagined Joey alone in that room, waiting for me, nervous and growing increasingly paranoid, until finally he gave into his despair. I hoped, curiously enough, that the water had been warm, that it had made him feel full and sleepy. I had read in novels that death could be like that. Every once in a while the impulse came over me to return to the hotel, to sneak up to the fourth floor, to force my way into Joey's room. I kept careful track of the hands as they moved in a circle around the face of my watch, wondering how long they would leave him in the bathtub, how long it would be until the coroner arrived, how long until Joey's body – his once beautiful body – would be loaded into the hearse and taken away.

Something – some kind of stone-shaped object – was worrying my hip through my coat pocket, and I reached in to discover the almond cookies from the historian's house, the ones I had accepted thinking Joey might like them. A queer choking came over me and I shoved all of them into my mouth, chewed them, and swallowed them. Then I got up from where I sat and retched into the rocks, the stomach acid of the vomit burning my nose and throat. I wiped my mouth on my coat sleeve and staggered over to where the bicycle lay, picked it up, and prepared to ride home. But the bicycle was useless. It was so cold, the wheels had frozen to the frame and they would not turn.

75

CLIFF

After the phone call with My Old Man, I was in no rush to hurry back to the apartment, where Eden would be surely waiting. Instead, I went looking for Rusty, and as I made the rounds of all the watering holes in the Village, sure enough I bumped into Swish. I hadn't seen old Swish in some time; he hadn't been present that terrible day when Gene bad-mouthed me at the tavern but I'd more or less begun avoiding the whole pack of 'em. My big plan had been to avoid them until my novel was published and then I had the idea I would invite them all to the fancy book party I was bound to have. I wouldn't let on that I knew how crummy they had been and instead I would be generous as hell as I basked in my success, and then they could all eat crow – Gene especially. But now that wasn't going to happen, not unless I could change My Old Man's mind or else come up with an alternate plan to get the book published . . . which was where Rusty came into the picture.

Anyway, I didn't find Rusty that night, but I did find Swish, and when I did we went right back into our old Heckle and Jeckle routine and we got good and drunk and stayed out all night together. I crashed on Swish's couch and in the morning, while nursing a headache over Swish's strong black cowboy coffee, I got up the nerve to ask if I could crash with him on a regular basis. I told him Eden and I were having problems, which was the truth, or at least it was one part of the larger truth. Swish said yes of course, and to his credit I thought I caught only the tiniest gleam of smug satisfaction in it when he said it. I guess I could've gotten all bent out of shape to think that maybe Swish was glad to see Eden and I were having problems but I was grateful to have an alternate place to stay so I didn't say anything. The truth was I didn't want to see Eden if I could help it; it was obvious now in retrospect that she had known damned well what My Old Man's news was going to be and she hadn't had the decency to warn me before sending me off to go make that phone call. And maybe if I'm being very honest, another part of me didn't want to see her because I felt pretty lousy about the whole business, like I had let her down.

In any case, Swish said yes and I waited until Eden was bound to be at work and then I went back to the apartment and packed a little bag. I considered scribbling her a letter and leaving it on the table but I didn't know what to write so I decided it would be best to just leave it alone. She would figure out soon enough that I was staying away on purpose and had found some other place to sleep.

My biggest problem was that I also still wanted to hash things out with My Old Man or at least tell him my side of the story and argue my case but seeing as how I was now avoiding Eden, I didn't exactly want to call him at work, where she would be likely to pick up the phone. I decided to call my mother instead.

She answered on the third ring. I heard her diamond earring clatter against the phone, and then a brief pause as she quickly removed it.

'Hello?' She sounded tired and harried, but maybe this was only because she'd had to answer the phone. Usually the maid answered our calls.

'Mother?'

'Clifford.' Her voice was tight, and it was not a question. 'What is it? I'm in the middle of setting up for the ladies to come over and play bridge. They'll be here any minute. Annabelle?' she cupped the receiver and called to the maid. 'I said use the *crystal* pitcher for the lemonade!'

Of course, I thought. Like an idiot I'd gone and forgotten about her bridge club. This was not entirely my fault: there were too many goddamned social events on my mother's agenda to keep track of anyway.

'Look, Mother, I'll make this quick,' I said. 'I was wondering if you could put me in touch with Father somehow.'

'Oh,' she said. 'Well, why don't you call him at the office? He's been spending a lot of time at work lately, and staying in the city most nights. I'm not sure what good I can do you.'

'Will you at least pass along the message that I'm trying to reach him?'

'Of course, Clifford. I know the two of you have had a little spat. I'm sure it will all blow over soon. Perhaps it's best if you just give it time.'

Little spat? I thought. It really bowled me over sometimes how my mother insisted on minimising things. I could tell from the tight, stretched quality in her voice that she knew all about the situation and about how My Old Man was cancelling the publication of my novel and avoiding me on purpose and although my mother liked to play dumb the truth was she was sharp as a tack and very likely knew damned well how serious this cancellation business truly was. It was the kind of thing from which my writing career might never recover and that might cause a rift between me and My Old Man for ever.

'I'll be sure to tell him you want a word with him when I see him next,' she persisted, and hung up the phone to finish preparing the drawing room for her bridge club.

I was disappointed but not surprised, I guess. I sat there thinking, looking around at Swish's apartment. For an eccentric bicycle messenger and devoted anarchist, Swish's pad was surprisingly homey and had all the comforts, even if he had found some of the furnishings on the street. Maybe he and Eden made for a better match than I'd have guessed. But anyway that didn't matter now because I had bigger fish to fry. I picked up a pencil on the kitchen counter and absent-mindedly chewed on it as I mulled over what to do next.

If I didn't want to go looking for My Old Man at his office, and he wasn't coming home at all, there was only one other place I might find him. I sure as hell didn't want to go there but it looked as if I didn't really have a choice. After a few nips of Swish's stash of whiskey for courage, I left the apartment and went to catch the subway.

The ride to Brooklyn was slow and terrible, and at every stop I thought about getting off and had to make the decision each and every goddamn time to stay on the train all over again. I cursed myself several times for not having thought to bring Swish's bottle of whiskey along with me. By the time I arrived in Bensonhurst my resolve had weakened considerably but I told myself I had come this far, I might as well see this thing through. I found my way through the streets, retracing the steps from so many years ago with that sensation of strange familiarity like the kind you feel in a dream.

The house looked smaller than I remembered it. I walked up the steps of the stoop and rang the buzzer. I couldn't help but notice my hand was trembling like a goddamn rummy in withdrawal. A few minutes passed and I rang the buzzer again. For a few seconds I thought maybe no one was home after all and I felt a wave of relief flood over me but this was cut short by the sound of footsteps approaching from inside. The door opened.

'Can I help you?' a woman with short black hair and full red lips asked. I recognised her immediately; I had found my way back to the right house.

'I'm here to see Roger Nelson,' I said, then added, 'My father.' She squinted at me and pushed the screen door open to get a better look.

'He ain't home yet,' she replied in a flat voice.

I don't know what I expected her to say, but not this. The words *He ain't home yet* made my stomach turn sour. I wanted to point out that My Old Man's 'home' was Greenwich, Connecticut, not this goddamned row house in Italian Brooklyn, but I bit my tongue.

'So you are expecting him, then?' I said instead.

She shrugged. 'When he's through at the office.'

'I'll wait for him here, in that case.' I stared at her and I could see she understood my expectation even if she wasn't exactly crazy about it.

'That so, huh?' She gave me a begrudging look. 'Well, fine. I guess you better come in, then,' she said, and held the screen door open for me. Her voice was unwelcoming as hell but I didn't care. I was determined to see My Old Man and maybe if he came home and saw me sitting in Dolores's living room the shock of it would wake him up and make him realise what a lousy father he was and what I had been through as his son. I relished the picture of this as I imagined it, and my confidence grew as I stepped into the dark foyer that led into the house.

I watched Dolores's grotesque bottom switch back and forth as she led me into the living room. I understood she was exactly the curvy type of woman a lot of men like but I found her repulsive as hell.

'Have a seat,' she said, but her voice was so low and rude, she might as well have said *Drop dead*. I ignored her command and stood there looking around the room and inspecting the details with scorn. It was a plain, ratty living room, with a little rundown fireplace and a bunch of yellowing lacy doilies covering what was likely a series of holes in the upholstery of the sofa and armchair.

I went over to the mantel and picked up a photo in a cheap brass frame. I knew right away who it was in the picture without having to ask because even though he was older and taller now he still had that same thick neck and thuggish nose and dark colouring I'd glimpsed at that Little League game all those years ago.

'He has Roger's eyes,' Dolores said. She said it in that rote, knee-jerk way people have when they've made the same comment plenty times over again and I knew this was likely the same remark she always made to anyone who happened to pick up that particular photo for closer inspection. Common sense told me she didn't mean anything by it, but I turned now and glared at her something awful all the same.

Dolores caught the sentiment behind my look and merely shrugged again. She knew her son was a sore subject for me but the shrug said she wasn't about to apologise for it.

'I know,' I replied in a flat voice to her remark about the eyes. 'I've seen him before.'

I was satisfied to see this made her jump with surprise.

'When I was eleven,' I continued, 'I followed My Old Man on the train. He went to watch a Little League game.' I put the photo in its lousy frame back on the mantel with a thud that was less than reverent.

'Oh, Little League.' Dolores nodded. She took a cigarette from her apron pocket and lit up and I watched her eyes through a veil of smoke. 'Yeah, Johnny did all the sports. Good at all o' them, too. A regular Babe Ruth at bat, his father used to always say.'

The stink-eye I'd been shooting her a few minutes ago intensified. Dolores was certainly rough around the edges in a lot of ways but it dawned on me now that there was a sharpness to her despite her obvious lack of education. She had a mean streak; she knew exactly what to say to kick a fella where it counted. She chatted to me, as casual as anything, and yet you could see in her eye that spark of intelligence and cruelty. And she was tenacious. The damn bitch refused to wilt under my terrible gaze.

'Well? You can act all bent outta shape, but what do you want?' She shook her head to show her indifference. 'You want his father should ignore him? Pretend he ain't his own flesh and blood? Real heart of gold you got there. Sure.'

'What do I want?' I echoed. I knew she hadn't meant the question in earnest and anyway it was rhetorical and full of sarcasm, but suddenly I wanted to answer it.

'Look,' I said, 'I'm all for a man living his life any way he damn well pleases, but it's the dishonesty.'

I could feel my mouth puckering and taking on an ugly shape in disgust, but Dolores only shrugged again in that damned infuriatingly blasé manner.

'Dishonesty? Hah. You're one to talk about that. Anyway, your mother knows,' Dolores said in a dry voice. 'Oh, I'm sure she doesn't talk about it at bridge club with her girlfriends or nothin' like that, but she knows.'

It was rotten as hell of her to say it, but nonetheless I didn't have a comeback for this, because I knew it was true. I thought back to the time I'd snuck out to Brooklyn on the train, and how my mother had come alone to pick me up in the Hudson, and how she hadn't sounded a bit surprised on the phone when I told her where I was.

'That's the thing about you rich people,' Dolores continued. 'You think you're too good to ever play second fiddle, and you can go on a hundred years pretending that's not the case! That's called arrogance, and it's like a bad tooth, only you rich folk are too hoity-toity to notice it in the mirror. At least down here when you got it, people take the trouble to knock it out of you.'

I was pretty sure Dolores had just called my mother second fiddle, but I brushed it aside.

'How did you meet My Old Man, anyway?'

'Huh,' she guffawed, her bow-tie lips puckering with scorn. 'Shows how much you know. Roger and I've been sweethearts since we was kids. He may stray, but he always comes back to me. The question you oughta be asking is how Roger met your *mother*.'

I shot her a wary look. She lifted an ashtray off the mantel and smiled.

'She was pregnant. Country club boyfriend of hers wouldn't marry her, and I guess she didn't want to have to "go away to visit her aunt" for nine months. If you ask me, Roger did her a favour. They was foolin' around some at the time, sure, but he don't even know if the baby was his.'

I looked at her, my stomach suddenly in my throat.

'That's right,' Dolores said, narrowing her eyes and lowering her lousy voice. 'You heard me.'

I could feel myself losing my cool, and I began to sweat. It was just like that telephone call with My Old Man all over again. I'd barely had anything to drink that day but I was still goddamn hungover and I thought maybe it was really taking its toll now, because the walls of the room were moving, just like they had all those months ago when I had passed out cold at the Sweet Spot.

I stumbled away from her and headed for the front door.

Dolores called after me, spite brimming in her voice, 'Roger ain't even sure you're his, and now after that monkey business you pulled, it looks like he might be losin' his job over you. He said to me the other day, the way he sees it, he only ever had one true son. And guess what? It ain't you.'

I fumbled for the front door and once I got it open I charged through it and didn't look back. The plan had been to wait there and I had been looking forward to the look on My Old Man's face when he arrived and saw that I knew all about Dolores and about his crummy double-life, and I thought maybe if he realised the cat was out of the bag he'd see what a rotten father he'd been and have some decency and sympathy and do right by me about the publishing contract.

But seeing Dolores, seeing her boldness and her vitriol, had convinced me I was on a fool's errand. My Old Man was a rat, and that was the truth of it. He wasn't going to come to his senses and defend me, and if I wanted to fight rattyness with rattyness, there was only one thing to do now. I'd be damned if I was going to give up this book contract quietly.

I went to look for Rusty.

76

EDEN

'You ought to give your notice, Eden,' Mr Nelson said.

A week had passed since the anonymous tip about Cliff's plagiarism. I knew this was coming, but it still shocked and saddened me. I looked at Mr Nelson, dismayed.

'I'm telling you this out of courtesy,' he said. 'Because of the appearance of nepotism – not to mention the possible plagiarism – they've asked me to resign quietly, and I doubt this will be a good place for you to stay on, given . . . everything.'

I nodded. We were sitting in his office. It was Monday morning, and he'd pulled me in for a quiet conference before the workday got under way. Mr Nelson had dark eggplant-hued circles under his eyes. Now he sighed, got up, and poured two glasses of Scotch. He handed one to me, and I accepted it.

The Scotch tasted like peat moss, and a little like licking a frog.

Mr Nelson got up and gazed out the window at the sea of high-rises. It was something he did when he was troubled.

'He's managed to buy out the contract and move the book to another house,' he said, meaning Cliff.

'I know.'

'This other house, they're willing to take the risk. Some character named Rusty Morrisdale arranged it. Some no-good beatnik friend of Cliff's, I imagine.'

'I heard that, too.' I hadn't spoken to Cliff directly; to my knowledge, he hadn't come home to our apartment a single time that week. Eventually, we'd have to cross paths. It would only be a matter of time before I'd have to find someone to draw up divorce papers.

'I'm outraged, if you want to know the truth,' Mr Nelson said. 'If it's plagiarism, and there's proof, it *will* catch up with him, sooner or later. He's getting off with far too little consequence at present.'

'What would you prefer?' I asked Mr Nelson.

He shrugged and looked down into his Scotch glass. 'I don't know.' He turned around to face me. For a moment his eyes watered. Uncomfortable, I stood up and smoothed my skirt. Sensing my impending exit, Mr Nelson asked me the only question he really wanted to ask me.

'Do you think he did it?' he asked. I paused and held him in my gaze, steady and flat and obvious.

'I don't know,' I said. At this, Mr Nelson looked crushed, and I realised he'd been counting on me to say something definite. It was funny to see that it mattered to Mr Nelson, that he was hoping for the best but still expecting the worst from Cliff. For the first time, it dawned on me that Mr Nelson's prickly attitude towards Cliff derived from something other than simple disdain. However, their relationship had already caused enough damage to them both, and to the people around them. It was no longer my concern.

'If it's all the same to you, I don't think I want to give two weeks,' I said. 'I'd like to start looking right away.' Mr Nelson gazed at me with a startled expression. 'Shall I telephone for a temporary girl?'

He gathered himself. 'Please do,' he answered.

I set down the empty glass on his desk and turned to go.

'I'll write you a letter of recommendation,' he said in a generous voice. 'I can have my girl make several copies of it, in case you need to hunt around a bit to find something.'

My girl, he had said. I'd been 'his girl', but as of that moment I was no longer. It was a simple phrase – loads of editors used it – but it revealed exactly how interchangeable I'd always been.

'I only want one copy,' I said. 'Make it out to Ms Mavis Singer of Farbman & Company.'

'All right,' Mr Nelson said in a weary voice.

'And, sir?'

'Yes?'

'Make it out in the name of "Eden Katz".'

Mr Nelson blinked. 'I'm not sure I understand . . .' he said, frowning.

'Eden Katz,' I repeated, and spelt it for him. 'That's my name. It always was.'

77

MILES

Once I left the shore of the Hudson River, the reality of the nightmare began to set in and take its toll, and while I am not a doctor, I believe I entered a sort of fugue state. I have a vague recollection of lifting my bicycle in anger and heaving it into the Hudson . . . watching the icy chunks floating on the river's surface bob like ice cubes.

After that, I must've sought out an appropriately wretched bar, for the next thing I remembered was waking up in my bedroom at my mother's apartment with a fat lip and a swollen eye, the taste of terrible cheap sour mash on my breath. I have no memory of the man – or men, perhaps – who left the souvenirs I discovered on my face.

There was only one monster, as far as I was concerned. And if I wanted to find him, all I had to do was look in the mirror.

But I didn't look in the mirror. I hardly wanted to see this new, fresh set of bruises, much less the more grotesque countenance I knew lurked beneath them. I stayed in bed, staring at the ceiling as the golden light of morning transformed itself, the window became a study of blues, and the light finally turned to ash. I passed the better part of a week like this, watching the same cycle repeat itself.

When my mother came in to scold me, prodding me to get up, I gave her such a look, she did not press the issue, nor did she attempt to prod again. Instead, she seemed to understand my distress, even if she couldn't see its source. She took a gentler tack and began bringing me trays of food – trays I did not touch, that she later cleared away.

It occurred to me I had fallen into a similar state once before, just after Rusty attacked me on Cliff and Eden's roof. But that was nothing compared this. I remembered what it had been like to heal, to board that Greyhound bus, trying not to notice people staring with curiosity at my beaten-up face, bruises swimming to the surface of my skin like yellow and purple jellyfish.

How foolish I was, I realise now, to latch onto that image of Cob's cicada moulting. *I am moulting,* I had thought at the time. I had identified with the insect, but I see now I was wrong. If I am anything in this metaphor, I am the moulted shell the cicada leaves clinging to the branch. San Francisco. Those days with Joey on the houseboat. I had lived and left all the living I'd done in that strange, perfectly sculpted yet empty echo of my life.

Days passed, then weeks.

A letter arrived, tucked neatly beside a bowl of soup on one of the trays my mother brought in. Its existence sent an electric shock through me, and yet, I knew who it was from immediately. He must have written it in his hotel room, just before. Four times, I attempted to open it, but failed. Whatever it said, it was everything I had left. Every time I touched the paper, my hand trembled, certain that its contents could only seal my passage to hell.

I was staring at the unopened envelope one day when my mother poked her head into my room.

'Janet come to see you,' she announced. 'I still don' know what all this about, but she got a right to know where you been at least.'

It was understood this meant my mother was going to send

Janet in, whether I wanted her to or not. I shoved the envelope into my bathrobe pocket and sat up on the edge of the bed, and my mother retreated to fetch my visitor.

Janet entered the room trembling.

'Miles . . .' came her soft voice. She perched on the bed next to me. 'I've been trying to reach you.'

I should've felt apologetic but I didn't, couldn't. My hands were still in my pockets and I could feel the envelope crinkled up in a ball there. For the first time in two weeks, I detected the alien tickle of emotion begin to pierce the veil of the numbing fog that surrounded me. Tears began to fill my eyes. The timing was terrible.

'Miles . . . ?' Janet murmured upon reading the small ripple of tiny earthquakes that was passing over the surface of my face. Her reaction, her expression of concern . . . these were enough to loosen the storm. I felt my face crumple and I reached for her and buried my face in her chest, just as the mad heaving began to take over.

'Miles!' I heard her voice shout softly, as if from far away. I understood she was alarmed. Why shouldn't she be? But I could not help it. I allowed the shaking to take me over.

'Miles!' she shouted again.

This crack in my mask, she would have none of it.

'Miles, please . . .' Janet begged me now. 'Miles, I have news.'

There was something in her voice. I sat up, wiped my face until I could hold her gaze like the steady, solid man I was supposed to be. I waited for her to continue.

EPILOGUE

CLIFF

March 30, 1980

I was dying and I was stuck in the lousiest hospital I had ever been in. When you are yellow from liver disease you might as well paint jail stripes on yourself because that is how they are going to treat you. They figure you did this to yourself and consequently you don't deserve to take up space in the good beds or talk to the good doctors and you don't really deserve to get better because you'll only go out and make yourself sick again. It's the nurses that are the worst because in the really bad hospitals they are washed-up old prudes who can't wait to judge you. They purse their hard little mouths at you and either barely touch you when it's time for your sponge bath, leaving you dirty and depressed, or else they scrub you so raw you wind up with red patches on your already-swollen belly.

I wouldn't have picked this hospital but I didn't have any choice because the guy driving the ambulance did all the choosing. The morning I was admitted had started out peaceful enough; we were living in Scarsdale just then and I'd been reading the newspaper and drinking some coffee with a little Irish in it while my wife, Carolyn, did some ironing. Carolyn wasn't like Eden at all. She wasn't a career gal and she was happy enough to do all the little things like iron her fella's shirt and fix him a nice stiff drink every afternoon when cocktail hour rolled around. Even though she wanted children and we hadn't been able to have them we still made the best of things and got along like a house on fire, mostly because Carolyn was solid as the earth and always knew when to look the other way, and never once forgot about cocktail hour. In any case, the trouble didn't start during cocktail hour but rather in the morning that day. I had an upset stomach and that was common enough but when I went to the bathroom I started throwing up and when I saw it was blood I called for Carolyn and she began to get pretty hysterical the way most women do and she called for an ambulance and reported my condition before I could stop her.

Once Carolyn called the ambulance I was stuck. The doctors told me later I'd had some kind of haemorrhage in my oesophagus and that my damaged liver meant my blood wouldn't clot and that was why there had been so much blood. They had put me under for a little surgery and had given me a transfusion and for a little while I was feeling better but in the end it was no good because I began to haemorrhage in other places. The way the doctor explained it to me, my body is like a bullet-ridden warship springing leak after leak. I don't know if I buy it, because I'd had problems before but no one had ever called an ambulance and things had always turned out fine and after I'd had a chance to dry out for a day or two I always felt as good as new.

Anyway that wasn't what had happened this time around. What had happened was I was trapped in the lousy hospital with the lousy doctors and their lousy prognosis and if they were right I was facing the inevitable very soon. I'd only had a few regrets in life and I'd asked Carolyn to fetch one of them out of our safety-deposit box down at the bank. She did and brought it to the hospital, along with a manila envelope. I sealed it up and asked Carolyn to look up the address for Eden Katz at Farbman & Company and put the whole business in the mail. Carolyn knew about my marriage to Eden and also how it had been annulled and all that jazz and if it ever bothered her she had the good calm practical sense not to let it show. She found the address and brought it to me scribbled in her very lovely and very neat handwriting on the back of a grocery receipt. Next I asked her to bring Rusty Morrisdale to the hospital during visiting hours, and he agreed to come, although the rat-fink made me wait a few days on account of his busy schedule. What kind of asshole makes a dying man wait? But I knew all about Rusty and his character and the only reason I wanted to see him was to settle a matter of unfinished business from twenty-two years ago.

Rusty was my agent but he had only ever represented me in one deal that we'd done when we moved my novel from Bonwright to another house and Rusty had really put the screws to me with that deal because he'd made sure that while the deal was decent enough for me, he made out with more than twice the commission a regular agent would have taken. It was very sneaky of him but at the time there was nothing to be done about it, because Rusty knew a certain secret about my book and Lord knows the rat-fink wasn't above blackmail.

Now, after all these years, Rusty finally was standing in the doorway of my hospital room, his beady eyes taking in the whole scene. His hair had turned a dirty iron-grey since I last saw him but the rest of him still looked the same and he still had that slouchy posture that made him look like a teenage girl with a bad attitude. I had never known him to need an invitation but nonetheless I waved him in and he came in and said a sheepish hello. I guess he could see I was really dying.

'You know why I asked for you here, Rusty,' I said, 'and it's about those things we did all those years ago.'

Carolyn had already come and gone for visiting hours and there was no point in beating around the bush but I could see Rusty was unnerved that I was being so frank because he glanced around nervously. My room was not private because in the lousy hospitals they never are and Rusty looked at the other beds in the room to see if anyone was listening to us. Even now, all these years later, there was still a minor swirl of controversy surrounding my book. Rusty had been able to get the book over the transom at Torchon & Lyle, but the publishing world is a very small place after all and he wasn't able to keep the rumours at bay indefinitely. Everyone knew about the big literary prize the novel had won but they also knew how the jury had later gone and taken the prize back due to the insinuations swirling around about the book being plagiarised. I was never formally charged and nothing was ever proven – not in a court of law, anyway – but those slobs took the prize back all the same. This in turn had the ironic effect of igniting people's interest even more and so the joke was really on that prize jury, because after that the book sold like hotcakes for a good long while. Rusty was naturally cagey about the rumours and I knew this was not necessarily for my sake but because the book was his bread and butter, too. At the same time rumours were good for business, a confirmation of these rumours would kill it. With his racket of a crooked commission, Rusty had done rather well in the end, and I could see he didn't want this prosperous run to end, and he certainly didn't want to be sued or have to repay the money to anybody.

'You should know I think of you as the devil, Rusty,' I said now, levelling an unfriendly look his way. 'A dirty, rotten bastard of a devil in elbow patches.'

'C'mon, cut it out with that stuff, old buddy. Things worked out all right. You got your deal, didn't you? Best to focus on that,' Rusty said in an encouraging voice. It was almost as if he were trying to cheer me up.

'Why did you do it?' I asked. There had been newspaper clippings in that safety-deposit box along with the composition book. I had mailed the book but not the clippings and I pushed them towards Rusty now, across the little hospital table over my bed.

'Do what? Help you move the book to a new publisher?'

I pointed to the article about a young man under investigation with the State Department who had committed suicide in a New York City hotel. 'This wasn't part of our plan. You didn't have to do it.' I tapped the headline and when Rusty looked at it his eyes went wide.

'Cliff, I didn't do that,' he said. I looked at him and he could see I didn't believe him.

'It was your big idea . . . the tip off. You said one anonymous phone call was all it would take.'

'I didn't call anybody, I swear.'

'All right, Rusty. Have it your way,' I said, irritated. There was no getting anywhere with this guy and it was plain he would never accept any blame for anything he had ever done. I looked at him. Here we were, a couple of forty-seven-year-old men, and he was still trying to play me.

'Get out, Rusty,' I said, suddenly exhausted and overwhelmed. 'I'm through talking.'

'Is there anything I can do for you, Cliff?'

'Get out!' I yelled more forcefully.

'We ought to discuss the future, Cliff, and your estate—'

At this, I picked up the water pitcher on the nightstand beside me and threw it at Rusty's head. I missed but I'd made my point anyway and Rusty scurried out on his little rat legs. A couple of nurses came in to scold me.

It was in that moment as I sat there watching the nurses waddling around with their fat posteriors, cleaning up the mess and clucking at me, that my brain began to work things over and consider possibilities I hadn't considered before. It bothered me that Rusty had denied having anything to do with phoning in the tip to the State Department. After all, it was his idea in the first place and it was certainly something he would do. It bugged me that he'd played it so cool and acted so dumb just now. I assumed Rusty had phoned in the tip, and I had assumed Miles had mailed the anonymous letter to Bonwright.

But now it dawned on me that these assumptions had been just that: assumptions. There were other possibilities, too, that I had never bothered to see.

I had already addressed the envelope to Farbman & Company and had put Eden's name on it and it was on its way to her right this very second. *Eden.* How could I have been so blind? It was right there before me, for decades, and I had never suspected. They say dying men see things more clearly and as I sat there in my lousy dump of a hospital room I thought about what a shame it was to finally see it all so clearly and to not be able to do a damn thing about it.

EDEN

April 21, 1980

I had been waiting a long time for that envelope.

When it finally arrived, I'd been at Farbman & Company for over twenty years. I followed in the footsteps of my mentor, the great Mavis Singer, until she eventually retired and I stepped into her shoes as editor-in-chief and associate publisher. It seemed as though the years had flown by rather quickly, and yet I knew I was not the same person any more. There were times I fantasised about going back in time and shaking hands with my former self, that nervous, excited girl, fresh out of college, young and energetic and at the same time a little bit exhausted from the bus ride that took her from Indiana to New York. She would be so shocked to see where I wound up; perhaps she might not even believe it. But then I reminded myself: I hardly needed a time machine. Every time I interview a new secretary, I know I am looking at a former version of myself. The bouffants and shoulder pads may shift in the tides of time, but some things remain the same.

I suppose the truth is there will always be young Edens pouring into this city, some of them hoping to end up in publishing. The second version of myself – the version I'd become after leaving Bonwright and after Cliff and I annulled our marriage; the version of myself who'd managed to stick it out in New York and make it as an editor after all – she was more rare. I didn't realise I'd become this second version of myself until I finally bumped into Miss Everett at a publishing party, a year or so after Ms Singer hired me to work at Farbman. It was bound to happen, our bumping into each other; we may live in a large metropolis, but the publishing business is a very small world. She was icy to me, as I had expected. But what I hadn't expected was how little I'd care. I had been afraid that seeing her would remind me of my terrible failure at Torchon & Lyle. But standing there, suddenly realising Miss Everett had no power over me, I also realised I did not regret my journey. I did not even regret the mistakes. It had been a mistake to allow myself to be bullied, but that had forced me to learn how to stand up for myself. It had been a bigger mistake still to abandon my last name and everything that came with it. But having recovered it since, I'd learnt just how precious it was to me.

No, there was only one thing I regretted, one thing I would take back if I could.

I had never been truly sure that envelope would come, but when it landed on my desk, I recognised the handwriting immediately. I opened the envelope; the contents were exactly what I'd expected. I picked up the telephone and booked a flight. I'd long ago decided this was something I would deliver in person.

I'd been keeping track of Miles from a distance. I knew that he'd written poetry, gone to graduate school, and eventually settled down in Berkeley, California, to teach poetry at the university. The travel agent was able to book me on a Pan Am flight in two weeks' time. I confirmed immediately and gave her my Visa card number. By that time, my life had long since taken on a simple, straightforward shape. There was no husband to phone at work and tell about my little business trip, no children whose care would need to be coordinated. Not even a cat for which a cat-sitter must be arranged. I suppose that sounds awfully sad, but the truth was I enjoyed my life. Books were my children; their spines smiled out at me from on the shelf. I worked with colleagues I admired and respected. And I knew I had, myself, become something of a character. I first took note of this development about a decade or so ago, when I came into the office one morning wearing one of my impeccably tailored suits (Mavis had given me the name of her seamstress), wrapped in a fox coat, two freshly-edited manuscripts peeking from my attaché case, and saw myself through my assistant's rather wide, expressive eyes. I laughed to understand what a caricature I'd become, but I wasn't bothered a bit. No, my life was a creation of my own making, and I embraced it. There was only one thing I regretted, and when that envelope arrived, I saw in it my chance to set right what little I could.

And so, two weeks, a six-hour flight, and one rental car later, I found myself wandering Telegraph Avenue, a sea of lively young people milling about and the smells of ethnic food thick in the crisp bay air.

I missed him at his office, but a group of his students told me which bar I'd be most likely to find him in. They were somewhat charming about it; they seemed to have sympathy for him as a romantic figure. His wife had recently died of cancer, they told me. 'I think he just likes to sit by himself and write poetry,' one girl said. I wondered how much he'd changed, whether I'd recognise him, but as soon as I entered the bar I spotted him: the same handsome face, even the same horn-rimmed glasses, and now the tiniest bit of grey at the temples.

'Hullo, Miles,' I said, pulling out the bar stool next to his and sitting down. He turned to study my face and I wondered how much I'd changed. A woman never knows. But I saw the spark of recognition in his eyes, even if he didn't smile.

'Hello, Eden,' he replied in a neutral voice, as if we'd just bumped into each other in the Village.

'I hear you're teaching poetry these days,' I said. 'I stopped by your office, but you weren't there. Your students seem to like you.'

'They tolerate me. They're good students.'

I paused, trying to think of what to say next. As soon as I had opened the envelope with Cliff's return address on it, I knew what I needed to do. But now that I'd come clear across the country, it was awkward trying to figure out how to bring the subject up.

'Cliff passed away two days ago,' I said. 'I got the news just before I left for the airport.' I paused, to give him a chance to absorb this information, and eventually Miles nodded. He didn't ask what had become of my marriage to Cliff, though he seemed to intuitively know. He also didn't say *I'm sorry*, which was fine, because we both knew he couldn't be.

'Before he died, he mailed me this.' I pulled the composition book out of my purse and put it on the bar. Miles's eyebrows shot up and his brow furrowed. I could tell he never thought he would see that composition book ever again. He lifted a hand and, with trembling fingers, lightly touched the cover.

'With Cliff,' I said, 'it's difficult to tell whether this is an apology, or a confession . . . or just an impulse. But this belongs to you.' I paused and cleared my throat. 'It always belonged to you.'

He picked up the composition book, stuffed thick with papers and wrapped in rubber bands, and gazed at it with a faraway look in his eyes.

'You had a near-complete draft of your own in there,' I said. 'I ought to know. I edited Cliff's manuscript until I was close to exhaustion. Before . . . before everything that happened at Bonwright.'

'I suppose,' Miles murmured. 'I don't know what complete would be – I wasn't sure what I was aiming for. I was just writing. It felt important to write it, whatever it was.'

'The events you wrote about . . . the parts with the war stories, that is . . . I did a little digging, and most of what you describe matches up with the 369th Regiment. They were known as the Harlem Hellfighters,' I said. 'Your father was one of them, wasn't he? These are his stories.'

'Yes,' Miles replied, and he frowned as though something had just occurred to him. 'Why would you look up battles fought by a black regiment from New York?'

I felt my cheeks colour slightly with shame. 'I knew the manuscript was yours,' I confessed. 'Cliff never admitted it to me, but I found the composition book hidden in our apartment after Cliff's father had acquired the manuscript as a novel.'

Miles looked at me and I could see he was rethinking his way through the past, determining what matched up and what didn't.

He stared at me for a long moment. 'You tipped off your own publishing company against your husband,' he said abruptly. There was no question in it, and little accusation. He was simply stating a fact.

'Yes,' I said. 'And I've come to apologise to you. I'm sorry I didn't do more. There are, well . . . there are reasons I didn't.' Hearing it for the first time, I was aware of how feeble my apology sounded. There was too much to explain, and now that we were middle-aged, explanations didn't seem to matter as much as they used to. At the time, I'd thought reporting the plagiarism via the anonymous letter would be enough to make Cliff back down and do the right thing. But I underestimated Cliff's pride, his stubborn streak, and I hadn't counted on Rusty getting involved. Before I even knew what was happening, Cliff and Rusty had moved the manuscript to a different publishing house – Torchon & Lyle, as a matter of fact. I knew then that Cliff was done with me and, what's more, that I was done with him. When I went to look under the floorboard for the composition book a second time, it was gone. I was a girl working under a false name accusing somebody of plagiarism, and I hadn't a shred of proof to show anyone.

'You didn't put up much of a fuss,' I said to Miles now. I'd wondered about the way Miles had quietly disappeared and not fought back. 'Not that I'm shifting the blame onto your shoulders,' I continued. 'Only that I assumed they had something on you.'

He looked at me.

'Whatever it is, Cliff's gone now.'

'Rusty's not,' he said, then paused. 'But it wasn't about that anyway,' he added in a much quieter voice.

Ready to make my final plea, I took a breath. 'I think you should come forward and set the record straight. It goes without saying, I'll support you. It would be my honour to support you.'

Miles didn't reply. I took another breath and continued.

'Something else, too . . .' I said. He turned and raised an eyebrow at me. 'I wish you'd write about it,' I plunged forward. 'It was a special time in Greenwich Village, in Harlem. Lots of people have written about it, but none with your story, none with your voice. I'm not saying this because I'm trying to buy your story – work with another editor if you'd rather, or another publishing house if you must – but . . . I know this hardly makes sense, and you have no reason to trust me, but sometimes editors, we're passionate about certain books . . . We simply want them to exist, to point to them on a shelf and to tell another person: "Here. Read this."'

'You want me to write about . . .' His voice trailed off.

'Yes . . . about what happened with Cliff, with Rusty . . . about all of it. Everything that happened. No matter how it makes any of us look, including me. You are the right man for the job, Miles. You always were.'

I took a business card out of my purse and laid it on the bar next to the composition book. Miles stared at the card with a pained expression. My spirits sank, but it had been worth a try.

'Think about it,' I said, and rose to go. We shook hands and I left him there, nursing a glass of whiskey, one hand lying on the composition book, staring blankly into the mirror behind the bar.

MILES

April 21,1980

I left the bar to go home shortly after Eden departed. Cob would be there, taking a nap on the living room couch and waiting for me. It had become our custom to eat dinner together. 'You shouldn't eat your meals alone,' Cob was always warning me. 'It's not good for you.' He had come out to California to help with the arrangements for Janet's funeral, and he'd stayed on for several weeks. We had not discussed when he would leave, but I knew he was waiting for some incremental shift in me, some small sign that I would be all right. I told him not to worry, that he had his own wife and family to worry about, and I had Marcus. But Cob knew that despite the fact Marcus lived at home – Marcus was twenty-one and preparing to graduate soon – we didn't see much of each other. Janet and I had kept Marcus far too close for too long, cajoling him into attending Berkeley for the discounted tuition and guilting him into living at home while his mother was sick.

Now he was angry. I understood this. The parent he had loved most had died, and he was stuck rattling around the house with me. Mostly he went out these days, making a life for himself anywhere but here.

So Cob had come to save me from myself, to weed the yard and mow the lawn and buy a barbecue from the hardware store.

It was a warm spring and California was bursting with flowers and humming with bees, the Pacific breeze blowing gently and gulls squawking in the distance over the bay. It was a strange time to lose someone, during a California spring. It made it not quite real somehow.

That evening, when I got home, Cob had already woken up from his nap and was in the backyard adding briquettes to the grill. He held up a package of hot dogs.

'I was listening to the game,' he said. 'It gave me an idea for dinner.' He grinned, and I caught a glimpse of his seven-year-old self lurking just beneath the surface of his thirty-year-old face.

I went into the kitchen and filled a bucket with ice and six bottles of beer, and brought them, along with an opener, back outside. Cob roasted the franks until they were a deep reddish brown and splitting at the seams like ripe fruit. We loaded them up with mustard and relish and ate, cutting the salty brine of the franks with sips of cold, bitter ale.

We were slow to make conversation at first, but eventually I told him about Eden, and about the composition book I'd kept long ago.

'I remember seeing that notebook,' he said.

I had never told him about what had become of the composition book, about Cliff and all the rest of it. I never saw a reason to. Cob had grown up to be an intelligent man and an engineer, but he did not keep up with the literary world. I had preferred to spare him the insult of it all. Now I told a dumbed-down version of it, and how Eden had petitioned me to set the record straight by writing a longer, more encompassing memoir.

'Will you do it?' Cob asked.

'I don't know,' I said. 'I think of . . . Marcus,' and as I said it I knew that this was true. I let my mind drift. There were so many complications knotted into the past, things I wanted to remember, things I didn't want to remember, and things I couldn't bear to remember.

'Do you remember that young man you saw at the museum?' I asked Cob abruptly.

Cob looked at me. 'I do,' he replied. 'I remember him.'

'I met him out here in San Francisco,' I said. 'He helped me find our father's journal from the war. The locker Mama mentioned wasn't as easy to find as I had thought it would be. I began to think the story Father told Mama had been made up, that it was just his crazy talk, that maybe there was no journal to find, but Joey – my friend – he wouldn't let me give up. He was a good friend to me.'

Cob looked at me for a long time, saying nothing. 'Where is he now?' Cob asked finally.

'Dead,' I answered, and suddenly I found it difficult to breathe.

We fell into silence. Cob detected my difficulty and, wisely, knew just to sit there with me. The glow of dusk slowly faded from the sky, the light leaving with a steady certainty, like water draining from a bathtub. Somewhere a mourning dove called for its mate. I thought, strangely, of Mister Gus.

After a while Cob got up. He reached to clear my plate. I leant over to pick up the bucket of beer, now full of six empty bottles knocking around in the cool water. We tidied everything, made a plate for Marcus – in case he decided to come home – and watered down the remaining coals in the barbecue. In the kitchen Cob announced he was going to bed, and I reloaded the bucket with ice and beer from the refrigerator.

'Miles?' Cob said.

'Yes?'

'About the memoir . . . I don't know much, but I think the

best kind of role model a guy can be is a truthful one.' He bid me goodnight, and I heard the sound of the stairs creaking.

I went back out into the yard and sat down on the lawn chair. I thought about what Cob had said. Children didn't always want the truth, but withholding it only accomplished so much, because the lie was always felt. I understood that now; it was something you understood after you had children of your own, after you had tried to protect them with lies and failed.

It was good advice, but too simple. Cob believed he knew the extent of my shame, but he did not. Eden had confessed to being the one who'd tipped off Bonwright, but she had not been the only one to betray the person she loved. I'd gotten the idea from Cliff, of all people. The threat was clear: all it would take was one call to the State Department. At first I was afraid for Joey: I wanted to protect him. But something changed, and all too quickly I went from being afraid *for* Joey to being afraid of Joey.

That phone call marked the darkest hour of my life.

I made up some bogus claims to communist ties – claims that could never be substantiated – and I figured at worst he would be investigated, only to be absolved. I thought it would make Joey back off a bit. The plan was to distance myself until there were no ties between us – none that anyone could prove – and we would revert to the strangers we were intended to be. I had the notion in my head that, when it was safe, I could use my father's journal to stake my claim against Cliff.

But Joey must've been more careless in his personal life than I knew, for while the FBI didn't find evidence of communism, the agents found plenty of other fodder. Their interrogations had been enough to make even the sanest person paranoid, fragile. And then I had been late – too late.

I was lost in these thoughts again when I heard the back door open and saw a long square of light stretch out upon the lawn.

'Dad?'

It was Marcus.

'Out here,' I called. I listened to the hushed swishing of his feet moving over the grass. He sat down in the lawn chair next to me. I bent over and lifted a beer from the bucket.

'Thanks,' he said. I heard the faint, high-pitched sound of the beer splashing in the neck of the bottle as he took a deep swig. We sat in silence together and looked at the stars. I stole surreptitious glances at Marcus. As a child, he resembled the handsome boy in the photo, the uncle he never knew but for whom he was named. He had grown up tall and strong, with a steady, loyal spirit I knew his friends loved in him. So did his mother. His teachers praised him for his diligence, his persistence, his discipline.

There'd been a time, after Joey had died, that I'd wanted to stand up for him, to claim the love between us, to confess my betrayal. But the day Janet came to see me at my mother's apartment, she told me she was pregnant. A result of that night in the hotel room, my attempt to purge Joey from my heart. It had been a foolish mistake, but one that had made me a father, and in thinking about fathers I had to consider what kind of father I wanted to be. In the end, Janet and I had built a peaceful, quiet life together. It had been love, but not the kind born of passion; more like two trains headed towards the same destination, their tracks running in perfect parallel to each other, never to cross. I never told her about Joey, and if she discerned his ghostly presence in our lives, she never let on. We were creatures who relied on harmony and shared a deep mistrust of the joy we were never quite certain we deserved.

But now, with Janet gone and Eden returning my old

composition book to me, goading me to put the unspeakable into words, I found myself considering the question of what kind of father I wanted to be all over again. Perhaps that's what it is to be a parent: you never stop considering it. I wondered if I was strong enough to put pen to paper again and write the truth. I wondered, selfishly, if Marcus was strong enough to love me in spite of the truth. *I wish you would write about it,* Eden had said to me. *About all of it. Everything that happened. No matter how it makes any of us look. You are the right man for the job, Miles. You always were.* Memoirs are a tricky genre. It is a little-known secret: we are never the heroes of our own stories, unless we are lying.

If we choose to count ourselves among the brave, we write ourselves as the villains we are, hoping for redemption.

ACKNOWLEDGEMENTS

First, the people.

I am very blessed to have a wonderful agent, Emily Forland. My thanks to her, Emma, Gail, and everyone at Brandt & Hochman.

I am extremely grateful for the editorial guidance I received from Amy Einhorn and Jake Morrissey, both of whom were very patient and encouraging. Thanks, too, to Liz Stein for her hard work when this book was in its early stages. Thank you to Kevin Murphy.

Thank you to Putnam and Ivan Held for publishing this book, and thank you to my publicist at Putnam, Stephanie Hargadon. I'd like to retroactively thank the very kind, very enthusiastic Penguin folks I came into contact with during the time my first book debuted: Kelly Welsh (now Rudolph), Lauren Truskowski, Heather Connor, Kayleigh Clark, Lydia Hirt, Katie McKee, Kate Stark, Alexis Welby, Tom Dussel, Dominique Jenkins, Alan Walker, Brian Wilson, Lisa Amoroso, Karl Krueger, Patrick Mcneirney, Lindsay Wood, Wendy Pearl, Tom Benton – and gosh, I'm sure I'm forgetting a ton of people! Please forgive me. As this second book moves forward, I look forward to seeing some familiar faces and also meeting those folks I haven't met yet.

I am very thankful for the wisdom of my early readers who gave excellent feedback: Eva Talmadge, Julie Fogh, Brendan Jones, Will

Chancellor, Susan Shin, Julia Masnik, Susan Wood, and Joe Campana. I am also very thankful for those who have shown friendship and support over the years: Jayme Yeo, Brian Shin, Ning Zhou, Melissa 'MRC' Ryan Clark, Lyndsay Faye, Elizabeth Romanski, Matt Schwartz, Andy Knuesel, Sophie Guinet, Cecile Pradillon, Noah Ballard, Laura Van Der Veer, and Hana Landes. Thank you to Rice University professors Bob Patten and Collen Lamos, who were kind enough to come to my fiction readings. Thank you to my family, Arthur, Sharon, Laurie, Melissa, and now Philippe.

And last but not least, thank you to Atom Sharp for being my loving partner.

Now, the sources.

This book was born in large part from a desire to put several books in conversation with one another: Jack Kerouac's *On the Road*, Rona Jaffe's *The Best of Everything*, James Baldwin's *Giovanni's Room*, Truman Capote's *Breakfast at Tiffany's*, Sylvia Plath's *The Bell Jar* . . . the list goes on. Anatole Broyard's *Kafka Was the Rage* was a very helpful memoir about life in Greenwich Village. I constructed much of Joey's interrogation scene from various testimonies recorded in David K. Johnson's *The Lavender Scare*. I gleaned details that went into Marvin Tillman's journal from Sammons and Morrow's *Harlem's Rattlers and the Great War*. I am ever grateful for the stimulus of all of these sources and more, all of which combined to create the cocktail that became *Three-Martini Lunch*.